Psychoanalytic Explorations in Music

Second Series

Psychoanalytic Explorations in Music

Second Series

Edited by
STUART FEDER, M.D.
RICHARD L. KARMEL, Ph.D.
GEORGE H. POLLOCK, M.D., Ph.D.

INTERNATIONAL UNIVERSITIES PRESS, INC.

Madison, Connecticut

Library of Congress Cataloging in Publication Data

Psychoanalytic explorations in music : second series / edited by
  Stuart Feder, Richard L. Karmel, George H. Pollock.
    p. cm.
   Includes bibliographical references and indexes.
   ISBN 0-8236-4408-1
   1. Music—Psychology. 2. Psychoanalysis. I. Feder, Stuart,
1930–   . II. Karmel, Richard L. III. Pollock, George H.
ML3830.P39 1993
781′.11—dc20   93-575
                                                  CIP
                                                  MN

International Universities Press and IUP (& design) ® are registered trademarks of International Universities Press, Inc.

Manufactured in the United States of America

Contents

Contributors   vii
Introduction   ix

I. On Music and Method

1. "Promissory Notes": Method in Music and Applied
   Psychoanalysis—*Stuart Feder*   3
2. The Composer's Experience: Variations on Several
   Themes—*Martin L. Nass*   21

II. On Affect in Music

3. Reflections on the Communication of Affect and Idea
   Through Music—*Leo Treitler*   43
4. On Form and Feeling in Music—*Gilbert J. Rose*   63
5. The Anlage of Feeling: Its Fate in Form (Discussion
   of Chapter 4)—*Eugene L. Goldberg*   83
6. On Affect and Musical Motion–*David Epstein*   91
7. How Music Conveys Emotion—*Pinchas Noy*   125

III. Studies of Composers and Compositions

8. Bach and Mozart: Styles of Musical Genius—*Robert L.
   Marshall*   153
9. A Tale of Two Fathers: Bach and Mozart (Discussion
   of Chapter 8)—*Stuart Feder*   171
10. Communication of Affect and Idea Through Song:
    Schumann's "I was Crying in my Dream" (op. 48,
    no. 13)—*Peter Ostwald*   179
11. Notes on Incest Themes in Wagner's *Ring*
    Cycle—*George H. Pollock*   195
12. Wagner's Use of the Leitmotif to Communicate
    Understanding—*Morton F. Reiser*   217
13. Erik Satie: Musicality and Ego Identity—*Richard L.
    Karmel*   229

IV. HISTORICAL ESSAYS

14. Richard Wagner's Life and Music: What Freud
    Knew—*Cora L. Díaz de Chumaceiro*   249
15. Freud and Max Graf: On the Psychoanalysis of
    Music—*David M. Abrams*   279

    Name Index   309
    Subject Index   315

Contributors

DAVID M. ABRAMS, PH.D.
Clinical Associate Professor in Clinical Psychology, City University of New York
Faculty, Institute of Child, Adolescent and Family Studies, New York

CORA L. DÍAZ DE CHUMACEIRO, PH.D.
Clinical Psychologist, Professor of Music, Caracas, Venezuela

DAVID EPSTEIN, PH.D.
Professor of Music, Massachusetts Institute of Technology

STUART FEDER, M.D.
Faculty, The New York Psychoanalytic Institute

EUGENE L. GOLDBERG, M.D.
Training and Supervising Analyst, Columbia University Psychoanalytic Center for Training and Research

RICHARD L. KARMEL, PH.D.
Senior Staff Psychologist, Department of Psychiatry, Montreal General Hospital
Member, Canadian Psychoanalytic Society

ROBERT L. MARSHALL, PH.D.
Louis, Frances and Jeffrey Sachar Professor of Music, Brandeis University

MARTIN L. NASS, PH.D.
Clinical Professor of Psychology, New York University Postdoctoral Program
Faculty, Training and Supervising Analyst, New York Freudian Society

PINCHAS NOY, M.D.
Training and Supervising Analyst, Israel Institute for Psychoanalysis
Associate Professor, Hebrew University, Jerusalem

PETER OSTWALD, M.D.
Professor of Psychiatry and Medical Director, Health Program for Performing Artists, University of California, San Francisco

GEORGE H. POLLOCK, M.D., PH.D.
  Ruth and Evelyn Dunbar Distinguished Professor of Psychiatry and
    Behavioral Sciences, Northwestern University Medical School

MORTON F. REISER, M.D.
  Albert E. Kent Professor of Psychiatry Emeritus, Yale University
    School of Medicine

GILBERT J. ROSE, M.D.
  Formerly Faculty, Yale University School of Medicine
  Western New England Psychoanalytic Institute

LEO TREITLER, PH.D.
  Distinguished Professor of Music, The Graduate Center, City Uni-
    versity of New York

Introduction

With the publication of this Second Series of contributions in psychoanalysis and music, it is clear that a field of inquiry has been established that both analysts and musicians are finding to be of considerable interest. In addition, a forum now exists for the exchange of ideas along with a venue for their publication.

Our first volume, published in 1990 (Feder, Karmel, and Pollock, 1990), was a survey of the literature in a discipline still to be defined. More in the nature of an anthology than a collection of original papers, it sought to present what were in our opinion some of the best papers on psychoanalysis applied to music by psychoanalysts and others with a psychoanalytic orientation.

The current selection represents a further stage of development, and reflects a different and better defined point of view. Two things made this possible. First, the friendly reception that the initial volume received, and with it a greater awareness of both the possibilities and pitfalls of working in this area. Second, a small but growing following of a unique sort.

There are a number of psychoanalysts and others in the mental health professions who have a serious interest in music, either currently or earlier in their careers, not infrequently on a professional level. For some, the chance to connect this interest with current professional involvement has proved to be stimulating and personally integrating. Others have been curious about possible parallels and connections with clinical work, particularly in the areas of affect and nonverbal communication. To be sure, still others have remained unconvinced by the interdisciplinary efforts of the earlier volume and have preferred their interests and involvement in each of the areas to be uncontaminated by the other.

On the other hand, there has been a small but dedicated group of writers in music who have been seeking innovative and less conventional methods in their studies. Few have attempted psychoanalytic studies for the same reason that few analysts have attempted crossover studies; namely, lack of facility in the other field. Yet, as can be seen below, some writers on music have been drawn to both subject matter and method that interface with those that engage the analyst. With regard to subject, affect and nonverbal communication may again be mentioned in addition to issues of structure as well as formal considerations. As to method, there has been increased interest in both disciplines, for example, in the nature of narrative. Certainly hermeneutics have perennially engaged both areas. Although essential in the psychoanalytic craft of interpretation, musicologists until quite recently have viewed it askance. Several musicians and music historians have engaged in a dialogue with psychoanalysts, as have those in such fields as art history and aesthetics. The work of four such writers appears in this volume.

Finally, an impetus has been given to the application of psychoanalysis to music by interdisciplinary meetings initially held under the auspices of the American Psychoanalytic Association. Currently, these meetings are under the joint sponsorship of the Academy of the Humanities and Sciences of the City University of New York and the Department of Psychiatry of Mount Sinai School of Medicine.

These meetings have stimulated the original contributions that form the core of the present volume and largely determine its central themes.

This second volume of papers is introduced by a section, "On Music and Method," consisting of two papers that stem from the 1990 meeting of the above noted Colloquium in Psychoanalysis and Music. The title of the first chapter, "Promissory Notes" (a term borrowed from musicologist Edward T. Cone), indicates the purpose of the conference, an exploration of possibilities. It also serves, in part, as the title of the opening paper by Stuart Feder. This paper is an attempt to develop a reliable and responsible method in the application of psychoanalysis to music. It is followed by a preliminary report by Martin L. Nass of an eighteen-year study of contemporary composers based on extensive interviews conducted by Dr. Nass. (This paper served as a basis for a roundtable discussion with a group of composers and others at the 1990 Colloquium.)

In a first paper that extends his psychoanalytic work in art to music, Gilbert J. Rose presents a theory of affect in music. Eugene L. Goldberg's discussion of the Rose paper also provides a wide-ranging review of recent developments in related fields.

These contributions pointed the way to the theme of the 1991 conference, "Communication of Affect and Idea in Music," in which the six participants were equally divided between psychoanalyst/psychiatrists and musicologist/music historians, all of whose papers are published in the following two parts of this volume. In the second section, "Affect in Music," two of these papers may be found in addition to those by Rose and Goldberg: David Epstein, a conductor and music theorist, discussed material from a forthcoming book relating musical motion to affective "emotion" and the nature of its communication among a triad of composer, performer, and listener. The paper that appears here is an abridged version of one of the chapters. His annotations and citations of the literature are extensive, and along with those provided by Leo Treitler, another participant and contributor to this volume, provide a unique bibliography for the interested reader. Treitler's paper "Reflections" imaginatively explores the interface between music and psychoanalysis noted earlier. He deals not only with structure, narrative, hermeneutics, and other aspects of meaning and interpretation, but strives to place the very study of these elements in its historical and cultural context. In a final paper in this section, Pinchas Noy pursues his long-standing interest in the psychoanalytic understanding of art, in a comprehensive exploration of emotion in music.

The third section, "Studies of Composers," begins with a paper on Bach and Mozart by Robert L. Marshall, a Mozart scholar. Marshall writes of the interface of music and psychoanalysis that relates to character and style in both mental life and art. It is this feature that Feder seeks to emphasize and develop in his discussion of Marshall's paper. Peter Ostwald's rich study of Robert Schumann informs the next contribution which seeks to analyze a single Schumann song against the biographical background of its composer. There follows George H. Pollock's application of his extensive studies on the human course of life—here, oedipal issues and aging—to a consideration of the *Ring* of Richard Wagner. Morton F. Reiser similarly extends his psychoanalytic explorations in dream imagery, memory, and neuroscience to the study of music. His focus in this paper is the nature of the *leitmotif* in the music of Richard Wagner. Richard L. Karmel's psychoanalytic study of a unique modern composer, Erik Satie, who was a controversial avant-garde figure in his time, brings this section to a close.

The fourth and final section of this volume, "Historical Essays," brings together two studies relating to Freud. The first, by Cora L. Díaz de Chumaceiro, explores the myth of the place of music—or lack of it—in the life of Sigmund Freud, putting it in a historical and cultural perspective. In particular, she focuses on Freud's knowledge of the life and work of Richard Wagner. Complementing this is David M. Abrams' study of Max Graf, the only psychoanalytic pioneer who was also a professional in music, a critic. Of further historical interest, Graf was the father of Freud's "Little Hans," the "colleague" through whom Freud conducted his correspondence-analysis of the child.

Owing to space considerations in the earlier volume and, as a result of the decision to publish only original articles in the present volume (with the exception of David Epstein's abridged chapter), several outstanding contributions to the literature of psychoanalysis and music have been omitted. Particularly noteworthy are Stanley M. Friedman (1960), "One Aspect of the Structure of Music: A Study of Regressive Transformations of Musical Themes"; Martin L. Nass (1989), "The Building of Psychic Structure from Transformed Scream through Mourning: A Critical Review of the Literature on Music and Psychoanalysis"; Eero Rechardt (1985), "Experiencing Music"; Gilbert Rose (1987) "In Pursuit of Slow Time: Modern Music and a Clinical Vignette"; and Ellen Handler Spitz (1985) "Ancient Voices of Children: A Psychoanalytic Interpretation." All are readily available elsewhere.

We anticipate that in future issues of this serial but aperiodic publication, other aspects of psychoanalysis and music will be considered. The nature and inherent problems of performance will be an area to develop in more detail. In addition, clinical aspects of musical performance and creativity will also be covered. In addition to these and other areas already explored to a degree in the first two volumes, we now anticipate seeking only new papers as we move further away from an anthology form and more toward a journal of original contributions.

S.F.
R.L.K.
G.H.P.

REFERENCES

Feder, S., Karmel, R. L., & Pollock, eds. (1990), *Psychoanalytic Explorations in Music.* Madison, CT: International Universities Press.

Friedman, S. (1960), One aspect of the structure of music: A study of regressive transformations of musical themes. *J. Amer. Psychoanal. Assn.*, 8/3:427–449.

Nass, M. L. (1989), The building of psychic structure from transformed scream through mourning: A critical review of the literature on music and psychoanalysis. *The Annual of Psychoanalysis*, 18:159–181. Hillsdale, NJ: Analytic Press.

Rechardt, E. (1985), Experiencing music. *Scand. Psychoanal. Rev.*, 8:95–113.

Rose, G. (1987), In pursuit of slow time: Modern music and a clinical vignette. In: *Trauma and Mastery in Life and Art,* ed. G. Rose. New Haven, CT: Yale University Press.

Spitz, E. H. (1985), Ancient Voices of Children: A psychoanalytic interpretation. *Curr. Musicol.*, 40:7–21.

I

On Music and Method

Chapter 1

"Promissory Notes": Method in Music and Applied Psychoanalysis

Stuart Feder, M.D.

Psychoanalysis, applied to the arts, has long been considered the unruly stepchild of clinical orthodoxy. From the viewpoints of both psychoanalysis and the individual arts, the borderland field of study has acquired the reputation of being the least disciplined of the disciplines and woefully unprincipled. The matter is frequently complicated by what is a relative lack of literacy in the area of application on the part of applied psycho-analysts working in the arts, and conversely, by a lack of famil-iarity with psychoanalysis on the part of scholars in other fields.

Music provides a particularly good example of the above state of affairs in both practice and promise. For here the training and communication gap has resulted in analytic contributions far less successful than those in the visual and literary arts, which have been more characteristic of applied psychoanalysis (Feder, Karmel, and Pollock, 1990). Contributions in music are frequently found by musicians to be unrealistic and amateurish. On the other hand quasi-analytic applications on the part of music historians and other writers in music are often found by analysts to be facile and unconvincing—more likely to be dismissed as journalistic examples of parlor psychology than responsible applications of psychoanalysis. Thus the gap widens.

Yet there is something fundamental to music which seems promising and applicable to the study of all of the arts, which particularly commends it for interdisciplinary study. This is its essentially formal property, which was perhaps put best more than a century ago by the art historian and aesthetician, Walter

Pater, when he wrote, "All art constantly aspires to the condition of music" (1873, p. 16). What is important here is that a
consideration of form might provide a bridge between a work
of art and the mental life of its creator. It might, for example,
link elements of character and style seen in or out of a clinical
setting with stylistic features of art. Further, it might illuminate
elements of the underlying structures of mind.

What follows is an attempt to derive and develop guidelines
and governing principles which might be useful in the application of psychoanalysis to art—music serving here as the extreme
but not unique example, since these principles are applicable
elsewhere as well.

In doing so, I have engaged the literary collaboration of
the musicologist and theorist Edward T. Cone in the form of
an article of his which also provides the musical specimen illus-
trating this discussion and, in part, its title as well. More than
this, Professor Cone thus serves the role of applied *musicologist*
complementary to the writer as applied *psychoanalyst*. From the
two approaches, it is hoped a framework can be established for
the consideration of some useful guidelines, the above mentioned "principles." Cone's paper is: "Schubert's Promissory
Note: An Exercise in Musical Hermeneutics" (1982). Thus, although the example is intended here chiefly as background for
the discussion to follow, we start with a consideration of his
article regarding Schubert's poignant *Moment Musical* in A flat,
op. 94 (D780), number 6, written in 1824 (Figure 1.1).

MUSIC, AFFECT, AND HERMENEUTICS

In describing the music as "poignant," one immediately and
spontaneously falls into a mode of discourse which links two
issues equally germane to psychoanalysis and music: feeling
and meaning. We have entered the realm of affect and idea.
In doing so one also falls almost inadvertently into a kind of
common aesthetic judgment which uncritically combines interpretation with listener response, of the order frequently encountered in program notes and the like. If then, Schubert's
Moment Musical can properly be said to be "poignant" (according to Webster, "painfully affecting the feelings: pierc-
ing"), there are at least two implications: first, the music seems

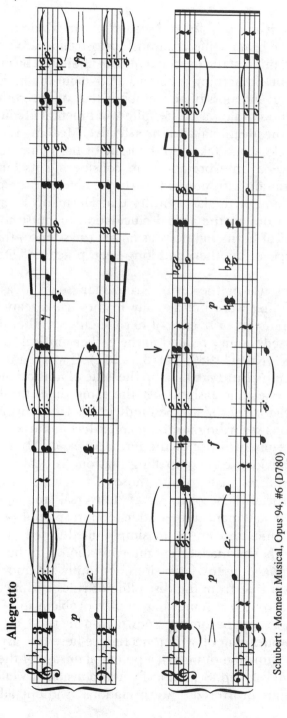

Schubert: Moment Musical, Opus 94, #6 (D780)

Figure 1.1. Schubert, F.: *Moment Musical* in A flat, op. 94 (D780), number 6.

to be inherently meaningful and second, the meaning conveyed
to the listener bears some relationship to feelings. Why these
issues should interest the psychoanalyst at all should be immediately apparent. Something is being stated about the mental life
of the listener and possibly even about that of the composer,
although in no simple way. The spheres of mental life involved
are specific: the ideational and the affective. Meaning is central.

In his article, Cone takes up the issue of hermeneutics, "the
art or science of interpretation" in considering its long and
uneasy association with music. Clearly, he notes, by the period,
"toward the end of the last century that Hermann Kretchmar
applied the word to the verbal elucidation of musical meaning, . . . musical hermeneutics was an art (or science) that, under one rubric or another, had long been practiced" (1982, p.
233).

Despite his use of the term, Kretchmar's own ideas about
musical meaning were not actually in the mainstream of the
then developing art or science of hermeneutics; rather, his was
a more focused inquiry related to the earlier musical "doctrine
of affections" (Kneif, 1980, Vol. 8, p. 511). It was left to others
in the twentieth century to take up the issue of musical meaning
in a more systematic fashion. At the same time, the lack of
method or theory never stopped individuals from formulating
interpretations regarding meaning and affect in music, such as,
for example, my own use of the term, *poignant*. After all, the
experiential evidence is compelling that one is dealing with a
system of symbols analogous to those of language. If this led
to the superficial cliché of music as "universal language," it is
nonetheless a statement to be understood in spite of personal-
ized or pedantic, unscientific or simply uneducated, or—as in
the instance above—inadvertent interpretation. For the universality of language in any form does not imply a democracy of
interpretation free from the discipline of rules and method.

Freud confronted a somewhat similar problem in 1910. As
psychoanalysis was becoming known as a method of understanding the meaning of symptoms (hence here too, aspects of
the symbolic function of mind), a potential misuse of the growing science developed. Scientifically irresponsible if well-mean-
ing individuals proffered "interpretations" without adequate

understanding of the principles involved or the technical constraints necessary in their application. Freud coined the term *wild psycho-analysis* (1910). " 'Wild' analysts" he wrote, "do more harm to the cause of psychoanalysis than to individual patients" (p. 226).

By further analogy, this may be one of the reasons the field of musicology has until relatively recently taken a cautious, if not frankly phobic, stance toward musical hermeneutics. It would be equally suspect among colleagues to be considered a "wild musicologist" as a "wild psychoanalyst." Musicology not only developed during the same period as did psychoanalysis, but like it, aspired to science. Its given name, "Musikwissenschaft," was first used by Guido Adler in 1885 (Sadie, 1980), five years before Freud's publication of *The Interpretation of Dreams* (1900). A full century later, in 1985, Joseph Kerman observed that a point had been reached where "semiotics, hermeneutics, and phenomenology are being drawn upon only by the boldest of musical studies today" (1985, p. 17). This represented a radical shift from the musicology of the 1950s when, as he puts it, "a virtual blackout was imposed on critical interpretation" of this sort (Kerman, 1985, p. 42). Donald Francis Tovey's 1935 seven-volume *Essays in Musical Analysis* has been subject to ridicule. Tovey's "madcap metaphors by which dominant chords 'whisper', motifs 'stagger', [and] phrases are caught in the momentum of a planet in its orbit . . . " (p. 74), must have served to condemn Tovey as the champion Wild Musicologist by subsequent generations of writers. Kerman notes that by the 1950s "analysis" had "come to mean the detailed 'internalist' explication of the structure of particular compositions" (p. 17). Both the merit and the limitation of this approach was its seeming objectivity, which not only avoided the putative excesses of Tovey but even such minor violations as my own above in calling the Schubert piece "poignant." (The musical *analyst* [or music theoretician] is contrasted here to the musicologist whose more broadly based interests might subsume *other* musical meanings than those which are purely intrinsic.)

In the early seventies, an interesting compromise position with regard to multiple meanings in music was taken by Wilson Coker in his *Music and Meaning* (1972). Coker distinguished two types of musical meaning which he terms *congeneric* and *extrageneric*. The *extrageneric* is intuitively more easily accessible, that is, essentially any reference in a musical work to the non-musical be it object, event, mood, emotion, or idea. *Congeneric* meaning refers to relationships intrinsic to the music which can only be revealed by a detailed analysis of the music itself. Returning now to Professor Cone and Schubert, we find that Cone takes things a bit further. He suggests that Coker's dichotomy is misleading; that if "any verbalization of true content . . . is possible at all, it must *depend* on close structural analysis." Putting it another way, he asserts, "extrageneric meaning can only be explained in terms of congeneric" (Cone, 1982, p. 235). With this, he undertakes to derive from a *structural* analysis of the Schubert *Moment Musical* in A flat, an account of its *expressive* content, calling his impressive 3000-word analytic essay only "partial." I will summarize that in only very general terms here.

SCHUBERT: THE MUSICAL SPECIMEN

For our purposes here our considerations of Cone's extensive essay will be the more "partial" and the reader who is interested in more detail is referred to the article and, of course, to the music, which is readily available in both score and recording. (A somewhat more detailed account appears in a footnote below, which, also "partial," fails to do justice to Cone's rich musical analysis.)

Cone's account hinges on the musical and extramusical significance of a single note—its congeneric meaning in the context of the tonality and the structure of the brief work, and the extrageneric meaning to which it leads him.

The note in question is the E natural first occurring in measure 12 where, in context, it strongly implies a modulation to another key within Schubert's system of musical syntax. Introducing a strong interpretive implication of his own (and admittedly so) Cone calls the errant E natural "a promissory note" because it "has strongly suggested an obligation that it has failed to discharge" (p. 235). Thus he considers a "troubling element" to have been introduced, although Schubert devises inventive,

alternate musical solutions. Cone's entire musical (or congeneric) interpretation, as well as the extramusical (extrageneric)
interpretation that follows, hinges on a discussion of this singular E natural. His analysis makes rewarding reading, only a few
details of which will be described here.[1]

SCHUBERT INTERPRETED: CONTENT AND AFFECT

As Cone moves on from the above technical aspects of the music
to a consideration of its expressive potential, he asserts: "We
subconsciously ascribe to the music a content based on the correspondence between musical gestures and their patterns on
the one hand, and isomorphically analogous experiences, inner
or outer, on the other" (Cone, 1974, p. 166). This is a principle
perhaps first advanced by Suzanne Langer (1967) and discussed
by Peter Kivy in his book *The Corded Shell: Reflections on Musical
Expression* (1980). In my own "The Nostalgia of Charles Ives:
Essay on Music and Affects" (1990), I suggested that music can
both represent *and* communicate affect "through an intrinsic
morphology which mirrors the mental organization underlying
the affect" (p. 265).

As Cone apprehends the Schubert *Moment Musical* he finds
a congeneric, or intrinsically musical situation to obtain which
he essays to describe verbally as:

> [T]he injection of a strange unsettling element into an otherwise
> peaceful situation. At first ignored or suppressed, that element

[1]For example, Schubert, hardly eager to settle the case, dwells on the ambiguity of
the note, emphasizing its peculiar connection to E flat. By changing its musical spelling
to F flat in the following section, for example, he has now placed the two notes in the
relationship of the sixth and fifth (or dominant) tone in A flat minor (measure 24).
Shortly (measures 28–29), as the key of E major is asserted, and E flat in turn is
respelled D sharp, the relationship of the two notes is reinterpreted as leading tone
and tonic. The intricacies continue until the expectable reprise in tonic key (measure
46) followed by the by now inevitable arrival of the *promised* key (measures 47–53). The
obligation is fulfilled but hardly settled as the reprise unfolds. The unruly E natural
returns (disguised now as F flat) and in the following phrase of the reprise wreaks a
harmonic havoc which Cone analyzes in a kind of technical detail that would make it
impossible to separate out the congeneric from possible extrageneric implications. He
summarizes: "The harmonic detail of the development, then, has infiltrated the reprise
with devastating effect . . . [and] . . . the rhythmic irregularity, experienced in the development as an agreeable loosening . . . has almost destroyed the original balance.
[The] expansion of the consequent phrase is terrifying in its intensity" (Cone, 1982, p.
239).

persistently returns . . . and . . . seems to have become completely assimilated. But that appearance is deceptive. The element has not been tamed; it bursts out with even greater force,
revealing itself as basically inimical to its surroundings, which it
proceeds to demolish [p. 240].

In an attempt to adduce some "isomorphically analogous experience"—and it is precisely here that the writer makes *the critical
leap from music to mental life*—he asserts "the arrival of the 'for-
eign element' to be symbolic of the occurrence of a disquieting
thought to one of a tranquil, easy-going nature. Disquieting, but
at the same time exciting, for it suggests unusual and interesting
courses of action" (p. 240). Before the yielding to temptation
an investigation is made:

[T]he protagonist becoming more and more fascinated by his
discoveries, letting them assume control of his life as they reveal
hitherto unknown and possibly forbidden sources of pleasure.
Although when "recalled to duty" he attempts to "sublimate
the thoughts," successfully at first, . . . the past cannot remain
hidden. What was repressed eventually returns and rises in the
end to overwhelm him [1982, p. 240].

Cone now takes the final plunge in an attempt to relate the
music not only to the "emotional life" of its composer, the inner
events of mental life, but to those external events that constitute
biography. He cites very briefly Schubert's suffering from syphilis, contracted probably in 1822, and of course incurable at the
time. He speculates whether "Schubert's realization of that fact,
and of its implications, induce, or at least intensify, the sense
of desolation, even dread, that penetrates much of his music
from then on" (p. 241). As for the *Moment Musical* No. 6, written
in 1824, he wonders whether one finds something comparable
to Shakespeare's, "The gods are just, and of our pleasant vices/
Make instruments to plague us" (Cone, 1982, p. 241).

ON THE "MYSTERIOUS LEAP" FROM MIND TO ART

Cone's essay might be considered an example of applied musicology; that is, musicology applied to psychology in some general sense; to mental life in specific; and psychoanalysis tangen-
tially. As such, it may be viewed as complementary to applied

psychoanalysis in those instances where psychoanalysis has been applied to music. Both endeavors attempt to bridge a conceptual chasm.

We cannot help but note that in his account Professor Cone uses such terms as *subconscious, sublimate,* and not only *repressed* but the *return of the repressed.* More than this, there is a passing consideration of symbolism and a description of mental process which subsumes a strong element of conflict, although the term itself is not used. Similarly, drive and drive derivatives are touched upon in the form of impulse, fantasy, and the seeking of forbidden pleasure. Has the musicologist here become the wild psychoanalyst of whom I spoke earlier? I think not and propose to devote the remainder of this discussion to reasons why. What is central is the issue of method in applied psychoanalysis. In a comparable instance years ago with regard to psychosomatic medicine, Felix Deutsch coined a phrase that served as title to his book "On the mysterious leap from mind to body" (1959). In applied psychoanalysis or applied art, scholars on either side are confronted with the mysterious leap from mind to art, in the present instance, music.

THREE PRINCIPLES FOR APPLIED PSYCHOANALYSIS

Few if any general principles have ever been postulated which might serve as guide or even as point of entry in bridging the gap between mind and art. And few writers in applied psychoanalysis have specifically addressed themselves to method. Among the exceptions have been Gilbert Rose (1980) and Francis Baudry (1992), writing respectively on art and literature. Others, like the proverbial Wild Psychoanalyst, have jumped into the breach with explanation and interpretation, but without adequate exploration of either method or underlying assumptions. This has been one of the chief sources of both justified criticism of such endeavors and mistrust as to the reliability of method.

What can psychoanalysis bring to these considerations? I propose to briefly outline three principles germane to psychoanalysis and appropriate, if not essential in their applications outside of the clinical setting. That said, a caveat will be required as addendum, acknowledging the ways in which clinical and applied analysis necessarily differ, without diluting the potential explanatory force of the applied. Certainly, no comprehensive approach is intended, or for that matter is even possible at this point. I mean only to continue the discourse initiated by Cone from the point of view of a psychoanalyst.

The first, the principle of overdeterminism, is historically one of the earliest and most fundamental concepts in a psychoanalytic view of mental life (Freud, 1900). In discussing it I include a related concept generated by clinical psychoanalysis, that of multiple function (Waelder, 1930). The two remaining principles are essentially perspectives which have emerged from my own work rather than having served as starting points, but which stem from some of Freud's earliest writings on the nature of representation (1900, pp. 509–622). I believe all of these principles are latent in Professor Cone's analysis, and where they are not, an area of discussion is at least highlighted.

First Principle: Overdeterminism and Multiple Function

Any single interpretation may in itself tend toward the reductionistic unless put into a broader interpretive context. This is true whether one is dealing with the interpretation of clinical material, talmudic text, or artistic product. The principle of overdeterminism (Eidelberg, 1968) states simply that "a phenomenon may be caused by more than one factor, some being more important than others." This renders the result of any mental activity, including the creative, a compromise of diverse elements. A creative act is not merely complicated by its constituent, contributory strands, but enriched by them. They are necessary for a depth of meaning. Psychoanalysis has long since understood that this mechanism "is of wide application and not confined to the sphere of neurosis" (Eidelberg, 1968, p. 288).

One psychoanalytic scholar, Roy Schafer, makes the point that the psychoanalyst does not speak of what something "really" means. "For to speak of what something 'really' means" disregards not only the principle of overdeterminism but another important principle as well, that of multiple function. Schafer (1983) writes, "That one has discovered further meaning, weightier meaning, more disturbing meaning, more archaic meaning, or more carefully disguised meaning than that which first met the eye or ear does not justify the claim that one has discovered the ultimate truth that lies behind the world of appearances—the 'real' world . . . " (p. 8).

Applied specifically to the Schubert example, this principle suggests a universe of factors motivating the composer in what would seem manifestly to be purely "artistic choice" in the invention of a selection of even a single note or musical idea—for instance, the compositional selection of the troublesome E natural. To be sure, in the network of multiple motivations which might prompt the composer, such factors as taste, education, and tradition are of critical importance, but would ordinarily constitute the conflict-free element in artistic choice; that is, free from *neurotic* conflict, but not necessarily free from other inner creative struggles.

With regard to tradition, Cone considers the nature of its influence in musical decision making in a discussion of the technical and aesthetic aspects of the ambiguous "promissory situation" in music of the eighteenth and nineteenth centuries (Cone, 1974, p. 236). It seems to me that where there is a preponderance of the traditional element in artistic choice—or only the traditional—we are dealing with the cumulative effect of many minds in which traces of individual motivation may well have been diminished, obliterated, or even expunged. At the extreme of such a trend one may encounter works which are derivative and uninteresting, lacking in depth of any kind. In contrast, in the relative absence of purely traditional influence we may find not only individual psychology exerting itself but the originality of the innovator.

Overdeterminism accounts for multiple motivations including (although not limited to) those resulting from psychic conflict. Indeed, in any art worthy of its name, such multiplicity is required. For example, Cone's brief sortie into the world of interpretation does not preempt the possible importance of Maynard Solomon's later and fuller development of Schubert's character and motivational patterns in his *Schubert and the Peacocks* (1989). Rather, it is thus enhanced. (We will return to Solomon's contribution later.)

A related and reciprocal principle is that termed by Waelder, multiple function (1930). "According to this principle, every attempt to solve a task is necessarily, at the same time, an attempt to solve other tasks, even if incompletely" (p. 45). Applied to the concept of a creative act the requirements of several psychological functions may be satisfied. Waelder conceptualized this in terms of the requirements of the psychic agencies of mental life (id, ego, superego), the outer world, and the unconscious human imperative to repeat, the repetition compulsion.

I suggest that even so spare an artistic act as Schubert's invention of the "promissory E-natural" can be fruitfully viewed in this framework with appropriate caveats regarding interpretation. (Here, of course, I refer to fundamental differences between interpretation in a clinical and an applied setting.) For example, the single note in this instance as an ambiguous and pivotal nodal point may be viewed as a mental organizer and integrator. It may thus satisfy an ego function in the service of creativity while at the same time, the resulting creative product consists of a precipitate of the act. Simultaneously, the other requirements are also met. Not only the adherence to the harmonic "rules" but the stretching and breaking of them are in the province of superego function. And the id may be thought of as generating the sexual impulses described in Cone's "strange, unsettling element" which is "untamed." That such impulses may be forbidden and result in conflict speaks to the contribution of the superego of a different nature than a technical issue. Similarly, the tendency to repeat may be seen not only in its technical realization, but perhaps more deeply with regard to whatever unconsious wish or striving is symbolized. Further, the tendency to repeat may result in those idiosyncratic stylistic gestures which identify a piece of music as characteristic of its composer, his creative fingerprint, as it were. Reciprocally, an act of musical invention which results from the psychic demands of these agencies, in turn satisfies each of their requirements. It is thus that to speak reductionistically of what something "really" means is to parody psychoanalysis rather than to represent it fully. The creative act of composition, even in the choice of a single element, must be viewed as an multifaceted psychic compromise which inevitably includes unconscious as well as conscious elements.

Second Principle—Infinite Displaceability

There is a fluidity and flexibility in mental function which is well known clinically such that every aspect of mentation can potentially articulate with every other aspect. As a result one thing can readily come to represent another. This is perhaps clearest in the dream but certainly not confined to it. Put another way, *mental representations are infinitely displaceable*. Thus, whatever the discrete element identifiable in mental life, what can become represented in one *form* can assume another, and yet another form ad infinitum. We know, for example, that such diverse products of mind as symptom, character trait, parapraxis, joke and dream may be fundamentally related. Similarly, whatever can be represented, for example, in *visual* dream symbolism should be capable of representation in the *auditory* sphere. This in fact occurs in certain dreams which are primarily auditory. Indeed, it is the very bias of psychoanalysis toward the visual and away from the auditory that has been a strong element in rendering possible applications of psychoanalysis to music so elusive.

A recent article by Susan McClary, "Schubert's Sexuality and His Music" (1992), attempts to relate aspects of Schubert's character and sexuality to symbolic representations in his music. In considering Schubert's *Unfinished Symphony*, she suggests that "[W]hile sexual orientation need not have any influence whatsoever on creativity, Schubert may be deliberately exploring alternative constructions of subjectivity and affect in his music." A psychoanalytic view would of course add "unconsciously" to "deliberately." Whether or not one finds the working through of this idea completely satisfying in this widely criticized article, it is important to note its underlying assumption (Rothstein, 1992). It would be the infinite possibilities of displacement in intrapsychic life that would create the possibility that such a representation could be accomplished. In this regard I believe McClary's approach, if not conclusive, has a psychological authenticity.

Let us return to Cone's Schubert. Cone adduces a conflict in the mind of the composer, a "psychic pattern" as he says, which becomes "*embodied in the musical structure of the Moment Musical.*" (The emphasis here is mine but note its similarity to McClary's assumptions.) Seen as "a model of the effect of vice on a sensitive personality," it consists of strivings of a dangerous and compelling attractiveness which may overwhelm mastery and self-control and is associated with "indelible and painful marks on the personality" (1974, p. 240). Thus one avenue of displacement of the content and structure of mental life is seen as character. Another finds representation in the auditory sphere in musical symbol: the musical idea expressed in the promissory E natural.

If we were to adduce Solomon's separate formulations about Schubert, we might bring the conflict to a finer point — an analysis of what may be yet another avenue of displacement, actual sexual behavior, indeed perversion. He writes not only of the clandestine homosexuality of Schubert's circle but, more offensive to Viennese society, "the prospect of sexual relations between a man and a youth, with its connotations of child molestation and its glimpse of a taboo realm of experience" (Solomon, 1989, p. 203).

With this in mind might we bring the issue of infinite displacement full circle back to the music if one were to explore further musical examples in the same composer. Does this complex of psychic elements as described find further and more varied symbolic representation in other works of Schubert? McClary selected the *Unfinished Symphony*. Perhaps a song which would have the additional association of text would provide a further point of entry. One such, which would pursue the line of Solomon's thinking, would be Schubert's *Ganymede*. It is a setting from Goethe regarding the beautiful Trojan youth who was abducted by Jupiter and carried to Olympus and made immortal as cup-bearer to the gods. Goethe's poem ends passionately: "In your lap/ upwards!/ /Embracing, embraced!/ Upwards to your bosom,/ all-loving father!" (In German: In eurerm Schosse/ Aufwärts!/Umfangend umfangen!/ Aufwärts an deinen Busen,/ Alliebender Vater!) What might it yield upon the detailed musical analysis Cone performed on the *Moment Musical* or McClary on the *Unfinished Symphony*?

Third Principle—Infinite Representation

We come finally to a brief consideration of the multiple meanings any single creative element may bear. Viewed from the vantage point of a given symbol—*every symbol is capable of infinite representation*. (Thus, the two further principles are complementary, the principle of infinite *displaceability* and the principle of infinite *representability*.)

As a kind of compromise, a musical idea may bear multiple meaning of the kind discussed simultaneously. More than this, other meanings may accrue over the course of time and others become obscured. Again, Schubert provides two interesting examples, both in the direction of trivializing his music. The unfortunate, if well-meant, attempts on the part of music educators of the last generation to help students "appreciate" music—in this case, Schubert—led to putting words to the theme of Schubert's *Unfinished Symphony*. ("This is the symphon-y, etc.") It is an interesting although banal example of a meaning accrued which for many unfortunate students created a barrier to accessing other representations and meanings.

Finally, Schubert's *Moment Musical* in A flat itself had an interesting later history in this direction. In 1916, Heinrich Berte created an operetta based on a biographical novel of Schubert's life called *Schwammerl* (Mushroom). The operetta, *Das Dreimaderlhaus*, enjoyed enormous popularity and "must be considered one of the most successful stage works ever" (Hilmar, 1992, pp. 42–43). The last lines of its final lied, a lament, consists of the first section of our *Moment Musical*. Its words are:

> Nicht klagen, nicht klagen!
> Was Dir bestimmt musst Du ertragen!
> Halt Stille, halt stille,
> es ist des Schiksals Wille.
> Voruber, voruber, vorbei!

(Don't grieve, don't grieve!/ You must suffer your fate!/ Be calm, be calm, it is destiny's will./ It's over, it's over, it's over!) (Hilmar, 1992, p. 43).

Despite all, this and every other musical symbol retains its potential for other meanings—technical meanings, historical meanings, and a vast array of personal, psychological meanings. The complexity is compounded when one considers the contribution not only of composer and listener but performer as well. It is, I believe, this wealth of potential, the result in part of the "elaborate psychic compromise" noted earlier, that endows art. Indeed it is a necessary condition. It is this potential which makes it possible for the performer to return again and again to a work with renewed interest and for the listener to find a lifetime of fascination in an oft-heard work.

REFERENCES

Baudry, F. (1992), Faulkner's *As I Lay Dying*: Issues of method in applied psychoanalysis. *Psychoanal. Quart.*, 61/1:65–84.

Coker, W. (1972), *Music and Meaning*. New York: Free Press.

Cone, E. T. (1974), *The Composer's Voice*. Berkeley & Los Angeles: University of California Press.

——— (1982), Schubert's promissory note: An exercise in musical hermeneutics. *19th Cent. Music*, 5/3:233–241.

Deutsch, F. (1959), *On the Mysterious Leap from the Mind to the Body—A Workshop on the Theory of Conversion*. New York: International Universities Press.

Duckles, V. (1980), Musicology. In: *The New Grove Dictionary of Music and Musicians*, Vol. 8. London: Macmillan.

Eidelberg, L. (1968), *Encyclopedia of Psychoanalysis*. New York: Free Press.

Feder, S. (1990), The nostalgia of Charles Ives: An essay in music and affect. In: *Psychoanalytic Explorations in Music*, First Series ed. S. Feder, R. L. Karmel, & G. H. Pollock. Madison, CT: International Universities Press, 1990.

——— Karmel, R. L., & Pollock, G. H., eds. (1990), *Psychoanalytic Explorations in Music*, First Series. Madison, CT: International Universities Press.

Freud, S. (1900), The Interpretation of Dreams. *Standard Edition*, 5. London: Hogarth Press, 1953.

——— (1910), "Wild" psychoanalysis. *Standard Edition*, 11:221–227. London: Hogarth Press, 1957.

Hilmar, E. (1992), Observations on the "Trivialized" Schubert. Symposium "Perspectives on Schubert," Schubertiade, Tisch Center, 92nd Street Y, New York, January 25 to February 2.

Kerman, J. (1985), *Contemplating Music*. Cambridge, MA: Harvard University Press.

Kivy, P. (1980), *The Corded Shell: Reflections on Musical Expression*. Princeton, NJ: Princeton University Press.

Kneif, T. (1980), Hermeneutics. In: *The New Grove Dictionary of Music and Musicians*, Vol. 8. London: Macmillan.

Langer, S. (1967), On significance in music. In: *Mind: An Essay on Human Feeling*. Baltimore: Johns Hopkins University Press.

McClary, S. (1992), Schubert's sexuality and his music. Paper presented at Tisch Center for the Arts, 92nd Street Y, Symposium: Schubert the Man—Myth versus Reality, February.

Pater, W. (1873), The Renaissance, "The School of Giorgione." In: *MacGill's Quotations in Context*. New York: Harper, 1969.

Rose, G. (1980), *The Power of Form: A Psychoanalytic Approach to Aesthetic Form*. New York: International Universities Press.

Rothstein, E. (1992), Was Schubert gay? If he was, so what? Debate turns testy. *NY Times*, C11.

Sadie, S., ed. (1980), *The New Grove Dictionary of Music and Musicians*, 20 vols. London: Macmillan.

Schafer, R. (1983), *The Analytic Attitude*. New York: Basic Books.

Solomon, M. (1989), Schubert and the peacocks. *19th Cent. Music*, 12/3:193–206.

Tovey, D. F. (1935), *Essays in Musical Analysis*, 6 vols. & supplementary vol. London: Oxford University Press.

Waelder, R. (1930), The principle of multiple function. *Psychoanal. Quart.*, 5:45–62.

Chapter 2

The Composer's Experience: Variations on Several Themes

Martin L. Nass, Ph.D.

I have been studying the process of creativity for many years. This research has involved interviewing composers regarding their experiences during the inspirational phase of their work. The findings have supported the notion that the creative process is an autonomous function in the creative individual and serves to build and to maintain psychic structure. It can be involved in conflict, it can be related to conflict, but for the most part it is an aspect of the individual's "craft or sullen art" which is often accessible to him or her even under the most trying of circumstances.

There has been a long-standing notion among many psychoanalysts and biographers that the creative process and psychopathology are linked. A number of such studies have appeared over the years which I have discussed in a review of the literature (Nass, 1989). In the past few years, several works have appeared which have taken a similar, or even stronger position regarding the causal connection between creative activity and emotional and physical illness; that is, the illness is a necessary condition for the creative process. Their titles reveal their point of view; for example, *Creativity and Perversion* (Chasseguet-Smirgel, 1984), and *Creativity and Disease* (Sandblom, 1982). Oddly enough, in a work entitled *Creativity and Psychopathology* by Robert Prentky (1980), a cognitive psychologist takes a somewhat different position on creativity and psychopathology. While he documents scores of prominent men and women in the creative arts who had severe emotional difficulties, he uses information processing theory to conclude that the creative act entails a manner of processing information that is markedly different from the more conventional strategies used by less creative people and causes these people to appear "weird" to the average bystander (Prentky, 1980, p. 19). I disagree with his conclusion that research on mental illness may provide insights to the sources of creativity. My contention is that the best manner in which to study the creative process is to speak with the creators themselves. In the material to follow, I will cite several such works which discuss the issue of the relationship between creativity and pathology, offer alternative positions to their central thesis, and then present some illustrations of the creative process from some of my interviews with composers.

Dr. Philip Sandblom, a Swedish surgeon and art collector, has written a book entitled *Creativity and Disease* (1982). His thesis is that creative activity is enhanced by illness and disease. Thus, according to Dr. Sandblom, Matisse became an artist because his mother introduced him to paints as a diversion during his year-long bout with appendicitis. This resulted in his becoming an artist instead of a lawyer. Had modern surgical and antiseptic techniques been available at that time he would have become a lawyer instead of a painter and his art would probably have been lost to the world.

Simplistic as this reasoning is, it is a rather popular position in the explanation of creativity. Talent is not dealt with in this example of the relationship of creativity to disease. Reductionism is the order of the day. A similar thesis is presented in the study by Richards, Kinney, Lunde, Benet, and Merzel (1988) in which they conclude that "liability for manic-depressive illness may carry advantages for creativity" (p. 461). Creativity, however, is defined more in terms of originality than it is in artistic terms.

Sandblom (1982) also goes on to discuss the great violinist, Niccolò Paganini.

There was no end to [Paganini's] suffering—he was plagued by tuberculosis and syphilis, osteomyelitis of the jaw, diarrhea, hemorrhoids, urinary retention and infection. The diseases and the treatment he received gave him an increasingly strange and emaciated appearance. . . . But the most remarkable feat in his pathology was a congenital disorder, the Ehlers-Danlos' syndrome (It has also been referred to as Marfan's syndrome), which at the same time *constituted the basis for his violinistic virtuosity*. The condition is characterized by laxity of the connective

tissue and an excessive flexibility of the joints which enabled
Paganini to perform the astonishing double-stoppings and rou-
lades for which he was so famous. His wrist was so loose that he
could move and twist it in all directions and he could bend his
thumb back to the extent of touching the little finger! [Here,
one of the famous Paganini drawings is inserted to illustrate the
point]. . . . This kind of disorder which usually is detrimental to
the individual became in Paganini's instance artistically beneficial—it was a "blessing in disguise." . . . *The Devils Trill* was a trill
of disease [Sandblom, 1982, pp. 59–60; emphasis added].

By contrast, and I must say in a stroke of good timing to
support the thesis which I am advancing, the June 1990 issue
of *The Strad* magazine was devoted to Paganini on the 150th
anniversary of his death. I would like to cite some material from
one of the articles on Paganini by the violinist and writer Henry
Roth. Roth says:

Several years ago Dr. Myron R. Schoenfeld wrote, "there is good
reason to believe that Paganini was afflicted with (or perhaps it
would be more correct to say endowed with) Marfan's Syndrome. The long, sinuous, hyper-extensible fingers of his left
hand gave his fingers an extraordinary range of motion and
freedom of independent movement on the fingerboard . . . " Dr.
Schoenfeld then cites Pagnini's "cadaverous appearance" as further proof that the violinist had Marfan's syndrome.
  Apparently the good doctor made his judgments from the
surfeit of the violinist's portraits which in the main were imaginative artists' conceptions. True, Paganini was a picturesque personality who did all he could to emphasize his eerie, skeletal
image in dress and carriage. And who knows, he might have
had Marfan's Syndrome along with his heritage of tuberculosis,
colitis . . . syphilis. . . . But while . . . his infirmities undoubtedly
sapped his strength to a serious degree, it is not logical to believe
that either these debilitations or any supposed physical advantages contributed to his technical accomplishments. Rather, it is
more logical to assume that Paganini achieved supremacy *despite*
his physical handicaps.
  Paganini's son Achille testified that "Niccolò's fingers were
one-half inch longer than a medium-sized hand." . . . Insofar as
the factors of size and pliancy of the left hand and fingers are
concerned, as emphasized so strongly by Dr. Schoenfeld (and
Dr. Sandblom) these factors are practically nullified inasmuch
as today, petite teenage girls with small hands and fingers often
perform and record Paganini's caprices, concertos and other of
his works with exceptional virtuosity [p. 461].

I am quite certain that Mr. Roth had the young violinist Midori in mind.

There has also been a recent renewed spate of writing regarding the emotional status of Vincent van Gogh, partly prompted by the appearance of two relatively new biographies (Hulsker, 1990; Sweetman, 1990) and partly stimulated by the recent article in the *Journal of the American Medical Association* (Arenberg, Countryman, Bernstein, and Shambaugh, 1990) which hypothesizes that he suffered from Menière's syndrome and not epilepsy. Sandblom also had some comments about van Gogh's art and I will quote a small section of it:

> Vincent van Gogh had both manic and depressive components in his constitution, sometimes intensified by absinthe intoxication and complicated by his fits of epilepsy. . . . In a letter from his last summer he wrote: "I am painting immense expanses of wheat beneath troubled skies, and I have not hesitated to express sadness, extreme solitude." In the last of these pictures, *The Wheatfield*, the extreme traits of his personality combine in a harrowing epitome. The manic component is reflected in the tempestuous whirling brush strokes, the depression in the flock of black birds which incarnate the dismal thoughts that would soon drive him to suicide [Sandblom, 1982, pp. 51–54].

Sandblom's conclusion seems to be a good example of how writers in the fields of psychoanalysis, medicine, and psychology extend their expertise to analyze the creative process by examining the psychopathology of the artist and do not consider the role of talent in the lives of these people. In the *New York Times Book Review* of August 12, 1990, the two van Gogh biographies were reviewed by Michael Kimmelman who commented on the conclusions of both books: "In the end as both (authors) wisely acknowledge, the truth about van Gogh is that *as a painter* he demonstrated no evidence of insanity. Only someone in control of his artistic sensibilities could have turned out 70 such well-considered paintings in as many days, or could have executed the careful, varied landscape drawings he produced during one period of supposed mental instability" (p. 461, emphasis added).

Kohut (Panel, 1960), in some of his introductory remarks to a panel on "Childhood Experience and Creative Imagination" adopted a position similar to the one which I am propounding. He stated:

> The great in art and the truly creative in science seem to have preserved the capacity to experience reality, at least temporarily, with less of the buffering structures that protect the average adult from traumatization—but also from creativeness and discovery. . . . I would therefore be inclined to consider characteristic for the psychological makeup of the great creators, not firmly organized neurotic structures—though neurosis *may* be present—but rather the childlike aspects of their personality . . . and intense but shifting object cathexes [Panel, 1960].

This is also the position of Phyllis Greenacre (1957) who talks about the developmental issues of the gifted, including their hyperacuity to sensory stimulation, their intense empathic ability, and their retention of sensorimotor styles which enable them to build up projective motor discharges for expressive function. As I have stated elsewhere (Nass, 1984), their hypersensitivity and strong empathic ability quite often result in a narrowing of object distance, in increased narcissistic vulnerability, and in special self-esteem problems which become organized around their talent (Coltrera, 1965, 1981, pp. 3–73).

The artist's accessibility and continuance of developmentally early vicissitudes places him in a most vulnerable position, and threats to his integrity call forth threats to survival. The work commands a most special position in his psychic economy and overall functioning. To me it is a sign of greater ego strength for the creative individual to have constant access to the material of early development and to rework it   a creative endeavor, than to seal it off as most of us do. Our understanding of the nature of nonverbal thinking and nonverbal learning needs to be revised. Psychoanalysts are taught that primary process thinking is more primitive than secondary process thinking, which involves words and discursive language. If this is so, how is it that some of man's highest level of creative achievement—music, visual arts, and dance—are nonverbal? It should be emphasized that later does not necessarily mean better or more developed, and earlier does not mean more disorganized.

In this connection, I used to read the following quotation to a class of graduate students and ask them for their diagnostic formulation:

> The words or the language, as they are written or spoken do not seem to play any role in my mechanism of thought. The psychical entities which seem to serve as elements in thought are certain signs and more or less clear images which can be voluntarily reproduced and combined. . . . (These) elements are visual or muscular in type. Conventional words . . . have to be sought laboriously in a secondary stage [Hadamard, 1945, p. 142].

After they discovered that this was a description by Albert Einstein of his experience during the process of inspiration the class then had the opportunity to discuss the relationship between the creative act and psychopathology and how easily it is misunderstood and misinterpreted. I must emphasize again that there is not a point for point relationship between creativity and psychopathology. The creative individual has the capacity to call forth earlier ego states with their less structured cognitive organization and the resulting ambiguity between internal and external. This shift enables the artist to work with earlier forms of thought, which of necessity involve a more loosely organized separation between inner and outer stimulation. The artist's own impulses are often experienced as external in origin, thus feeling that they are the copyist and not the creator. One sees this attitude particularly in the literature involving nineteenth century composers, although several of the contemporary composers with whom I spoke also felt that their inspirational source was external. The experience of passivity and of recapturing early ambiguous states is present. Thus, the late Roger Sessions, through his writings and my interviews with him, noted that composers think in terms of musical sounds (this is incidentally true for many, but several with whom I spoke think in visual or kinesthetic terms).

The auditory sensory style in many composers and the fact that the ear and auditory pathways are hypersensitized in many musicians and composers raises some important questions. What are the physiological or experiential factors which sensitize an individual to sound? Some large percentage of musicians and composers have had hearing disturbances. Experiences of pain in the ear and ringing or buzzing during childhood appear frequently in biographical and clinical material. Among the world's great composers, Beethoven, Schumann, Smetana, and Fauré had serious auditory symptoms with related confusion over inside–outside differentiation. I must point out that difficulty with the auditory apparatus is but one of several possible sources of auditory hyperacuity in composers. The chief determinant of a low threshold for sound beginning in infancy and an auditory acuity and hypersensitivity common among musicians is probably constitutional. The use of sound as the central vehicle of communication between mother and child is also important. To my way of thinking, studies of the creative process which make use of this type of material through interviews with gifted people are the direction for us to take. In this way we can increase our understanding of a complex process and fill a severe lack in psychoanalytic theory in the understanding of the creative process.

My studies of composers (Nass, 1984) have been an ongoing attempt to apply a developmental perspective to the process of inspiration by relating some of the descriptive accounts given by composers to a framework which draws from the works of a number of contemporary psychoanalysts. My contention is that musicians have dealt with separation issues in a unique way, organizing a part of them around experiences dealing with sound or experiences which in some way have been integrated into a musical matrix. Thus, some developmental tasks, for example, the development and maintenance of object constancy, may be handled by the musically gifted child by incorporating them into his special auditory sensitivity and extending them through experiences involving sound. The musician is thus able to deal with the separation issues in a less concrete form and maintain a greater distance from the object.

I will now present what I have found to be some of the key elements in the development of creative imagination in composers and illustrate them with a sampling of material from interviews which I have conducted with a large number of prominent American composers:

1. Heightened sensory awareness, be it auditory, visual, or kinesthetic together with the capacity to retain early (nonverbal) experiences from childhood.
2. The capacity to deal with loss and use one's work as a means of doing so and working out issues of mourning.
3. The ability to take the difficult path when there is a less anxiety provoking alternative and to "own" one's work rather than view oneself as a passive receiver of ideas.
4. The capacity to tolerate and maintain ambiguity and unclosure.

I will discuss each of these in more detail and illustrate their operation.

Gifted people have heightened sensitivity to stimuli and a lower sensory threshold than do most other people. They seem to have many more receptive antennae out to receive stimuli. This style has been well documented in studies of the gifted. I, too, found this to be true. They also are close to early memory experiences and can retain them in vivid form over long periods of time. One such composer, the late Roger Sessions, described in detail to me his being wheeled in a perambulator to the Brooklyn Heights waterfront to see Admiral Dewey return from the Spanish-American War. He remembered the crowds, the colors, and the excitement. Another described his early experience as a toddler in trying to compose music by copying columns from a book of his father's and trying to imitate notations and then play them on the piano. Still another told me that the stories and the games which he played with his Romanian father appear in all of his music as do visual and other sensory experiences.

In my talks with these composers over the years, I have been most impressed by their auditory acuity and auditory sensitivity. For the most part, the musical impulse is auditory, and it is given shape, time, and dynamic value by the composer. It is a link to the composer's past and a line of mastery of the world of sound. Many composers speak of constantly hearing sounds and musical phrases in their consciousness. One told me that he had music in his head all of the time and that this had been true since childhood. "I realized that it was music that I couldn't identify so I knew I must have thought of it myself." Another, who grew up in a river town in Appalachia, told me that the echoing of sounds is in his music, and it reflects his hearing experiences growing up. There was always an echo to sound as he heard it resound among the mountains. Another composer discussed in detail how sensory experiences appear in much of his music and how he is so attuned to experience of touch and movement. He said, "Words are impositions. I learned to talk with instruments rather than words."

That the creative act can be a means of dealing with the mourning of a loss has been well documented, witness the many requiems which have been written over the years. In the psychoanalytic field a number of papers have been written on memorialization in music and on the creative act as serving the function of dealing with a loss by the composer or artist. George Pollock has been one of the pioneers in this area (Pollock, 1974, 1975). He makes it clear, however, that musical creativity and creativity in general are not dependent upon object loss, but given such loss, the direction of the creative act will be influenced by the intrapsychic processes of mourning. This has been noted in the case of Rossini whose creative output took a radical drop for the last forty years of his life following the death of his mother (Schwartz, 1965).

A similar point has been made by Stuart Feder (1980) in the case of Charles Ives, whose musical productivity dropped during the last thirty years of his life. Feder attributes this to Ives having reached the age that his own father was when he died. One composer told me that several of his most powerful pieces were written as a means of dealing with the tragic death of his college-aged son. "The music was a quest for an answer or a solution to the question of 'why,' but I suppose there is no answer." Another was inspired to write a piece to deal with feelings at the end of an intense love affair. However, a number of composers with whom I have spoken told me that they do not believe that a single experience can produce a piece; rather there is an ongoing process which may become organized around a particular experience, just as an external event in a person's life can organize a particular set of actions which are looking for an occasion—a phenomenon with which psychoanalysts are quite familiar. This makes the most sense, and also that the triggering experience in reality becomes the catalyst.

Some composers I have spoken with have consciously tied compositions to specific experiences, such as a view of New York
from a plane, or a rural village at sunrise. While respecting
their subjective view of their creative process, one can entertain
the possibility that more complexities may be involved. It is
quite possible that their understanding may mask some other
levels of meaning in their creative experience.

Several composers have been quite specific as to the complicated nature of inspirational impulses. That is, a piece is not
seen to be connected to a particular experience. One of these
composers, György Ligeti, was not interviewed by me but related his opinions to Péter Várnai. This was published as a book
entitled *György Ligeti in Conversation*. He said:

> Creative activity in music, painting or literature is not directly
> prompted by an experience you have just been through. You
> have to look for it in your genes or in childhood experi-
> ences. . . . There is no doubt that external circumstances, both
> personal and shared experiences . . . leave their mark on a piece
> of music. But for the . . . piece of music . . . to take actual shape
> you need an individual creative will, an artist's talent. The exter-
> nal world does not affect this inner core of creativity . . . if you
> try to understand a work from the actual circumstances of the
> artist, you will get nowhere. It is a rather childish idea that a
> composer will write music in the minor key when he is sad, it is
> rather too simplistic. There is no doubt, however, that the stance
> of the artist, his whole approach to his art, his means of expres-
> sion are all of them greatly influenced by experiences he has
> accumulated in the course of day-to-day living [Ligeti, 1983, pp.
> 20–21].

I have been given similar interpretations by two composers in
quite recent interviews. One said: "If there's a direct connection
between a composition and an event, they will end up being
more distant. Music isn't set up that way" (as in writing a poem).
Another told me:

> I tend to think it's not a one-to-one relationship where some-
> thing happens and then I say I'm going to write a piece. I think
> that all of life is constantly influencing you. One's art is a reflec-
> tion of the life one leads. It's all there. I wrote a piece after the
> death of a special uncle of mine and suddenly I started hearing
> this beautiful cello piece and started to compose that. It must

have been though that there was a cello piece inside of me waiting to come out anyway at some point and that it meshed with
an actual experience. I tend to think that more than to think
that the event actually triggered something that wouldn't have
been there in some fashion otherwise.

In reviewing the writings of some nineteenth century composers (Nass, 1975), I found that they attributed some of their
creative impulses to external sources, be it God, some supernat-
ural spirit, or some external muse. One of the questions which
I frequently asked the composers I interviewed dealt with this
issue, and one finds a sense that for many this self-created work
has taken on a life of its own and is viewed as outside of the
composer. Of course, when there is more careful examination
and questioning, the composers acknowledge that the piece
comes from inside of them, but this is an area which has raised
some questions regarding "owning" one's creation and dealing
with what I feel to be the awesome sense of aloneness and
separateness in truly creative work. It seems to fill an adaptive
need to feel that the work has an independent existence even
during the creative act. Thus in a recent interview with a composer, I picked up on a statement regarding "where the piece
is taking me." In response, the composer said,

> I'm making up the piece and the further it goes the more it
> seems to have a life of its own. I have to wait till the next step
> presents itself. Then suddenly it takes me there and I say, "OK,
> this is where the piece has to go." It only happens in context.
> There's the sense that I am the slave of the piece. I suppose I'm
> its master on the one level but I'm also its slave. If I don't listen
> to it, then the piece doesn't go. It feels as though it's coming
> from somewhere else.

Another, in a similar vein, talked about *his* sense of outside and
inside:

> There's the notational representation. It's a separate entity. It
> takes on its own life. I find—and I'm sure most composers are
> like this—the more concrete the work becomes, the more it be-
> comes "other" and that has advantages because it means you're
> not stuck inside, and disadvantages because you begin to lose
> your grasp in some sense. These are such profound and complex
> questions about the mind.

In past writings (Nass, 1984) I have attributed this characteristic to the creator's issues around facing and dealing with separation trauma which is a feature of all work involving creative imagination. This was and continues to be one of my fundamental conclusions and a consequence of the creative act. There seem to be phases during which the composer shifts in and out of this posture. To own one's production and truly be separate involves facing the most profound issues of aloneness and the continuous experience of separation. This is the burden carried by the creative individual.

In this context, one would wonder whether a commissioned piece with certain parameters set would limit the composer's spontaneity or independence. It was interesting to discover that a vast majority of successful contemporary composers mostly write works which have been commissioned, and while they feel that there are confines because of these parameters there is still unlimited freedom to compose. At times the composer is given the freedom even in the commission to set the instrumentation. One was working on a piece for two pianos and two cellos and was wondering why he chose that particular instrumentation.

> They needed to know what combination I was writing for a year before I even began to work on the piece, so I did a kind of frivolous thing. I invented something off the top of my head and now I'm trying to respect whatever the voice was that told me to do it that way. On the surface of it, it seems like a completely capricious idea. I'm trying to believe that there was a reason for that and it will emerge. . . . I must have been hearing something when I said that combination of instruments.

Another told me that from the beginning most of his works were externally set by some kind of circumstance. He said:

> I now have about 153 works in my catalogue and I imagine there must be a few in there whose nature I chose myself but, in general, even the ones earlier on which I wrote without a fee were written for specific performers and friends of mine. I began a professional career very early and right from the start was asked to do things for performers who wanted to play them. . . . There is one case where I wrote a flute concerto for a colleague and I chose the instrumentation for that . . . a group of instruments I had an interest in at that moment.

The commission thus can set the timbre of the piece, the combination of the instruments, and also the length of the piece, but the freedom within these parameters is extremely broad and the composer has access to a wide range of possibilities within the limits. However, it must have some effect on creating a constraint on the virtual freedom one has to express one's ideas completely.

Another critical area is one I refer to as the capacity to tolerate ambiguity. The ability to tolerate unclosure, to live with it as a part of one's functioning, is a necessary condition for creative activity. It involves the capacity to wait, to discard quick, glib answers to problems, to deal with not knowing for long periods of time rather than supplying a ready answer as a means of obtaining completion. As I noted in my paper on composers (Nass, 1984), the ability to deal with not knowing differentiates the outstanding artist from the more routine one. Maintaining unclosure enables the more gifted artist to look at and work with path-breaking alternative solutions to problems. It also requires the ability to deal with intense feelings of anxiety during the process of looking inward, not unlike some intense periods of psychoanalysis. It also requires the capacity for self-reflection and self-awareness and an understanding of one's style of working. Two composers had most interesting perspectives on this issue:

> I can work for many months and not feel that I understand what the piece I am working on is about. And I'm usually waiting for a . . . I think of it as a kind of crisis. This involves doubting the sketches, doubting the quality of the ideas, doubting the concept of the form. In short, doubting whether you can make a piece at all. And then, hopefully at about that time, there's some sort of little twist in the way of ideas coming together. It may throw things in a different light. I mention this because it happens so consistently . . . and it never gets easier. One would think that with experience you would learn to prepare for that or to bring that on much earlier. I haven't learned to do that. As a matter of fact, I think the tendency is the other way. As you write more, you can feel too experienced, like you know, "I can handle this" and then you don't open yourself up and you're less apt to. I sense a danger in becoming too systematic or too methodical, too much of a routine.

Another dealt with an additional problem of the pull against finding a routine solution to a problem in composing:

> There is a sense that one has explored every reasonable alternative that applied to that moment and there comes that time when you say "I absolutely cannot think of anything better than that." You think that having explored all the alternatives you have now the best solution at hand. It's a feeling, not an absolute knowledge. It can be subject to reversal, refinement, addition or amendment. The facile composer is the one who sorts all this out quickly, maybe in his head and arrives at them quickly. A superficial composer arrives at them too quickly because he looks only at the easiest alternatives; he doesn't look at the path-breaking alternatives, the overwhelming alternatives, you know, the ones that you can't quite face.

New ideas involve another separation experience and a reexposure to the unknown. They involve a move away from ritualized stances and routines as a way of dealing with the anxiety of facing the new and the awesome. It is far easier to repeat a well-tried approach than to attempt a completely innovative way to deal with a problem. It seems to me that this is true in every creative field including my own where all too often psychoanalysts use rather routine interpretations where an imaginative, unique formulation is indicated, one that calls for more uncertainty and requires a more creative integration. One also sees it in the visual arts where a painter's style does not change even over a lifetime of work. Also characteristic of the process of inspiration and composition is the ability to be open, to shift into and out of a more loosely organized state of consciousness at some point in the work. In fact, creative individuals during the act of creation often lose a sense of time and may work for long periods without being aware of how much time has elapsed. Or they can have great difficulty in "breaking the ice." Several composers described these kinds of experiences to me:

> It was my 2nd string quartet and I remember I sat and wrote and it was in the middle of the night and there was a film of white light in front of me. I couldn't see. All I remember is this white light. I don't remember what I wrote. I finally put the pencil down and slept 24 hours. When I got up I looked at

it and I don't remember writing that. . . . It was one of those experiences.

Another stated, regarding beginnings: "The first weeks and months can be a kind of agony and a torture because nothing's coming out. You can't understand how you could possibly write any music. You begin to think, 'I'm shot. There's nothing left. I have nothing new.' And then, little by little it begins to happen." Some have developed styles of beginning work which help them move on to new material:

> The conception of an idea. . . . I think it's very inconsistent. But I suppose that there are over the long periods resemblances, you know, to what happens. I sketch a lot, so I have sketch books where I have thematic material and I mark them down by ear. And I have this stuff which I play over frequently every time I prepare a piece, and it's like letting something hatch inside.

Another described a rather similar approach:

> I don't plan out my compositions the way some composers do. . . . I go from the opening to the matrix. I hear it in my mind. I don't hear the specific pitch, but I hear duration and time values. Sometimes I find the pitch at the keyboard. That takes me a while to find, but when I find it, I recognize it as something I want to work with. And that's always the start. It's very often a harmony, a vertical setup and from that point on I hear the next thing in my mind.

Another variation on planning a piece of music was expressed by a different composer: "I frequently start at the end of a piece. I like to pin down that end and I've done that in most of my music. It gives me psychological confidence."

He stated further:

> For most of my music there's some basic impulse, the next step is to find the overall shape. . . . I would describe this as a psycho-logical curve. It's the hardest thing for me. I encounter this with every piece and try to find a shape that seems logical. . . . I never dare write down the details of the opening of a piece unless I have a very clear idea of the total piece. . . . I must have the total conception of the piece otherwise I'm never going to finish. . . . I experience the music in an unrealized sense.

Clearly, issues of the composer's character enter into these styles of working and one must view these modes as an adaptive factor which puts the creator in a more comfortable position vis-à-vis his work. An analogous description was given by another composer:

> For me, the beginnings of all of the important sections of a piece need to be located before I can begin to compose the piece. I can't go to a crucial destination unless I know something about the goal point. I often go through a period where I'm waiting a lot with things I could begin, but I don't want to unless I have a sense of what they're pointing toward. . . . Eventually, those guideposts are there. I may then not know the order of the movements, but I know they are there.

The development of this self-observing function in the composer has struck me as a crucial necessity in artistic work. It is a function which then provides the artist with insight into his individual style, which can then serve as a regulator and help him through periods of difficulty during the creative process. For example, if a composer experiences the intense despair which occasionally arises during a phase of work, and recognizes this as a necessary part of the process of creation, it is more possible to "go with it" when it is understood as a natural course of events in the development of the piece. One can view this as analogous to a piece of regressive recall during a difficult phase of psychoanalysis where early memories are recalled through their being relived and the person is in a profound state of despair.

That it is difficult to hold onto and to effectuate is evident in the following comment by one of the composers with whom I spoke:

> I have the impression over the past few years that what I do now is a great deal more straightforward than what I did 15–20 years ago, which is not the result of any conscious effort on my part, but simply perhaps the result of learning enough to eliminate certain unnecessary things. Some people agree with that, but others tell me that it's pretty much the same consistently throughout. I'm in no position to judge. One can't ever step back far enough.

This self-observing function and the ability to wait and tolerate unclosure and not knowing is one of the basic characteristics of the creative mind. As seen from some of the statements of the composers, it involves the ability to sit with uncertainty and all of the anxiety which it entails and to wait until a solution to a problem is worked out in a manner which is fulfilling. It involves a degree of self-knowledge and trust in oneself and one's abilities which requires a high level of autonomy and ego strength. To view this as connected with a form of pathology is to me an absurdity. It is tantamount to saying that free artistic expression which draws on less structured thinking is pathological because pathological thinking is less structured. Were this logic applied to other fields of endeavor it would probably be seen more as a demonstration of the disorganized thinking of the formulator than as a valid scientific hypothesis. However, one sees this rampant in psychoanalytic writings. As mentioned earlier in this paper, this approach seems to be having a renaissance in psychoanalysis and is going a long way toward making our studies of the creative process somewhat distasteful to artists. The artist's capacity to remain open, to continually face the awesome, keeps him continually open to his own internal processes, and I feel this has resulted in this distorted notion that greater accessibility to internal processes is a sign of psychopathology. The individual who has contact with feelings and has the capacity to shape them in a unique view of the world has a greater degree of ego strength, is able to experience the onslaught of powerful feelings, and is able to do so over long periods of time.

The issue of self-trust is further exemplified by the following statement: "I write something and something else goes inside and composes by itself and comes back to me fresh. You have to trust your instincts as an artist."

Another composer, speaking to the same issue, talked about his learning to trust new ideas which emerged when he was working on something else. His impulse during an earlier phase of his career was to discard the "distraction" and to stay with the major work of his current project. He now stated:

I've had to train myself that it not necessarily be the project I'm working on. In fact, some of my best work started when I wasn't

working on something and got an idea. . . . I have also learned
that if you go in too soon to write something you can cause
yourself a lot of pain and screw it up. . . . This work takes time
and patience.

One could conclude on the basis of these statements that self-
knowledge and knowledge of one's own style of work is a major
issue in the work of the composer and may be an important
differentiating factor in the truly gifted artist. I have found this
one issue to be present in a consistent fashion in the interviews
with the composers. A final statement of this nature is in order:

For me the process has been to learn enough about the way I
can be productive through years of disciplining myself in certain
ways, to learn to allow myself not to set up a rule about the way
it's done. In each one of my projects, I've often found that I had
an idea, I wrote a piece and it was successful and I did it this
way. The next time I'm a different person and it's a different
project and it doesn't work that way. So what I've learned to try
to do is to be responsive to who I am in any given moment and
to allow it to work that way.

The artist is in a unique position to draw upon his fundamental autonomous stance and to trust what is inside of him. He is
able to listen to small cues, and to learn to attend and respond
to an inner voice which becomes a kind of self-guiding gyro-
scope in his work. In his artistic development this becomes
clearer and louder in the course of time and bears the individual stamp of the composer.

After many years of interviewing composers, this study has
resulted in the following conclusions: First, there is no single
way that gifted composers write, nor is there a consistent way
that an individual composer applies himself to his work. Each
piece is different and has its own methodology. Second, composers are not necessarily auditory people but use a variety of
sensory skills. They are also visual, kinesthetic, use tactile cues,
and tap all possible sense modalities in their work. Further,
there are as many individual variations in style of work as there
are character styles in people, and the composers with whom
I've spoken reflect this in their mode of working. Some need
to have clear conceptions of all parts of the pieces which they
are writing, some need to know where it will end before they

feel comfortable in beginning, and others have a style which is less structured and more open. Another major area which appears over and over in the discussions which I have had with composers is the necessity to have the ability to deal with waiting, doubt, and uncertainty. This capacity to tolerate not knowing and to be able to wait is what I have observed to be one characteristic of the highly creative mind. Most of the composers with whom I spoke had descriptions of their work which reflected the same point of view. Sometimes it is most difficult to continue the faith in one's ability during the most trying times of composing or dealing with the feeling of running "dry."

Finally, there is a consistent theme which one could best describe as being able to "take a chance." To risk trying something new, to go with one's gut instinct and use an innovative idea, to overcome the pull to be more conservative, these characterize the style of so many of the people I've spoken with over the years.

REFERENCES

Arenberg, I. K., Countryman, L. F., Bernstein, L. M., & Shambaugh, G. E. (1990), Van Gogh had Menière's disease and not epilepsy. *J. Amer. Med. Assn.*, 264:491–493.

Chasseguet-Smirgel, J. (1984), *Creativity and Perversion.* New York: W. W. Norton.

Coltrera, J. T. (1965), On the creation of beauty and thought: The unique as vicissitude. *J. Amer. Psychoanal. Assn.*, 13:634–703.

——— (1981), *Lives, Events and Other Players: Directions in Psychobiography.* New York: Jason Aronson.

Feder, S. (1980), Decoration Day: A boyhood memory of Charles Ives. *Musical Quart.*, 46:232–261.

Greenacre, P. (1957), The childhood of the artist: Libidinal phase development and giftedness. *The Psychoanalytic Study of the Child*, 12:47–72. New York: International Universities Press.

Hadamard, J. (1945), *The Psychology of Invention in the Mathematical Field.* Princeton, NJ: Princeton University Press.

Hulsker, J. (1990), *Vincent and Theo Van Gogh. A Dual Biography.* Ann Arbor, MI: Fuller Publications.

Kimmelman, M. (1990), Vincent observed. *NY Times Book Rev.*, August 12:1, 22–23.

Ligeti, G. (1983), *Györgi Ligeti in Conversation.* London: Eulenburg Books.

Nass, M. L. (1975), On hearing and inspiration in the composition of music. *Psychoanal. Quart.*, 44:431–449.

——— (1984), The development of creative imagination in composers. *Internat. Rev. Psycho-Anal.*, 11:481–491.

——— (1989), From transformed scream, through mourning, to the building of psychic structure: A critical review of the literature on music and psychoanalysis. *Ann. Psychoanal.*, 17:159–181.

Panel (1960), Childhood experience and creative imagination. *J. Amer. Psychoanal. Assn.*, 8:159–166.

Pollock, G. (1974), Mourning through music: Gustav Mahler. In: *The Mourning-Liberation Process*. New York: International Universities Press, 1989.

——— (1975), Mourning and memorialization through music. *Ann. Psychoanal.*, 3:423–436.

Prentky, R. A. (1980), *Creativity and Psychopathology*. New York: Praeger.

Richards, R., Kinney, D. K., Lunde, I., Benet, M., & Merzel, A. P. C. (1988), Creativity in manic depressives, cyclothymes, their normal relatives, and control subjects. *J. Abn. Psychol.*, 97:281–288.

Roth, H. (1990), The greatest violinist who ever lived. *The Strad,* 101:458–462.

Sandblom, P. (1982), *Creativity and Disease*. Philadelphia: George F. Stickley.

Schwartz, D. W. (1965), Rossini: A psychological approach to the "Great Renunciation." *J. Amer. Psychoanal. Assn.*, 13:551–569.

Sweetman, D. (1990), *Van Gogh. His Life and His Art*. New York: Crown Publishers.

II

ON AFFECT IN MUSIC

Chapter 3

Reflections on the Communication of Affect and Idea Through Music

Leo Treitler, Ph.D.

I shall engage our topic through observations about a little piece by Béla Bartók from the sixth and last book of the *Mikrokosmos,* Bartók's *Gradus ad Parnassum* for pianists (Figure 3.1). The piece is at once of interest because of Bartók's title for it: in Hungarian, "Mese a kis légyröl," "A Tale About a Little Fly" (this is a literal translation; I shall take up the translations in the published editions later on). If titles are labels then the piece itself is that tale, just as Dickens's novel is itself the *Tale of Two Cities*; Bartók's music, like Dickens's prose, is the medium of narration. How can that be? How can music convey action and suggest why it takes place? How can it portray character and feeling; interpret the past and anticipate the future? There is no doubt that Bartók thought these things to be within music's capabilities; he wrote these indications in the score: about the middle of the piece, "molto agitato e lamentoso" and just above, "Yikes! a cobweb!" (a better translation than what is in the edition; measure 49) and 10 measures later, "con gioia, leggero" (joyfully, lightly). Another piece in the *Mikrokosmos* (Book 3, no. 94) he titled "Hol Volt, Hol Nem Volt . . . " (Where Was? Where Was It?). This is a formula for beginning stories that corresponds to "Once upon a time. . . . " It is the piece itself that is a story, given *in music,* but this time there is no hint at all of what it might be about. How can that be?

Attempts to formulate answers to this question and the other ones I have posed fill volumes of philosophical literature. On the whole musicians and musical scholars act on the belief that it *is* so, without troubling about how it might be so. Bartók

43

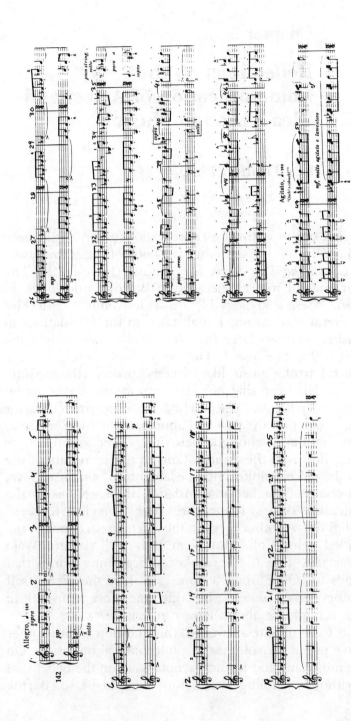

Figure 3.1a–b. Bartok, Bela: "From the Diary of a Fly." *Mikrokosmos.* Copyright 1940, Hawkes and Son (London) Ltd. Used by permission of Boosey and Hawkes, Inc.

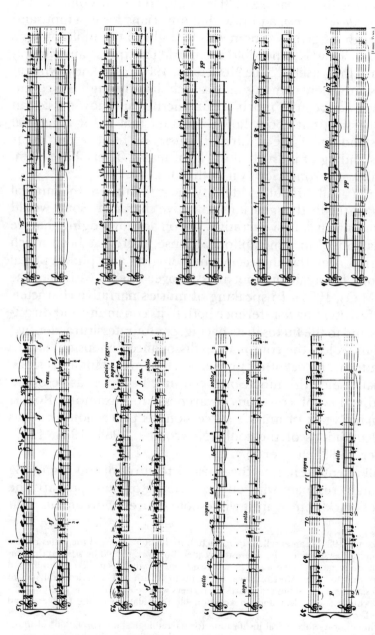

Figure 3.1c–d. Bartok, Bela: "From the Diary of a Fly." *Mikrokosmos.* Copyright 1940, Hawkes and Son (London) Ltd. Used by permission of Boosey and Hawkes, Inc.

wrote in the first measure of "Hol Volt, Hol Nem Volt . . . " the words *molto espressivo,* a phrase that musicians see in a thousand scores without giving a moment's thought to the philosopher's question, "How is it possible for music to express anything at all, other than itself?" (see Newcomb, 1984)[1] We know what to do. Disagreements among musical scholars through the centuries have not been so much about whether and how music can be expressive, but about how important that is for a general understanding of the nature of music, or for the particular understanding of individual works of music. There have been, and still are, strong views on both sides.

It is not at all difficult to identify those features of the musical tale about the fly that give it its narrative character. Some would insist on saying "quasi narrative," or on acknowledging that we say "narrative" in a metaphorical sense; there has been much discussion over this in recent musicological and philosophical literature, but again, it is not an issue over which I wish to pause here (Maus, 1991). In speaking of music's narrative character, or narrativity, I have reference both to its continuity and directedness and to the fluxes in its pacing, contour, tessitura, density, harmonic color, the consonance–dissonance dimension, rhythmic pattern, and yet other properties, that musicians and critics, especially since the nineteenth century, have felt as resonant with the flow of conscious awareness; for example, Robert Schumann's talk of music's successions as processions of ideas or of conditions of the soul[2] (Newcombe, 1983, 1984, 1987; Treitler, 1989, chapter 7).

I call attention first to the musical features of the beginning that might resonate with our experience of flies: perhaps the clash of black-note against white-note figures between the right

---

[1]Newcomb (1984) is an excellent introduction to the literature and the issues from a musicologist's perspective. The interested reader, however, should be advised that this excellent study cannot serve as an exhaustive guide to what seems like an unlimited literature on this topic. Most of it will be found in British and American journals of aesthetics, and may be of limited interest to readers who do not share the philosopher's primary concern with clear and unexceptionable formulations of the problems and proposed solutions.

[2]A contemporary theoretical justification for narratological interpretations of music can be distinguished from a historical one, that is, through evidence that composers or critics who were their contemporaries believed their music to have a narrative character. While such evidence should not be granted unquestioned authority, it provides sufficient grounds for a narratological approach as a hypothesis.

and left hands, resulting in a generally chromatic sonority, reminds us of the buzzing of flies. Or perhaps, instead, that clashing irritates us in a way that resonates with our irritation at flies, which is quite a different matter. Or something else, again, the way that the hands must be on top of one another and the fingers clustered to play this passage, reminds us of the smallness and the swarming of flies. Or all three. It is interesting that the latter two have more to do with the way we feel—emotionally and kinaesthetically—about flies than about the way we would describe them objectively. They are about our relation to flies, our identification with them, even if negative (why is it negative?).

These are the prominent dynamic features: the circling about at the beginning that goes nowhere but grows rhythmically more impatient, that is, compressed (measures 1–11); the shift to another locale (measures 11–26) where there is more of the same sort of circling about (26–30); a two-stage move upward to the highest place in the piece, the first stage tripping on its way, the second stage sharply directed to its goal, growing louder and faster as it goes (30–34, 35–41); eighteen bars of frenetic activity marked by increasing density of texture and dissonance in an ever narrower and more crowded sound-space, rhythmic compression punctuated by sharp accents (42–59). Then there is a sudden reduction of the texture to two threads, descending out of the region of crisis, matching the earlier ascent but with more energy (the alternation of the rising fourth and falling fifth in the right hand, mm. 59–68, pulls the music down), first rushing past the original point of departure (to measure 67), then making a chromatic return to it (68–75), and then a last stretch of becalmed activity that gradually subsides altogether.

Under the provocation of the title and those few indications in the score, this sequence is easily imagined as a scenario in which a fly is aimlessly buzzing about, now here, now there, then takes off for some goal that has attracted it, first uncertain, then moving faster and faster until it is caught in a spider web; panicked, it struggles to get loose, finally succeeds, and flies swiftly and happily back to its home ground—first flying right past it, then returning—where it buzzes about for a bit longer and finally settles down, perhaps dozes off. This scenario is

easily imagined because it matches the course of the piece so
closely. But the piece has this storylike action and affective
contour even without our imagining this or any other scenario.
We don't know at all that Bartók set out to write a piece about
the adventures of a fly; perhaps he wrote the piece and then
amused himself by giving it that very appropriate title and writing in those few indications in support of it. Other scenarios
can be imagined and matched just as closely to the same musical
narrative—including some in which the protagonists are nothing other than configurations of notes. Another piece in the
same volume carries the abstract title "Minor Seconds, Major
Sevenths" (there are many such titles throughout the *Mikrokosmos*). It, too, has a narrative quality, but of a different character, hinted at by the indication at the beginning: Molto adagio,
mesto (very slowly, mournful).

For the Boosey and Hawkes edition of the *Mikrokosmos* (1940),
the translations of the titles were reportedly provided by Bartók's associate Matyas Seiber (Benjamin Suchoff, personal communication). (Figure 3.1 is taken from Peter Bartók's Boosey
and Hawkes edition of 1987, in which some of the translations
have been changed, but not these particular ones.) In the case
of the piece we have been looking at, Seiber performed an
interesting transformation. With the Hungarian title the music
presents, mediates, forms, reacts to the episodes and internal
states in the life of the protagonist. Like the teller or singer of
all tales, the composer is free to shape the tale, through music,
to achieve whatever effect he wishes. The translations introduce
an evasion of this responsibility and control. The French title
claims that it is a report from the protagonist that we hear, but
at second hand, and the English and German titles claim that
it is at first hand; it would be, perhaps, closest to an enactment.
Each title identifies a different "I" and a different mix of direct-
ness and mediation. And thereby it locates the "I" of the listener
differently vis-à-vis the piece. It is that interaction of the selves
of the listener with those in the music—no, better put: the
awareness of the self (selves) in the music through its (their)
interaction with the listener's self—that interests me here; musical communication as a function of the interaction of identities.

But the piece itself is not altered by the title. I wonder
whether any one of the three titles is a more accurate label for

it than the others. There are two reasons why that question cannot be given a straightforward answer. First, any answer would presuppose that it is always the same voice that we hear throughout the piece, and that is rarely so for any piece. Doesn't it address us in a different way in the Agitato section, than in the enchanting little contrapuntal games between the two hands that divert our attention at the beginning and end? At the beginning, the hands mimick one another in inversion on the black and white keys, at the end playing arpeggios together, the right hand with five notes up-and-down on the black keys against the left hand with four on the white keys, so that they coincide with one another always in different tonal and rhythmic configurations with something like the effect of change-ringing. But again, that question has no straightforward answer. And second, it depends how we play it. After I had learned the piece (before learning the meaning of the Hungarian title) I listened to Bartók's performance on record (Hungaroton, side 9, LPX 12330-A), and I was surprised by the restrained character of his agitato, by the relative muting of the pain that I wanted to bring out in my (first person) performance.

A moment of Mozart, as reinforcement for much of this. The F sharp minor Adagio movement of the 23rd piano concerto (K488, A Major) is initiated by the piano with a song in a slow, steady rhythm that, if we know the convention, we recognize as a *Siciliana*, a kind of aria with pastoral and melancholy character. (I think it is safe to say that the melancholy character, at least, comes through even if we don't know the convention. See Figure 3.2.) But the steady, lulling pastoral character imparted by the rhythm is contradicted by the eccentric jagged contour that the melody begins to trace almost immediately. This leaves a corona of lingering dissonance (we can identify it as a first-inversion dominant seventh chord if we are interested in doing so) that is relieved only by the harmony of the orchestra when it enters. The resolution makes for a logical connection in the sense of the tonal grammar of the musical system.

But then the violins and winds, out of the blue, step forward and belt out an air of their own, with a very different character. I make an affective connection: to the disjointed lament of the piano a composed, strong, sympathetic, but nevertheless

Figure 3.2a,b. Mozart, W. A.: Piano Concerto #23 (K. 488), *Adagio*, in two piano reduction.

upstaging response. The piano comes back, inconsolable, sobbing even. The orchestra never takes up the *Siciliana,* but the piano eventually joins the orchestra's song—in self pity? in resignation? How we apprehend this movement—its structure and its expressive character both—depends on the vantage point in the piece from which we hear it. A very likely perspective is with the orchestra, calmly regarding the piano as a pathetic or even pathological figure. But what if we found an ironic, or even parodistic aspect in the successive escalations of the piano's moanings alternating with the orchestra's repeated display—even posture—of mature, serene, superior beauty? Such a response might turn the piece into social commentary, with the piano becoming a victim of the orchestra's haughty authority.

This becomes a question about what kinds of resonances the piece has with the collective experiences that contribute to the makeup of our conscious and unconscious selves. Indeed that is so about virtually everything that I have said about both pieces: Agitato, lamentoso, con gioia, melancholy, lulling, sympathetic commentary, consolation, calm, mature and serene beauty.

I emphasize that it is not only the communication of the movement's affective progression but also our apprehension of its structure that depends on its resonances with our inner selves, for its structural idea is certainly a matter of this interaction of the two voices, however *we* apprehend that. The resonance is reciprocal between the music and ourselves. Neither its constitution nor our response is a given.

One last point about the imperatives of the title of the little Bartók piece. I have called attention to some mimetic aspects. I think it important to say both that the piece plays on things that we know about ourselves, and that there is something about the musical details that resonates with our experience of flies. That must be so on at least two levels: the chromaticism suggests buzzing, but also the way that the two hands are physically in the same space, virtually on top of one another, getting in each other's way, mimics the intimacy that flies manage to have with us, whether we like it or not; the piece can reach the feeling of irritation with which we might react to that. But it does not evoke such a feeling necessarily; it depends whether we have it

about flies. William Blake conveyed the possibility of rising
above it, in his poem "The Fly," from his *Songs of Innocence and
of Experience*:

> Little Fly
> Thy summers play,
> My thoughtless hand
> Has brushed away.
>
> Am not I
> A fly like thee?
> Or art not thou
> A man like me?
>
> For I dance
> And drink & sing:
> Till some blind hand
> Shall brush my wing.
>
> If thought is life
> And strength & breath:
> And the want
> Of thought is death;
>
> Then am I
> A happy fly,
> If I live,
> Or if I die.

The poet's identification of himself with the fly goes along with
my suggestion about the resonance between the selves of the
music and our own selves. The parallel helps me to see that in
recognizing that resonance, I must be reaching over to a self in
the music. So does not the thought of the poem, like the expression of the piece, arise ultimately out of that resonance itself,
to which the words or the notes give us access? This reminds
me of the central thesis of the philosopher Roman Ingarden's
remark that "The work [of music] itself remains like an ideal
boundary [perhaps "horizon" would be a better translation] at
which the composer's intentional conjectures of creative acts

and the listener's acts of perception aim," for listeners' acts of perception are themselves intentional conjectures (Ingarden [1986]; see Berger [1988] for a resumé of Ingarden [1986]). But it also resonates with T. S. Eliot's praise of music as the only art that can reach "that fringe of feeling . . . beyond the nameable, classifiable emotions and motives of our lives . . . which we can detect, so to speak, out of the corner of our eye" (1951, p. 12).

What I have said so far I consider as introductory and heuristic remarks, made in order to enable me to get on to my next subject, which is the shifting place of our topic in musical studies during modern times. I return to my earlier observation that "disagreements among musical scholars through the centuries have not been so much about whether and how music can be expressive, but about how important that is for a general understanding of the nature of music, or for the particular understanding of individual works of music."

Music historians have been interested in systems of musical content, character, and expression that have been active as conventions in particular traditions; for example, the overall conception of music as a coded affective discourse that was active in theory and practice from the seventeenth into the nineteenth century,[3] and the "plot archetypes" that were conventionalized as "narrative strategies" in nineteenth-century symphonic music (Newcomb, 1984, 1987).[4] Based on the study of such systems historians have been giving out interpretations of particular works with the serious claim that they are solidly grounded in semantic fields that functioned in the time of their composition and initial performances. Such interpretations are not in the domain of subjective interpretive criticism; they embody a claim to be historically verifiable.

I hope to engage the reader's interest in a different kind of historical question, and one to which I think a psychoanalytical perspective can contribute significantly. What place has talk

---

[3]I am referring here to what music historians generally call "the doctrine of the affections." A brief and reliable account can be found in the *New Harvard Dictionary of Music*, p. 16.

[4]This conception has not had nearly the exposure and acceptance that the doctrine of affects has had among music historians. This is reported without implying any reservations on my part.

about the communication of affect and idea through music had
in musical studies, and what are the historical factors bearing
on changes in the kind of attention that this topic has received?
I construe "historical factors" quite broadly, to touch matters
of culture, ideology, and psychological style. Conversely, then,
what wider significance can we read out of the attitudes that
musical scholars have displayed toward our topic? If we can
frame the topic in this broader context, that might allow us
greater freedom in dealing with it in particular cases.

I'm going to consider musical studies during a relatively brief
time span, entirely within my memory: from the tradition of
problems, methods, and attitudes that was transmitted to me
through literature, teaching, and that commanding transmitter
of paradigms, the doctoral examination, during my graduate
studies in musicology beginning in 1958, to the present. What
I will have to say has application to a much longer time span,
but I want to speak out of my own memory.

To put it bluntly, there was no place for our topic in that
tradition. An exception is the first category of historian's questions that I mentioned, especially the investigation of the theory
of affects, which is open to descriptive and analytical investigation on the grounds of substantial documentary evidence, but
not to analysis in terms of interaction with the listener's subjective apprehensions. There might have been an opening
through the study of music aesthetics, but on the whole in the
American academic-scholarly construction of musical studies,
aesthetics has been an outsider, housed in philosophy (to the
detriment, I have to say, of all three fields, philosophy, aesthetics, and musicology). But I say "*might* have been," because musical studies remained well into the twentieth century under the
powerful influence of the music critic and aesthetician Eduard
Hanslick who, in 1854, wrote that music may very well be considered to have expressive effect, but that could not be the
concern of a scientific music-aesthetics.

That was then. For a sample of now, I have decided to look
at the topics of papers presented in the national meetings of
the American Musicological Society in 1990 and 1991. No
doubt that choice skews the sample toward the new and the
formerly marginal, as compared to, say, recent journals. But
that serves my present purpose.

Here are some titles from the 1991 meeting.

"Abstractions of Desire in Skryabin's Fifth Sonata"
"Sexual Signifying: Cinematic Representations of the Jazz
    Trumpet"
" 'Schwarze Gredel' in Mozart's Operas: Tonal Hierarchy and
    the Engendered Minor Mode"

("Schwarze Gredel" was the name given by the eighteenth-century theorist Joseph Riepel to the parallel minor tonic, which
he considered androgynous and destabilizing.)
    And here are some from the 1990 meeting:

"*Carneval*, Cross-Dressing, and Women in the Mirror" (the last
part of the title refers to the author's interpretation of musical
mirror images in Schumann's work as projection of gender
mobility).
" 'Das Land der Griechen mit der Seele Suchend': The Ambivalent Subject in Brahms' *Gesang der Parzen.*" ("Ambivalent Subject" refers to the author's interpretation about intentional ambiguities created by shifts of narrative voice in the music,
particularly ambiguities of gender that she associates with "the
manifold ambivalences" in his relationship to the painter An-
selm Feuerbach, with whose paintings she links Brahms' song.)
"The Proper Role of Metaphor in a Theory of Musical Expres-
    sive Meaning"
"Emotion and Drama in Instrumental Music"
"Schoenberg's *Erwartung*: Art as the Representation of Inner
    Events"
"Affect, Meaning, and Cultural Codes"

I don't want to give the impression that such topics are now
typical (far from it, they represent some 3 percent of the papers
presented). But the field is open to them and they are on the
increase, whereas I think it is not conceivable that any one of
these papers would have been given a place on a program
around 1960. What is more, the authors of these papers are in
the main in the junior ranks of faculties, but there is already a
foundation of books on related topics by their senior colleagues.

Joseph Kerman has offered two successive interpretations of this phenomenon: first it was "the ebbing tide of positivism" (1985, p. 201). More recently it was a "paradigm shift" (Kerman, 1991). I doubt that either of these slogans has much explanatory or even descriptive value. Philosophical orientations like positivism or idealism do not just ebb and flow as autonomous natural processes, and to say that we are in the midst of a paradigm shift is something like saying "I am in my middle period." I would hope that we could locate this change in a context broader than that set by the ostensible boundaries of daily musicological practice.

To reach beyond those boundaries, however, I shall first try to identify some tendencies within them that I believe were then associated with the scruples about what are the proper questions for musical study. I emphasize "tendencies," allowing that there are always fine differentiations to be made and conflicting tendencies to be recognized that I will not be able to deal with because of time constraints.

1. There has been a tendency to construe music history in images of the unfolding of styles, genres, techniques, theories, and so on, following immanent principles, like the growth of a plant—images, that is, with little or no highlighting of human will, intention, desire, or need on the one hand, or societal, cultural, or ideological pressures, on the other, as shaping influences. The articulation of such images had a high status as the framing work for the whole field.

2. There has been a tendency for serious musical analysis to focus on structure as an end in itself, avoiding questions of expression or communication, of affect or nonstructural idea. The possibility of musical expression was not disputed, it was simply circumvented as irrelevant or even incoherent. That means, too, avoidance of questions of apprehension or reception and, hence, avoidance of consideration of the listener as a variable in the determination of the musical object. Actually "the listener" was often posited, but as an empty concept, an a priori construct assumed to have exactly the competencies that the analysis required of it. (Analysts would speak of what "we hear," as though they were making phenomenological observations, when they were really making ontological statements.) The identity of the musical object was defined by its structure

and was not at all contingent on its reception by listeners. And as professional analysis tended to be conducted as though it were a puzzle-solving activity aimed at finding correct solutions, the musical object was assured the authority of a stable, determinate meaning.

3. While the musical object was defined for the analyst by its structure, for the historian it was defined by its genesis, how it came to take on the stable and determinate form by which it is known. The study of the production of the work shared priority with the establishing of its authentic mode of being: in the correct analysis, in the critical edition, and in the authentic performance.

4. As the ideology of musical studies demanded a stable object, it had to demand a stable subject, for one depended on the other. The guiding principle of objectivity was the conception of a neutral observer (subject) who functioned as a window, transmitting without intervention the object as it presented itself, and split off from the self that is the seat of emotional and volitional processes. This conception was manifested in an aversion to the appearance of personal involvement in the production of scholarship, an exclusion of the scholar's state of mind as a factor in determining what is reported, a quest for proof such that the reader had no more choice about accepting the conclusion than a mouse caught in a trap has about accepting its fate.

What all of these features of work have in common is depersonalization. But what of the composer's work? It could hardly be denied that it was the product of will and intention. But one of the most commonly raised banners in that time carried the motto about the "intentional fallacy." Composers were denied credit for their work in favor of the processes of history. A historian writes that Schoenberg's *Erwartung* was a piece that "had to be written." But Schoenberg himself tells an admirer who asked whether he was *the* Arnold Schoenberg, "Somebody had to be, so I volunteered." Stravinsky says "I am the vessel through which *The Rite of Spring* passed," a claim rich in implications: for the perfect, stable, and determinate status of the work, for the absence of personal involvement in and responsibility for its production, for its authority as the product of some sphere of divinity or nature (as a long-time student of

Gregorian chant, it reminds me of the claims implicit in medieval representations of St. Gregory the Great, receiving the chant from a dove who is an embodiment of the Holy Spirit, cooing it into his ear). Not quite the image of Beethoven, making decision after agonizing decision in laboring over the work. The ideology of depersonalization was everywhere, and may be said to be an aspect of modernism (although its roots, paradoxically enough, are in romanticism). And that brings me back to the exclusion of the expressing and signifying functions of music from the canon of subjects worth pursuing. In the atmosphere that I have been describing that should hardly be surprising, for those functions cannot be dealt with at all without taking account of the listener's active self, and its interactions with the selves of music.

I have tried to shape my description in order to steer it away from the temptation to interpret these attitudes in the light of the emphasis that has been placed on objectivity in Western culture since the seventeenth century and of the philosophy of logical positivism that embraced it in the nineteenth. As I wrote in the Introduction to my book, *Music and the Historical Imagination* (1989b): "The idea that a culture would have evolved such distinctive, pervasive, and deeply etched personality traits, which have after all to do with the individual's very way of being in the world, just in response to the epistemological requirements of its science and scholarship seems hard to credit" (p. 9). I wonder whether it would not profit us to think of the standard of objectivity not only as an epistemological first principle of scholarly methodology, but also as a rationalization for a depersonalized interactional style of broader application and deeper and broader associations.

What I suggest, first, is that the scruples with regard to the exclusion of subjectivity from judgment have functioned to provide security against the loss of control—I mean for the moment self-control; I could say control over others, but that would take me in a different, though equally relevant, direction—in the struggle between reason and impulse. Anxiety over that threat is documented in our literature at least as far back as Plato's *Phaedrus* (245B), in the image of the soul as a chariot, with the charioteer, who is Reason, struggling to control the twin steeds of Passion and Desire, lest they run away with the

chariot. But it is daily documented in the contemporary literature of musical studies.

Second, I suggest that the demand for stable and determinate
objects has been a hedge against a fear articulated in 1981, for
example, by the literary scholar Jerome McGann, that a criticism separated from the solidity of textual scholarship (regarded by some as a quintessentially positivistic enterprise)
might "slip loose from its ground and . . . dissipate its analytical
rigor" (McGann, 1981), and echoed in 1987 in a presidential
speech to the American Musicological Society with a caveat
about "reliance on ephemeral and subjective verbal formulations to describe musical content" (Lockwood, 1988).

This reminds me of a passage from Robert Jay Lifton's 1967
essay "Protean Man."

> [O]ne can observe in contemporary man a tendency which seems
> to be precisely the opposite of the protean style. I refer to the
> closing-off of identity or constriction of self-process, to a
> straight-and-narrow specialization in psychological as well as in
> intellectual life, and to a reluctance to let in any "extraneous"
> influences. But I would emphasize that where this kind of con-
> stricted or "one-dimensional" self-process exists, it has an essen-
> tially reactive and compensatory quality. In this it differs from
> earlier characterological styles it may seem to resemble (such as
> the "inner-directed" man described by Riesman, and still earlier
> patterns in traditional society). For these were direct outgrowths
> of societies which then existed, and in harmony with those socie-
> ties, while at the present time a constricted self-process requires
> continuous psychological work to fend off protean influences
> which are always abroad [Lifton, 1967, 323–324].

What is meant by "protean style" can be reached through a
description of the Greek sea-god Proteus, who could see into
the future and who always told the truth, but who had to be
caught and forced to tell what he saw. And in order to escape
capture he could change shape at will—into a lion, a dragon, a
panther, water, fire, a tree. But he was unable to commit himself
to any one of these forms. Lifton sees Proteus as a symbol of
the struggle for coherence and integration of the self, in the
midst of the shapeshifting process. He sees this struggle having
been intensified by three modern historical experiences: a psy-
chohistorical dislocation through the breakdown of traditional

symbols, a bombardment with multiple images and styles, and the constant presence of an apocalyptic imagery of extinction. (I am struck by the fact that in the year of the first publication of Lifton's essay, I published an essay in which I called attention to the apocalyptic theme that ran through then current historical writing on music of the twentieth century [Treitler, 1967].)

I believe that the avoidance of our topic in mainstream musical study can be usefully interpreted as a reflection of a protean struggle for identity, in two senses: first, a difficulty over the kind of self-projection into the work that I suggested at the beginning must be entailed in the reception of music with respect to its affective contents, and second the need for objects that can be relied upon to be recognizably the same from one interpretation to another—a need that cannot be satisfied by a criticism built on the interactive reception of music.

And that, finally, raises the question: How can we interpret the new opening to our topic of which there seem to be signs? I suggest that it is not necessary to regard this as a change—on the model of paradigm shifts or any other model. It can be understood as another side of the same larger phenomenon, viewed positively rather than negatively, a tolerance for the possibility that the work, in its collaboration with interpreters, may appear in protean multiple manifestations. I am interested to notice, in this connection, that alongside these forays into listener-oriented criticism there have been attacks on what could be regarded as the backbone of the work concept, the ideal of unity. After all, to say that a work is unified is to say that everything about it is in its place and could not be otherwise. That is the guarantee of a single stable meaning. But this kind of writing has not displaced the previous attitude in a progression. My colleague at CUNY, Carl Schachter, has recently published an essay bearing the provocative title "Either/ Or," which, in ironic contrast to the sense of perplexity that Kierkegaard meant to convey with it, is to be understood as though it were preceded by the phrase "make up your mind" (1990). When confronted by two paths, Schachter asserts, "the analyst cannot choose both. . . . The larger shape [of a work] manifests itself to the listener only after he has correctly understood certain crucial details . . . " (1990, p. 128).

In a review of Kerman's book I wondered why the fear of a loss of control of which I have spoken here should have exercised so much greater an influence in musical studies than in the study of literature. I suggested that "perhaps an answer lies in the paradoxical position that music has occupied in the history of Western thought: on one side the senses and passions are held to be more vulnerable to music . . . , and on the other music, of all the arts, has been most closely associated with rationality. There is more to lose, and it is more easily lost (Treitler, 1989a, p. 402).

About 400 A.D. Saint Augustine wrote movingly of his anxiety over the powerful feelings aroused by the sound of music:

> I used to be much more fascinated by the pleasures of sound than the pleasures of smell. I was enthralled by them, but you broke my bonds and set me free. . . . But if I am not to turn a deaf ear to music, which is the setting for the words that give it life, I must allow it a position of some honor in my heart. . . . I realize that when they are sung these sacred words stir my mind to greater religious fervour and kindle in me a more ardent flame of piety than they would if they were not sung. . . . But I ought not to allow my mind to be paralyzed by the gratification of my senses, which often lead it astray. For the senses are not content to take second place. Simply because I allow them their due, as adjuncts to reason, they attempt to take precedence and forge ahead with it, with the result that I sometimes sin in this way but am not aware of it until later. . . . So I waver between the danger that lies in gratifying the senses and the benefits which, as I know from experience, can accrue from singing. . . .
>
> This, then, is my present state. Let those of my readers whose hearts are filled with charity, from which good actions spring, weep with me and weep for me. . . . But I beg you, O Lord my God, to look upon me and listen to me. Have pity on me and heal me, for you see that I have become a problem to myself, and this is the ailment from which I suffer [pp. 238–239].

REFERENCES

Bartók, B. (1945), Mese a kis légyröl (A tale about a little fly). In: *Centenary Edition of Bartok's Records*. LPZ 12330-A. Hungaraton Records.

Berger, K. (1988), Review of R. Ingarden. *Music and the Problem of Its Identity*. J. Amer. Musicol. Soc., 41:558–565.

Eliot, T. S. (1951), *Poetry and Drama*. Cambridge, MA: Harvard University Press.

Ingarden, R. (1986), *The Work of Music and the Problem of Its Identity*, tr. A. Czerniawski, ed. J. H. Harrell. Berkeley, CA: University of California Press.

Kerman, J. (1985), *Contemplating Music: Challenges to Musicology*. Cambridge, MA: Harvard University Press.

——— (1991), American musicology in the 1990's. *J. Musicol.*, 9:131–144.

Lifton, R. J. (1967), Protean man. In: *History and Human Survival*. New York: Random House.

Lockwood, L. (1988), President's address. *College Music Symposium*, 28:1–9.

Maus, F.E. (1991), Music as narrative. *Indiana Theory Rev.*, Vol. 12.

McGann, J. (1981), Shall these bones live? *Text*, 1:21–40.

Newcomb, A. (1983), Those images that yet fresh images beget. *J. Musicol.*, 2:227–245.

——— (1984a), Once more between absolute music and program music: Schumann's Second Symphony. *19th Cent. Music.*, 7:223–250.

——— (1984b), Sound and feeling. *Critical Inqui.*, 10:610–643.

——— (1987), Schumann and late 18th century narrative strategies. *19th Cent. Music.*, 11:164–174.

New Harvard Dictionary of Music (1986), Cambridge, MA: Harvard University Press.

Schachter, C. (1990), Either/or. In: *Schenker Studies*, ed. H. Siegel. Cambridge, U.K.: Cambridge University Press.

St. Augustine (c. A.D. 400), *Confessions*, tr. R. S. Pine-Coffin. Harmondsworth, U.K.: Penguin Books, 1961.

Treitler, L. (1967), The present as history. In: *Music and the Historical Imagination*. Cambridge, MA: Harvard University Press, 1989.

——— (1989a), Mozart and the idea of absolute music. In: *Music and the Historical Imagination*. Cambridge, MA: Harvard University Press.

——— (1989b), *Music and the Historical Imagination*. Cambridge, MA: Harvard University Press.

Chapter 4

On Form and Feeling in Music

Gilbert J. Rose, M.D.

The relation betwen music and the emotions has been debated for centuries. What, if anything, can psychoanalysis say about this, and what is the point of entry?

These modest but promising questions were raised at the conclusion of *Psychoanalytic Explorations in Music,* First Series (Feder, Karmel, and Pollock, 1990). They are a welcome change from the usual practice: cite Freud (1928) about psychoanalysis laying down its arms before the problem of the creative artist, and then proceed to rediscover universal unconscious motivation buried within artistic content. Neither taking up nor laying down arms, better to open one's arms to the spirit of interdisciplinary discourse—in order to continue to inform oneself while testing whether a particular psychoanalytic perspective might add a useful dimension to the question under study.

Accordingly, the present paper explores the question: How do the formal structures of art—music, specifically—become transduced to a new level of personal emotional experience on the part of the listener? The term *transduce* is borrowed from physics to refer to the process by which one form of energy or signal—in this case, acoustic stimuli—becomes converted into a different one—affect.

My previous work in this area (Rose, 1980, 1987, 1990a,b, 1991) has sought to demonstrate that art may be taken as an ideal model of how the ego operates in the moment by moment "creativity of everyday life": integrating primary and secondary process modes of organization in thought and perception, to reconcile change and constancy, the familiar with the strange,

Based on Rose (1980), *The Power of Form,* expanded edition. Madison, CT: International Universities Press, 1992.

unity and separateness. Art fosters ego development in specific ways, increasing the scope of its mastery, honing its orientation in a reality which, more and more, has come to be seen as dynamically shifting, multiple, and permeable rather than static, single, and established. Hence, its necessity.

This frame of reference emphasizes form more than content, perception and reality more than motivation, adaptation more than conflict. It is directed less toward psychopathology than to autonomous, nonconflictual psychic structure. It views sublimation as significant beyond being yet another ego defense against instinct; it shares the view, going back at least as far as the Renaissance, that *both* art and science are prime ways of exploring the universe and that both, in so doing, transform and enhance reality.

In contrast to the earlier psychoanalytic literature centering on repression and the *content* of art, it draws on the increasing realization that "regression in the service of the ego" is misleading when applied to the chains of subliminal, less differentiated precursors and accompaniments of conscious thought and perception. The former (recapturable experimentally, cf. Fisher [1954, 1956]), when raised to the level of enduring structures in art, show us primary and secondary process modes of organization—imagination and knowledge—in dynamic equilibrium, and in such a way as to invigorate everyday thought and perception with vividness and fresh feeling.

Recent studies of Freud's writing style (Mahony, 1987) reveal this interplay of primary process imaginative freedom with secondary process logical control. The resulting "music" of his prose "enacts" the ideational content, "instancing the allusivity, elusivity, and illusivity of unconscious mental processes" (p. 167). Freud played joyfully with language, loosening its confining rigidity with creative metaphors; image interacts with idea, perspectives shift, even "objective" language is sometimes eroticized. The primary process of Freud's prose has an accumulative impact on the reader so that the interplay of rational and affective processes "constitutes a masterful acting out in the writing in" (p. 50).

Like all art, Freud's prose style, neither in the details of its formal structure nor in its effect on the reader, is compatible with the pejorative connotation of regression even when in the service of the ego. In attempting to render some account of how the structure of literary style or any other artistic form evokes emotional response, it may be more useful to turn from the clinical pathological concept of regression and recruit psychoanalytic ideas having to do with the primary and secondary processes.

Let us summarize these briefly. An interplay of primary process imagination and secondary process knowledge of reality underlies all thought and perception. As a consequence, a cyclic interplay takes place between their respective modes of attention and organization. On the one hand, there is a widely scanning receptivity to data, organized unconsciously according to familiar primary process principles of condensation, displacement, and symbolism. On the other hand, there is sharply focused, selective, conscious attention to data organized according to secondary process common sense, logic, and accepted knowledge of reality. There is also the matter of the different types of discharge. The interplay is accompanied by a building up of tension associated with the long circuited, highly controlled, slow discharge of the secondary process, and a release of tension and greater freedom from control associated with the rapid discharge of the primary process.

The key idea that extends my previous work in this area and relates the forms of art to personal emotional experience is based on Freud's (1915, 1924) speculations that changes in stimulus strength account for pleasure/unpleasure. The latter, in turn, lies at the core of emotion. If we reason that changes in stimulus strength, in the form of building and resolving tension, is also central to the structure of aesthetic form, we have, I propose, one "point of entry" for psychoanalysis to contribute to the fundamental question of the relationship between the formal structures of art, including music, and emotional responses to it.

Before spelling this out in greater detail it will be useful to take some historical perspective on the question of form and feeling in art and music.

Until relatively recent times, neither art nor music were considered to be expressive free-standing forms in their own right. Art, for example, was clearly in the service of religion. The significance of a beautiful work, indeed its sole meaning, lay in its conveying a religious *idea*. It had no meaning apart from the idea of paying tribute to God. Contemporary hermeneuticists would agree up to a point, arguing that whether art conveys a religious idea or some other, its meaning can only be ideational; this, moreover, requires the mediation of language. Nonobjective art presuming to stand on its own by dint of its very presence is an impossible fiction because "there is no presence unmediated by words, uncontaminated by ideas" (Harries, 1982, p. 23).

It was against this long-standing and still vigorous tradition that the aesthetic approach to art began to arise in the enlightenment. It was, however, the Cubist revolution at the beginning of our own century that "questioned the basic assumptions underlying the tradition of Western art, assumptions that had prevailed for many centuries. . . . The means by which images could be formalized in a painting changed more during the years from 1907 to 1914 than they had since the Renaissance" (Chipp, 1968, p. 193).

Of the many schools of formalist, abstract, and nonfigurative painting that came to dominate the art of the twentieth century, the most radical statement of the ideal of absolute art came from Moscow. Kasimir Malevich, for example,

> [A]lthough he had never been outside of Russia, assimilated both he Fauvist and Cubist styles while they were still new and pressed onward toward the ideal of a purely abstract painting. . . . He painted the purest and most radical abstract picture yet seen, a black square on a white ground. He explains that "In 1913, trying desperately to liberate art from the ballast of the representational world, I sought refuge in the form of the square" [quoted in Chipp (1968, pp. 311–312)].

His "Suprematist" art aimed at nothing less than transporting the viewer out of the constrictions both of language and the relationship to objects of the visible world into the realm of aesthetic contemplation. Here, the only meaning to a work of art lies in its being perfect with nothing missing, nothing superfluous; its content is its form; its subject is itself.

Music, like art, did not stand on its own until recent times. Until the seventeenth century, Plato's doctrine of musical structure was never doubted. Music was made up of *harmonia*, *rhythmos*, and *logos*. *Harmonia* meant regular, rationally system-atized relationships among tones; *rhythmos*, the system of musi-cal time, which in ancient times included dance and organized motion; and *logos*, language as the expression of human reason. Only with the great aesthetic debates of the seventeenth and eighteenth centuries did the idea of "absolute music" arise. "It consists of the conviction that instrumental music purely and clearly expresses the true nature of music by its very lack of concept, object, and purpose. . . . Instrumental music, as pure 'structure' represents itself" (Dahlhaus, 1978, p. 7).

Like art, which became independent of conventional theist religion only to become enmeshed in the aesthetic contempla-tion of the Absolute, music, too, took on a quasi-religious func-tion. The aesthetic contemplation of music became a kind of art religion, affording a glimpse of the infinite beyond ideas, images, things. The Beethoven quartets became the paradigm of music as a revelation of the absolute beyond the ability of words to express—a language above language. Some believe that music as art religion still underlies our own musical canon (Dahlhaus, 1978, p. 7).

When art ceased being a vehicle for conventional religious expression, and the social setting for music was freed from the constraint of being merely an accompaniment to dance or language, their "frame" became changed. This is a way of stat-ing that it became possible to experience each in a profoundly different way. For, according to the main tenet of frame analy-sis, "The frame is first and foremost a declaration that any view of reality *is* but a view—that any story or perception is framed—that we experience experience by applying a frame" (Goffman, 1974, p. 23). For example, "any found object [may] be turned into visual art by an act of selection and display" (Scholes, 1977, p. 106). Mounting music or art in a special setting of their own, defamiliarizes and enhances their aesthetic qualities. Concentrating on the experience of music or art per se revealing their own nature, rather than serving some ulterior supportive or communicative purpose, renders the inner struc-ture of their expressive forms more evident.

What can be said in general terms about this inner structure of aesthetic forms and how is it related to perception? Perhaps the broadest definition of an expressive artistic form is that it consists of a symmetrical resolution of opposing forces of tension and resolution (Toch, 1948, p. 157). An idea of fundamental importance because of its bridging nature is that these same forces of tension and resolution already exist in perception itself. There they constitute the expressive quality of perception—the capacity to perceive with feeling. This, according to Arnheim (1954, p. 430), is the most elementary attribute of perception and the primary content of vision.

The biological basis of the expressive quality of perception lies in the fact that the first task of the organism in any new situation is to make an immediate practical decision about its perceived friendliness or hostility and thus know what to do about it in terms of approach, withdrawal, or watchful waiting. Perceiving with feeling makes such an evaluation possible on the basis of hedonic tone and strength of stimulation.

In the expressive dynamics of visual perception, all the visual perceptual categories—shape, color, location, space, light—are experienced as expansion, contraction, rising, falling, approach, and withdrawal. They arouse tension and are counterbalanced by an opposite tendency in perception to resolve tension by creating unity, simplicity, symmetry, and balance. These are experienced as harmony, rest, and stability.

In other words, lines and shapes are seen as forces or gestures striving in certain directions. They convey a happening of directed tensions rather than a being. Obliqueness produces an effect of potential energy or tension in contrast to the horizontal and vertical positions which are experienced as stable and static. A rectangular or oval shape conveys more movement than a square or circle; a parabolic curve looks more dynamic than a circular one; shaded or blurred surfaces give the impression of movement as do wedge shapes; unequal intervals between objects, deformations of familiar shapes or multiple stroboscopic reduplications and textures all produce a strong dynamic quality, as do brightness, high saturation, and particular admixtures of color (Arnheim, 1954).

This is the field of expressive forces inherent in ordinary perceptual experience. Drawing on the media of his own particular palette, the artist works to select, intensify, and compose the quality of experience in such a way as to express it more energetically and clearly than the original from which it was extracted. If successful, the enhanced rhythms of tension and release in the art work will be experienced by the receptive viewer with an accompanying responsive emotion.

Can something analogous be said about musical structure and experience? Stravinsky (Stravinsky and Crafat, 1959) warned, "How misleading are all literary descriptions of musical form" (p. 17). Yet, in his *Poetics of Music* (1942), he had ventured: "All music is nothing more than a succession of impulses that converge towards a definite point of repose" (p. 35). In a similar spirit, Roger Sessions (1950) said that the most important ingredient of music and the essence of hearing it is hearing the dynamic quality of tones, their direction, their movement; each musical phrase is a unique gesture that moves constantly toward the goal of completing a cadence.

More specifically: music is based on a *symmetrical yet unbalanced* structure—namely, on musical scales that derive from the physical phenomenon of overtones making up the harmonic series. Musical theorists beginning with the Greeks tried to enforce an equal distance between the twelve notes arranged in the scale progression of the chromatic scale, producing a system which is not only symmetrical but circular—the circle of fifths. This so-called equal temperament distorts the notes' relation to the natural overtones. That is to say, following the natural harmonics of the tones, D double flat is not the same note as B sharp, and neither coincides with C.

The resulting built-in *imbalance* of harmonic structure gives the sharp direction greater strength over the flat direction. Sharp keys imply an *increase of tension*; flat keys, a *lower tension*. Different tonalities have different "characters." "F Major, [for example, is] by 'nature' a tonality with a subdominant quality of a *release of tension* relative to C-Major . . . the first tonality every musician learns as a child . . . " (Rosen, 1971, p. 28, emphasis added).

"This [built-in] imbalance [of harmonic structure] is essential to an understanding of almost all tonal music, and from it is derived the possibility of *tension and resolution on which the art of music depended for centuries*" (Rosen, 1971, p. 24, emphasis added). Tension exists between any two adjacent tones of melodic progressions or two tones sounded simultaneously. This tension is imagined in terms of distances in space and lapses of time. These intervals and the tension embodied within them are the basic musical building blocks.

The tension implicit in intervals sequential in time or sounded simultaneously in chords can be intensified or attenuated in various ways. It would be well beyond the scope of this paper to attempt to discuss the elements of musical structure that either charge a score with energy or bring about its resolution. We may, however, rely on musical authority to mention some of them (Meyer, 1956, 1967; Rosen, 1971).

Beethoven's masterful use of simple repetition is an example of one way to build tension: stimulate the demand for resolution and at the same time withhold it. Similarly, after a point of great tension is reached, and one expects the return to the tonic to resolve the tension, a long sequence may serve to extend the melody, avoid the cadence and raise anticipation still further. A short repeated motif, especially a rising chromatic one, increases speed and gains in intensity; a descending sequence implies a loss of energy. Other devices to build tension and intensify feeling are ornamentation, the minor key, moving from one key to another, fragmentation, contrapuntal imitation, remote harmonies, and dissonance.

Some musical devices combine or juxtapose *logically* contradictory possibilities: an increase with a decrease of tension. For example, many of the melodic, rhythmic, and harmonic variations introduced for the sake of apparent variety are actually repetitions and recurrences in disguise (Bernstein, 1976). To the extent that they are experienced as novel they are associated with mounting tension; but to the extent that they may also be experienced as disguised returns to the familiar, they are associated with the reduction of tension.

In this connection, rhythm deserves special mention for it fuses sameness and difference, constancy and change. The uninterrupted pattern of periodic recurrence stands for unity and this tends to reduce tension; but its changing movement shows off the variety of its contrasting details and this heightens tension. Essentially, rhythm embodies the paradox of Time, itself: forever constant yet ever changing.

Studying the way different styles build, sustain, and resolve tension may be used to differentiate one from the other. Rosen (1971), for example, claims that in a classical work of Haydn,

Mozart, or Beethoven tension is concentrated in the middle section where the movement to a new key is dramatized between a stable beginning and end. In contrast to this, Baroque music maintains a relatively low level of tension, generated by rhythm, harmonies, choruses, diffused throughout the piece with certain fluctuations, and resolved only in the final cadence.

Returning to our central problem: how to explicate the relationship between an aesthetic structure and the emotional force it appears to generate. To put the question somewhat more precisely: How do acoustic or visual stimuli become transduced into a genuine aesthetic emotional experience?

Before this problem musicology, unassisted, "lays down its arms," acknowledging that the complex relationship between affect and structure "may require an interdisciplinary approach encroaching as it does upon such areas as aesthetics, linguistics, psychology and biology" (Epstein, 1979, p. 205). It is apparent that perceptual, physiological events on the one hand, and psychological meanings on the other, are phenomena of a profoundly different order; even an interdisciplinary approach, while reflecting the complexity of the problem, provides no key to translate these two different realms into each other's code.

To begin with the obvious, human emotion cannot exist *embedded in* the inorganic structure of aesthetic form. The structure can only offer the necessary perceptual conditions for an emotional response to occur. When this happens it may feel as though the structure were the mechanism whereby affect is developed and resolved (Epstein, 1979, p. 204), and that the emotion was then "communicated" directly to the recipient.

It might be more accurate to say that the structure *evokes* emotion on some primary level. In any case, emotions are not communicated either reliably or in full to the audience even when the composer intends to do so. Mahler believed that his whole life was laid out in his First and Second Symphonies "to anyone who knows how to listen" (quoted by Feder [1981]). Yet, Feder (1981) has shown that Mahler's Second Symphony contains sections that lend themselves equally well to being heard as musical representations of falling asleep—replete with an allusion to Brahms' famous lullaby—as to awakening. From this, as well as other musical examples, textual and biographical analysis, he persuasively argues that Mahler's "latent" program of fratricidal impulses is detectable and perhaps preconsciously responded to along with the composer's "manifest" program.

Aside from a composer's "latent" intent existing alongside his consciously intended "manifest" one, however, it may be stated that the model of linguistic communication from sender to receiver does not adequately encompass or perhaps is not even applicable to the expressive power of art. Art does not transmit information in the same sense or as dependably as language (which, according to deconstructionists, also cannot be relied upon to carry stable connotations). Kivy (1990) has described music as a kind of middle ground between representation and noninterpretive perception; it is an area of emotional expressiveness analogous to passionate human speech. As an example of how music lends itself to different listeners, Hindemith (1952) notes that the second movement of Beethoven's Seventh Symphony "leads some people into a pseudofeeling of profound melancholy, while another group takes it for a kind of scurrilous scherzo, and a third for a subdued pastorale. Each group is justified in judging as it does" (p. 47).

In other words, the emotional impact of art or music depends on many things beyond a univocal embedded "message." Perhaps above all, it involves elements of knowledge as to the code and context. In pictorial art, the latter frequently determines the meaning. For example, both comic caricature and the sublime make use of anatomical foreshortening; often it is only the context that allows one to tell which is intended (Posèq, 1988).

As for the code, just as Rosen (1971) summarizes harmonic common practice and differentiates classical from Baroque styles on the basis of the diffusion or concentration of tension and release, one may assume that this underlying dynamic could apply to other styles such as serial music. Experienced listeners to contemporary music insist that while at first it may sound random, expectancies inevitably emerge and order the musical experience—even that of John Cage. Since expectancies of any kind involve rising tension, and their fulfillment brings resolution of tension (Meyer, 1956), the same structural principle would appear to hold. But would it be true also for oriental music? A Westerner listening to oriental music for the first time is unlikely to hear anything remotely musical, whereas the initiated may feel any number of different emotions.

The question appears to involve more fundamental matters than mere familiarity. For argument's sake, an electrocardiogram may look just about "the same" as a Hokusai drawing of Mt. Fuji. They are distinguished because the EKG's meaning relies primarily upon the ordinate and the abscissa, whereas in the Hokusai drawing all the visual characteristics are significant: "any thickening or thinning of the line, its color, its contrast with the background, its size, even the qualities of the paper—none of these is ruled out, none can be ignored" (Goodman, 1976, p. 229).

Hindemith (1952) points in the right direction: not embedded or communicated feelings but the *memories* of feelings. "The reactions music evokes are not feelings, but they are the images, memories of feelings . . . " (p. 45). He goes on to state that if the music is so strange and unfamiliar as to correspond with no other musical experience we have had, we still do our best to find in our memory some feeling that would correspond with how we felt when confronted with some former nonmusical experience that similarly puzzled us. "This theory," he continues, "gives us a reasonable explanation for the fact that one given piece of music may cause remarkably diversified reactions with different listeners . . . since different listeners will experience different images, and even one and the same listener will not react uniformly to reappearing musical stimuli . . . " (pp. 47–51).

With the aid of psychoanalysis it is possible to extend this theory in both depth and precision. The response to any stimulus will depend in large measure on the conscious and unconscious ideation, memories, images provoked by the stimulus—its cognitive meaning in the light of past experience. But for there to be an *emotional* response of any significant degree, pleasure/unpleasure sensations must be involved.

And on what does this depend? At first, Freud (1915) believed that it was the *quantitative* change of stimulus that accounted for pleasure/unpleasure. Later (1924), he speculated that it depended rather on *qualitative* rises and falls of excitation such as *rhythm*. Either way—quantitative increase or decrease, or optimal, rhythmical changes in stimulus quality—we are dealing with the idea that degrees of tension and resolution underlie the sensations of pleasure/unpleasure which in turn constitute the matrix of emotion.

The particular quality of an emotion may well depend on the conscious and unconscious *ideas* that come to be associated with it in the course of time (Brenner, 1974). However, the important point for our purpose is that because the central nervous system is constructed the way it is, all experience including thought is intertwined with emotion. More technically, affective reactions are the subcortical contributions to cognitive processes in the service of adaptation (Basch, 1976). In infancy, thinking and feeling may be considered as one—facets of a total experience serving the function of communication as well as acting as a precursor of the ego to establish internal structure (Panel, 1974; Ross, 1975).

Let us recapitulate before continuing. (1) According to contemporary psychoanalytic thinking and the open system model of the organism, all thought and perception are accompanied by an interplay of primary process imagination and secondary process knowledge of reality. The former is associated with a release of tension; the latter with tension buildup. (2) An interplay of tension and resolution in perception accounts for an elementary biological aspect of perception, namely, its expressive quality—the capacity to perceive with feeling,. (3) As we have seen, a central dynamic of musical and artistic form involves a balanced structure of tension and release. (4) Thus, there is a correspondence in type of structure between the symmetrical, opposing forces of tension and resolution in art and music and these same forces making up the basic expressive quality of perception.

Lacking a more precise key with which to translate the language of these different realms into each other's terms, we now resort to homology and analogy to speculate as follows:

Homology: does the *correspondence* between the expressive structure of tension and release in aesthetic form, on the one hand, and, on the other, the perceptual expressive capacity to respond with tension and release, result in a "responsive resonance"? By "responsive resonance" I mean that a viewer or listener has an intensified experience—one invested with both emotion and clarity—rather than the jaded semiawareness of everyday life? In other words, I am setting forth the aesthetic experience as an enriched affective state stemming from the resonance between corresponding structures: aesthetic form and a receptive person's psychic structure, each being described in terms of an interplay of primary and secondary processes involving tension and release, the dynamic core of affect.

This is an abstract and general formulation that focuses on tension and release in both musical structure and perceptual apparatus. It is consonant with Feder's (1990) specific conclusion about the music of Charles Ives and the affect of nostalgia. Pointing to the elements of pleasure/unpleasure, idea, and mood structure of nostalgia, he finds an "isomorphism" or mirroring between nostalgia and the formal features of Ives' organized musical structure, with the result that the music "both represents and communicates nostalgia" (p. 265).

With the aid of a psychoanalytic analogy we may now expand both formulations into one which is both more comprehensive and specific. Does the homology—or isomorphism—just described resemble in function and form the emotional ambience of a therapeutic situation? Let me make clear that I am not referring to clinical detachment or benevolent neutrality, as important as they may be in treatment. Rather, I mean the emotional underpinnings that make a therapeutic alliance possible between patient and therapist, and thus a therapeutic situation.

In therapy the patient experiences a dynamic balance of closeness and distance that conveys the assurance that one can experience one's self and be one's self without being dropped metaphorically. That is, the attempt to understand compassionately yet neutrally can be depended upon as a steady backdrop in treatment; thus, the patient can leave the beaten track of convention and explore his own thoughts and feelings without risking the threat of discontinuity. In short, I am referring to the establishment of a safe holding environment, with all its undertones (or overtones) of an early state of security (Winnicott, 1960).

Just as nonverbal elements in therapy are conducive to a readiness for transference, the right to be different yet secure, and the encouragement to think feelingly and remember, the structure of aesthetic form also provides the security and freedom conducive to feeling-memory. One feels oneself to be "in good hands," fully to receive, respond, even "participate."

During the period of ambiguity in a musical piece, in the negative space of a painting, through the passage involving loss of
discursive meaning and regularity in a poem, the audience is on
its own. If the art form has stimulated needs as well as encouraged the participating ego to join in forming new integrations,
if it has provided a favorable proportion of freedom and control,
the audience will be able to put up with the discontinuities and
continue to respond in resonance. It will be able to intensify and
enrich the carefully withheld ingredients with its own sympathetic, supplementary vibrations. During chromatic wanderings
from one key to another, the absent tonic will be understood as
immanent, if not obvious, until it appears later in time. As in a
painting, the composition will restore stability in another place.
The art form is trusted to bring us back safely to the home key
[Rose, 1980, pp. 198–199].

Perhaps the homology between aesthetic structure and perceptual response—analogous to the attunement between patient and therapist in the safe holding environment of a therapeutic alliance—also provides a nonverbal ambience likely to
trigger conscious and unconscious feelings and memories
rooted in psychological issues of one's own personal history.
We now know from neuroscience that memories are stored in
association with the dominant feelings of the moment and regain access to consciousness when the original feelings are re-
aroused. This is the basis of Proust's *madeleine* phenomenon as
well as common psychoanalytic clinical experience.

What are some of the psychological issues of one's past likely
to be evoked in the safe holding environment provided by the
secure ambience of an aesthetic structure? It has long been
suspected that the creation of and response to a work of art
bears some relationship to the work of mourning. For example,
a nostalgic work of art may aid the work of mourning and lead
to enhanced internalization; or it may bypass mourning and
preserve the lost object in the form of an aesthetic externaliza-
tion; or it may represent an elaborate compromise formation
that, "from a formal point of view, [is] congruent with and
parallel to the mental condition that engendered it" (Feder,
1990, p. 244). One may suspect that any and all of the above
outcomes are possible and that nothing short of *clinical* psychoanalysis can disclose the particular mix of elements that seems
to hold in an individual case.

Other psychological issues, indirectly related to mourning, are likely to be drawn into the response to music and art. The dynamic patterns of tension and release in the aesthetic structure succeed in offering ideal examples of the reconciliation of familiarity with strangeness, continuity and change, synthesis with separation. Thus, they encourage the hope that one can have it both ways in the perpetual cycle of differentiation and dedifferentiation. The thrust toward individuation as against "mourning" the "loss" of replenishment through reunion, blurring the boundaries between self and object representations, is never "resolved." It is ever available to be drawn into a present reality and the response to art.

Theoretically at least, there is hardly any limit to the depth of feeling-memories that are "on tap," so to speak, to lend a richness of personal emotional response to the *nonverbal* ambience of aesthetically balanced tension and release. For we also know from infant research that the "communicational matrix" of infant and caregiver is organized around an optimal degree of tension and resolution. This provides the *preverbal* backdrop for the child's "affective core." While this "primary affectivity" recedes with the development of language, defense mechanisms and self-awareness, it is likely that aspects of it remain unconsciously and continue to influence emotional responsiveness (Wilson and Malatesta, 1989). This may be especially relevant to the emotional response to art and music.

Let us be more specific. Knowledge about the infant from recent research reported to a panel (Panel, 1980) shows that from birth on the infant gives rapt attention to the caretaker's facial expressions and speech sounds. From the first day of life the baby's interest in listening to voice sounds is so intense that it can overpower interest in food even when he is hungry. Significantly, the *musical* aspects of speech are the ones that most compel the infant's attention: rhythm and timing at first, then, by 6 months, the variations of intonation and a tonal range at a particular pitch. Intuitively sensing this, parents across cultures automatically *exaggerate the musical features* of speech, speaking or sing-songing to the infant in a higher and more variable pitch than in adult conversation; they imitate the baby's facial and vocal expressions, repeat her babbling syllables, amplify them with bursts of manifest pleasure, and spark things up with expressions of mock surprise (Emde, 1983, pp. 171–172). The baby on his side, responding in kind well before 6 months of age, can match the pitch, intensity, melodic contour and rhythmic structure of mother's songs.

Thus, investigators observe what they interpret to be a biologically based system of affective signaling between parent and infant as it unfolds over time. They concur that it is rhythmical and recurrent. It is comprised largely of tonal (and visual) repetitiveness perked with surprise, soothing familiarity spiced with graded doses of excitement. In short, it is composed of the various elements making for the build-up of tension and its resolution.

Would it be an exaggeration to refer to this as Opus No. 1, the first duet?

Or that it finds a resonance in later intimate relationships—not excluding the therapeutic, where active recreation and mastery are possible—or the aesthetic, where symbolic repetition and reexperiencing may take place (Klein, 1976; Rose, 1987)?

Let us return to our analogy with therapy. Many clinicians have long known that meaning in psychoanalysis depends less on language than on feelings (Modell, 1978). Also, that in addition to analytic work and the central importance of transference, the *art* of psychoanalysis is "primarily an aesthetics of care [involving] timing, spacing, wording, intoning [that evokes] . . . the infant's relation to the mother" (Bollas, 1978, p. 393).

Developmental research supports clinical as well as life experience: the empathic feed-back of intimate relationships at any time in life can reactivate very early motivational processes and spur ongoing development (Emde, 1983).

Might music be counted among these potentiating experiences?

During those special times in therapy when empathy touches on the primary affective core, "things come together." Patient and therapist share a sense of rightness and wholeness. The fleeting experience has attributes of the aesthetic moment in that everything is there, nothing is superfluous. One patient compared it to his favorite music: "Mozart could deliver this essential good to me—putting myself right with my body and myself with the world."

SUMMARY

Psychoanalysis, in concert with some findings of neuroscience and developmental research, may be justified in suggesting the metaphor of art as *transmuter*: art facilitates bridging between and transforming perceptual stimuli, on the one hand, and affective meanings, on the other. Music provides the perceptual preconditions for affect, namely the nonverbal ambience of a safe holding environment conducive to affect and memory-readiness. A predisposed listener may respond to the dynamic structure of carefully balanced tension and release with an attunement of his own perceptual receptivity to tension and release. This will entail a range of sensations of pleasure/unpleasure, eliciting conscious and unconscious thoughts, feelings and reminiscenses and resulting in an emotional experience. For the particular individual this may involve a variable mix of regressive reexperiencing, mourning, and mastery, as well as a progressive reintegration of thoughts, feelings, and memories related to the ongoing need to relate continuity with change, familiarity with strangeness, separateness, and reunion. Conscious and unconscious feeling-memories may reverberate as far back as the first *preverbal* affective interactions between parent and infant, adding depth and intensity of emotional experience to the response to music and art—structures which have themselves been constructed in such a way as to maximize the tension and release inherent in ordinary perceptual experience.

REFERENCES

Arnheim, R. (1954), *Art and Visual Perception: A Psychology of the Creative Eye*. Berkeley & Los Angeles: University of California Press, 1957.
Basch, M. F. (1976), The concept of affect: A re-examination. *J. Amer. Psychoanal. Assn.*, 24:759–777.
Bernstein, L. (1976), *The Unanswered Question: Six Talks at Harvard*. Cambridge, MA: Harvard University Press.
Bollas, C. (1978), The aesthetic moment and the search for transformation. In: *The Annual of Psychoanalysis*, 6:385–394. New York: International Universities Press.

Brenner, C. (1974), On the nature and development of affects: A unified theory. *Psychoanal. Quart.*, 44:532–556.

Chipp, H. B. (1968), *Theories of Modern Art: A Source Book by Artists and Critics.* Berkeley & Los Angeles: University of California Press.

Dahlhaus, C. (1978), *The Idea of Absolute Music.* Chicago: University of Chicago Press, 1989.

Emde, R. N. (1983), The prerepresentational self and its affective core. In: *The Psychoanalytic Study of the Child,* 38:165–192. New Haven, CT: Yale University Press.

Epstein, D. (1979), *Beyond Orpheus. Studies in Musical Structure.* New York: Oxford University Press, 1987.

Feder, S. (1981), Gustav Mahler: The music of fratricide. *Internat. Rev. Psychoanal.,* 8:257–284.

——— (1990), The nostalgia of Charles Ives: An essay in affects and music. In: *Psychoanalytic Explorations in Music,* First Series, ed. S. Feder, R. L. Karmel, & G. H. Pollock. Madison, CT.: International Universities Press, pp. 233–266.

——— Karmel, R. L., & Pollock, G. H., eds. (1990), *Psychoanalytic Explorations in Music,* First Series. Madison, CT: International Universities Press.

Fisher, C. (1954), Dreams and perception. *J. Amer. Psychoanal. Assn.,* 2:389–445.

——— (1956), Dreams, images and perception. *J. Amer. Psychoanal. Assn.,* 4:5–48.

Freud, S. (1915), Instincts and their vicissitudes. *Standard Edition,* 14:117–140. London: Hogarth Press, 1957.

——— (1924), The economic problem of masochism. *Standard Edition,* 19:157–170. London: Hogarth Press, 1961.

——— (1928), Dostoevsky and parracide. *Standard Edition,* 21:175–194. London: Hogarth Press, 1961.

Goffman, E. (1974), *Frame Analysis: An Essay on the Organization of Experience.* Cambridge, MA: Harvard University Press.

Goodman, N. (1976), *Languages of Art: An Approach to a Theory of Symbols.* Indianapolis: Hackett.

Harries, K. (1982), The painter and the word. *Bennington Rev.,* 13:19–25.

Hindemith, P. (1952), *A Composer's World.* Garden City, NY: Doubleday/Anchor Books, 1961.

Kivy, P. (1990), *Music Alone.* Ithaca & London: Cornell University Press.

Klein, G. (1976), *Psychoanalytic Theory: A Study of Essentials.* New York: International Universities Press.

Mahony, P. J. (1987), *Freud as a Writer.* New Haven & London: Yale University Press.

Meyer, L. B. (1956), *Emotion and Meaning in Music.* Chicago: University of Chicago Press.

——— (1967), *Music, the Arts and Idea.* Chicago: University of Chicago Press.

Modell, A. H. (1978), Affects and the complementarity of biologic and historical meaning. In: *The Annual of Psychoanalysis,* 6:167–180. New York: International Universities Press.

Panel (1974), Toward a theory of affects. Castelnuovo-Tedesco, P. (reporter). *J. Amer. Psychoanal. Assn.,* 22:612–625.

——— New knowledge about the infant from current research: Implications for psychoanalysis. Sander, L. (reporter). *J. Amer. Psychoanal. Assn.,* 28:181–198.

Posèq, A. W. G. (1988), An affinity between the comic and the sublime in pictorial imagery. In: *Psychoanalytic Perspectives on Art,* 3:3–17. Hillsdale, NJ: Analytic Press.

Rose, G. J. (1980), *The Power of Form: A Psychoanalytic Approach to Aesthetic Form,* expanded ed. New York: International Universities Press, 1992.

———— (1987), *Trauma and Mastery in Life and Art*. New Haven & London: Yale University Press.

———— (1990a), From ego defense to reality enhancement: Updating the analytic perspective on art. *Amer. Imago*, 47:69–79.

———— (1990b), Paul Gauguin: Art, androgyny, and the fantasy of rebirth. In: *The Homosexualities and the Therapeutic Process*, ed. C. Socarides & V. Volkan. Madison, CT: International Universities Press, pp. 259–270.

———— (1991), Abstract art and emotion: Expressive form and the sense of wholeness. *J. Amer. Psychoanal. Assn.*, 39:131–156.

Rosen, C. (1971), *The Classical Style*. New York: Viking Press.

Ross, N. (1975), Affect as cognition: With observations on the meanings of mystical states. *Internat. Rev. Psychoanal.*, 2:79–93.

Scholes, R. (1977), Towards a semiotics of literature. *Crit. Inqui.*, 4/1.

Sessions, R. (1950), *The Musical Experience of Composer, Performer, Listener*. Princeton, NJ: Princeton University Press.

Stravinsky, I. (1942), *Poetics of Music*. Cambridge & London: Harvard University Press.

———— Crafat, R. (1959), *Conversations with Igor Stravinsky*. Garden City, NY: Doubleday.

Toch, E. (1948), *The Shaping Forces in Music*. New York: Criterion Music.

Wilson, A., & Malatesta, C. (1989), Affect and the compulsion to repeat: Freud's repetition compulsion revisited. *Psychoanal. & Contemp. Thought*, 12:265–312.

Winnicott, D. W. (1960), The theory of the parent–infant relationship. In: *The Maturational Processes and the Facilitating Environment*, New York: International Universities Press, pp. 37–55.

Chapter 5

The Anlage of Feeling: Its Fate in Form (Discussion of Chapter 4)

Eugene L. Goldberg, M.D.

Dr. Rose's paper is a creative and imaginative extension of his lifelong endeavor to enrich our aesthetic response with his humanistically perfused psychoanalytic understanding by asking: "How do the formal structures of art—music, specifically—become transduced to a new level of personal emotional experience on the part of the listener?"

From its beginning music was employed in the service of religion, to convey an idea. The belief in the Platonic doctrine of musical structure, consisting of harmonia, rhythmos, and logos, was eventually followed in the eighteenth century by the doctrine of *affektenlehre*, formulated by Quant and Phillip Emanuel Bach, in which it is presented as a formulary for the musical expression of certain typical emotions. After the great aesthetic debates of the seventeenth and eighteenth centuries, instrumental music, like art, was able to reach a point where its true nature, by its "very lack of concept, object and purpose" became a "structure representing itself" in the words of Dalhaus (1989, p. 7). But in its rejection of a specific language, music took on a "quasi religious function," with the description of certain music as revelatory experience. This attempt at a lucid portrayal of musical expression through metaphor, poetic description, analogy, and image is "at variance with the realities of musical communication . . . through a medium-sound and time—that is unique, intrinsic unto itself, and incapable of translation" (Dahlhaus, 1989, p. 7).

The aesthetic core of Dr. Rose's presentation, in both visual and musical modes, is that "the broadest definition of an artistic form is that it consists of a symmetrical resolution of opposing forces of tension and resolution." This is consistent with Leonard Meyer's early explication of *Emotion and Meaning in Music* (1956), and is in line with Arnheim's Gestalt theories, Charles Rosen's elegant evocation of the classical style with emphasis on this tension producing effect in the harmonic structure (1971), and in Hindemith's writings. In the latter's *Craft of Musical Composition* (1945) he graphically presents the rise and fall of tension in both the melodic and harmonic realms, with an almost mathematically developed thesis on the tension produced between various melodic intervals and between various harmonic permutations. It is also equally relevant to mention the linear-analytic technique of Schenkerian analysis (Salzer, 1962), which attempts to define structure by the Urlinie, a graphing of the melodic and bass line. This structural perspective led next to Schöenberg's Grundgestalt or basic shape (Schöenberg, 1967). Both of these individuals have played a major role in the development of the work of David Epstein, author of the next chapter, who expanded his exploration of the structural aspects of music through motion and time, the primary affectual elements (1987).

With this as a background, Dr. Rose returns to his central thesis: how to "explicate the relationship between an aesthetic structure and the emotional force it appears to generate." The tension and release of the nonverbal ambient aesthetic stimulus is "likely to trigger conscious and unconscious feelings and memories rooted in the psychological issue of one's own personal history." These memories are initially stored with affectual bonds which are rereleased with the arousal of the original feelings. I find this idea totally consistent with the work one encounters in the holding environment of the analytic session which is convincingly analogized to the musical experience.

I was particularly intrigued with Dr. Rose's emphasis on the "communicational matrix" of infant and caregiver, as the anlage of the "primary affectivity" of early life. Studies of neonatal behavior, particularly the ideas of Daniel Stern, are most relevant here (Stern, 1985). In the first stage, which Stern calls the emergent self, there is no clear differentiation between the inner and outer world; perception is "amodal," sound may be seen visually or felt motorically, in addition to being heard acoustically. These psychobiologically based feelings are global, and can be productive of a powerful "vitality" affect which is felt as rushing or waves of emotion, akin to the oceanic feelings experienced later on during trance states, orgasm, or intense aesthetic pleasure. One might suggest that this type of feeling is expressed perfectly by T. S. Eliot in "The Dry Salvages" when he says:

> music heard so deeply
> That it is not heard at all, but you are the music
> While the music lasts.

In this early relationship affective experiences are accurately registered before the onset of defensive operations, leavening an "affective core" that guarantees a continuity of experiencing across a life span that resists transformation.

Between 3 and 8 months Stern describes a second stage, with the development of a "core self," where the separation and individuation may lead to the creation of a transitional object. As McDonald has beautifully illustrated, a tune, such as a lullaby, often subsumes this function in the musically sensitive infant (1970). In the third stage, with the establishment of the "subjective self" (8–15 months) the "attunement" is focused on the process whereby the child and his caretaker achieve mutuality and empathy. It is this empathic resonance that is responsible for the therapeutic alliance essential to clinical work. In a recent paper exploring the learning of this process, which I originally called "Dissonance in the Well Tempered Listener" (unpublished), I examined our "analyzing instrument" analogizing the therapist as a musical listener. Dr. Nass had written on this previously and noted that the "cognitive quality of the hearing experience is of necessity a more ambiguous one. Thus the ambiguity may induce a more fluid state of consciousness" (1975, p. 308). These early forms of cognition arise out of the primordial transferential dyad.

This relationship is exquisitely described in the writings of Winnicott who pictured the interaction between mother and child, or analyst and patient, as an area of play, the safe holding environment. "This intermediate area of experience, unchanged in respect of its belonging to the inner or external (shared) reality, constitutes the greater part of the infant's experience, and throughout life is retained in the intense experiencing that belong to the arts and to religion and to imaginative living and creative scientific work" (1953, p. 97).

With the development of the "symbolic self" in the fourth stage, there is the semiotic acquisition of language and symbolic behavior, with which the child can create his own external world through fantasy and play. As we have emphasized, certain vital emotional experiences escape the net of lexical appropriation, remain outside of conscious awareness, and are the basis of feeling states.

As I was thinking about this fascinating paper, I ran across a remark by the composer George Rochberg who argued that "music is a secondary 'language' system whose logic is closely related to the primary alpha logic of the central nervous system itself, i.e. of the human body. If I am right, then it follows that the perception of music is simply the process reversed, i.e. we listen with our bodies, with our nervous systems and their primary parallel/serial memory functions" (1971, p. 97). As I indicated, this is quite in line with David Epstein's ideas of music as an affectosensorimotor language, in his idea that "you play like you are" (personal communication). To further this idea, the word *emotion* itself is literally derived "from" motion.

These concepts provoked an attempt to unearth some possible neurophysiological correlates, in line with my initial interdisciplinary training and research on the psychophysiological responses to affectively charged stimuli.

Following the suggestion of Oliver Sacks, I discovered the proceedings of a group studying the Biology of Music Making, whose 1987 Denver conference was investigating the relationship between musical experience and child development, from a cognitive, emotional, ethnomusicological (social) and motorically developing perspective. I recommend this volume and regret I can merely touch on a few items (Wilson and Roehmann, 1988).

We are all aware anecdotally, or as participants in gestation, of the prenatal responses to auditory stimuli. We know that the cochlea and the middle ear (auditory apparatus) is fully developed by the fifth month of fetal life. We also know from PET scans that the sensorimotor cortex and the cerebellum of infants are quite active at birth while the visual areas are not. These findings suggest that musical development and responsivity may actually start before the baby is born, reflected in the Chinese and Japanese custom of reckoning the child's age at birth as one year.

In a project at the Eastman School of Music, Donald Shelter, deeply influenced by his association with Suzuki, has been approaching this in a more organized fashion with pregnant mothers from the academic and musical community (1988). During the in-utero stimulation period, monophonic music is presented by applying high fidelity stereophonic earphones directly on the abdomenal skin for five- to ten-minute periods. Two types of musical stimuli were presented, a stimulating (rapid tempo) and a calmer one. In ten out of thirty subjects the fetus responded with sharp, rapid, or agitated movement to the stimulating music and rolling, soft, or muted movements to the "sedative" selection. This is consistent with an earlier study by Olds (1984) who thought that tempo was the most important variable for the fetal response. One of the most intriguing suggestions from this study is that one finds the early development of highly organized and remarkably articulate speech in those children exposed to this prenatal music stimulation.

Van DeCarr (1985), who considers the womb a "prenatal university," exposed his fetal subjects to music, poetry, and the mother's and father's reading of *The Cat in the Hat*. They found that the neonate evinces recognition of specific phonetic patterns from the book in the neonatal period. This suggests that the infant must have an innate capacity to process the basic elements of speech, such as prevoiced and delayed voice onset time, positions of stops in articulations, categories of vowels, liquids, glides, and pitch contours. As Roger Sessions emphasized in his monograph, *The Musical Experience of Composer, Performer and Listener*, "From almost the first moments of our existence the impulse to produce vocal sound is a familiar one, almost as familiar as the impulse to breath. . . . Is it not clear that much of our melodic feeling derives from this source . . . with the vital act of breathing" (1950).

In a study at the Langley Porter Institute, Peter Ostwald (1988, p. 13) has demonstrated that newborn babies produce sounds that have melodic structures and rhythms which seem to be fixed by the neurophysiological and respiratory apparatuses of the infant, supporting Sessions' hypothesis, and lending support to a belief that "there is an appreciation for acoustical nuances built into the brain in embryonic development, which is linked to both language acqusition and the experience of primary affect" (Ostwald, 1988). The Papouseks, highly respected developmental researchers from Germany, report that infants as young as 2 months can match the pitch, intensity, and melodic contour of mother's songs, and by 4 months can match the rhythmic structure as well (cited in Rogers, 1988, pp. 2–3). Other researchers have found that infants between 5 and 8 months can discriminate pitch differences of less than half a tone.

Perhaps children with these sensitivities have the embryonic potentiality to react to the subtle changes in stimulus strength and intensity to which Dr. Rose refers, and develop into artists who are able to select and energize the quality of the aesthetic experience.

Musical stimuli are processed in the brain separately from nonmusical stimuli. For example, if musical tones are presented stereophonically to nonmusicians, they are registered in the nondominant hemisphere; whereas for musicians they are registered in the dominant hemisphere. The presumptive hypothesis is that in the course of training, music moves to the dominant hemisphere and actually takes on the characteristic of a discrete language.

A condition called amusia, with the loss of recognition of known music, is due to a lesion in the nondominant hemisphere, where the affective response occurs prior to cognitive processing, and is clearly linked to and intensified by subcortical and limbic system connections and reinforcement. The contribution of neurotransmitters and neurohormonal agents has also been demonstrated recently. At Stanford, a group of volunteers experienced deeply felt emotional responses to favorite pieces of music—"tingles up the spine." When the same individual was given Naloxone, an agent which blocked the effect of endorphins, our natural opiates, the same music "just lay flat. The body feels nothing. The rapture is gone" (Ackerman, 1990, pp. 219–220).

I have touched on these recent neurophysiological observations because I feel that they provide a presumptive correlation to Dr. Rose's richly imaginative thesis, and point the way to further studies. As a conclusion to my remarks, I should like to go back to the work of Dr. Oliver Sacks, a neurologist with a profound analytic understanding. He reported a case of an 80-year-old woman (1987), who after a stroke had a period of musical hallucinations of Irish songs of her youth, presumably due to a temporal lobe focus. She reported to him: "I know I'm an old woman with a stroke in an old people's home, but I feel I'm a child in Ireland again—I feel my mother's arms, I see her, I hear her singing." In understanding what Thomas Mann calls the "world behind the music," Sacks sought out her associations. Her father had died before she was born, and her mother before she was 5. Orphaned and alone, she was sent to America. She had previously had no memory of the first five years of her life, and had experienced this as a painful sadness. With this musical recall, it was "like the opening of a door." When the hallucinations ceased, after three months, she said wistfully, "The door is closing, I'm losing it again." She was glad it occurred and felt it was a healing experience.

REFERENCES

Ackerman, D. (1990), *Natural History of the Senses*. New York: Random House.
Dalhaus, C. (1989), *The Idea of Absolute Music*. Chicago: University of Chicago Press.
Epstein, D. (1987), *Beyond Orpheus: Studies in Musical Structure*. New York: Oxford University Press.
Goldberg, E. (unpublished), Dissonance in the well-tempered listener.
Hindemith, P. (1945), *Craft of Musical Composition (Revised Edition)*. New York: Associated Music Publishers.
McDonald, M. (1970), Transitional tunes and music development. *The Psychoanalytic Study of the Child*, 25:503–520. New York: International Universities Press.
Meyer, L. B. (1956), *Emotion and Meaning in Music*. Chicago: University of Chicago Press.
Nass, M. L. (1975), On hearing and inspiration in the composition of music. *Psychoanal. Quart.*, 44:431–449.
Olds, C. (1984), Fetal response to music. Wickford, Essex: Runwell Hospital.
Ostwald, P. F. (1988), Music in the organization of childhood experience and emotion. In: *Music and Child Development, the Biology of Music Making: Proceedings of the 1984 Denver Conference*, ed. F. R. Wilson & F. L. Roehmann. St. Louis, MO: MMB Music, pp. 11–27.
Rochberg, G. (1971), The avant garde and the aesthetics of survival. *New Lit. Hist.*, 3:71–92.

Rogers, S. (1988), Theories of child development and musical ability. In: *Music and Child Development, the Biology of Music Making: Proceedings of the 1984 Denver Conference*, ed. F. R. Wilson & F. L. Roehmann. St. Louis, MO: MMB Music.

Rosen, C. (1971), *The Classical Style*. New York: Viking Press.

Sacks, O. (1987), Reminiscence. In: *The Man Who Mistook His Wife for a Hat*. New York: Harper & Row Perennial Library.

Salzer, F. (1962), *Structural Hearing*. New York: Dover.

Schöenberg, A. (1967), *Fundamentals of Music Composition*. New York: St. Martin's Press.

Sessions, R. (1950), *The Musical Experience of Composer, Performer, Listener*. Princeton, NJ: Princeton University Press.

Shelter, D. J. (1988), The inquiry into prenatal musical experiences: A report of the Eastman project. In: *Music and Child Development, the Biology of Music Making: Proceedings of the 1984 Denver Conference*, ed. F. R. Wilson & F. L. Roehmann. St. Louis, MO: MMB Music, pp. 44–62.

Stern, D. (1985), *The Interpersonal World of the Infant*. New York: Basic Books.

Van DeCarr, R. (1985), The prenatal university. *U.S.A. Weekend*.

Wilson, F. R., & Roehmann, F. L., eds. (1988), *Music and Child Development, the Biology of Music Making: Proceedings of the 1984 Denver Conference*. St. Louis, MO: MMB Music.

Winnicott, D. W. (1953), Transitional objects and transitional phenomena. *Internat. J. Psycho-Anal.*, 34:89–97.

Chapter 6

On Affect and Musical Motion*

David Epstein, Ph.D.

Does music express emotion? Does it convey feelings? Can these feelings, this affect, be described, elaborated upon, "explained" through the medium of words?

Questions like these have been part of the dialogue about music, certainly since the time of the ancient Greeks. Plato, writing in *The Republic*, not only recognizes the sensual qualities of music and its power to move people emotionally; he in fact expresses concern over the potential consequences of this power.[1] Ultimately, his is a political view of the arts. He advocates the temperate in music, as opposed to the sensual, so that music may not arouse passion and possibly disturb the status quo.

A similar awareness of the sensuous in music informed the policies of the early church authorities, who saw in the Gregorian modes a proper set of affective qualities for religious expression. This concern over the musically sensuous further permeated the musical dialogues of the church in the late Middle Ages and early Renaissance. With the development of polyphonic music, the affective aspects of intervals themselves became a concern, particularly that "devil in music," the tritone;

---

*Reproduced by permission of Schirmer Books, an imprint of Macmillan Publishing Company, a division of Macmillan, Inc. (U.S.A.), from *The Sounding Streams: Studies of Time in Music*, by David Epstein. Copyright © 1993 by David Epstein. In press.

[1]Musical training is a more potent instrument than any other, because rhythm and harmony find their way into the inward places of the soul, on which they mightily fasten, imparting grace, and making the soul of him who is rightly educated graceful, or of him who is ill-educated ungraceful . . . he who received this true education of the inner being will most shrewdly perceive omissions or faults in art and . . . while he praises and rejoices over and receives into his soul the good . . . he will justly blame and hate the bad, now in the days of his youth, even before he is able to know the reason why [Plato, *The Republic*, Book III, p. 289].

certain chromatic alterations; even the properties of the harmonic interval of the third, whose capacity to arouse improp-
erly unspiritual feelings led to its circumscription.

Late baroque and early classical musicians had no doubts
about the reality of musical feeling and its expression. The
"doctrine of the affections" that stemmed from this period
sought in fact to classify the musical effects that might be used
to express particular emotions—joy, sorrow, languor, passion,
and the like.

If anything, it has been our own century that has looked upon
questions of musical affect and expression with a jaundiced eye.
Possibly this was a result of the nineteenth-century development of program music, with its growing tendency throughout
the century to describe, or presume to describe, not only feelings but events, ideas, philosophies, places—things intrinsically
extramusical. That view, augmented by the increasingly hyper-
emotional qualities of late romantic music, led writers on music
to presume far more about musical expression than could be
justified by, or specifically related to, the musical text itself—a
tendency that spilled over well into the twentieth century.[2]

A reaction was perhaps inevitable. Its arrival coincided in
part with the development of logical positivism which, while it
involved largely a critique of the philosophical use of language

[2]As an example, among hundreds of candidates, consider the following:

> [Q]uick melodies without great deviations are cheerful; slow melodies, striking
> painful discords, and only winding back through many bars to the key-note
> are . . . sad. . . . The short intelligible subjects of quick dance-music seem to
> speak only of easily attained common pleasure. On the other hand, the Allegro
> maestoso, in elaborate movements, long passages, and wide deviations, signifies
> a greater, nobler effort towards a more distant end, and its final attainment.
> The Adagio speaks of the pain of a great and noble effort which despises a
> trifling happiness. . . . The Adagio lengthens in the minor the expression of the
> keenest pain, and becomes even a convulsive wail. . . . The inexhaustibleness of
> possible melodies corresponds to the inexhaustibleness of Nature in difference
> of individuals, physiognomies, and courses of life [Schopenhauer, 1947, p. 448].

Schopenhauer was, in fact, quite sophisticated about music, and he makes clear in
the pages following this quote that his descriptions must be seen as analogies, that
music has only an indirect relation to these things, since it can never express the
phenomena themselves but only the inner nature of these phenomena; that is, the will,
itself. His descriptions, however, are typical of writing about music in this period—a
mixture of analogy and subjective imputation of properties and qualities, none of them
objectively demonstrable. Interestingly, these thoughts, in Schopenhauer and others,
are at times counterbalanced by analogs of process and structure that our own age
would find legitimate, indeed, potentially rich.

in describing the real world, also purported to deal essentially with factual knowledge, knowledge that was objectively verifiable. Such would be our view of music as well, said the new critical thinking of musicians. Let us deal with that which we can demonstrate—namely, musical structure.

Curiously, these emerging views of the world, which put such faith in the scientific approach to fact and data, were in conflict with some of the most compelling ideas in the evolution of modern science. Einstein's principles of relativity, for example, recognized that the world was an observed universe in which the observer was not only inevitable but intrinsic. Quantum theory, via the concepts of Bohr, Born, Heisenberg, Schrödinger, posited not only that the act of observation affected the nature of what was observed, but further that one could not be certain of what was being observed—it could be energy (a wave) or matter (a particle), and could change its state depending upon various conditions. The ultimate stage of scientific verification, moreover, came not to be *proof*, as earlier generations had viewed that term, but the fact of correlation. Scientific thinking sought confirmation via highly correlated relationships of data, relationships subjected to stringent evaluation. The permanence of such explication was not a prime concern; it was presumed that different, more economical, better correlated explanations, incorporating new evidence, further phenomena, might displace theories that previously reigned (Rahm, 1989). "Truth," as other generations knew it, has absented itself from scientific discourse, and "proof" has changed its clothing.[3]

Whatever its inconsistencies with what has evolved as contemporary science, logical positivism had considerable impact upon critical thinking in the arts. Its musical embodiment, as seen in the disdain for the musically subjective and emotional, was expressed by, among others, Igor Stravinsky, who wrote about the issue of musical expression at least twice in his life, in his *Autobiography* and *Poetics of Music*.[4] Logical positivism led to the

---

[3]Replication and predictability, those other staples of scientific theory, particularly of theory as confirmed by experiment, themselves fall under the rubric of correlation. Replication presumes correlated prior performance carried out under controlled test conditions. Predictability rests upon past replication.

[4]I consider that music is, by its very nature, essentially powerless to express anything at all, whether a feeling, an attitude of mind, a psychological mood, a phenomenon of nature, etc. . . . Expression has never been an inherent property

New Criticism in poetry, which deals with demonstrable elements of syntax, structure, linguistic meaning and the like. Ultimately, it led to structuralism, which in musical thinking found expression through analysis of the presumably objective, demonstrable elements of organization.

The inadequacies of musical structuralism have been clear for some time. Boretz, writing in 1979, recognized that with music, as with science, the observer influences the nature of what is observed. As he put it, "while we may not speak as we perceive, we will soon enough be perceiving as we have spoken. For the rhetoric of discourse is coercive on our senses, as is any mode of description or thought: description transforms the described. . . . If we . . . influence . . . the perceptions . . . of others by how we speak descriptively . . . we must be even more profoundly influencing our own" (p. 174).

Guck demonstrates this effect of the observer upon music observed (1990). Drawing upon the writings of some of our best theorists, she pinpoints particular uses of language that implant upon the music a special, indeed "favored," point of view. One example comes from Cone: "It is not surprising, therefore, that E-natural *dominates* the contrasting section of the song form. But unlike the development of the Beethoven sonata . . . this one . . . *prefers* . . . *to dwell* on the promissory note and *to investigate further its peculiar connection* with Eb." (1986, p. 20; Guck's emphases). Guck notes that Cone deals with the structure of Schubert's *Moment Musical* in A flat, op. 94, no. 6, in the context of mental reflections of a persona, an individual, who pursues the implications of a musical event. The music itself is drawn into this portrayal; it is itself seen as

---

of music. That is by no means the purpose of its existence. If, as is nearly always the case, music appears to express something, this is only an illusion and not a reality. It is simply an additional attribute which, by tacit and inveterate agreement, we have lent it, thrust upon it, as a label, a convention—in short, an aspect unconsciously or by force of habit, we have come to confuse with its essential being. . . .

The phenomenon of music is given to us with the sole purpose of establishing an order in things, including, and particularly, the coordination between man and time. To be put into practice, its indispensable and single requirement is construction. Construction once completed, this order has been attained, and there is nothing more to be said. It would be futile to look for, or expect anything else from it [Stravinsky, 1936, pp. 53–54].

"Do we not in truth, ask the impossible of music when we expect it to express feelings, to translate dramatic situations, even to imitate nature?" (Stravinsky, 1947, p. 77).

an individual, one that can enlist support for its efforts. We as observers are drawn into a drama that is internal to the music.

By such examples, Guck lays bare the perceptual lenses through which musical works may be viewed. The perspectives are resonant with our times, dealing with structure, function, process. The contexts are worlds removed from the emotional qualities imputed by an earlier age to musical works. What is inescapable, however, is the fact of mind-set: the way a mind orients itself to the properties of a piece. As with Heisenberg's law in physics, so here, too, the observer becomes part of the observed.

Our preoccupation with the formal and the structural in music has not been unproductive. We are more cognizant today than ever before of the manifest, wide-ranging, and subtle aspects of control and of meanings (however we may define their aspects) that structure exerts upon music. The selectivity of the structuralist approach has left the affective side of music, however, in limbo.

Some recent writers have resumed the ages-long exploration of musical expression. We have not, as a consequence, come full circle to where musical philosophy was a century ago. If anything, we have made a revolution upon a spiral rather than a circle, for we examine these matters now from a higher vantage point, one marked by an intellectual sophistication that has benefited from contemporary science, from theories of language, from modern philosophy of science.

Meyer (1967) and Narmour (1977), in their pursuit of these matters, have dealt with information theory and cognitive aspects of perception. Cognition and the psychology of music have spawned new journals (*Psychomusicology, Music Perception, Psychology of Music*), as well as a spate of books (Clynes, 1982; Deutsch, 1982; Bruhn, Oerter, and Rosing, 1985; Sloboda, 1985). Maus and Micznik have found in current literary theory richly suggestive approaches to musical affect (narrative theory of Genette, Barthes' concept of connotation, intertextuality as viewed by Kristeva and Riffaterre—Micznik; story and discourse theory; theories of drama—Maus) (Maus, 1988a,b; Micznik, 1988).

The philosophical contexts within which issues of musical expression have been seen in past eras leave questions that merit a further look. The phenomenon of musical motion has something to offer these questions; the synthesis of motion and affect will be the focus of this chapter.

In her study of the arts, *Philosophy in a New Key*, Suzanne Langer makes a number of points that are critical to this discussion (1948, pp. 165–199). For one, she argues convincingly that the contents of a work of art, particularly its symbolic aspects, cannot be expressed in terms other than what they are. The contents, that is, are untranslatable. They are unique and specific to the medium in which they exist, be it musical sound, the shapes, colors, forms of paintings, the images of poetry.

Moreover, these contents are uniquely embodied within their artistic medium—their specific musical sounds and shapes, specific poetic images. Thus, although we can describe and discuss the inner essence of a work, we cannot penetrate this essence to its core by these secondary means of description. That essence, that core, remains inviolate, intrinsic to the medium, the "language," of the work. It must ultimately be experienced through the music, poem, painting itself, speaking in its own terms.

Langer further suggests that the feelings communicated by works of art are essentially symbolic, providing insight into the morphology of feeling itself. Music, she suggests, can articulate with clarity and precision subtle complexes of feeling that language, for all its denotative power, cannot even name, let alone set forth.

The essence of this argument is that music, in its affective connotations, provides a symbolic representation of an inner state. On this insight rests much of the discussion that follows in these pages. For if music presents us with this kind of symbolic representation, then our insight into this affective state may be more precisely grasped if we can determine the nature of the symbolism itself.[5]

---

[5]Langer carried forward her discussion of art and affect in a later book, *Feeling and Form* (1953). The major summary of her philosophical work in aesthetics is found in the three-volume set, *Mind: An Essay on Human Feeling* (1967). In these pages, in addition to concerns about art and expression, she is involved with issues of perception, cognition, the processing of information and other matters which, over the decades since, have evolved into current foci in the brain sciences, artificial intelligence, and computer science.

We have little trouble grasping some kinds of symbolic statements—those, for example, that are couched in specifically musical terms. Horn calls, folk songs and dances, bird calls (Mahler [First Symphony: Wayfarer songs], Beethoven's Pastorale Symphony [close of the slow movement]) are cases in point. Parodies of these genres, such as the bitter or ironic ones that Mahler effects (again, the First Symphony, middle section of the slow movement) we find equally clear in their references, as we do Mahler's waltz passages, with their sense of longing, their *Rückblick* toward a bygone age (the Scherzi of the First Symphony [the Trio] and Fifth Symphony).

Parody and satire, as done by Stravinsky with merciless wit in the Tango, Fox Trot, and Ragtime in *L'Histoire du Soldat*; even the destruction of musical genre, as Ravel does at the close of *La Valse*—these are equally clear in their affective implications. For the commentary in these cases is couched in musical terms. The effect of that commentary, in fact, is achieved by working against the genres themselves.

Though this use of musical genre, and deliberate distortion of genre, may be clear in its affective implications, it occupies a small segment of the musical literature. Other, less obvious, more abstract aspects of musical expression are not always so clear, though they are far more pervasive in our repertoire. Do these instances also embody some symbolic representation of an inner affective state? Can they be explicated?

Perhaps so, though to what extent remains to be seen.

We examine some cases in the examples that follow. Invariably, in these instances, the element in which this symbolism seems to lie is connected with motion—motion embodied in one of its many aspects, be it the sense of forward movement or lack of it, the tension and release exerted by harmony, the qualities of articulation that control the character of a phrase, the use of tempo as an element of affect.

Gilbert Rose (chapter 4), dealing with the relationship of the formal structures of art to affect, speaks in much the same terms we have discussed above. He suggests that the structures of works of art are transduced to a new level of personal emotional experience on the part of the perceiver. ("Transduced" is used as in the world of physics, denoting the process by which one form of energy or signal [in the case of music, acoustic stimuli] becomes converted into a different one—here, affect.)

This transduction involves particular processes. Rose (chapter 4) refers to two: the primary process of imagination, and the secondary process of knowledge. Further, he speaks of the modes of organization intrinsic to both processes, lying in dynamic equilibrium such that they invigorate everyday thought and perception with vividness and fresh feeling. As he puts it:

> An interplay of primary process imagination and secondary process knowledge of reality underlies all thought and perception. As a consequence, a cyclic interplay takes place between their respective modes of attention and organization. . . . a widely scanning receptivity to data, organized unconsciously according to familiar primary process principles of condensation, displacement, and symbolism, . . . sharply focused, selective, conscious attention to data organized according to secondary process common sense, logic and accepted knowledge of reality. . . . The interplay is accompanied by a building up of tension associated with the long circuited, highly controlled, slow discharge of the secondary process, and a release of tension and greater freedom from control associated with the rapid discharge of the primary process [p. 65, this volume].

The changes in stimulus strength account for pleasure/unpleasure, sensations that in turn lie at the core of emotion. The result is characterized by Rose as a "happening of directed tensions." The enhanced rhythms of tension and release in the art work will be experienced by the receptive perceiver with an accompanying emotional response (see Rose, chapter 4).[6]

[6]Rose carries these ideas further. Human emotion, he suggests, cannot exist embedded in the inorganic structure of aesthetic form (i.e., within a work itself). The structure can only offer the necessary perceptual conditions for an emotional response to occur. Degrees of tension and resolution underlie pleasure/unpleasure. These sensations in turn constitute the undifferentiated matrix of all later emotions; their particular quality will depend on the conscious and unconscious ideas that come to be associated with them in the course of time. Rose points out that affects, according to Brenner's unified theory, consist of both sensations and ideas (Brenner, 1974).

Motion as the embodiment of rhythm, temporal process, duration and tension is discussed from a contemporary composer's perspective, though with many points in common with concepts advocated here, by Xavier Alvarez (1989). Alvarez suggests that "meaning in musical language is in fact a 'discovery' of satisfactory relations between the motion of music structures and physical human experience." By discovering this relation, the listener becomes engaged in apprehending musical form. He sees rhythmic structures as perhaps the strongest and most crucial references in music, and finds that by shaping motion in music, musical time and form are articulated in a way that has poetic meaning to the listener (p. 203).

Stuart Feder has explored what might be considered those underlying mental structures which subserve such operations from a psychoanalytic point of view. He suggests that "through the medium of auditory form with its symbolic implications, the composer achieves an organized musical structure that is expressive of an affect." Such structures while stable are not rigid; rather, they may have the kinetic quality revealed in Rose's formulation. Feder suggests that both representation and communication of an affect occur "through an intrinsic morphology which mirrors the mental organization underlying the affect" (1990, p. 265).

It is but a small and logical step from the dynamic buildup and release of tensions described above to the factor of motion, as it operates in music as the carrier of these tensions and as the means through which tensions are controlled, modulated, and ultimately resolved. For our sense of musical motion is in part felt physically (muscularly) and psychologically in terms of tension and release. Tension/release may indeed be the essential factor, conveying the sensation of movement, of motion, in the absence of true physical motion in space.[7]

David B. Green also sees the temporal passage through a musical work as intrinsically connected with affective meanings. These meanings have in large part to do with anticipations and perceptions of rhythmic as well as formal processes (1982, 1984).

[7]Rose discusses affect, with its concomitants of tension/release and pleasure/pain, phenomenologically, concerned with the processes of sensory experience. The brain scientist would approach affect on a different level, focused upon the physiological mechanisms that underlie these processes. These involve the transmission of impulses and data through the nervous system, preparation mechanisms that precede the establishment of affect, the electro- and biochemical roles of neurotransmitters, of endocrine secretions, of endorphins such as dopamine, which control the sensation of pleasure and pain.

The two approaches are not antithetical, but complementary, focused upon different levels and aspects of physical mechanisms. Neither approach, in fact, is sufficient in the sense of explicating all. If anything, we still lack the essential connecting link between the two. We can know fully, that is, the neurophysiological elements that may effect a particular feeling, yet that information cannot describe the feeling itself but only its determinants. It seems impossible, in fact, to convey the experience of feeling by any means but metaphor, simile, adjective, and the like. The impenetrability of affect, in a descriptive sense, thus exists in the scientific approach to the matter much as it does in philosophic–aesthetic discourse.

Nevertheless, it is a step forward, in the musical encounter with affect, to see the matter in terms of motion, tension–release, pleasure/pain, as well as with an understanding of the physiology that underlies these elements. What is attained is a more precise awareness of the mechanisms by which motion is controlled, even if that motion, or more precisely our experiences of its affective character, remain impervious. The principal goal of this discussion is a practical one—a more finely delineated understanding of motion–affect that can allow us as performers to shape it with greater awareness and to greater effect. This, too, is a matter of mechanism, musical mechanism, which seems capable of description.

It is no accident, perhaps, that motion should be so intimately tied to musical affect, and thus tied to musical symbols that carry affective sensibility. The etymology of the word *emotion* itself is related to the experience of motion. *Emovere, emotus* are the Latin roots (*e*, out of, *motus*, motion; stemming from motion; moving out, stirring up). A sense of motion underlies our emotional life itself. We describe ourselves as being "moved" by emotional experience—in English, in the other romance languages, in German.[8]

Motion has long been recognized as a prime component of musical feeling. It has been little examined, however, in terms of its mechanisms, or how they may relate to musical affect, or indeed control it. What follows here is in no sense a complete discussion of the topic. Like other studies in these pages, it must be seen more as a pilot venture, a preliminary inquiry.

Some of the examples that follow are, admittedly, programmatic works. That is not to say that motion and its affective connotations apply only to such music. In fact, the programs in these works serve a utilitarian purpose at best, in terms of these studies. They provide a basis for methodology—a check upon the emotional properties sensed in the music, and the symbols that are seen as their purveyors. Presumably, since the composers have provided programmatic descriptions, the affective properties of the music and their symbolic embodiments can be interpreted as deliberate attributes, rather than the subjective impressions of listeners. The final work, a Mozart concerto, is absolute music, though connotations are traced to elements beyond the pale of pure music.

It would seem that the insights these examples offer can be extended to abstract, supposedly "pure" music. That possibility forms the final discussion in these pages, allied with additional musical examples.

Perhaps the most striking aspect of the examples that follow is the structural role filled by motion. Also, the connection with musical feeling that motion effects. All elements of the music—melodies, rhythms, harmonies, whatever, are not seen as

---

[8]French: emouvant—moving (emotionally); Spanish, Portuguese: comover—to move; Italian: commuovere. German shares the same expression. The adjective for being affectively moved (bewegt) stems from the word for motion (Bewegung).

elements (or functions) in themselves. As such, they are of limited interest. It is only when these elements are related to musical motion that they take on new interest, and their functional roles assume a higher level of meaning.[9]

Motion thus occupies the highest level of the structural hierarchy. It is motion, with its correlated affect, that makes ultimate sense of the music, that ultimately guides, indeed dictates, the direction of the music, the nature of its flow—in brief, how it will "go." In this respect, motion subsumes, integrates, and provides the broadest context for all other musical elements.

Equally interesting is the handle that motion provides for elusive and often enigmatic musical problems—in many instances, performance problems. This fact speaks to a situation fairly common with serious and experienced performers, a situation found during the preparation of a work or perhaps in a reexamination of it after performances over many years. At such times one may find that in all obvious respects, the piece is "known": it lies comfortably beneath the hands; its technical hazards are no longer hazardous; its structure is understood on a sophisticated level; its style, phrasing, shaping are "right," integrated, beyond contention. Yet in some way, the piece remains unknown; its inner content seems to elude intuition.

The search for this missing element can be agonizing, not least because of the intangibility of what one seeks. Often it is the affective grasp of the music that feels insufficient. But affect is an intuitive matter, a sense of how the music falls on the nerve endings, so to speak. How does one use reason, analysis, to grasp what is fundamentally not understood via reason?

In the examples that follow, motion is found to be the clue. Within the sense of motion—a sense that can be delineated, refined, grasped with precision, there seems to lie that liaison of form, structure, and affect. Each example is a case study of this amalgamation. Together they suggest ways that these elements may be synthesized, ways as varied as the imaginations of the composers themselves.

---

[9]Often, in the discussion that follows here, musical symbol and structural detail are referred to interchangeably. That fact reflects the inseparable nature of structure and symbol, the intrinsic wedding of one with the other—confirmation, really, of Langer's view about the role of symbols as structural carriers of expression.

MENDELSSOHN—FINGAL'S CAVE OVERTURE (THE HEBRIDES)

Our point regarding this well-known piece is its opening phrases, the first of which is shown in Figure 6.1. Given an orchestra of professional competence, a performance of these segments (and, as a consequence, perhaps, much of the work) is likely to be of one of two qualities. These are less a matter of "good" or "bad" than of interesting, and hence effective, or dull. One frequent cause of the latter species is the way the opening phrases are shaped.

To be sure, one could make the same claim about any piece—that how it is shaped will have much to do with its effectiveness. In this work, however, the quality of the phrasing lies in an aspect of affect not readily discernable at first glance.

One often hears the opening phrases, particularly their melodic line, played in a somewhat "flat" manner, the dynamics level and steady, the rhythmic shape of the melody, in its succession of eighths, sixteenths, and quarters, played "straight." In this may lie the shortcoming. For though there are no signs or symbols to suggest it, other than the programmatic title of the overture itself, the phrase cannot be read in a purely straightforward manner, concerned only with an exclusively musical line. Its affect has to do with other things as well, matters that hinge upon the sense of motion within the line.

"Fingal's Cave" was admittedly inspired by the seacoast cave of this name, which impressed Mendelssohn during his visit to the Hebrides in 1829. The stormy character of the sea heard in the latter part of the overture is obvious. The calm quality of the sea in the opening bars is overlooked in some performances, however. Therein lies the problem.

In a more general sense, "Fingal's Cave" is concerned with the sea, particularly in its opening passages, with the *quality of motion* of the calmly rolling seascape. Motion is the key symbol to this passage.

The music is not a "description" of the sea, but more the embodiment of its motion—more precisely, the "feel" of its unique sense of movement. That feeling may be accessible to one standing upon the coast, observing the gently rolling waves of a calm sea as they ebb and swell in their journey toward the land. If ever one has been upon this sea, particularly in a small

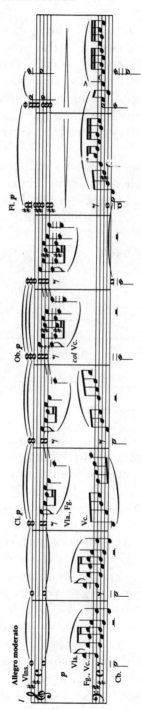

Figure 6.1. Mendelssohn: Fingal's Cave Overture.

boat (and unhindered by *mal de mer*), the motion is unforgetta-
ble. Wave motion on a calm ocean, as the water moves over a
bottom of moderate depth, creates what Yankee sailors long
ago termed "rollers"—long waves of moderate height (from
eight to perhaps twenty feet), built up over distances as great as
hundreds of miles. The periods of these waves are impressively
long, extending as much as two hundred yards from crest to
crest.

Experiencing this wave motion in a small boat, one feels an
acceleration, suggested in the drawing in Figure 6.2, as the boat
slides down the wave toward its trough. As the craft rises upon
the back of the next wave, the uphill motion creates a retar-
dation.

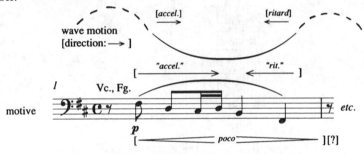

Figure. 6.2

Acceleration and ritard are inadequate terms to describe this
motion, though they are part of it. Beyond matters of speed,
there is also an intensification of movement on that downward
slide—not just the tightening of the muscles as one braces
against the descent, but an internal *feeling* of greater intensity
as well, which slacks off with the slowed uphill rise.

The physical reality of this accelerated forward motion,
which is associated with the down-wave movement, is built into
the opening motive of the overture, as indicated in Figure 6.2.
The intensifying forward movement resides in the rhythms,
which quicken from eighths to sixteenths. Conversely, consistent with the uphill climb, the rhythms slow to quarter notes at
the end of the bar.

Here, then, is the musical symbolism that is the key to the
affect of the passage. To establish this quality, more than just
the rhythms must be played, however. One must capture as

well the sense of intensifying and slowed down motion that lies behind these rhythmic shapes. That is a quality that must be felt; it is a matter for the body, less for the mind. Its shadings of intensities must further translate into the bassoonist's breathing, the cellists' bowing.

No exterior signs, such as crescendo/decrescendo, can convey such a feeling with certainty. It is a crescendo/decrescendo of intensities that one seeks here, not the conventional sense of louder/softer that hairpin dynamics generally connote.

This may explain why these dynamics are not found in this passage, though we cannot know for certain, obviously. If our reading of the phrase is accurate, though, its affect could as easily be distorted as helped by such markings, for they could be read as purely "dynamics" (in the conventional musical sense), markings devoid of the deeper sense of movement. Alternatively, they could result in an exaggerated louder/softer *expressivo* affect—a plausible interpretation, if one has no other reference frame.

There probably is no marking adequate to convey this affect of motion. Musical signs are a paltry collection of indications, unable to imply subtleties like the ones discussed here, qualities that may inhere on deeper levels within a phrase. Those qualities may be elusive, but once grasped, they are precise and clear. The search for them is carried out as much by intuition and imagination as by any literal reading of musical signs.

A final observation: It has been observed by seamen that wave action has a further pattern—that waves come often in groups, the seventh one commonly larger than the preceding six. How verified this may be by oceanography is a question, and it is equally uncertain whether Mendelssohn was aware of this sailing lore. What is clear, however, is the presence of this wave pattern in the music itself (see again Figure 6.1). The first six bars of the overture represent six statements of the wave motion discussed above. The next two bars convey the surge and ebb, even the physical, durational dimensions of a larger wave, its intensity explicitly augmented here by crescendo/diminuendo signs.[10]

---

[10]Peter Kivy, in discussing representation in music as expression, sees this opening of *Fingal's Cave* with much the same perception of periodic wave motion as suggested here, though he deals with it more briefly, and more with concern for general effect than with details of specific musical mechanisms by which the effect is created (Kivy,

WAGNER—PRELUDE TO TRISTAN AND ISOLDE

Wagner's prelude to the opening act of *Tristan and Isolde*, in its theoretical implications, may be the nineteenth century's most discussed work. For over a century, the debate has prevailed. The music, whose first 12 bars are seen in Figure 6.3, has been seen as the singular death-knell to tonality, its harmonic and tonal wanderings destroying any sense of a stable tonal base. To the contrary, it has been suggested that the tonal departures are local only, all of them cohering within the larger domain of a single tonality, that of A minor (Hindemith, 1945).

What purpose do these harmonically and tonally complex passages serve? Curiously, the *Tristan* Prelude is understood in two seemingly unconnected respects, those of its harmonic/tonal structure, however it may be viewed vis-à-vis coherence, and its affective character. The last term of its tempo direction, "schmachtend" (languishing, pining, yearning), seems the key to that character.

If there is a central feeling that underlies this opera, it is that of love and desire unfulfilled. Eros infuses all, love not only on a sensual plane, but in the total complexity of feelings, passions, aspirations, and desires by which two people wish a complete union with one another. That union is withheld, thwarted, frustrated throughout the playing-out of the drama, attained only by way of death. (The original Celtic legend upon which Wagner drew withheld this union even upon death, for the characters are separated through burial on opposite sides of a church. From their graves, however, grow oak trees whose branches in time intertwine above the roof of the church.)

1984, pp. 137–140).

Kivy, who has devoted considerable thought to questions of musical affect and expression, seen primarily from the perspective of a philosopher, though one with musical training and understanding, agrees with many of the tenets of our discussion. Among other things, he, as Langer, recognizes the intrinsic and untranslatable aspect of affect in music, concluding thereby that affective aspects must be seen in musical terms. As he says in a discussion of instrumental music, "The function of an expressive property in a work of pure instrumental music is no different from the function of any other *musical* property of such a work . . . an expressive property *is a musical* property . . . and its function is to be musically exploited, musically developed, musically played with, musically built with and built upon, along with the rest of the musical qualities it may be in company with" (Kivy, 1990, pp. 185–186). This is a somewhat different viewpoint than found in Kivy's earlier work (1980), where he sees two essentially separate languages for describing music, one of them involved with technical aspects, the other with emotive, or expressive, aspects.

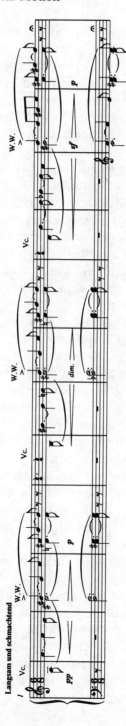

Figure 6.3. Wagner: Prelude to *Tristan and Isolde* (excerpt).

If we counterpose these two elements of the opera (or, in this discussion, the opening Prelude)—its structural anomalies and its underlying affect—the connection between them seems evident. The link has to do with tension and, with respect to tension, the way in which the music moves.

Intrinsic to the central element of unfulfilled love that infuses the psyches of the central characters, is a physiological correlate of tension—generated by desire, by longing, by hope, by the frustration—that is the ongoing trajectory of this consuming passion. Every scene, every action of these personae, whether external or internalized as thought and reflection, is underlain by tensions that relate to this theme. Every moment of the opera as a consequence reveals levels and degrees of tension that, in a sense, are variants upon a central affect—tensions not of the ordinary sort that underlie all motion within all music, but tensions of this special character, tensions continually bound to this overarching motivation.

It is by these unique qualities of tension, embodied in musical structure, that the music of *Tristan* moves, most particularly, its opening prelude. That prelude functions much like a baroque or classical introduction to an overture or symphonic opening, stating the motif upon which the subsequent music will build. Wagner turns the concept of an introduction to yet another purpose as well, establishing from the outset the affective character that will dominate the entire work. Establishing this elemental affect in such a condensed manner at the initial notes of the Prelude is a stunning stroke of artistry. By the close of the first phrase of the Prelude, within a mere three bars, we are set, caught in the grip of the issue to be joined, bound by the dramatic attitude that is the elemental property of the plot, the personae, the total work.

This elemental affect not only links the emotive side of the opera to the anomalous musical syntax of the Prelude, but by this linkage lifts our view of the music and its syntax to a higher level of structural hierarchy. It forces us to consider not harmonic functions alone, be they local or global, but the more interesting question of why such an anomaly may exist.

Again, tension and its control of motion, both of these uniquely fashioned in this music, are the integrating agents that bind musical construct and feeling. For just as the pervasive affect of tension, the product of unrest and frustrated desire, is encapsulated by this 111-bar Prelude, lying in disturbed quiescence in its opening bars, rising to passionate heights in its central section, so is the musical structure of the Prelude, in its harmonic, tonal, rhythmic and melodic aspects, similarly underlain by tension. The tension is graduated by finely distinguished degrees, ever regulating the particular ways in which the music moves. The structure is thus an analog of the affect, an analog supremely shaped, matching in degree and kind the tensions that inhabit both spheres.

The overriding impact of the opening bars is indefiniteness, its tensions compounded by suspense and ambiguity. The inner lives of Tristan and Isolde are built into the musical structure and the motion of that structure, the product of compositional technique utilized on an almost cunning level of imagination and control. Ambiguity, the progenitor of this uncertainty, these tensions, lies yet deeper in the music, announced by the very opening note of the Prelude. For how we are to hear that note, in the sense of understanding it contextually, is replete with contradictions.[11]

The tensions, the ambiguities, the sense of unrest, unquiet, with implications both syntactical and affective, remain as the music progresses from this obliquely turned opening. The dialogue of the first three bars continues through the next phrase, though implanted upon a higher tonal center, one some degrees removed from the initial framework of an ambiguous A minor. How this new tonal focus is to be heard, how it relates to the prior tonal level, is unclear. Thus another element of uncertainty, structural ambiguity, affective unrest is introduced to the compositional mix, seemingly without preparation or compositional context. This fact alone lifts the level of tension and, as well, enriches the qualitative sense of that tension, as it pertains to the central affect of the drama.[12]

[11]As early as measure 3, we sense that the opening pitch, A, functions in the background as a tonic—in the view of some analysts, *the* tonic. It could not be less forceful in that role, however, in that manner by which it initially sounds, for it is placed upon the weakest point in the meter and quickly moves to F, which suggests contexts of D minor or F major more immediately than the more subtle and complex context of A minor.

[12]Phrase 3 (measures 8–11) carries the compositional dialogue a step farther. The initial motive alters. Its phrase length is expanded, the answering wind line (measures 10–11) rising an additional step. Its cello line, likewise, descends by an additional chromatic step to reach a different if equally tense chord in measure 10 (intensified by

Even as viewed this far, in an incomplete discussion, it is clear that Wagner creates in the Prelude a continual state of uncertainty, of unrest, unease, a state whose counterpart is tension that is ongoing, changing in degree and intensity, but never fully resolved. Ambiguity plays a role in this process, effecting uncertainties of harmony, harmonic direction, resolution and context, further leaving uncertain how we are to construe passages that traverse distant tonal climes. Rhythm, meter, phrasing, and articulations, by their unique disposition at the service of a special sense of motion, further enhance this condition of unrelenting uncertainty.[13]

By these many means, the Prelude lies in continual tension. Its slow tempo, long-sustained, often languorous lines, dynamic increments and decrements contribute to its unique sense of

---

the *sf*). Further, the pause preceding the phrase is reduced from the prior 7 beats to only 4, in the process metrically displacing the phrase within the bar.

Adding to this expansion of the phrase, in effect to the broader, more intense "breath" of the music and the sighing, longing, of its affect, are the rhythms that carry the cello line downward. For that line, with its intensifying crescendo, is not only extended over a wider span in this phrase; a sense of acceleration is further built into the music, contributing to the forcefulness of the descent. The cello line feels inexorable in its movement toward G sharp, this sense of a goal-directed fall incremented through the step-by-step rhythmic diminution of the notes approaching the climax.

[13]This view of the Prelude is not unique, though it does embrace a particular concern with the mechanisms of motion, whereby affect may be both embodied in music and controlled. Roger Sessions reflects a view of the Prelude in many ways parallel to that expressed here. He, too, is concerned with movement, with gesture, with affect, and with aspects of structure as they bear upon these matters, though his focus is oriented primarily upon harmonic progression (Cone, 1979, pp. 3–26).

Sessions eloquently describes music in terms of movement and feeling, pointing out "how intimately our musical impulses are connected with those primitive movements which are among the very conditions of our existence," and "how vivid is our response to the primitive elements of musical movement." In a subsequent passage concerned with "expression" in music, he shows that "emotion is specific, individual and conscious," that:

[M]usic goes deeper than this, to the energies which animate our psychic life, and out of these creates a pattern which has an existence, laws, and human significance of its own. It reproduces for us the most intimate essence, the tempo and the energy, of our spiritual being; our tranquility and our restlessness, our animation and our discouragement, our vitality and our weakness—all, in fact, of the fine shades of dynamic variation of our inner life. It reproduces these far more directly and more specifically than is possible through any other medium of human communication [Cone, 1979, p. 19].

It is notable how these thoughts clearly parallel Langer's portrayal of music as a symbolic representation of our inner life, an inner life untranslatable to another medium. Session's discussion of emotion, as opposed to the term *affect* which is preferred in this discussion, also parallels Langer's view of these matters, as well as ours in this chapter.

motion, which in effect is an analog that mirrors the affective tensions that underlie both Prelude and opera as a whole. The unique motion, the special sense of pacing are only partly a function of tempo; they are more a consequence of the sustained phrases, with their slowly, only partially resolving tensions, that pervade the music.

There are practical consequences of this marriage of structure and affect that have a bearing upon performance. Among them are, paradoxically, issues of tempo. Though the motion of the Prelude is in part paced by the mix of line, harmony, shift of tonality, and the like, as we have discussed, the unfolding of the music is also controlled, as with all music, by tempo. The Tristan *Prelude*, as in works of Brahms, cannot be let down in tension because of performance, for its tensions are intrinsic to the structure. The music can languish, however, as a consequence of tempo. In this respect, the Prelude has suffered something of the same fate as Mahler's music: it has been over-interpreted, the in-built qualities of the phrases exaggerated in performance. Prime among the musical offenses in this case are tempos that are unfortunately slow, not to mention flexibilities of tempo and pulse that can render phrases rhythmically out of shape.

Pöppel has pointed out that a specific time interval seems to function as an integrating mechanism within which we fuse sequential events into integral forms. It is the interval which, psychologically speaking, determines our sense of the present as distinguished from past and future. In most people, the upper limit of this psychological present lies in the neighborhood of 2.5 to 3 seconds. It is notable that within this period fit virtually all phrases, as spoken in all languages. Also fitting this period are virtually all motifs in music (Pöppel, 1988).[14]

In the case of the Tristan *Prelude*, Wagner's opening phrases stretch this perceptual capacity in the extreme. If, in addition, an exaggerated, slow tempo is taken, the boundaries within which we must perceive these units may be beyond our capaci-

---

[14]Note that we speak of phrases and motifs only, which serve as minimal building blocks, or smallest ideational units. Larger concepts like sentences in language, phrases in music consist of a number of such units strung together. These minimal units are significant in that they seem to be the basic ideational quanta involved in the cognitive processing of information that constitutes thought.

ties.[15] As a consequence, we hear not motifs nor phrases, but notes. Time does not flow, even by Wagner's languorous schedule, and affect is distorted—the victim of a misconception that sees surface effect as primary *desideratum*, a substitute for an underlying union of feeling and temporal construct.

MOZART—PIANO CONCERTO NO. 20 IN D MINOR, K. 466. MOVEMENT I

The question of affect, as well as how to shape the music of this movement, arises with the opening bars of the concerto. The initial phrase, seen in Figure 6.4, can be and often is played much as the music stands on the page. The syncopated chords in the strings are heard detached, in a slightly angular, articulated manner; the dynamic is generally quiet; the bass figures are more or less "neutral" in character; and something of a melodic line is heard in the first violins in bars 3 and 4.

Much the same approach marks the later entrance of the piano (in measure 77). Though the phrase is marked legato, the notes come out as somewhat individual and independent, which is to say, less than cantando, underlain by a dynamic level that seems more the result of the playing than a causative element.

Such performances are remarkable: they have the power to turn one of Mozart's deeper works into *ennui*.

The alternative approach, to these ears less often heard, embraces a different affective frame. The dynamics of the orchestra in the opening bars, while fundamentally piano, are differentiated in level, the object being a hushed, subdued overall effect. The violins and violas (measure 1ff) are slightly softer than normal piano (*ben p*), their figures made less distinct by being linked under extended bows. The cello/bass line is mysterious, a character enhanced by the lower and darker sonorities of the basses, which prevail over the celli. The color of the entire ensemble is evanescent, any brightness of sound avoided by playing somewhat over the fingerboard (*sul tasto*), possibly curving the bow as well to engage fewer hairs on the string. And the melody in measure 3 does not so much "begin" as emerge—indefinite, obscured, as if emanating from a fog.

---

[15]Tempos extending from M.M.52 to the M.M. mid-40s are not uncommon in some performances.

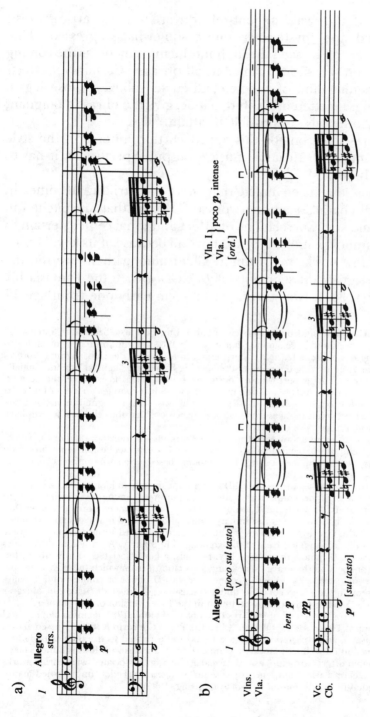

Figure 6.4. Mozart: Piano Concerto No. 20 in D Minor, K. 466, I.

Heard this way, an entirely different piece arises, music haunted and mysterious, music somewhat depressed. That character can be seen throughout the movement, as the coming discussion will show. It inhabits all phrases. Certainly it affects the opening line of the solo, discussed above, whose legato markings, abetted by a soft dynamic, give the phrase a poignant quality otherwise impossible to attain.[16]

There is reason for this approach that inheres in the style and context of Mozart's musical output. Specifically, it has to do with key.

It has long been noted that there are striking affinities in musical character among works of Mozart that are pitched in the same key. Correlations of affect and tonal center pertain to the D minor piano concerto, above all because of its key. Mozart wrote few works in D minor. Chief among them are the *Requiem*, significant segments of *Don Giovanni*[17], the Fantasia for piano (K.397), two string quartets—an early one from age 17

---

[16]Musicians who find this approach unfaithful to the music because it "interprets" Mozart's score should reexamine what may be a false assumption that neutral, literal rendering of a score is feasible. Interpreting, in a sense of decisions about a score, is inevitable. Even playing the notes of the opening bars in the "neutral" manner initially described here entails performance decisions, in this case, for example, the decision that the opening violin/viola phrase in measures 1–2 incorporates no longer line to be brought out through bowings or articulations; likewise, that no significant melodic line lies in the first violins in measures 3–4; or the decisions that the cello/bass figures have no particular expressive character.

Even nondecisions about performance are decisions—by omission, rather than commission. Neutrality in performance does not exist. The central question is not "to decide or not to decide," but what kinds of decisions, based upon what criteria, may best penetrate and reveal a score.

[17]D is the central key of the opera. D minor appears only in limited places, however, ones that have distinct connections with death. Foremost among these is the music in the Finale of Act II when the statue of the murdered Commendatore, accepting Don Giovanni's invitation, arrives for dinner—music also reflected in the opening D minor section of the Overture. Passages in this scene are diverted toward other harmonic regions, only to be pulled back to this commanding tonality. A paradigm thus exerts tonal control: D minor, the central key, prevails, a key associated with death, with a statue from beyond the grave—a key, and associations, from which there is no escape. (A somewhat similar paradigm in connection with D minor as commanding tonality will be seen in the piano concerto under discussion.) A fuller discussion of Mozart's use of the D minor tonality may be found in the fuller version of this chapter.

Feder has traced a trend of Mozart's D minor works after 1781 against a biographical background. These are the Quartet K421, the Piano Concerto K466, discussed above, *Don Giovanni*, and the *Requiem*. All are found to be related to the themes of father, fathering and fatherhood; Mozart's oedipal conflict; and his wish for his father's blessing. Related affects are emphasized, in particular rage, associated with earlier works such as Elektra's aria, "Tutte nel cor vi sento" in *Idomeneo* (Feder, unpublished manuscript, cited in *The American Psychoanalyst*, Spring, 1991).

(K.173), and the later K.421, a Kyrie (K.341) of 1781, and the present piano concerto. Of an output which modern scholarship now recognizes as numbering some 800 works, this collection in D minor is significant by its limited size alone.

It is more significant still for the character of these works. Of them, two deal explicitly with death—the Requiem, and portions of *Don Giovanni*.[18] Of the other major works in this key, the prevalent affect is one of depression, gloom. Those qualities are inescapable in the Piano Fantasia, as they are in the older string quartet's opening movement, whose initial phrase is underlined in this regard with the direction "sotto voce." Spare textures, somber, serious, and somewhat depressed music characterize the earlier quartet in its D minor outer movements, its concluding fugue ending with darkly colored, long-sustained chords. This same dark, depressed quality pervades the opening movement of the D minor Piano Concerto. It is this quality, mixed with a sense of the ineffable, the mysterious, that suggests the performance decisions discussed here.

This concerto is, of course, absolute music—instrumental music without an additional programmatic agenda, in contrast to the works studied earlier in this chapter. Absence of a program does not mean absence of an affective agenda, however. The apparent significance of D minor for Mozart is a compelling argument that the K.466 concerto does, in fact, share qualities of feeling that this key seemed to connote for the composer. We use this fact here much as we used the fact of programmatic associations in the works discussed earlier, that is, as a check, a means for evaluating affective properties that we might attribute to this music.

Two aspects of the music seem important from the standpoint of affect, both found in the opening D minor movement. One is a sense of entrapment; the other, related to entrapment, a sense of struggle. Both can be seen in purely structural

---

[18]It may be an index of Mozart's personality that a number of these works in D minor, a key with such foreboding connotations for the composer, turn to the bright region of D major for their conclusion. This is the case in the Finale of the piano concerto, whose last movement shares in large degree the sense of struggle against unrelenting conditions shortly to be discussed in the opening movement. Yet its D major conclusion is music of wit and lighthearted motivic byplay. Likewise, *Don Giovanni* ends with a chorus in D major that celebrates the triumph of righteousness (and, really, life).

terms—as musical constructs turned to particular account. They can also be seen as structural analogs of affective content. Therein lies precisely the connection between a work of music seen in its own positivistic terms, and Langer's view of an art work as symbolic representation of an interior (affective) state. The all-important need is the connection between these perspectives: How can musical symbol, as structure, be joined to affective state? If we can denote the means of this union, our interpretive power is augmented in large degree, for we know ever more precisely what is to happen with a work in performance—where it is to occur, and how.

Entrapment is evident in a number of passages within this movement. It is a tonal entrapment, a confinement to the tonality of D minor. Allied with this, indeed heightening the sense of tonal imprisonment, are efforts to "break out" of these tonal confines, efforts that may appear hopeful in the short run, but which ultimately are fruitless—the music turns otherwise and remains in the tonic. In view of Mozart's affective connections with D minor, the emotional connotations of these musical structures are obvious. We need not go so far as to connect this music with death per se, though the view of death as inescapable is tempting. It is equally valid to view the music through the affective lens of depression, or gloom. These states, too, have an imprisoning quality about them, as common experience can attest. They, too, require effort, at times struggle, for one to break out of their grip.

The reader is referred to the full chapter for several extended examples in which the sense of entrapment and the effort to break out harmonically are in evidence (Epstein, in press). Such a structural program necessarily affects the feeling of the music and its performance.

In a further example, the sense of struggle that is part of the structural–affective paradigm is illustrated in the passage which occurs in the first *forte* phrase in the concerto (Figure 6.5). The question of tonality is not at issue here. To the contrary, it is explicitly clear. That, in fact, is the point. What one draws from the music is struggle in two dimensions, one of them lying in the virtually physical, slashing motions of the strings in the triplet figures (they must be played by a quick and emphatic

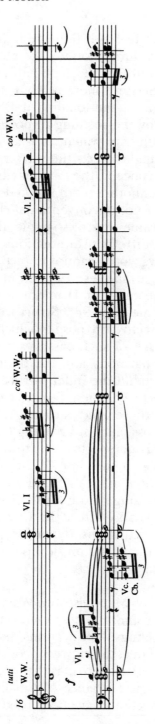

Figure 6.5

Figure 6.5. Mozart: Measures 16ff. Piano Concerto No. 20 in D Minor, K.466, I.

martellato stroke) that feel as if they are fighting against confining bonds. These slashing motions are abetted by the *staccato
marcato* articulations of the quarter-, half-, and whole notes of
the thematic lines. Second, there is a harmonic struggle in the
music, a conflict against the tonality of D minor itself that at
times is intensified by the seeming impossibility of leaving the
key. D minor is not just prevalent; it is an immovable force.

This sense of struggle affects the way one plays the passage.
For without such a concept, the *forte* may be just another *forte*,
the articulations just another set of marked *staccati*, the progressions merely a set of not unconventional chords in minor key.
Played within the framework of struggle, these factors assume
greater dimensions, different connotations, all of which inevitably come out in ways words cannot depict.

In this (and other examples provided in detail in the longer
chapter) the inescapability of D minor is heightened (a final
example occurs at measure 98). Structure is enriched by an
awareness of the affective purpose to which it is put. The posi-
tivist–structuralist view of such passages would focus upon the
technical details of harmony and the periodicity of harmonic
rhythm. This is valid, but the fuller picture comes into focus in
the light of the affective element behind these bars. The effect
of this passage and those cited earlier is to heighten the sense
of struggle, the impossibility of breaking out of the confines of
D minor. Seen in this perspective, the quickening of harmonic
rhythm, for example, at the close of the phrase, is more than
technical manipulation; it is the final stage of a heightened
frustration, a maximizing of the sense of imprisonment. That
awareness must inevitably affect the way in which these bars
are played—their articulations, dynamics, pressure of forward
motion, in brief, in their total musical persona, as seen by both
soloist and orchestra.

As noted, the works by Mendelssohn, Wagner, and Mozart discussed above have some affective connection with the world
of places, events, feelings—connections that can be reasonably
denoted by words. Thus, the express programmatic agendas of
the Mendelssohn overture; eros, as the affective substratum of
Tristan; a morphological alliance of tonality and feeling with
Mozart. These connections have been used as a check, a means

of ascertaining that values of affect and feeling attributed to these works are those of the composers, to the extent that can be suggested by the inadequate means of language, rather than "subjective" values imputed to the music by others.

The argument holds as well for "abstract" music, that much wider class of instrumental works for which no external handle, no specific affective connotations, exist. These works, too, embody a fusion of affective qualities and musical structures, often symbolic structures. If a significant difference pertains, it is that we cannot and need not describe, by means of language, the feelings evoked by the music. Langer's point prevails here—the affect of the art work is unique, impervious to translation across media.

Translation is not a necessity, however. What is crucial is that our affective concept itself be shaped and precise. What can be so vexing when grappling with a work and the way it should "go" is not the need to describe the music but to pinpoint its elusive qualities. We may feel the music, but not feel it exactly, with definition. To shape it for performance is thus impossible, for we are unsure what particular aspects of phrase, line, articulation, and the like should receive just what particular quality, emphasis, coloration. Conversely, we know intuitively and immediately when we have the passage "in hand," when it is "right."

In the search for an intuitive grasp of music, it is helpful to recall not only the fused state in which affect and structure exist, but the role that motion plays in this fusion. More often than not, it is the nuances of motion that effect, modulate, and ultimately control musical affect. This is considered in detail in the fuller version of this chapter (Epstein, in press).

What we see there and in those examples considered here—Mendelssohn, Mozart, and Wagner—is that affect is deeply and intrinsically wed to structure, and structure inseparably tied to motion. The means for creating motion, as well as controlling it, are numerous, and are differently embedded in each instance. Such means and their applications we might well expect; they represent the oft delineated procedure of an artist working with the materials of an art, as conformed by style and practice, to achieve individual and unique effect.

The perspective of this chapter lends a new element to this discussion. Philosophers concerned with aesthetics, with affect and expression, by and large have been content to delineate in an abstract way how these elements may exist—within works, and in our perception of works. Omitted from these discussions, and indeed beyond the pale of most philosophical purviews, are the technical specifics of how the affective and the structural interrelate.

Those specifics are of the essence of musical discussion, however. They are the key to the pragmatic decisions that continually beset performers and composers, decisions of structure and creation, of shaping and expression. In the realm of musical motion, the bases of these phenomena seem to reside. Motion, as the quintessential element of temporal passage, has found in tonal music specific embodiments, as well as elements that structure its intensities, control its forward progression, regulate its temporal unfolding. Thus time, motion, tempo, the constructs of rhythm, harmony, tonality, the subtle inflections of articulation, dynamics, timbre, and the host of other qualities of musical speech, coalesce in the service of controlled affective statement.

We have dealt with affect not in the fruitless sense of seeking to describe it with words, but in the context of the mechanisms by which it is controlled and shaped. Those mechanisms extend beyond musical structure alone. They encompass the nervous system as well, with its functions, propensities, and tendencies that relate to periodicity, coupled oscillations, and other aspects of timing—the physical substrata of musical timing in its broadest sense.

These neural propensities have an aspect related to the satisfaction, or pleasure/unpleasure, that we experience in our temporal anticipations and expectations, and the fulfillment of these expectations. The mechanisms function on physical as well as psychological levels, their physiologically controlled timing tendencies intertwined with our perceptions of these expectations, and further with the tempi, drives, energies, indeed animation of our psychic lives—processes described eloquently by Sessions (see p. 110).

Cognitive aspects of these timing proclivities are discussed elsewhere in connection with musical acceleration/ritard. We spoke there of an apparent innate tendency of the nervous system to control this changing time series via a cubic curve, a curve that at times extends to a cubic spline. Hearing the initial tempo points as a ritard or acceleration gets underway, it seems likely that we as listeners, drawing upon this same proclivity, project an ideal pattern of the complete curve, a pattern that serves as something of a timing template against which we inevitably compare the actual curve being performed.

Thus we anticipate the event with a set of expectations. When the reality approximates these expectations, even perhaps, with some surprising twists and turns of timing, we experience pleasure-anticipation fulfilled. That pleasure would be diluted by a poorer match, seemingly in direct proportion to the degree by which the performance is discrepant from our projection.

Our proclivities are not limited to accelerations and ritards; they extend to all aspects of timing in music, stemming from the periodic nature of the nervous system and its innate tendency to process time via equal quanta. That tendency, as we have seen, is the basis for beat and pulse, and for the periodic hierarchies built from these fundamental units.

It is also the basis for proportional tempos in music, wherein expectation and fulfillment are further experienced. Tempos that fall into meaningful proportional relationships seem to gratify a physiological as well as psychological need for periodicity. They are thus congruent with our neural functioning, and thereby gratify deep-seated anticipations.

Tempo rubato deals with these same neural proclivities. Indeed, that is its essence. Rubato seems the ultimate degree of playing with time. In its stretching and compression of phrase, it tantalizes and dares us, exerting a kind of musical brinkmanship which at times carries us to the edge, to the danger point where our sense of periodicity—our temporal "form"—may be decoupled. Done well, it rescues us from the edge, falling back into phase with our expectations. This, too, is exciting; the play with time gives special vitality to phrasing, and by its preservation of periodicity, its ultimate retention of phase, it provides yet another source of gratification.

These various modes by which our innate sense of periodicity is played with exert affective effect. In their special ways, they deal with this fundamental aspect of our humanity—our need to organize the passage of time, and with a physiology has evolved in a way that makes this organization possible. Music that speaks to this innateness, which deals congruently with these propensities, is, not surprisingly, a source of deep fulfillment.

Obviously this congruence enjoys a broad spectrum of means. All of them play with our expectations, and ultimately, respect them. The satisfactions that result complement those other aspects of affect that deal with musical symbolism, and through it, probe our inner states of being. All of this relies upon mechanism, for these modes of temporal by-play operate via their particular brands of mechanism. If we can grasp these mechanisms, understand how they work, we move some steps closer to that goal of all serious musicians—the most refined shaping of music; the ever better performance.[19]

REFERENCES

Alvarez, X. (1989), Rhythm as motion discovered. *Contemp. Music Rev.*, 3:203–231.
Boretz, B. (1979), Language as music. *Perspect. New Music*, 17/2.
Brenner, C. (1974), On the nature and development of affects: A unified theory. *Psychoanal. Quart.*, 44:532–556.
Bronstein, D., Krikorian, Y., & Wiener, P., eds. (1947), *Basic Problems of Philosophy*. New York: Prentice-Hall.
Bruhn, H., Oerter, R., & Rosing, H., eds. (1985), *Musikpsychologie*. Baltimore: Urban and Schwarzenberg.
Clynes, M., ed. (1982), *Music, Mind and Brain*. London: Plenum.
Cone, E. T., ed. (1979), *Roger Sessions on Music*. Princeton, NJ: Princeton University Press.
———— (1986), Schubert's promissory note: An exercise in musical hermeneutics. In: *Schubert: Critical and Analytical Studies*, ed. W. Frisch. Lincoln: University of Nebraska Press.
Deutsch, D., ed. (1982), *The Psychology of Music*. New York: Academic Press.
Epstein, D. (in press), *The Sounding Streams: Studies of Time in Music*. New York: Schirmer.
———— (in press), *Affect and Musical Motion*. New York: Schirmer Books.
Feder, S. (1990), The nostalgia of Charles Ives: An essay on affects and music. In: *Psychoanalytic Explorations in Music*, First Series, ed. S. Feder, H. L. Karmel, & G. H. Pollock. Madison, CT: International Universities Press.
———— (unpublished), Mozart in D Minor: Mental conflict, musical forum. Typescript.
Green, D. B. (1982), *Temporal Processes in Beethoven's Music*. New York: Gordon & Breach.

---

[19]The topics mentioned on pp. 120–121 are discussed in depth in the full version of this article (Epstein, in press).

—— (1984), *Mahler: Consciousness and Temporality*. New York: Gordon & Breach.

Guck, M. A. (1990), Analytical fictions. Paper presented at the Society for Music Theory, Oakland, CA.

Hindemith, P. (1945), *The Craft of Musical Composition*, Book 1, tr. A. Mendel. New York: Associated Music Publishers.

Kivy, P. (1980), *The Corded Shell*. Princeton, NJ: Princeton University Press.

—— (1984), *Sound and Semblance: Reflections on Musical Representation*. Princeton, NJ: Princeton University Press.

—— (1990), *Music Alone: Philosophical Reflections on the Purely Musical Experience*. Ithaca, NY: Cornell University Press.

Langer, S. (1948), *Philosophy in a New Key*. New York: Mentor Books.

—— (1953), *Feeling and Form*. New York: Scribner's.

—— (1967), *Mind: An Essay on Human Feeling*, Vols. 1, 2, 3. Baltimore: Johns Hopkins University Press.

Maus, F. E. (1988a), Music as drama. *Music Theory Spectrum*, 10:56–73.

—— (1988b), Story and discourse in music. Paper presented at the meetings of the American Musicological Society, Baltimore, November.

Meyer, L. (1967), *Music, the Arts and Ideas*. Chicago: University of Chicago Press.

Micznik, V. (1988), Intertext vs. narrative in Mahler's music. Paper presented at the meetings of the American Musicological Society, Baltimore, November.

Narmour, E. (1977), *Beyond Schenkerism: The Need for Alternatives in Musical Analysis*. Chicago: University of Chicago Press.

Plato, *The Republic*, tr. J. Jowett, ed. L. R. Loomis. New York: Van Nostrand.

Pöppel, E. (1988), *Time and Conscious Experience*, tr. T. Artin. New York: Harcourt, Brace, Jovanovich.

Rahm, J. (1989), New research paradigms. *Music Theory Spectrum*, 11/1:84–94.

Schopenhauer, A. (1947), The Platonic idea and the object of art. In: *The World as Will and Idea*, found in: *Basic Problems of Philosophy*, ed. D. Bronstein, Y. Krikorian, & P. Wiener. New York: Prentice-Hall.

Schwartz, H., Schwartz, D., & Berger, A., eds. (1985), Symposium: On the nature of music. Fall-Winter.

Sessions, R. (1979), The composer and his message. In: *Roger Sessions on Music*, ed. E. T. Cone. Princeton, NJ: Princeton University Press.

Sloboda, J. (1985), *The Musical Mind*. Oxford: Clarendon Press.

Stravinsky, I. (1936), *An Autobiography*. New York: W. W. Norton, 1962.

—— (1947), *Poetics of Music*. Cambridge, MA: Harvard University Press.

Chapter 7

How Music Conveys Emotion

*To the memory of my late wife and my best friend
for thirty years—Hanna Noy-Lichtner*

Pinchas Noy, M.D.

OVERTURE

Art is but one of several media of human communication. It differs from all others not only in communicating information, but also in conveying emotions, and/or evoking emotional response in the receiver. However, there is no agreement among professionals involved in art—artists, art theoreticians, and aestheticians—as to either how art conveys emotions, or the nature of the "emotional response" art is expected to evoke.

Theoreticians studying the "arts of form," music, dance, architecture, ornamentation and abstract painting, have been perhaps more interested in finding the answer than theoreticians studying the "arts of content," literature, poetry, drama, and representational painting. The latter know that any art based on content is in fact telling us some story, and the creative story-teller is endowed with the talent to tell us his story in such manner as to activate the imagination. One becomes involved in the story as if it were one's own experience; by identifying with one or several of the heroes and their deeds, one experiences the emotions appropriate to the situation. This process is the main route for conveying emotions in all arts which communicate meanings through content. I would call it the route of "narration-imagination-identification."

In fact, most of what is regarded today as "psychoanalytic interpretation of art" is based on the tacit assumption that meanings are always related to a narrative, and the function of interpretation is therefore to reconstruct the hidden narrative line out of its unconscious symbolizations, displacements, condensations, and other distortions. The problem is that such an approach is justified only in the case of interpreting *content*, but not for interpretating *form*. Although we know that form too may represent in some cases an unconscious content, in other cases it may represent nothing beyond itself. If so, perhaps many of the interpretations that assign varieties of latent meaning to elements of form are nothing more than the projections of the creative imagination of the interpreter himself.

Theoreticians interested in these arts have never been satisfied with a psychoanalytic approach attributing the emotional effect only to the ability of the receiver to identify with some narrative however latently represented by the elements of form. Rather, they have felt that form itself may have some *direct* effect on the receiver to arouse, induce, or entice him into an emotional response.

Although this belief in the eventually direct emotional impact of form was repeatedly expressed in the aesthetic literature concerning all media of art, it was only in the field of musicology that some testable theories have been formulated, controlled research has been done, and the various, sometimes contrasting theories have been systematically discussed and criticized. Music seems therefore to be the *preferred* field of art for presenting and investigating the general problems of the emotional impact of art. Accordingly, I will confine the discussion of the emotional impact of art in the present paper to *music*, with only short passages to examine whether some of the findings can also be applied to other arts, or to art in general.

The view attributing emotional effects to music originated in the aesthetics of the Renaissance, as reflected in the writings of the Camerata of Florence. Vincenzo Galile, a member of that group, wrote in 1581: "Music exists primarily to express the passions with greater effectiveness and to communicate these passions with equal force to the minds of mortals for their benefit and advantage" (p. 306). The 300-year-old discussion of the possible ways in which music may affect the listener's emotions has been surveyed by Kivy (1980). A significant breakthrough occurred only in the last fifty years with the formulation of two different theories worthy of serious consideration: the theory of isomorphism by Suzanne Langer (1942) and C.

C. Pratt (1952), and the theory of ego mastery by H. Kohut and S. Levarie (1950).

1. According to Langer and Pratt, every affect has its specific form or "Gestalt," and any message used in human communication that has a form similar to one of the affects (isomorphism) may activate this particular affect. As S. Langer said (1953): "The tonal structures we call 'music' bear a close logical similarity to the forms of human feelings . . . music is a tonal analogy of emotive life" (p. 27). And Pratt (1952) explains: "Music presents to the ear an array of auditory patterns which at a purely formal level are very similar to, if not identical with, the bodily patterns which are the basis of real emotion. The two kinds of pattern are with respect to their forms practically the same, but the auditory pattern makes music, whereas the organic and visceral pattern make emotion" (p. 17). He concludes: "Music sounds the way emotion feels" (p. 24).

2. Kohut and Levarie (1950) claimed that music may reach the listener's ear as a chaotic and unorganized stimulus which, owing to its association with some archaic, frightening sounds, may arouse anxiety. The ego, in its efforts to control anxiety, tries to master these potentially frightening auditory stimuli by organizing and transforming them into lawful and recognizable forms of music. The affect felt is the result of the ego's mastering activity—pleasure, if it has succeeded in its organizing efforts to restore order and law into the chaos; frustration, irritation or disgust, if it has failed to accomplish it. This ego psychological theory represents a totally new approach to the centuries old discussion of the emotional effect of art. Common to all previous theories was the implicit view of the receiver of art as a passive recipient getting the emotion that has been communicated to him embedded in the message, and the question to ask was therefore only how is the emotion communicated and how does the receiver succeed in recognizing it. According to that new approach, the receiver of art is perceived as an active agent performing some organizing work on the artistic input, while there are no emotions whatsoever that have been communicated, transmitted, or suggested in the artistic message. All the emotions experienced as a response to music listening are only the by-product of that organizing activity itself.

To summarize, we now have three theories to explain the emotional effect of music: the theories of narration-imagination-identification, of isomorphism, and of ego mastery. These theories represent three different principles for explaining how art may convey emotions or, in other words, three different routes by which the artist may succeed in evoking his or her audience's emotions.

The first is the *narrative route*, luring the audience to identify with the experiences and emotions appropriate to the narrative by arousing imagination. The second is the *direct route*, using messages that may activate directly, by means of their form, the emotions the artist is interested in. The third is the *indirect route*, provoking the receiver's ego into that particular organizing activity that, according to the artist's experience, may result in the emotional response the artist intends to arouse. The gifted artist effectively utilizes all three routes. It is the point of view of the present paper that every art involves all three routes in conveying emotional meanings, while the difference between one art and another is the relative proportion each route is utilized. Although the "arts of content" predominantly use the narrative route, it is possible to demonstrate that they almost always utilize the two others as well. The same is true of the "arts of form" which, while predominantly involving the direct and indirect routes, also utilize the narrative one as well.

THE NARRATIVE ROUTE
VIA NARRATION-IMAGINATION-IDENTIFICATION

To what extent is this route, predominant in the "arts of content" utilized also in music? It is clearly involved in all music associated with a verbal text, such as the lied, opera, ballet, and program music in general. However, if a text were the only way for music to present a story, it would suggest that music alone is unable to communicate a narrative line. The question then is whether abstract music, in the absence of extramusical elements, can present a narrative line. Popular music criticism has always drawn attention to a narrative of sorts. For example, Gradenwitz (1950) writes of Beethoven's Piano Concerto no. 4, op. 58: "The second part . . . presents the opposition between the orchestra and the soloist to the highest degree of poetic expression . . . the strings speak firmly, forte, in one voice, fragmented, in sharp rhythm; the solo talks softly, in piano, continuously, in full accords, in a calm movement, and some elegaic spirit hover over it" (p. 127). Such writing attempts to show how the various instruments of the orchestra converse and interact one with another. They present the great creations of symphonic and chamber music, not only as a narrative but as a drama full of excitement, suspense, contradictions, and surprises.

Nor is the capacity of an "art of form" to tell a story without relying on any verbal means confined to music. Any nonrepresentational and modifiable form, if expanded over the axis of time, may create a narrative line, and hence may convey meaning just as a *content*. It may be said to constitute a "content" of its own.

If the narrative content of music may serve as one of the routes for the conveyance of emotional meanings, two further questions arise: (1) Can the average nonprofessional listener really "read" the story the composer intended to tell out of that highly sophisticated contrapuntal transformation in which the narrative line has supposedly been hidden? (2) Are the narratives of music really representative of the narratives of life with which the listener can identify?

If the average listener is expected to respond to the meanings the composer intended to convey by means of such subtle formal manipulations, he must in some way be able to discern and identify them. The problems, however, need not be completely conscious, although a degree of cultural competence in listening may be necessary. Psychoanalytically oriented art interpretation in revealing unexpected symbolic meanings or by demonstrating hitherto unnoticed formal manipulations may arouse an uneasy sense of "oversophistication" and questions as to whether the average audience is indeed capable of perceiving and responding to such intricate expressive means. But modern psychoanalysis no longer doubts the legitimacy of this form of interpretative approach, which is based on one of its chief contributions to the understanding of art: art is constructed according to the laws of the primary process. Most of the transformations of content and form in all arts are similar to the transformations done by the "dream-work," the unconscious processes producing the joke, the neurotic symptoms, and determining the forms of psychotic thought disorders and infantile cognition.

By 1935, this growing body of knowledge was applied to music by Mosonyi but was further developed only in the fifties. Ramana (1952) wrote: "In some ways musical production can be compared with dream process, with its similar mechanisms of condensation, displacement, symbolization, and transformation" (p. 240). Friedman (1960) studied music based on the hypothesis "that primary process transformations must frequently be found and also play an important role in the structure of serious music" (p. 430), and he managed to demonstrate eight such processes of transformation in various samples of classical music. He summarized his study with the assumption "that these transformations greatly enhance the affective impact of the melodies," and even suggested that "it may be related to our judgments of musical greatness in a manner not yet understood" (p. 448).

The question as to whether the listener is able to recognize the meanings encoded by such transformations was addressed by Ehrenzweig (1953): Even the most intricate transformations in music (as well as all other arts) are readily deciphered and comprehended by unconscious perception because they are already encoded according to the laws of the primary process governing the "language" of the unconscious. Ehrenzweig presents examples which demonstrate that the most sophisticated of formal transformations created by composers are hardly intellectual exercises or mathematical calculations, but rather originate like a complex dream in its creator's unconscious thought (see also Noy, 1969).

Clearly, primary process is not exclusively responsible for *all* intricate artistic creations. Training and musical literacy comprise a further element. The composer must learn the laws of musical transformation in harmony, counterpoint, and so on. However, there are composers who continue to pursue nothing more than intellectual exercises; more recently, technology of the computer and synthesizer. Accordingly, many novel, formal innovations are created not out of human creative imagination but are invented by a machine! The degree of involvement of the primary process in the creative process may well be regarded as one of the main measures for greatness in music, and perhaps, in any creative art. The reason for the failure of many musical compositions, especially those "modern" pieces composed with the aid of electronic devices, to reach the audience and induce an emotional response, may be that they are composed according to laws not comprehensible for the unconscious perceptual apparatus of the average listener.

With regard to whether the narratives of music truly parallel those narratives of life with which the listener can identify, the entire history of musical aesthetics is the story of the debate between the two parties—the absolutists and the referentialists (see also, Meyer [1956, p. 3]). The absolutists approach music as it would be a closed and self-sufficient system, not referring to any extramusical meanings. Music is based on its own set of rules, which are neither derived from nor applicable to any other system, and if there is any connection to any other set of rules, it is only to mathematics. If music induces in its listeners an experience, it is a purely aesthetic experience, not related to any other known human experience. Accordingly, music can be interpreted only by music; for example, the only interpretation of Haydn's St. Anthony chorale (from Divertimento no. 1 in B Major) is Brahm's "Haydn Variations" op. 56. The referentialists consider music to convey meanings that refer to human expressions, conflicts, and experience *outside* music. Accordingly, the function of music interpretation is to reveal these extramusical references in order to understand why, and to what, the listener is really responding.

It is clear that psychoanalysts, and all others attempting to apply psychological knowledge to music interpretation, belong to the party of referentialists, and therefore have to deal with a common theoretical problem: If music is regarded as referential, to what exactly does it refer? Or, put another way, if music can be interpreted as a narrative, what is the nature of the musical narrative?

An instructive example was provided in a class of art students to whom I assigned writing of two brief imaginative stories, one about a young man who became a success in his professional career, and one about a failure. Fifty stories of each type were categorized and analyzed according to various formal criteria.

It was interesting to note that despite the variety of content, one found striking uniformity in several of the formal criteria characteristic of each of the two groups of stories. For example, following the stories according to the criterion of the *rhythm* characterizing the development of the stories, we could see in the stories of "success," some sense of movement which became increasingly intense and vigorous, finally reaching a climax, after which there came a plateau of steady and happy rhythms. In contrast, the stories of "failure" that began with the same hasty and vigorous rhythm, instead of reaching a summit, disintegrated into an unorganized rhythm, finally becoming slower and weaker. (Similar uniformity was also found in several other formal criteria.)

This informal study suggests that every narrative of life—success, failure, love, hate, envy, competition—may have its own specific configuration which can, in turn, serve to represent that narrative. Art strives to reach some degree of generalization, to deal not with the particular and trivial but universal ideas and experiences. The difference between the "arts of content" and the "arts of form" is mainly in the different representational means they use to reach that universality. The "arts of content" represent the universal mostly by means of the particular, like representing the experience of "success" or "failure" by telling an individual story. The "arts of form," in contrast, represent the universal mostly by means of presenting only the configuration, the outline, or a formula of the story's structure. This configuration, outline, or formula can be presented by a variety of means—visual, auditory, tactile—and any art uses a different but specific sampling of means. Thus, music utilizes only one particular group of presentational means (i.e., sound), and is directed only to one sense (i.e., hearing), but succeeds in representing with that limited group of means the whole gamut of human narratives. The axis of time is, of course, of critical importance here.

There are also arts which combine the representative means of the "arts of content" and the "arts of form," such as opera, classical ballet, or theater, presenting their stories by the particular and the general together, but such a combination of means does not necessarily enhance their expressive power. The ability for expression is, and will always be, dependent not on the expressive means the artist chooses, but on his talent and creative ability to utilize even the most simple means for telling us a universal story. Bach, for example, in any of his solo violin sonatas might succeed better to convey a wider range of human emotional experiences than a less gifted composer in an opera equipped with all the expressive means that form can afford—drama, a picturesque stage, dance, and all the instruments of the orchestra.

Thus far, I have dealt with the nature of communication in music via the narrative, which bears emotional meaning. I now turn to the capacity of the listener to *respond* to the music emotionally. Here something additional is required which will be considered in the following sections.

THE DIRECT ROUTE

An assumption underlying music composition, performance, interpretation, and criticism for the last three hundred years is that the raw materials of music are not emotionally neutral, but rather the tones, phrases, melodies, and harmonies of music have each some emotional meaning of their own. Even the mode (major or minor) and the scale (C minor or E minor) carry a different emotional coloring. This is achieved not only by the narrative line already discussed, but created through the *direct* emotional impact of the listener, of the very building blocks of which this narrative is constructed. The theory of isomorphism, while the most significant contribution to this issue, is not capable of providing a completely satisfactory explanation of *all* the means by which music exercises its direct emotional effect on the listener. Therefore, I will not confine the forthcoming discussion to the theory of Pratt and Langer, but will try to examine the issue of music's direct emotional impact in its generality.

The group of "direct means" includes all the musical elements that may allude to, represent, or transmit some emotional meaning, or act as stimuli for arousing or enhancing an emotional response in the listener. There are two major groups: means that represent some meanings and means that do not represent meanings. The first group includes all those means that affect the listener, owing to the specific meaning they are representing; the second group includes all those means that affect the listener by activating directly, sometimes even accidentally, some of his emotions.

Via Representational Means

Over the course of the past three hundred years, two major theories explaining the expressiveness of music have emerged. These are, according to Kivy (1980), the "contour theory" and the "convention theory." The first considers music to be able to convey meanings owing to "the congruence of musical 'contour' with the structure of expressive features and behavior"; while the second "explains the expressiveness of music as a function, simply, of the *customary* association of certain musical features with certain emotive ones, quite apart from any structural analogy between them" (Kivy, 1980, p. 77; emphasis added). This historical debate reflects a wider controversy: the "Contourists," assuming that the expressiveness of a given musical element is derived from the similarity of its contour to the pattern of expression of one of the human emotions, ascribe to it a high degree of generality and universality. The expressive features of human emotions transcend the limits of languages, and are understood by all people; and so music. The meanings music conveys are universally comprehended by any human being open to get its message. The "Conventionists," in contrast, assuming that the expressiveness of musical elements is dependent on arbitrarily assigned meanings, regard the expressive power of any given piece of music to be limited only to that particular human group that shares the same language and cultural convention.

These views are not polar opposites and both parties have a point! Almost all the musical means representing some definite emotional meaning are related in some way to the vast group of nonverbal means used in human communication, a group that is compounded of all kinds of signs, signals, and symbols partly derived from universal features of emotive expression, and partly from arbitrarily agreed-upon means. Accordingly, the musical means too, representing the nonverbal means of human communication, are compounded of a similar admixture of universal and conventional meanings.

In a former paper (Noy, 1972), I described human communication as a two-level system. The secondary level includes all the symbols, signals, and signs conveying the meanings that had been assigned to them by agreed-upon social convention (words and other agreed-upon signals), and the primary level, which includes all means expressing directly and concretely human emotions, experiences, and other subjective states of mind. In regular communication, both levels participate in the process of information conveyance. On the secondary level, the objective knowledge is transmitted by means of language. On the primary level, the subjective experiences and feelings are expressed by means of all the accompanying gestures, inflation of voice, movements, and so on. While the signs utilized on the secondary level are mostly confined to a single medium of communication—the vocal–auditory medium in speech and the visual medium in writing and reading—the signs of the primary level are derived from all available media. Among these various media participating in primary communication, the vocal–auditory medium usually conveys the most significant part of information because it provides the main supporting system for speech, expressing most of the experiences and emotions accompanying verbal communication of ideas. Most of these experiences and emotions are expressed by means of the tone, pitch, intensity, rhythm, resonance, timbre, duration, and inflection of the speaking voice, in short, by all that we use to call "the music of speech."

A considerable part of music's representational means conveying emotional meanings derive their meanings out of these "musical" components of speech. Music uses a variety of techniques for representing all kinds of meaningful nonverbal signs comprehensible to any user of language, such as imitating various well-recognized expressions of emotions, like laughter or weeping (the laughter of the orchestra accompanying the aria of Leporello in Mozart's *Don Giovanni* or the weeping of Dido from the lament of *Dido and Aeneas* by Purcell), or by manipulating any of the expressive means presented above (i.e., tone, pitch, intensity). For example, Berlioz in the "Lacrymosa" of his Requiem, op. 5, presented the experience of weeping by imitating the nonrhythmical sighs characteristic of sobbing by means of disturbances in the line of regular rhythm.

The affinity of human speech and the expressiveness of music has long been observed. The specific contribution of psychoanalysis lies in reminding us repeatedly that the "nonverbal" means of communication also constitute the "preverbal" means. The infant, prior to the phase of acquisition of language, communicates with his human environment exclusively through the primary means of communication; that group of means, which only in a later phase are relegated by the emergence of the secondary means (language and other agreed-upon information-conveying signs and signals) to the "nonverbal" means.

In an earlier paper (Noy, 1968), I presented the theory that the origin of musical language lies in the preverbal phase of communication. This theory is based partly on the observation that in that phase the infant and his mother succeed in understanding one another effectively, although they rely only on the primary means of communication. In the twenty years since that paper, infant research has provided more evidence regarding the efficiency of primary communication. In the child's world, mother and all other objects are represented as experiences of vision, touch, voice, or sound. Music achieves a portion of its meanings by representing the auditory segment of such preverbal experiences. "If we could turn back and identify with the infant, hearing the world around us through infantile ears, might not the secrets of music unveil themselves before us, enabling us to understand its paths of expression?" (Noy, 1968, p. 335).

The problem in studying the preverbal experiences of adults is in the difficulty of retrieving them from the files of memory. These experiences have been stored in their primary sensual form and a considerable portion have never been reorganized according to the phase-appropriate categories of organization, therefore remaining forever stored in that primary form. Adult memory functioning in the secondary-process mode of organization can hardly integrate these primary experiences with the rest of experience. Thus, earlier content owing to their primary-process organization remain cut off from the rest of memory. Practically, they can be retrieved only by other primary-process organized perceptions or memories which may create some associative links with them. The specific power of artistic communication lies in its ready access to preverbal memory owing to its primary-process organization.

In my survey of the psychoanalytic theories of music (Noy, 1966, 1967a,b,c,d), I showed that except for the differences in terminology and formulation (regression, oceanic feelings, nonanalogic communication, coenesthetic organization, etc.), most authors related music in some manner to the earliest phases of development and were impressed with the special power of music to reach the preverbal levels of human memory and to evoke the earliest forms of experience. It is precisely this that accounts for the observation that the emotions evoked by music are not identical with the emotions aroused by everyday, interpersonal activity. Rather, they originate in the preverbal phase of development, and are therefore organized in a form that antedates the characteristic form of emotions that become stabilized only in later developmental phases. Schoen (1928), for example, wrote about the emotional effect of music: "this effect is always of the nature of a mood but never an emotion. Thus music may create a condition of sublimity, sadness, gaiety, but never produces anger, jealousy or fear" (p. 182); and Kate Hevner (1935): "the expressiveness of music is a general rather than specific nature arousing an affective state rather than one specific emotional experience" (p. 195).

In my paper about the psychoanalytic theory of affect (Noy, 1982), I described the three phases of affect development as: (1) Identification—the ability to identify the fleeting changes occurring in the body and mind as having some meaning; (2) Acknowledgment—to acknowledge the affect as a distinct psychophysiologic entity, having its specific quality, pattern of activation, and meaning; and (3) Differentiation—the differentiation of the global and diffuse primary affectual arousals into more refined and discrete affectual programs. If at least a part of the emotional response to music has its origin in a developmental phase antedating these three phases of affect development, it is clear that identification, acknowledgment and articulation, and differentiation cannot become established in such instances.

Via Nonrepresentational Means

Music has the power to arouse an emotional response in the listener in some direct way that is not dependent on any communication of meanings. The only current comprehensive theory which attempts to explain the emotional effect of music is the theory of isomorphism of Langer and Pratt noted earlier. The device or "trick" they consider the creative musician to utilize is the invention of a musical phrase similar in its form to the form of a given emotion, which is therefore mistakenly perceived by the listener as a communication of that emotion. I suggest below how this may occur.

In my paper about affect (Noy, 1982), I defined affect as an organized pattern of changes comprising several physiological and psychological systems, changes that include arousal of systems (such as the elevation of blood pressure and acceleration of the pulse in anger), suppression of systems (such as the reduction of gastrointestinal motility in aggression), or steering of the function of a system in a specific direction (such as imagination in anger which is channeled to represent exclusively only fantasies of revenge). The assumption is that each specific affect is characterized by a typical configuration of such changes, and therefore can also be identified by an outsider if he will perceive these changes and conceive the typical configuration. For example, if we see somebody with a red face, pounding vessels, strenuous breath, widened pupils, clenched fists, and hear his tense voice, we will certainly have no problem in recognizing that he is angry, even without having him tell us about it. The number of changes sufficient for us to recognize a given emotion varies according to the frequency of appearance, our acquaintance with that emotion, and our sensitivity to perceive the emotional expressions of others. There are emotions whose typical pattern we are able to identify after perceiving only two or three changes, while in others, we need a whole cluster of changes before its typical configuration becomes clear to us. The danger with the best recognized emotions, identified by only a minimal number of signs (observable typical changes) is that they may become also a source for errors in identification. For example, if one becomes so sensitive as to identify anger on the basis of only one sign, for example, the typical tremor of the speaker's voice, it would also be easier to be deceived by the presentation of some very similar voice.

Kivy (1980), attempting to demonstrate the theory of Langer, presented the example of the Saint Bernard dog, who is mistakenly identified by us as having "a sad face," only because nature created him with a mouth whose angles are declining downward.

Such an example demonstrates that, for the most prevalent emotions such as laughter and sadness, a cluster of changes to identify their typical pattern is not required; one or two signs may be sufficient. Unfortunately, that efficiency makes it also more amenable for errors in the identification of the affect, errors that may be the result of one's own misinterpretation.

Langer (1942, 1953) based her theory on the assumption that most of the signs indicating the activation of a given emotion (any psychophysiological change belonging to the typical activation pattern of an emotion can serve as a sign for identifying that emotion) can be communicated also by an alternative medium other than the original one; for example, the signs of mounting rage that can be communicated by bodily movements going faster and faster, increasing sounds, flashes of light, whirling red colors. By utilizing only its specific medium, any art is able to communicate the same wide spectrum of human emotions: music, through the auditory medium (such as the laughter of Richard Strauss' Till Eulenspiegel presented in the strings); painting, through the visual medium (such as sadness expressed by downward declining lines in the picture); dancing, through the medium of expressive movements. The novelty of the theory is in assuming that music, and perhaps any art, can represent in its specific medium not only any of the particular changes (signs), but also the form of the entire pattern of changes. That also means the less prevalent emotions, not identifiable by one or two isolated signs but only by the special configuration of the whole cluster of changes, can be communicated by music. An excellent example is presented in Stuart Feder's paper (1981) where, basing himself on Langer's theory, he showed how the composer Charles Ives succeeded in representing by his music a complex emotion such as nostalgia.

One of the main limitations of the Langer-Pratt theory is identical to that noted with regard to the narrative theory. That is, to explain how we are able to *recognize* the emotional experience that music is attempting to convey, does not explain why we *respond* to it emotionally. The fact that I am able to recognize the expression of sadness in Verdi's Requiem doesn't yet explain why I am moved by that music almost to tears. This question is relevant not only for music but also for the communication of affect in general. To answer the question, we will have to apply some additional knowledge about the psychology of the affect.

Basch (1976), in his reexamination of the concept of affect, summarized: "affect, so-called, is in fact an onto- and phylogenetically early form of communication" (p. 776). The communication of affect is based on genetically determined constitutional links. We are programmed in advance to respond to the perception of certain emotions with the arousal of our own emotions. In my paper about empathy (Noy, 1984), I suggested the term *primary empathy* for this kind of constitutionally determined human sensitivity and responsiveness to the manifestations of the other's emotions. I believe that the concept of empathy may assist us also in explaining the phenomenon of emotional responsiveness to music. It is of interest that the concept of "empathy" (Einfuehlung) was originally introduced in the professional literature by Th. Lipps (1903) as a concept for explaining the effect of art, and has only later been adopted for describing interpersonal emotional relations.

We may assume that the creative artist would not be content with presenting emotions only for the sake of enabling his audience to recognize them, but always wishes to arouse an emotional *response*. To achieve it, he will certainly choose first these "infective" emotions, the recognition of which will evoke an involuntary emotional response in the recipient. Problems involved in a detailed consideration of primary empathy are discussed elsewhere (Noy, 1984).

In order to predict a particular kind of emotional response to music, we have to take into consideration at least two factors: the specific emotion the form of which is supposedly transmitted by the music, and the listener's present state of preparedness. This state that varies normally from person to person, and within the same person from time to time, is responsible for individual responses to the same music or for the same person's response at different times. What is essential is that all these substitutions and transfers from one medium to another, and from one means to another, are part of the human-specific ability for *symbolic representation*. Langer (1942) states: "symbolism is the recognized key to that mental life which is characteristically human and above the level of sheer animality" (p. 28). According to Langer, what the artist expresses is "not his own actual feelings, but what he knows about human feeling" (p. 26). Peter Kivy (1980), discussing at length the relations between music and emotions in his book, *The Corded Shell*, describes music as being *expressive* of emotions, but not as an *expression* of emotion. I concur with Langer and Kivy in the belief that all that can be said about music is that, for the listener, music may be expressive of emotions if he is able to recognize in it certain emotions and respond with some emotional experience of his own. But this fact does not provide us with any evidence for stating that music can really express or transmit emotions, and certainly not, that the emotional experience the listener responds with is identical to the emotional experience of the composer while composing that piece of music. I would even be more extreme and say that what the composer experienced while composing that piece of music we are so fond of is simply not relevant either for the enjoyment or for the understanding of music. We know many great musical compositions that were composed as an expression of the composer's emotional experience, such as several Requiems and Stabat Maters which were composed to express the composer's own mourning about somebody especially close to him (see Pollock [1975], for many interesting examples). However, we know also about many great musical compositions that move our emotions deeply but were composed without any emotional involvement of the composer; rather only out of some economical necessity or for application to some competition. The truth is, if we didn't know about the emotional state of the composer from some historical source, nothing in the music itself can give us a clue regarding the emotional conditions of its composition.

I believe that the preoccupation with the question, What did the composer really feel? reflects our attitude to art in general. Art is always merely an illusion, and the creative artist is a master of "make-believe." Just as the little child, after listening to the fairy tale, asks "And what happened afterward?" so do adults want to know what really happened to the creative artist and what did he really feel while writing his poem or book, painting his picture, or composing his music. It seems that the very condition of art, of being moved emotionally, sometimes even to tears, laughter, or elation by something we know to be merely an illusion and by somebody we know is creating that illusion by artifice, never ceases to insult.

THE INDIRECT ROUTE VIA ORGANIZATIONAL ACTIVITY

So far, music has been treated as if it were a kind of message that communicated emotions, something similar (isomorphic) to emotions, or some meanings that may arouse emotions. Common to that approach is that in order to understand the emotional effect of a certain music, we have to look into that music. We will now explore the indirect route by which music is treated as if it were only an array of acoustic stimuli that does not include, transmit, or allude to any emotions but provokes the listener into some kind of organizational activity which may evoke in him some emotional response. In order to understand the emotional effect of a certain music, according to that approach, we have to look into the listener's reaction to that music; not asking as we did earlier, what the music is doing to the listener, but rather, what the listener is doing with the music. To answer this question, we will momentarily disregard the capacity of music to act as a communication, telling stories or conveying emotions, and treat it as if it were some stimulus to respond to, some material to deal with, or some problem to solve. This approach is not presented as an alternative theory to explain the emotional impact of music and art in general, but as an additional explanation to the former two in advancing that music, in addition to telling a story and in addition to evoking directly an emotional response, may also provoke the listener into doing some active work.

Almost all of the higher arts utilize that principle and invite or require the receiver to do some active mental work before he is permitted to understand. Many pieces of music engage us in that simple game of challenging us first to do some active work if we want to get the satisfaction music is expected to provide us. For example, many of the romantic symphonies present you with a simple and exciting melody, repeat it until you begin to love it, and then add more and more instruments and more and more distracting voices until it becomes harder and harder to follow the beloved melody. Sometimes, as in the fourth and fifth Symphonies of Tchaikovsky, it sounds as though we are attempting to listen to a lovely tune sung in the production hall of a noisy factory. In these cases, it is as if the composer is teasing you: "Why make it so easy for you? If you want to find your beloved melody again, then please make some effort!"

To my mind, the degree of active participation the listener is asked for in order to get his satisfaction from the music is one of the main criteria for differentiating higher music from the lesser one. Common or "pop" music is based on simple and recognizable themes, recurrent beats, and endless repetitions. "High" music, in contrast, is characterized by its variability and versatility, by presenting the already recognized themes in a different form each time they appear anew. If to arrange the various styles of music along a continuum from the "lowest" to the "highest" music, the difference is that while at the lower pole, music, by caressing, hypnotizing, or stimulating him directly, entices the listener into a passive and regressive attitude; at the higher pole, it always attempts to challenge him into some kind of active involvement. The listener has to always do something and invest some mental efforts in order to get his satisfaction.[1]

What is that "work" the listener is provoked into doing if he really wants to participate in the enjoyable experience music is luring him into? As the basic idea has been taken from Kohut and Levarie (1950), let us first see what they had to say about it.

> [U]norganized sound symbolizes primitive dread of destruction. The fear is made unnecessary by the intelligible, though nonverbal organization of sound in music. Elements in this organization

---

[1]By "passive and regressive attitude," I mean only passive from the aspect of cognitive activity, and I am, of course, aware that pop or rock music may entice the listeners into such an activity as to put the whole concert hall into ruins. But that belongs to "direct stimulation" and not to "organizing activity."

are the clear-cut beginning and end; the use of tones rather than
noises; a tonality to which the listener is conditioned, a statement
of the tonic at the beginning of the composition, regular rhythm;
repetition; traditional formal patterns (for example, fugues or
sonatas); and familiar instruments [p. 86].

This statement is derived from and reflects the basic premises
of the "ego psychology" of those days, regarding the function
of the "organizing processes" (Hartmann, 1947) as serving the
needs of the ego for reducing instinctual tension, alleviating
anxiety, or getting mastery over impulses and wish-derivatives.
But this kind of mental activity is not exactly the same as that
presented at the beginning of the present chapter, that of an
activity similar to solving crossword puzzles or other pastime
games. Here we are dealing with another kind of organizing
activity which, unlike the "ego mastery" activity which is moti-
vated by the defensive needs of the ego, is activated by some
other kind of motivation. To differentiate between the two
kinds of organizing activity, I would call the first, "defensive
organization" and the second, "cognitive organization." As the
first is described adequately by Kohut and Levarie (1950), it
remains only to explain what is meant by "cognitive organization."

The best presentation of that kind of organization is in *Emotion and Meaning in Music* by Leonard B. Meyer (1956). He
assumed that the knowledge of the laws according to which
music is composed creates in the listener expectancies about
what is going to follow after any given point in the sequence of
music:

> [T]he significance of a musical event—be it a tone, a motive, a
> phrase, or a section—lies in the fact that it leads the practiced
> listener to *expect*, consciously or unconsciously, the arrival of a
> subsequent event or a number of alternative subsequent events.
> Such expectations (or "subjective predictions") are entertained
> with varying degrees of certainty, depending upon what is felt
> to be the probability of any particular event in this specific set
> of musical circumstances [Meyer, 1961, p. 259].

When the music we are listening to proceeds otherwise than
we have expected it to, we are aroused to an emotional response: "Affect or emotion-felt is aroused when an expectation—a tendency to respond—activated by the musical stimulus

situation, is temporarily inhibited or permanently blocked. . . .
Hence deviations can be regarded as emotional or affective
stimuli" (Meyer, 1956, pp. 31–32). Meyer did not specify how
deviations arouse emotions, but in his paper of 1961, he wrote
about memorizing music. "Memory is not a mechanical device
for the immutable registration of stimuli. It is an *active* force
which, obeying the psychological 'law of good shape,' organizes,
modifies, and adjusts the impressions left by perception. In so
doing, it tends either to 'improve' (regularize) irregular but
well-structured patterns or to 'forget' poorly structured ones"
(p. 261).

Since Meyer presented this theory, psychology has learned
that not only memory but perception itself "is an active force
which . . . organizes, modifies, and adjusts the impressions" so
that everything Meyer assumed as being the function of memory can be regarded today as being also the function of perception. In revising Meyer's theory taking the above into account,
I would state that music is composed according to a set of laws
known to the musical community (the composers and listeners
of a given cultural group), and therefore any point in the sequence of music arouses certain expectations regarding what
will follow. If the music in its progression surprisingly deviates
from this expected sequence to present something unexpected,
the apparatus of perception will be called into action to edit
("organizes, modifies, and adjusts") the musical input to fit the
form as determined by the laws.

In my paper, "Why Do We Enjoy Art?" (Noy, 1989), I presented a theory about the pleasure provided by art based on
psychoanalytic and neurophysiological knowledge. Regular
daily cognitive activity, which is dominated by the secondary
process, is from the neurophysiological point of view a neural
activity confined to a limited number of highly differentiated
brain circuits and centers mostly located in the left hemisphere.
Dreaming, fantasizing, art production and consumption, which
are primary-process dominated cognitive activities, are, from
the neurophysiological point of view, characterized by a widespread neural activity involving brain circuits and centers in
both hemispheres. My conjecture is that the higher arts, by
provoking the perceptual apparatus to take active measures for
organizing the percept, force cognitive functions to shift from

a secondary-process dominated activity to a primary-process dominated one. From the neurophysiological point of view, there is a shift from a highly focused neural activity in which the great number of brain circuits and centers remain relatively "silent" to a widespread neural activity involving most of the circuits and centers of the brain. To demonstrate this theory in practice, let me quote the example presented in that paper.

> The fourth movement of Mozart's Jupiter Symphony, a monu-mental musical architectonic construction built on five different themes, is one example for us to study. You can enjoy listening to it, even if you follow nothing more than the simple melodic line and its rhythmical beats. Such listening does not require activation of additional circuits of music perception. . . . But you may receive an even greater pleasure by following various inge-nious combinations of the two, three or four themes, and their inversions, from beginning to end. In doing so you will have activated many hitherto inactive brain circuits, including spatial-perceiving centers in the right (opposite) hemisphere. And you will achieve the greatest pleasure of all if you succeed in follow-ing all five melodic lines of the symphony to their climax at the coda, where they converge into a magnificent five-part counter-pointal structure. Then, in order to attend to the whole orches-tra, your entire brain, on all available circuits, will have to orches-trate in concordance with the music perceived [pp. 129–130].

The function of the higher arts provoking the cognitive appa-ratus to be actively involved in the organization of the percept is, according to this theory, to entice the brain into a more widespread organizational activity, and, by that, to activate also many of the brain circuits that usually remain silent during most of the daily routine secondary-process dominated cogni-tive activity. The assumption is that the brain, in order to main-tain its flexible functional capacity, needs such periodic "pipe-cleaning," to drive into action from time to time those relatively silent circuits and centers. And as nature has assured the fulfill-ing of any of the biological survival functions by attaching to it a premium of pleasure, so also artistic activity which fulfills the vital function of enticing the brain into a widespread organiza-tional activity, provides such pleasure. The expectation for that kind of pleasure is in part the motivation that drives us to invest time and energy in exercising the organizing functions of the cognitive apparatus.

The problem with the "ego-mastery" theory or in its wider version, the "organization-provoking" theory, is in the relatively limited repertoire of emotion whose arousal can be explained according to this theory. The theory is based on the assumption that music is perceived as a stimulus that provokes the ego, the cognitive apparatus, or the brain (depending on your point of view) into some organizational activity. The emotions aroused are an outcome of the degree of success in this organizational task. As in any challenging task, success in performance will result in emotions of effectance, pride or grandiosity, and failure in performance will result in emotions of frustration, shame, or depression. The "ego-mastery" theory adds another group of emotions. Because the organizational task is supposed to neutralize the anxiety-arousing effect of the unorganized noises, success in it may result in feelings of relief, while failure may result in arousal of tension, anxiety and fear. This last eventual reaction is indeed what Kohut and Levarie (1950) described in cases where the music heard is too difficult to be organized. "Such is the case when he is confronted with music the form of which is entirely unfamiliar. Unable to cope with the unfamiliar sounds of atonal music, for example, large numbers of listeners trapped in the concert hall experience a gradual rise of anxious tension at the strange sounds which they cannot master" (p. 12). The first problem is that all these emotions, supposedly aroused as a result of listening to "organization-provoking" music, although belonging to the repertoire of emotional response to music, are not the most prevalent, while many more prevalent emotions, such as elation, nostalgia, elegy, or sadness, can hardly be explained as belonging to these responses. The second problem is that all these emotions, representing success or failure of a cognitive task, are of the quality of immediate emotions, while the repertoire of emotions evoked by music belong mostly to the quality of emotions described as mood, emotional tendency, or by the new term *self-state*. A fuller development of the ramifications of this for affect theory in general and music in specific will await a further contribution.

SUMMARY

Affect and the nature of its representation in art has been the central theme of this paper. Music has been considered not only in its own right but, in effect, as a model for other arts. Specifically, three pathways by which music encodes affect are discussed. The first is the *narrative* route; the second, a more immediate, *direct* route which manifests itself alternatively via representational and nonrepresentational means. A third, the *indirect* route is considered in terms of the organizational activity of the mind. Aspects of the latter which relate to the psychology of the self are cited and will be explored in more detail elsewhere.

REFERENCES

Basch, M. F. (1976), The concept of affect: A re-examination. *J. Amer. Psychoanal. Assn.*, 24:759–777.

Ehrenzweig, A. (1953), *The Psychoanalysis of Artistic Vision and Hearing*. New York: George Braziller.

Feder, S. (1981), The nostalgia of Charles Ives: An essay in affects and music. *Ann. Psychoanal.*, 10:301–332.

Friedman, S. (1960), One aspect of the structure of music: A study of regressive transformations of musical themes. *J. Amer. Psychoanal. Assn.*, 8:427–449.

Galile, V. (1581), Dialogo della musica antica e della moderna. In: *Source Reading in Music History*, ed. O. Strunk. New York: W. W. Norton, 1950.

Gradenwitz, P. E. (1950), *The World of the Symphony (Hebrew)*. Tel Aviv: Massadah.

Hartmann, H. (1947), On rational and irrational action. In: *Psychoanalysis and the Social Sciences*, Vol. 1. New York: International Universities Press.

Hevner, K. (1935), Expression in music: A discussion of experimental studies and theories. *Psychol. Rev.*, 42:186–204.

Kivy, P. (1980), *The Corded Shell: Reflections on Musical Expression*. Princeton, NJ: Princeton University Press.

Kohut, H., & Levarie, S. (1950), On the enjoyment of listening to music. *Psychoanal. Quart.*, 19:64–87.

Langer, S. K. (1942), *Philosophy in a New Key*. Cambridge, MA: Harvard University Press.

——— (1953), *Problems of Art*. New York: Charles Scribner's Sons.

Lipps, T. (1903), *Grundlagen der Aesthetic*. Leipzig-Hamburg: Voss.

Meyer, L. B. (1956), *Emotion and Meaning in Music*. Chicago: University of Chicago Press.

——— (1961), On rehearing music. *J. Amer. Musicol. Soc.*, 14:257–267.

Mosonyi, D. (1935), Die Irrationalen Grundlagen der Musik. *Imago*, 21:207–226.

Noy, P. (1966), The psychodynamics of music. I. *J. Music Ther.*, 3:126–134.

——— (1967a), The psychodynamics of music. II. *J. Music Ther.*, 4:7–23.

——— (1967b), The psychodynamics of music. III. *J. Music Ther.*, 4:45–51.

—— (1967c), The psychodynamics of music. IV. *J. Music Ther.*, 4:81–94.

—— (1967d), The psychodynamics of music. V. *J. Music Ther.*, 4:117–125.

—— (1968), The development of musical ability. *The Psychoanalytic Study of the Child*, 23:332–347. New York: International Universities Press.

—— (1969), A revision of the psychoanalytic theory of the primary process. *Internat. J. Psycho-Anal.*, 50:155–178.

—— (1972), About art and artistic talent. *Internat. J. Psycho-Anal.*, 53:243–249.

—— (1979), The psychoanalytic theory of cognitive development. *The Psychoanalytic Study of the Child*, 34:169–216. New Haven, CT: Yale University Press.

—— (1982), A revision of the psychoanalytic theory of affect. *Ann. Psychoanal.*, 10:139–185.

—— (1984), The three components of empathy: Normal and pathological development. In: *Empathy*, Vol. 1, ed. J. Lichtenberg, M. Bornstein, & D. Silver. Hillside, NJ: Analytic Press.

—— (1989), Why do we enjoy art?. *Israel J. Psychiat.*, 26:124–137.

Pollock, G. H., (1975), Mourning and memorialization through music. *Ann. Psychoanal.*, 3:423–436.

Pratt, C. C. (1952), *Music and the Language of Emotion*. Washington, DC: U.S. Library of Congress.

Ramana, C. V. (1952), Observation on the analysis of a musician. *Samiska*, 6:229–242.

Schoen, M. (1928), The aesthetic attitude in music. *Psycholog. Monogr.*, 39/178:162–183.

III

STUDIES OF COMPOSERS AND COMPOSITIONS

Chapter 8

Bach and Mozart: Styles of Musical Genius

Robert L. Marshall, Ph.D.

Johann Sebastian Bach and Wolfgang Amadeus Mozart represent the antipodes of eighteenth-century musical genius. As we have all been taught, Bach's music was the culmination of the so-called baroque era during the first half of the century; Mozart's, conversely, was the culmination of the antithetical classical style, during the second half.[1] But the antithesis is not just a technical matter of the contrast between the late baroque and high classical styles, rather, it extends into their personal lives as well. We know almost nothing about Bach's private life; we know almost too much about Mozart's. Bach was an orphan; Mozart was all too much the son of an autocratic father. Bach was the product of the Lutheran tradition of northern Germany; Mozart belonged to the Catholic, actually, the Italianate secular tradition of Austria. These starkly contrasting personal backgrounds inevitably affected their existential values—their understanding of their "purpose in life," their artistic missions. Such understanding, in turn, inevitably touched on the purpose

---

[1]It is no longer fashionable to divide the eighteenth century neatly into two equal parts and apportion the first half to Bach and Handel and the second to Mozart and Haydn. The recent trend in musical historiography, as in the writing of history generally, is to try to understand the history of music more in terms of its institutions rather than its "great men." Moreover, one now tends to define the eighteenth century as a largely continuous period. Rather than focus on the so-called style shift apparently bisecting the century at its midpoint into, roughly speaking, a "baroque" and a "classical" part; the current preference is to conceive of the century largely in terms of what, at least from the social perspective, was undeniably its dominant institution: Italian opera—especially opera seria. Such a conception, needless to say, is particularly unkind to J. S. Bach. Indeed, the revisionist version of music history, as postulated, for example, by Carl Dahlhaus (1985) dismisses Bach altogether as a historically irrelevant "outsider," an "esoteric who knowingly withdrew from the world and drew the compositional consequences from that" (see Marshall, 1987).

and, ultimately, the meaning of their music. Why did Bach and Mozart bother to compose at all? What did the effort and the resulting work mean to *them*? What were their fundamental objectives as artists?

I should like to begin exploring these issues somewhat indirectly. Rather than talking immediately about Bach or about Mozart, let us consider Mozart's Bach. As it turns out, Mozart instinctively understood a great deal about the creative impulse informing the music of Bach. In April of 1789, on the occasion of his visit to Leipzig (and his performance on the organ of the Thomaskirche—Bach's own organ), Mozart experienced a close encounter of the revelatory kind with the church music of J. S. Bach. The event was recorded by Friedrich Rochlitz, a pupil at the Thomasschule at the time of Mozart's visit, and later the founding editor of the influential Leipzig journal, the *Allgemeine Musikalische Zeitung*. Rochlitz writes "On the initiative of the late [Johann Friedrich] Doles, then Cantor of the Thomas-Schule, the choir surprised Mozart with a performance of the double-chorus motet, *Singet dem Herrn ein neues Lied* [BWV 225], by Sebastian Bach. . . . Hardly had the choir sung a few measures when Mozart sat up startled; a few measures more and he called out: 'What is this?' And now his whole soul seemed to be in his ears. When the singing was finished he cried out, full of joy: 'Now, there is something one can learn from!' " (Rochlitz, 1798; Solomon, 1991).

J. S. Bach, no doubt, would have been most gratified at Mozart's alleged response to his music. For it was Bach's explicitly stated intention to have his music serve as an object of study. On the title page of *The Well-Tempered Clavier* Bach had declared that this monumental collection of superbly crafted preludes and fugues was "for the Use and Profit of the Musical Youth Desirous of Learning," and he ended the title of the *Orgel-Büchlein* with the telling rhyme: "Dem Höchsten Gott allein zu Ehren / Dem Nechsten, draus sich zu belehren" ("In Praise of the Almighty's Will / And for my Neighbor's Greater Skill"). Bach, then, certainly thought of himself very much as a teacher.

Mozart, for his part, hated to teach. He declared to his father: "Giving lessons . . . is no joke. . . . You must not think that this is laziness on my part. No, indeed! It just goes utterly against my genius [his word] and my manner of life" (Paris, July 31, 1778).[2] Of course, Mozart is talking about giving keyboard lessons; Bach was teaching through the example of his compositions. Nonetheless, it is clear that there was a vast distance between the self-proclaimed artistic missions of J. S. Bach and W. A. Mozart.

There is more to be learned from Mozart's contact with Bach. The episode in the Thomaskirche did not represent his first serious encounter with the music of the Thomaskantor. That had occurred some seven years earlier. On April 10, 1782, about a year after he had settled in Vienna, Mozart reported home to his father: "I go every Sunday at twelve o'clock to the Baron van Swieten, where nothing is played but Handel and Bach. I am collecting at the moment the fugues of Bach" (Anderson, 1938). Indeed, under the auspices of the Baron Gottfried van Swieten, formerly the Austrian ambassador to Prussia and later the prefect of the Imperial Library in Vienna, Mozart, in April 1782, had embarked on a study of the fugues of J. S. Bach—specifically, the fugues of *The Well-Tempered Clavier* and *The Art of Fugue*, as well as the organ trios. He had soon prepared arrangements for string trio and string quartet of no fewer than a dozen of Bach's fugal compositions from those collections. They are listed as numbers 404a and 405 in the most recent Köchel catalogue (1964, pp. 436–439).[3] Even more than in the case of the motets, the austere preludes and fugues of *The Well-Tempered Clavier*, as Mozart undoubtedly recognized, constitute an art of *revelation*. They were never meant to be merely listened to, but rather to be played—and studied. In fact, Bach's most devoted admirers today, as in the past, developed their admiration of his music by playing or singing it themselves and thereby entering actively into an aesthetic realm of a particularly sublime, transcendental sort. This is a quite different experience from that of allowing oneself to be

[2]Mozart apparently uses "genius" here and elsewhere as a synonym for "talent."

[3]Mozart arranged three of the three-part fugues from *The Well-Tempered Clavier* for string trio; in addition, he provided them with newly composed introductions of his own. He also arranged Contrapunctus No. 8 from *The Art of Fugue* for string trio with the adagio from the Organ Trio, BWV 527, serving this time as the introduction; finally, Mozart scored two movements from the C minor Organ Trio, BWV 526, for string trio, as well. He similarly scored five of the four-voice fugues from Book 2 of *The Well-Tempered Clavier* for string quartet.

emotionally moved by more worldly, or "human" sentiments transmitted, that is, communicated, by intermediaries: by professional interpreters. For Mozart, on the other hand, music was, above all else, an art of communication and expression; and what it communicated and expressed was the "thoughts and feelings" of the composer. In a famous passage he had once confessed to his father (November 8, 1777): "I cannot write in verse, for I am no poet. I cannot arrange the parts of speech with such art as to produce effects of light and shade, for I am no painter. Even by signs and gestures I cannot *express my thoughts and feelings*, for I am no dancer. But *I can do so by means of sounds*, for I am a musician" (Anderson, 1938). In further contrast to Bach's explicit conviction that music must *teach* was Mozart's conviction that music must *please*. For Mozart it was part of the very definition of music. "Music . . . must never offend the ear, but must please the listener, or in other words must never cease to be music. . . . The Janissary chorus [from *Die Entführung aus dem Serail*] is . . . all that can be desired, that is, short, lively and written to please the Viennese" (September 26, 1781). Mozart also revealed to his father with reference to the "Haffner" Symphony: "I have composed my symphony in D major, *because you prefer that key*" (July 27, 1782). Whereas Bach composed the preludes and fugues of *The Well-Tempered Clavier* for the noble didactic purpose described earlier of instructing "the musical youth desirous of learning," the impetus behind the composition of Mozart's very Bachian fugue in C, K. 394, was a desire to please his wife: "My dear Constanze is really the cause of this fugue's coming into the world. . . . As she had so often heard me play fugues out of my head, she asked me if I had ever written any down, and when I said I had not, she scolded me roundly for not recording some of my compositions in this most artistic and beautiful of musical forms, and never ceased to entreat me until I wrote down a fugue for her. So that is its origin" (to Nannerl, April 20, 1782).

By no means, however, should Mozart's desire (indeed, his need) as a composer to please his audience be understood as pandering. Quite the contrary. If he was to compose a short, lively Janissary chorus to please the Viennese, then it would be a first-class Janissary chorus. Quality was not to be sacrificed for the sake of appeal. Nor need it be. Mozart would have both. As he explained in 1782, with reference to his recently completed piano concertos, K. 413 to 415, "There are passages here and there from which the connoisseurs alone can derive satisfaction, but these passages are written in such a way that the less learned cannot fail to be pleased, though without knowing why" (to Leopold Mozart, December 28, 1782). It was, for Mozart, a matter of honor. As he declared, "I am really unable to scribble off inferior stuff" (to Leopold Mozart, Vienna, July 31, 1782). Similarly, if we wished to make a favorable impression on the preeminent composer of Europe, Joseph Haydn, with a series of string quartets, then he would invest (as he reported in the dedication appended to the original publication) "long and laborious study" to produce string quartets of the very highest quality. The ambition (or compulsion), then, to please provided Mozart with a simply enormous artistic agenda. After all, the only way he could hope to please, variously, his wife, his father, Baron van Swieten, the Viennese audience, Emperor Joseph, and Joseph Haydn was to be the universal musician he was.

As striking as Mozart's desire to please was his high esteem for what he called "effect." "Ah, if only we had clarinets too [i.e., in Salzburg, as they had in Mannheim]! You cannot imagine the glorious effect of a symphony with flutes, oboes and clarinets" (to Leopold Mozart, Mannheim, December 3, 1778). "My new Haffner symphony [K. 385] has positively amazed me, for I had forgotten every single note of it. It must surely produce a good effect" (to Leopold Mozart, February 15, 1783).

Bach's music was little concerned with either of Mozart's declared objectives, appeal or effect. Bach's music by and large was not intended or expected to appeal to a concert audience in the modern sense. Bach had little occasion—although there was some—to write what we may call "public" music. Admittedly, his most popular compositions today, by far, are his instrumental concertos, especially the Brandenburg Concertos. This is completely understandable; for in them we find an emphasis not only on virtuosity and exuberant technical display but also on an intensity and immediacy of expression that strikes a sympathetic listener as "personal" in tone and feeling. But Bach wrote relatively few such compositions. Hardly two dozen concertos survive. On the other hand, he composed hundreds of church cantatas, close to two hundred of which survive. These compositions, however, for all their superb technical craftsmanship and profound expressivity, were primarily intended not for the "delectation" of a concert public at all, but rather for the "edification" of a church congregation. They may even have been conceived for, and dedicated to, the ultimately exclusive audience: for almost every one of Bach's cantata manuscripts closes with the inscription: *SDGl (Soli Deo Gloria)*, "To God alone the glory." All of this has been deliciously summarized by the Swiss theologian (and passionate Mozart enthusiast) Karl Barth in his famous bon mot: "It may or may not be the case that when the angels make music in praise of God they play Bach; but I am sure that when they are by themselves they play Mozart—and then God, too, is especially eager to listen in" (1956, p. 12).

We are now ready, I think, to reframe the questions I posed at the outset rather more specifically, as follows: *Why* did Bach perceive his music as "revelation"? Why did he conceive his artistic mission as one of teaching his neighbor and of praising God? Why did Mozart, on the other hand, understand *his* art as self-expression? Why did he feel obliged to please and impress his listeners? What, in a word, were the deeper forces driving the creativity of Bach and Mozart?

Let me turn first to Mozart whose life is less enigmatic than that of Bach, largely because it was so well documented from the beginning by the principals themselves. Indeed, there is probably more material of this kind bearing on Mozart than there is for any other artist before the nineteenth century. Over 1200 original copies of letters survive from Mozart and his immediate family alone. Furthermore, Mozart's father, Leopold, kept every document relating to his son, and saw to it that—at least during Wolfgang's childhood (i.e., when Leopold was on hand himself)—virtually every fact and movement of the boy was duly recorded, sometimes unduly exaggerated, either in a diary or in the form of extensive letters to acquaintances back in Salzburg, describing their experiences on their European tours.

The irony is that many of the most crucial pieces, especially those pertaining to Mozart's maturity, are missing. This is exactly the opposite of the usual situation. With most great figures of history we know little about their childhood but quite a bit about their adult years; for it is normally not obvious that a child is going to be a great man some day. With Mozart the case was the reverse. Leopold Mozart recognized Wolfgang's extraordinary musical talent and was convinced that he was going to be a great musician. Moreover, he planned to write a biography of his phenomenal child himself and, therefore, recorded everything. Finally, Wolfgang was more famous and celebrated as a child prodigy than as a man—known (and reported on) throughout Europe from London to Naples, Paris to Prague. As a consequence, material bearing on Mozart's childhood abounds. For our present purpose this constitutes, needless to say, an unalloyed boon. Childhood, after all, is the crucible of personality; and in the case of an artist, the seedbed of creativity.

But it really does not take exhaustive familiarity with Mozart's biography to recognize that by far the two most significant facts of his childhood were, first, his extraordinary musical talent, a natural gift perhaps unmatched in history, and, second, the extraordinarily powerful presence of his father

One can readily imagine that, with the exception perhaps of Franz Kafka, no great artist has ever had to cope with such a formidable father. Moreover, in Mozart's case, the life, talent, and fortunes of the son had become the father's all-consuming obsession. Mozart had clearly learned at a most early age that his enormous musical talent was a source of unbounded pride and pleasure to his parents whose praise and delight in his abilities were of course a source of great encouragement and gratification to himself. (By the age of 6, it had literally become Mozart's profession to please and delight others beside his parents with his talent.) Conversely, it must soon have become evident to the boy that he could appease his father, ward off his displeasure, by means of, perhaps *only* by means of, his musical accomplishments. There is every reason to suspect that Leopold made it clear to the boy that parental approval, and implicitly parental love, too, largely depended on his continued musical performance and production. We can be sure that Wolfgang quickly learned this lesson. No doubt he soon discovered as well that he could always reassure himself, as well as relieve pent-up emotional pressures, by drawing on the resources of his extraordinary creative talent. In short, music and composition had become for Mozart, in the language of the psychologist, an effective "ego defense": a source of self-esteem, a means of winning approval.

Such patterns of behavior, as they continue into adult life, can become a hallmark of the "depressive" personality, one unduly dependent on the opinions and on the approval of others, and therefore given to behavior designed to *ingratiate* oneself with others, potentially at the cost of suppressing one's own individuality (Storr, 1972, pp. 76–77).

Mozart has in fact been diagnosed before as an individual with mild "manic-depressive" or "cyclothymic" tendencies (Davies, 1989, pp. 145–160). This is of course not to say that he suffered from an emotional disorder in any significant clinical sense. But such ugly, clinical terminology, like it or not, has come to serve, in the modern era, as our preferred vocabulary for describing, understanding, and categorizing human nature. This is an enterprise that has engaged mankind since antiquity, when Hippocrates divided members of the species according to the four temperaments: the choleric, the sanguine, the phlegmatic, and the melancholic, and attempted to explain their behavior in terms of the preponderance of one or the other of the bodily fluids.

I am convinced that Mozart did not suffer from any serious pathological condition. The composer could hardly have been unaware of the phenomenal quality of his artistic achievements, for they were repaid, often enough, in the coin of worldly success: fame and money. And it would hardly have been abnormal, if such "ego reinforcement" at times produced a "manic" state of triumphant elation—and even excessive exuberance. Indeed, it is difficult to imagine how it could have failed to do so. As for his sad moods: Mozart himself was convinced that there was "always an [external] cause" for them. And there is evidence that he was not altogether wrong. Most but not all of the severe emotional difficulties he experienced can be associated with stressful circumstances of the moment: the death of his mother, loneliness, paternal browbeating, financial worries, separation from his wife. Yet, there is no denying that he was especially sensitive to the opinions of others.

He claimed not to care, but he clearly did. On August 8, 1781, he wrote to his father: "I played to [Countess Thun] what I have finished composing [from the first act of *Die Entführung*] and she told me afterwards that . . . what I have so far written cannot fail to please. But on this point I pay no attention whatever to *anybody's praise or blame*—I mean, until people have heard and seen the work as a whole" (Anderson, 1938). Two years later he asked his father "Please send me, if possible, *the reports* about my concert" (April 12, 1783). In the face of truly severe criticism, such as he experienced at the time of his break with his patron and protector, the formidable and frugal Prince-Archbishop of Salzburg, Hieronymus von Colloredo (with whom the Mozarts had had a difficult relationship for years), Mozart not only lost his ability to work but even suffered physical collapse. Vienna, May 12, 1781: "All the edifying things which the Archbishop [Colloredo] said to me during my three audiences . . . all the subsequent remarks which this fine servant of God made to me, had such an excellent effect on my health that in the evening I was obliged to leave the opera in the middle of the first act and go home and lie down. For I was very feverish, I was trembling in every limb, and I was staggering along the street like a drunkard. I also stayed at home the following day, yesterday, and spent the morning in bed" (Anderson, 1938). His moods of depression could also become intense. On June 27, 1788, he wrote to his fellow Mason and creditor, Michael Puchberg, "If such black thoughts did not come to me so often, thoughts which I banish by a tremendous effort, things would be . . . better." On July 7, 1791, just five months before his death, Mozart confessed to his wife, who was taking a cure at the time: "I can't describe what I have been feeling—a kind of emptiness, which hurts me dreadfully—a kind of longing, which is never satisfied, which never ceases, and which persists, nay rather increases daily. . . . Even my work gives me no pleasure." But it is important to add, as does Mozart, that the reason for this particular bout of melancholy was his separation from Constanze.

The recognition of Mozart's mildly manic-depressive temperament—let us just call it his "moodiness"—helps explain other features of his behavior. For example his scandalous, and

rather "manic," delight in scatological language. There is a series of letters Mozart wrote to his first cousin Maria Anna
Thekla Mozart (Bäsle), the daughter of Leopold Mozart's
brother, that contains almost nothing but obscenities of this
sort.

But it is important to realize, first of all, that there was a
sociological context for the "Bäsle" letters. Crude scatological
language was by no means taboo in the eighteenth century
among the European middle class. Body parts and functions
were called by their vernacular names, not their Latin euphe-
misms. The words were used openly and naturally, even between men and women. Talking about the excretory functions
in the late eighteenth century, it seems, was a bit like talking
about one's diet today—or perhaps about one's analysis—and
really no more gauche. I'd like to stress two further points about
the "Bäsle" letters. First, their obscenities are almost exclusively
scatological; they contain very few sexual references, and those
few are hedged in double entendre. The second point is this:
Bäsle must have been amused by them. This observation, as
obvious as it is, emphasizes the fact that, once again, Mozart
wished to please his audience. He seems to have been adept at
adjusting his language and his behavior, like his music, to suit
the occasion. In general, he knew how to behave, or, put another way, he knew how to "act" properly. This ability, I believe,
holds the key not only to much of Mozart's personality but also
to much of his art. Mozart apparently, for the reasons we have
been discussing, was a role-player throughout his life—a perpetual actor. This may also explain in part why he was a great
dramatist. Mozart was able to create such credible characters
on stage, characters ranging from Monostatos and Papageno
to Sarastro, from Zerlina to the Countess, because he possessed
an almost limitless capacity to empathize. And this capacity, I
submit, derived from the fact that he was obliged to play an
exceptionally wide range of roles in his own life—especially in
his childhood.

Mozart, after all, in addition to the powerful and no doubt
oppressive omnipresence of his father, did not grow up like
other children, developing his personality under stable circumstances in a more or less stable circle of peers. On the contrary,

he was constantly on the move, especially during the ten forma-
tive years from 1763 to 1773, that is, between the ages of 7 and
17. He was performing all the time—and not only on stage as
a pianist. He was also performing a constantly changing role in
a constantly changing social context: now at the court of Maria
Theresa or George III or Louis XVI; now in the often colorful
company of actors and singers; now among his fellow musicians
at home in Salzburg—men of dubious character and etiquette;
each time Mozart "fit in."

In a word, he was accommodating. As with his music, Mozart
behaved in the manner he thought would best please his com-
rades and companions of the moment. With Bäsle he was the
vulgarian. With his billiard and bowling companions he played
the clown and prankster. With his pupils—mostly women—he
may occasionally have played the seducer. With his wife Constanze the role had many facets. On the one hand, there was
the purely physical, robust, lovemaking. But Mozart also played
another part with her. Constanze had been shabbily treated by
her mother, and it is clear that Mozart thought of himself as
her protector and savior. At court, so far as is known, his man-
ners were beyond reproach; he was a convincing courtier. With
his father, Wolfgang was by turns the affectionate child, the
gentleman of lofty moral principles, the bold rebel, even the
mature, reflective man of thought. With his brethren from the
Masonic lodge, Mozart was the high-minded humanitarian.

Finally, this ability to adjust, to assume many roles, has its
counterpart in Mozart the musician. Mozart was the ultimate
eclectic. He was at home, like no other musician in history, with
literally every genre and style of his time: the concerto, the
symphony, the opera, church, keyboard, and chamber music.
His achievements in each were supreme but most impressive
perhaps in opera, where his ability as a person to absorb and
empathize with such a range of human behavior fused with his
unlimited technical resources and stylistic range as a musician
and composer.

It seems possible, then, to fit together a picture of Mozart the
man that not only does justice to even the less flattering facts
of his life, but seems to harmonize with his profile as a composer. Can the same be done in the case of J. S. Bach?

In stunning contrast to the situation with Mozart, we probably know less about the private life of Bach than we do about
that of any of the other supreme artistic figures of modern
history (with the exception, perhaps, of Shakespeare). The documents bearing on Bach's life that have survived, whether written by others or by Bach himself, are almost invariably "official"
in character: inspection reports on organs, bills, receipts, letters
of recommendation on behalf of pupils, complaints to or from
employers and other authorities. Not a single letter has survived
from Bach to any of his children, or to his first wife, Maria
Barbara, or his second wife, Anna Magdalena. We may assume
that not many were ever written.

If the decisive fact about Mozart's childhood, and perhaps
for his personality, generally, is that he was the son of an overwhelming and formidable father, then the decisive fact about
Bach's childhood is that he was an orphan. He lost both parents
within one year. His mother died in May 1694 when Johann
Sebastian was just 9 years old. His father, Johann Ambrosius
Bach, remarried six months later, in November, and died himself, three months thereafter, in February 1695—a month short
of Bach's tenth birthday. We can also wonder about the quality
of parental, or at least maternal, attention he had received in
his earliest childhood. Bach was the youngest of eight children.
It is likely that childhood sickness was always present in the
household. We know that death was a not infrequent visitor.
Just two months after Bach was born a brother died at the age
of 10. Exactly one year later, a sister died at the age of 6 (Freyse,
1955, pp. 103–107). Shortly after the death of his father, the
family broke up. The 10-year-old Johann Sebastian and a 13-
year-old brother were taken in by the oldest of the surviving
siblings, Johann Christoph, then 24 years old, and employed as
organist in the Thuringian town of Ohrdruf. We do not know
how well Bach got on with his oldest brother and protector.
Both C. P. E. Bach and Johann Nicolaus Forkel relate the famous story that Johann Christoph did not allow Bach to see a
certain music manuscript and that Bach surreptitiously made a
copy for himself at night by candlelight (David and Mendel,
1966, pp. 216–217, 302). If the story is true, it is significant
enough. If it is untrue, a legend created presumably by Bach
himself and passed down to his children and on to posterity,

then it is, if anything, even more significant. But the decisive fact about Bach's childhood, once again, was his status as an orphan. Whereas the child Mozart suffered under the *threat* of the *withdrawal* of parental love, the child Bach experienced the actual deprivation of his parents. This catastrophic deprivation, along with others, real or imaginary (as the story of Johann Christoph and the hidden manuscript reveals), understandably put the boy on his guard, engendering in him, we may be sure, an attitude of "basic distrust" against an unreliable, even treacherous world.

Under such circumstances, it is readily apparent why Bach would have been drawn to religion, especially to the Lutheran religion with its message of personal faith and salvation, combined with a determined rejection and distrust of the vain and deceptive pleasures of what is ultimately regarded as a meaningless world. Such a temperament as Bach seems to have developed, potentially vulnerable to a powerful sense of apathy, futility, meaninglessness should perhaps be dubbed "the Sebastian complex." At all events, in order to prevent this discussion from taking on an unduly clinical tone, I shall adopt the conceit of designating the two temperaments I have been describing up to now henceforth as the "Mozartian" and "Bachian."

Unlike the Mozartian personality, the Bachian is typically an introvert, detached and isolated, inclined to keep his fellow man "at arm's length," and evincing an air of coldness, superiority, and aloofness. He is reluctant to become emotionally involved with others. For example, we do possess one letter written by Bach that does touch, if ever so briefly, on his private situation. It is dated October 28, 1730, and is addressed to his childhood friend, Georg Erdmann. It is essentially, and typically, a business letter in which Bach expresses his interest in leaving Leipzig and asks his friend to see what he could do. Quite untypically, Bach appends a concluding paragraph, much in the manner of a reluctant afterthought, in which he notes:

> Now I must add a little about my domestic situation. I am married for the second time, my first wife having died in Cöthen. From the first marriage I have three sons and one daughter living. . . . From the second marriage I have one son and two

daughters living. . . . The children of my second marriage are
still small. . . . But they are all born musicians, and I can assure
you that I can already form an ensemble both *vocaliter* and *instru-
mentaliter* within my family, particularly since my present wife
sings a good, clear soprano, and my eldest daughter, too, joins
in not badly. I shall almost transgress the bounds of courtesy if
I burden Your Honor any further, and I therefore hasten to
close remaining. . . . Your Honor's most obedient and devoted
servant. Joh. Seb. Bach [David and Mendel, 1966, p. 126].

We should not be surprised to notice that while Bach may
have failed to mention to Erdmann the names of any of the
members of his family, he did not fail to mention that his second
wife was musical and even to offer a brief, if modest, assessment
of the nature of her talent. It is abundantly clear from Bach's
letter to Erdmann—from his having mentioned just about nothing else in connection with his "domestic situation"—that music
and music-making occupied a central position in Bach's private
life and was at the core of his relationship with his wife and
children. We learn virtually nothing for certain, either here
or from any other document, about the affective relationships
among the members of Bach's immediate family. His family, it
seems, was an extension of his profession—his "calling."

It is not difficult for this absence, distrust—even abhor-
rence—of personal emotional involvement, such as we can observe in Bach, to enhance the sense of meaninglessness I referred to before. Nor is it difficult to understand how a
formidably gifted individual like Bach could find in his own
creativity the compensating resources to create meaning.

The recourse to art, then, on the part of the talented and
creative individual of Bachian disposition has an altogether different motivation from that of an individual of Mozartian temperament. A Mozart hopes to win approval (and love) with his
display of talent and by providing pleasure. A Bach hopes, in
the absence of any perceived meaning in the outer world, to
create for himself his own world of meaning, and to proclaim
it, to *reveal* it, to others: disciples, congregants.

I don't think it is surprising that the Bachian temperament
is observed more frequently in brilliant scientists than in artists.
In a provocative study entitled *The Dynamics of Creation* (1972),
the British psychiatrist Anthony Storr suggests that both Albert

Einstein and Isaac Newton, had "an intense need to create an all-embracing, explanatory scheme which would alleviate the discomfort of living in an arbitrary or contradictory world." Storr adds that "[Isaac Newton,] like many a prophet, seems to have been convinced that he had a direct personal relationship with a God who inspired him." In other words, when the Bachian temperament appears in individuals "of religious bent," they are, according to Storr, "apt to substitute a relation with God with the human contacts they find so difficult" (p. 70). This is not a little reminiscent of J. S. Bach's practice of signing his church compositions *Soli Deo Gloria*.

The strong representation of scientists (rather than artists) of genius possessed of what I have been calling the Bachian personality gives us an important clue as to the musical consequences of Bach's psychological predisposition. For Bach music was destined to be far more than a mere object of aesthetic beauty. Rather it was, in two respects, a revelation, a manifestation of truth. First of all, his church cantatas, in connection with their liturgical texts, were designed to serve as explicit vehicles of theological truth. Second, and far more significantly, for Bach *all* "real" music, in its very substance and structure, bore witness to the divine order itself (Marshall, 1990). Bach once declared that the thorough-bass was "the most perfect foundation of music being played . . . in order to make a well-sounding harmony to the Glory of God," and admonished further that "where this is not observed there will be no real music." In fact, I am convinced that it was Bach's conviction that "real music" was the product of the *correct application of learnable and teachable principles* that informed his pedagogical commitment. With his convictions about the existence of universally valid principles, or "laws," governing the organization of musical phenomena, Bach revealed himself to be the product of the Age of Reason, the Age of Enlightenment.

Enlightenment thought provided both an external impetus and an intellectual justification for Bach's inborn and uniquely powerful synthesizing impulse—an impulse, as we have seen, that had for Bach (as for Newton and Einstein) deep psychological sources. Synthesis and unification were a characteristic preoccupation of the philosophers and scientists of the Enlightenment. The ultimate significance of the work of Isaac

Newton—for which he was duly celebrated during his own time—is that he had discovered in the laws of gravity the "unifying principle," the underlying unity that lay behind the new discoveries about the natural world that were being amassed in the course of the seventeenth century. Compare Bach's achievement in *The Well-Tempered Clavier* with that of Newton. On the one hand, the work embodies a fusion of the potentially antithetical principles of functional tonality and linear counterpoint; on the other, it constitutes an "encyclopedic" survey of the most diverse forms and styles of the era—dances, arias, motets, concertos—all developed in accordance with a single "unifying" compositional principle: that of the fugue. The parallel with the achievement of Newton is both palpable and profound.

It was certainly palpable to Johann Wolfgang von Goethe who exclaimed, after he had heard the fugues of *The Well-Tempered Clavier* for the first time: It was "as if the eternal harmony were communicating with itself as it might have happened in God's bosom shortly before the creation of the world" (for a more extensive discussion see Marshall [1989, pp. 65–79]). Goethe was more right than he could have imagined. God's bosom indeed! It seems to me that it is by no means inappropriate to picture Bach the orphan, the "fatherless father" (literally, the father of twenty children, figuratively, in his role as teacher, the father of dozens of students and disciples) feeling himself, for the reasons we have been discussing, predestined to don the mantle of the lawgiver and understanding his personal destiny to be nothing less than that of a Godlike maker of worlds—worlds, to be sure, of musical sounds that not only bore witness to, but indeed emulated the divine order itself.

What we witness in the case of both Bach and Mozart is the auspicious intersection of personality and history. Bach was born under the old aesthetic dispensation, according to which, the purpose of art was the imitation of nature, truth was beauty, that is, the aesthetic experience of beauty was the product issuing from the contemplation, or emulation, of divine order. For Mozart and his contemporaries, on the other hand, nature and the natural were redefined and understood in terms of amenity and grace, simplicity and immediacy, and personal, self-expression. For composers of the classical period, beauty was truth; that is, the creation of beauty, understood as that which is pleasing (or "effective," i.e., exciting to the senses) was the true objective of art. Despite their tragic personal destinies, Bach and Mozart each enjoyed the immensely good fortune of appearing at precisely the right time and place in history not only for the optimal cultivation of their prodigious natural gifts but for the expression of their particular spiritual needs, as these needs emerged from the crucible of their childhood experiences. The lesson seems to be this: for there to be art of the highest order there has to be a congruence of historic and personal circumstances—a perfect union of style and genius. There is more than one road to Parnassus.

REFERENCES

Anderson, E., tr. (1938), *The Letters of Mozart and His Family*, 3rd ed. London: W. W. Norton, 1985.
Barth, K. (1956), *Wolfgangs Amadeus Mozart*. Zurich: Theologischer Verlag.
Dahlhaus, C. (1985), *Das neue Handbuch der Musikwissenschaft*, Vol. 5. Laaber: Laaber Verlag.
David, H., & Mendel, A. (1966), *The Bach Reader*, rev. ed. New York: W. W. Norton.
Davies, P. J. (1989), *Mozart in Person: His Character and Health*. New York: Greenwood Press.
Freyse, C. (1955), Wieviel Geschwister hatte J. S. Bach? *Bach-Jahrbuch*, pp. 103–107.
von Köchel, L. R. (1964), *Chronologisch-thematisches Verzeichnis Sämtlicher Tonwerke Wolfgang Amade Mozarts*, 6th ed., ed. F. Giegling, A. Weinmann, & G. Sievers. Wiesbaden: Breitkopf & Härtel.
Marshall, R. L. (1987), The eighteenth century as a music-historical epoch. A different argument for the proposition. *Coll. Music Soc. Symposium*, 27:198–205.
——— (1989), On Bach's universality. In: *The Music of Johann Sebastian Bach: The Sources, the Style, the Significance*. New York: Schirmer Books.
——— (1990), Truth and beauty: J. S. Bach at the crossroads of cultural history. *Bach: J. Riemenschneider Bach Inst.*, 21:3–14.
Rochlitz, F. (1798), Verbürgte Anekdoten aus Wolfgang Gottlieb Mozarts Leben. *Allgemeine Musikalische Zeitung* (Nov. 21, 1798), Colls. 116–117. In: *The Bach Reader*, ed. H. David & A. Mendel. New York: W. W. Norton, 1966, pp. 359–360.
Solomon, M. (1991), The Rochlitz anecdotes: Issues of authenticity in early Mozart biography. In: *Mozart Studies*, ed. C. Eisen. Oxford: Clarendon Press, pp. 28–29.
Storr, A. (1972), *The Dynamics of Creation*. New York: Atheneum, 1985.

Chapter 9

A Tale of Two Fathers: Bach and Mozart (Discussion of Chapter 8)

Stuart Feder, M.D.

As a psychoanalyst, I found much to admire in Professor Marshall's paper, "Bach and Mozart: Styles of Musical Genius." First, he is a far better psychologist to his own data than the certified experts he consults, here chiefly Anthony Storr and Peter Davies. Second, his underlying assumptions regarding creativity—its sources, manifestations, and above all, its transformations—are consistent with a psychoanalytic point of view. My own aim in this discussion is a modest one: to highlight some of these correspondences and to briefly explore directions suggested by Marshall's work.

I draw the reader's attention first to his title where I would emphasize his use of the term *styles*. This is important because his focus is not psychopathology per se but rather *character*, comprised of those constant and enduring features of personality which normally originate in mental conflict but do not necessarily result in neurotic symptom. In particular, Marshall cites such character traits as Mozart's tendency "to please" and "to appease," and Bach's propensity "to teach." Style, in general, may be said to be the *expressive* pathway of character or personality—the manner in which persons reveal themselves in thought, language, gesture, and every other variety of behavior. Basically a function of organization and form in the mental sphere, it is more than reasonable to expect that a person's style will become symbolically encoded in art, and here, of course, we speak of music. From all we know of mental life, its manifestations and, above all, its transformations, that expectation is logically obligatory. Moreover, it is testable. The nature of style

171

is such that it is rooted in a fundamental displaceability of mental form and mental content. It is thus that mind can achieve representation in music (Feder, see chapter 4). For example, if Marshall's observation of Mozart's trait of pleasing and Bach's of teaching are authentic, they must have demonstrable musical, stylistic consequences. The task of applied musical analysis or applied psychoanalysis equally, is to responsibly demonstrate these artistic sequelae and to explore the means by which they come about.

A further thought on style before going on to fathers, which is what I chiefly want to discuss. No single trait can fully determine the complex overarching style of an individual human personality, although in some instances, an isolated trait might characterize a brief work of art. To infer that a single trait can be more than one building block of personality is to invite a frequent criticism of psychoanalysis: the fallacy of the "nothing but." Thinking such as this tends to suggest a caricature of both the human being studied and the psychoanalytic method which subserves observation. Using the example of Mozart's trait "to please" as discussed by Marshall, it is isolated in his paper only for purposes of analysis and discussion. The author nowhere implies that this accounts for all there is to Mozart's character let alone his music.

By the same token, any single given characteristic is likely to have multiple developmental determinants. For example, issues of pleasing, displeasing, and appeasing, issues of compliance and rebellion, symbiosis and autonomy are as if coordinates which reach back into a period of personal human anal history when the making of things was closer to body than to mind. The relationship of the parent to the child's body applied to the Mozart family brings us sharply not only to Mozart's father, but to his mother as well.

It seems likely from what we know that Anna Maria Pertl Mozart was at least enough of a "good enough" mother for Mozart to have been able to proceed through the very earliest phases of life with an appropriate degree of pleasure and gratification, yet a sufficient degree of renunciation of infantile satisfactions to progress developmentally. Some of these early pleasures could be revived relatively free of the conflict born of shame or guilt with Bäsle, the seductive little cousin (who, by the way, bore the same given names as Mozart's mother only, appropriately enough, backwards, Maria Anna); later, they could be revived with Constanze who had much in common with his mother in character. Like many artists, Mozart's *access* to earlier phases of life and states of mind was extraordinary—which is not the equivalent of being immature or childlike, although it might manifestly appear that way at times (Greenacre, 1963, pp. 15–18; 1971). What is essential in the artist is the ultimate creative use to which this access might be put. In any event, with regard to Mozart's mother—the limitations of eighteenth century biographical conventions aside—the chances are that the biographically "silent" and female parent was probably the parent who was relatively more silently loved, with less residual conflict stemming from childhood.

In contrast, the parent ostentatiously revered yet feared, and covertly hated, was the "too much" parent, Leopold Mozart, the parent of conflict. It was he who promoted the potential for regression and the continuation of childhood anxieties into his son's adult life at every level: oral—in his continuous, overweening concern about his son's very survival; anal—in the struggle for control and intrusive bid to be an active, ongoing presence in his son's creativity; genital—in his insistence upon being the arbiter of the choice of woman with whom his son would be permitted sexual gratification.

Yet, Leopold was full partner in creating an unparalleled musical ego in providing the child Mozart with opportunities for the fullest possible development of musical language and fostering its maturation. Nor is blame (or credit for that matter) to be assigned to the psychological compromises the individual, Mozart, devised for himself, given the father he had. However, it is of interest to note the biographical transformations of Leopold from Otto Jahn's shrewd but admiringly respectful portrait of 1855 to more modern treatments (Hildesheimer, 1983; Stafford, 1991). The task remains for a full psychological appreciation against the background of modern notions of child rearing, not to mention child abuse.

Even more remarkable than Mozart's attachment to Leopold was his ability finally to separate from him—more than this, his need to do so and the manner in which he carried it out, a mixture of mature ingenuity and adolescent bumbling. Separation, the cardinal psychological task of adolescence, could not be accomplished in physical proximity to Leopold. Even if Leopold's intrusiveness were tempered by now, it may have retained too many habitual, nonverbal, anxiety inducing body-meanings for Wolfgang; and perhaps too, there was a passive part of him wishing to yield. The sense of restrained urgency revealed in Mozart's letters of the time suggest what might have been at stake for him: nothing less than body and soul! This became manifest shortly before the climax of this human drama as 1782 approached, the year of his marriage. Mozart answered to his father for even "thinking of such a thing at an unseasonable time." Wolfgang begs:

> But, I entreat you, dearest, most beloved father, to listen to me. I have been obliged to reveal my intentions to you. You must therefore allow me to disclose to you my reasons, which, moreover, are very well founded. The voice of nature speaks as loud in me as in others, louder, perhaps than in many a big lout of a fellow. . . .

There is more in this letter (December 15, 1781), an entreaty for corporeal autonomy, which ends, "Please take pity on your son! I kiss your hands a thousand times and am as ever your most obedient son" (Anderson, 1938).

The frustration and rage that lay behind the submissive and tactful facade was displaced in a direction that even Leopold could appreciate: the Archbishop Colloredo. It was with him that Mozart most manifestly enacted the son's rebellion provoking at length the famous "kick on the arse" administered by Count Arco (Sadie, New Grove, 1980, Vol. 1, p. 780). While he took his punishment indignantly, the ultimate irony was that it was precisely Mozart's identification with Leopold that enabled him to handle his father: Wolfgang had learned much from observing Leopold's crafty, manipulative management of powerful authoritarian figures.

It was in 1782 that Mozart reported "collecting at the moment the fugues of Bach." By the time Mozart played the Bach organ in Leipzig in 1789, Leopold was dead. In fact, the Leipzig event took place a month before the second anniversary of his death. The need for a father endures as well as the need to come to terms with a father in life and in death. Could this have been one strand of motivation in Mozart's turning to Bach? When he exclaimed, "What is this? . . . Now there is something one can learn from," he already knew very well what the "this" of the music was. The insight had perhaps to do with the refinding of an earlier and more benign teacher, the father with whom the earliest learning of music had been shared. It will be recalled that Bach had his parallel in the teacher Leopold Mozart who published his famous *Versuch einer grundlichen Violinschule* in 1756, the year of Wolfgang's birth. Mozart's conflict with his father had involved intense feelings of love and hate, the latter strongly defended against. With Leopold dead, feelings of guilt for real and fantasied transgressions would have summated with those of longing for a lost object in the direction of a wish for restitution. Could the "discovery" of Bach then represent a rediscovery of a father? If so, a degree of the musical influence that Bach exerted might be considered to be an artifact of mourning. Indeed, if such is the case, can it be traced and corroborated in the music, a specific and testable example of how the mental life of the composer may influence the music he creates?

We turn now to a few comments on Marshall's discussion of Bach. There could be few figures in music—or any of the arts for that matter—who were more concerned with origins. What remains to this day "the most reliable documentary evidence of the family history" (New Grove, Vol. 1, p. 780), the Bach *Ursprung* (lit. source, or geneology) was drafted by J. S. Bach himself in 1735, perhaps in observation of passing his fiftieth birthday. Its relationship to a business letter to a childhood friend of five years earlier, of which Marshall makes mention, is a biographical puzzle worth solving. For the "business" related to a crisis in Bach's private and creative life had musical and stylistic sequelae of historical as well as personal importance. (This is beautifully described in an earlier essay by Marshall on "Bach, the Progressive" [1989].) Five years later, we find Bach tracing his origins.

Bach's "systematic investigation" of the "family heritage" was consistent with the pride he took in his children as "born *musici*" (New Grove, Vol. 1, p. 780). His was a dynasty whose very name spelled out in music: "B flat, A, C, B natural" in German nomenclature, a motif first used by Bach in his *Art of the Fugue* (cf. Schumann's *Six Fugues*, op. 60).

Extrapolating origins was a psychological necessity for Bach who, as Marshall indicates, was orphaned by the time he was 10. The fact that he could reliably trace an impressive array of forebears would not necessarily satisfy fully a wish for the legendary. (This is hinted by Marshall in the present paper.) The central, universal organizing fantasy of origins called the family romance, first described by Freud, harks back to "the child's longing for the happy vanished days when his father was the strongest of men and his mother the dearest and loveliest of women" (1909, p. 291). Several psychoanalytic writers have emphasized the specific family romance of the artist (Greenacre, 1971, Vol. 2). I have written elsewhere of its furthest and most grandiose reaches where the wish for utopian origins blends with the artist's fantasied identification with God the Creator (Feder, 1989, 1992). I believe this was the direction of Bach's family romance fantasy. The mythic father with whom he identified was God Himself. When Bach signed church compositions, "Soli Deo Gloria," it was not exclusively out of pious humility: in fantasy, they belonged to the same glorified family. More than this, the sense of the family connection, as it were, may have endowed Bach's grandest and most spiritual music.

Thus, I am in harmony with Professor Marshall who reaches a similar conclusion as he pictures "Bach the orphan, the 'fatherless father' . . . feeling himself . . . predestined to don the mantle of the lawgiver and understanding his personal destiny to be nothing less than that of a Godlike maker of worlds. . . ."

In what we like to call real life Mozart had too much father, Bach, too little. Both, however, had internalized fathers in mental representation. The imagery and fantasy generated by this particular compartment of mind were realized in very different styles of music which, in turn, implied very different content: Mozart's powerfully vengeful father endures in its D minor representation of the Commendatore of Don Giovanni; Bach's magnificent father in his B Minor Mass.

REFERENCES

Anderson, E., ed. tr. (1938), *The Letters of Mozart and His Family*. New York: W. W. Norton, 1966.

Blom, E. (1939), *Mozart*. London: J. M. Dent.

Feder, S. (1989), The family romance at ninety. Paper presented at the Mt. Sinai School of Medicine, Department of Psychiatry, April. Bernard S. Meyer Memorial Lecture.

—— (1992), *Charles Ives: My Father's Song*. New Haven, CT: Yale University Press.

Freud, S. (1909), Family romances. *Standard Edition*, 9:235–241. London: Hogarth Press, 1959.

Greenacre, P. (1963), *The Quest for the Father*. New York: International Universities Press.

—— (1971), The childhood of the artist: Libidinal phase development and giftedness. In: *Emotional Growth*, Vol. 2. New York: International Universities Press.

Hildesheimer, W. (1983), *Wolfgang Mozart*. London: J. M. Dent.

Jahn, O. (1855), *Life of Mozart*, tr. P. D. Townsend. New York: Cooper Square, 1970.

Marshall, R. L. (1989), *The Music of Johann Sebastian Bach: The Sources, the Style, the Significance*. New York: Schirmer.

Sadie, S., ed. (1980), *New Grove Dictionary of Music and Musicians*, 20 vols. London: Macmillan.

Stafford, W. (1991), *The Mozart Myths: A Critical Reassessment*. Stanford, CA: Stanford University Press.

Chapter 10

Communication of Affect and Idea Through Song; Schumann's "I was Crying in my Dream" (op. 48, no. 13)

Peter Ostwald, M.D.

One cannot truly appreciate the evocative power of a song by reading about it. The music must be heard! Before the following paper was presented to a "Psychoanalysis and Music" conference at Mount Sinai School of Medicine in New York, on November 23, 1991, we listened to a live performance of Schumann's lied "Ich hab' im Traum Geweinet" ("I was Crying in my Dream"), sung by baritone Boris Louschin, accompanied at the piano by Joanne Polk. Then, after discussing its origins and meaning, we heard the song performed once more. It was a moving experience, allowing us to share, empathically, the composer's grief and terror as he brooded over a deeply troubling memory from childhood. Thus I would urge you, before and after reading this article, to listen to Schumann's song, in your imagination if you are familiar with it, or from a recording, or better yet, a live performance.

The basic model for human communication was formulated nearly half a century ago by Jurgen Ruesch and Gregory Bateson in a pioneering contribution to psychiatry (1951). It stipulates that there be an exchange of discrete information between identified senders and receivers, with messages encoded in a context governed by collaborative feedback. Music, with its specifiable network of composers, performers, and auditors, as well as a system of notation that can be standardized, lends itself well to analysis. Investigators from different fields such as musicology, psychology, performance history, or psychoanalysis may interpret, from various points of view, the affects and ideas communicated by particular compositions.

179

XIII.

Figure 10.1a. Schumann: "Ich hab' in Traum Geweinet" ("I was Crying in my Dream").

Figure 10.1b. Continuation of Figure 10.1a.

Schumann's "Ich hab' im Traum Geweinet" ("I was Crying in my Dream") is one of sixteen lieder he assembled in 1840 for his well-known song cycle *Dichterliebe* (A Poet's Love), op. 48. The composer was then 30 years old and enduring a life crisis precipitated by the threatened loss of his fiancée, the pianist Clara Wieck. Using a psychobiographical approach, I would like to explore the conscious and unconscious meanings of this song. The analysis will proceed along four converging lines: (1) Schumann's memory of a disturbance in his attachment to his mother; (2) his evolution as a writer of songs; (3) his conflicted relationship with Clara Wieck; and (4) his resolution of personal conflicts through composition of this particular song.

SCHUMANN AND HIS MOTHER

Schumann's mother was close to menopause when Robert was conceived and had already given birth to five children. The one immediately preceding him had been a daughter who died at birth, leaving the mother depressed and exhausted. She recalled his birth in 1810 as "a hard struggle." Yet it was with his mother that Robert shared his first pleasurable musical experiences. She loved to sing, and although not a trained musician, it was said that because of her great familiarity with songs his mother merited being called "the living book of arias." The child evidently mirrored her behavior—as she described it, he would sing back to her "with beautiful intonation and in the right rhythm" (Ostwald, 1985, p. 16). Music no doubt was an important element in their early attachment. However, because of his mother's near-fatal illness, their bond was broken when Robert was 2 years old.

The Schumann family was then living in Zwickau, a small town directly in the path of Napoleon's Russian invasion. With the French defeat in 1812, thousands of starving and diseased soldiers entered the town, carrying a lethal typhus epidemic. Nine percent of the population was wiped out, and Schumann's mother became infected, which necessitated quarantine, and separation from her children. The 2-year-old Robert was placed with the family of Zwickau's mayor and apparently attached himself without too much difficulty to this man's wife,

Frau Ruppius. Detailed information is not available, but it seems that his foster mother provided adequate care for the next two-and-a-half years. We don't know whether she too was interested in music or singing, nor is it clear why the boy's separation from his biological mother was so prolonged. I assume it had something to do with the severity of her illness, and her slowness to recover. Robert's mother was generally a rather sickly person, as was his father; there was a history of depressive disorder on both sides of the family. In any event, we know that the discontinuity in young Schumann's relationship with his mother persisted for several years, and that there were serious problems in their relationship even after they were reunited.

In his first autobiography (1825), written when he was 15 years old, Schumann described his attachment to his foster mother (Frau Ruppius) as follows: "She accomplished a great deal in the education of children. I loved her. She was my second mother, and . . . I stayed under her maternal supervision for two and a half years" (Ostwald, 1985, p. 15). Contact with his family was not completely broken, however, and it seems that he visited his parents' home fairly regularly. An emotional distancing seems to have occurred, similar to the detachment described by John Bowlby and others who observed young children after separation from their mothers (1969). "Once every day I went over to my parents," writes Schumann, "but otherwise *I did not concern myself about them any longer.*" He mentions additional symptoms, related most likely to the discontinuities felt in relation to a lost maternal object: "Still very clear in my memory is that *I couldn't sleep* the night before moving out of this house, and that *I cried throughout the entire night.* Also once before, when Frau Ruppius was away on a trip, I got up *alone during the night* . . . and sat at the window, *crying bitterly,* so that early in the morning they found me, *asleep, with tears rolling down my cheeks*" (Ostwald, 1985, pp. 15–16; emphasis added).

It was this set of memories which Schumann seems later to have transformed, and creatively integrated, to compose his song "I was Crying in my Dream."

Schumann's Ambitions as a Songwriter

His desire for musical experience and self-expression was repeatedly frustrated. First came the disturbance of attachment to his aria-singing mother, just described. Then there was the stultifying effect of the small town, Zwickau, an artistically deprived environment lacking good music teachers. Piano lessons began at age 7 with a rather mediocre church organist, and continued sporadically until adolescence. Schumann, who generally had difficulty relating to authority figures, remained essentially self-taught. He excelled at improvisation, and achieved some fame in his community by doing musical portraits at the keyboard, capturing the mannerisms and speech patterns of his friends and neighbors. It was expected that he would enter the family publishing business, and this led to further conflict. Symptoms of anxiety, restlessness, interference with concentration, and self-doubt had been noted since age 9. Robert usually felt more comfortable when withdrawing from people and engaging in fantasy. "I much preferred going for walks all by myself, and I would pour my heart out to nature." Yet he attempted to form relationships, and during puberty fell in love with two girls from his neighborhood.

At age 15, Schumann experienced a sequence of object-losses, with serious consequences for his mental health. First, his sister Emilie, then 30 years old, became physically and mentally ill. She committed suicide, by drowning. This tragedy stimulated Schumann's preoccupation with self-destruction, and led to a lifelong fear of psychosis. Second, his father died, the only member of the family who was then actively supporting his musical ambitions. The father had encouraged Schumann in all kinds of ways, for example, by buying a piano for him, arranging concerts, and offering to finance his education as a musician. "I railed against fate," wrote Schumann, describing his loss. According to Wilhelm Wasielewski, his first biographer, following the loss of his father young Schumann's "demeanor reversed itself into almost the opposite [of the] predominantly cheerful disposition he had shown before" (Ostwald, 1985, p. 23). Deflected from his father's plan, which was that he go to Dresden and study at the Opera House with Carl Maria von Weber (who in the meantime also had died), Schumann was sent instead to the University of Leipzig, to study law, which he deeply resented because it involved self-discipline and a form of logical thinking that he found too constraining.

Already, before entering college, he had begun to develop his creative abilities as a writer, using a free-associational approach borrowed from romantic authors like Jean Paul Richter and E. T. A. Hoffmann. Schumann also helped his brothers in the family publishing business, producing books and dictionaries, which added to his literary skills. He wrote poetry, autobiographical sketches, and essays on such heady topics as "genius, intoxication, and originality." Indeed, as a college student he was intoxicated much of the time, experimenting with wine, champagne, strong coffee, and heavy cigars, hoping thus to expand his "originality." For a while, his desire to emulate and identify with his late father who had been a literary man was so strong that Schumann actually decided to become a professional writer. But he never completely gave up his earlier ambition, probably based on a strong identification with his aria-singing mother, to express himself musically and become an "artist of sounds" (Tonkünstler).

A psychotherapeutic experience during his turbulent adolescence was significant, in terms of both Schumann's personal growth and his development as a composer. He had met Dr. Ernst August Carus, the director of a mental hospital in Colditz, and later Professor of Medicine in Leipzig. Carus was himself an amateur musician, and his wife Agnes was a capable singer. Young Schumann would visit their home, bask in their encouragement of his musical talent, and accompany Agnes Carus's singing at the piano. It was like having yet another set of parents. It was also a way of becoming acquainted with the lieder of Franz Schubert, to which Agnes Carus had introduced him. Schubert's lieder were to serve as models for Schumann's first mature compositions, including the two songs he dedicated to Agnes Carus, "Light as Fluttering Sylphs," and "Transformation." Throughout this time, Dr. Carus tried to counsel the young man and advise him professionally in regard to various illnesses. It is in a letter to Dr. Carus that we find Schumann's first description, at age 19, of a psychosomatic hand disorder which will be mentioned again shortly.

Interestingly, his next set of songs, composed while he was still a law student, was set to poems written by a physician, Dr. Justinus Kerner, well known for his interest in psychotherapy and hypnosis. These early compositions were not well received. "Your songs have many defects, a great many, and I would like to call them the sins of youth," wrote Gottlob Wiedebein, a prominent Kapellmeister. It was after this painful rejection of his early musical efforts that Schumann decided to turn his talents and energies again in the direction of literary work, specifically music criticism. He successfully organized and published Leipzig's influential *New Journal for Music*. Schumann himself did most of the writing, and all of the editing. From time to time, usually very quickly and in a sudden burst of inspiration, he would also write music, and for ten years composed exclusively for the piano. These highly original works, for example *Carnaval, Davidsbündlertänze, Kreisleriana*, and the four great solo sonatas, were considered at that time to be almost unplayable, but today enjoy the reputation of keyboard masterworks. The composition of songs was totally suppressed during that decade.

Schumann's Relationship with the Young Pianist Clara Wieck

The first time they met, at a party given by Dr. and Mrs. Carus, Clara was a pretty, 8-year-old child prodigy performing miracles at the piano, while Robert was an unhappy law student of 18, yearning to take music lessons. There seems to have been a mixture of attraction and rivalry from the beginning of their relationship, which later became one of the most productive marriages in music history.

Schumann probably envied Clara Wieck's pianistic skills, which clearly surpassed his own. He would often tease and berate her for the brilliant but superficial virtuoso literature she excelled at and loved to play. He also resented the undivided attention Clara received from her father, Friedrich Wieck, who for a while was his piano teacher as well. Wieck had divorced Clara's mother and was grooming the girl to be Europe's leading star pianist. To her, Schumann was like an older brother.

They often played together, and she jealously observed his escapades with a succession of older girl friends, one of whom, Ernestine von Fricken, was her friend as well and became Schumann's fiancée for over a year. Growing up in Leipzig, where Schumann had become a prominent music critic, Clara was the only pianist willing and able to perform his highly original and extremely difficult piano compositions, and he wrote many of them expressly for her. After she entered puberty, there was a strong element of sexual attraction.

Schumann's own promising career as a performer had been shattered by the disability of his right hand, originating in prolonged, unsupervised practicing, and he had suffered a psychiatric breakdown at age 23, a suicidal panic and depression. Two years later, when Clara was 15, he kissed her erotically for the first time, and she nearly fainted. At this time, Schumann was living with a male companion, the pianist Ludwig Schunke, and harbored passionate feelings not only for women but also for men, the so-called "Davidsbündler." Some of these were imaginary companions, internal self-objects that he often projected into prose writings and musical compositions, especially the moody, feminine, masochistic "Eusebius," and the masculine, daringly aggressive "Florestan." Other "Davidsbündler" were fellow artists and musicians, drinking buddies, or journalists working for his newspaper. Wieck knew them all quite well, and he strenuously objected to any physical contact between his teenage daughter Clara, and the gifted but disturbed Schumann.

This attitude was not shared by Schumann's elderly mother. Indeed, following one of Clara's concerts in Zwickau, she broached the subject of marriage, and strongly urged Clara to be Robert's wife. The following year, Frau Schumann died, and Robert, not wanting to attend the funeral or see his family, visited Clara instead. With her he attempted to complete the work of mourning, and they finally decided, secretly, to become engaged. When Wieck found out about this, he tried in every way possible to keep the lovers apart, and to prevent their marriage. Since permission for a woman to marry before age 21 necessitated parental consent at that time, Clara with Robert's assistance, decided to take legal action against her father.

COMPOSITION OF "I WAS CRYING IN MY DREAM"

The year before his marriage, 1839, had been unrelentingly stressful for Schumann. An attempt to resettle in Vienna, where marriage would have been possible without Wieck's consent, had failed. There were several deaths in Schumann's family, including that of a brother, and he was again suicidally depressed. One can hear the melancholia in his gloomy *Corpse Fantasy* for solo piano, retitled (at Clara's suggestion) *Nightpieces* (*Nachtstücke*, op. 23). She urged him to postpone the marriage for another year, which made him very angry. "All hope has disappeared," he wrote her. "If you had been with me, Clara, I would have been ready to put you and me to death." On July 16, 1839, Clara went to court against her father, whose response was to argue for an exorbitant financial settlement, were she to marry Schumann. Wieck then introduced evidence of Schumann's alcoholism, womanizing, shifting career goals, and psychiatric problems, including his hand disability. He told the court that Clara was "crazy" for wanting to marry such a man, and she, in an alarming confusion of loyalties, began taking pity on Wieck and siding with him. In January 1840, Schumann, separated from his fiancée, was ready to give up the fight. "I'm certainly not going to stop you if you want to go back to your father," he wrote her (Ostwald, 1985, pp. 152–155).

It was in this setting of extreme stress and uncertainty that Schumann started composing songs again. He had recently been working on a new piano sonata for Clara, but rage stirred by the court battle with Wieck seems to have interfered with his creative process, and work on the sonata had ground to a complete halt. Felix Mendelssohn, conductor of Leipzig's Gewandhaus Orchestra and a personal friend, had been trying to help Schumann, first by testifying in court on his behalf, then by advising him to try to overcome his creative work block by writing shorter pieces, perhaps some songs. The first lied Schumann composed at that point was, significantly, "The Farewell Song of a Fool" (op. 127, no. 5), to words by Shakespeare, a tribute to Mendelssohn's highly successful incidental music for *A Midsummer Night's Dream*.

There followed an outpouring of ideas and feelings exclusively through songwriting. Having found his voice at last,

Schumann was now able to integrate his sensitivity for vocal sound, nurtured in infancy by his mother, with the literary skills he had acquired from his father and honed as a music critic. Songwriting also served as a symbolic union with the distant Clara. During their engagement, they had been compiling poems by their favorite authors, hoping later to enlarge and perhaps publish this collection. Now Schumann was fusing voice, poetry, and the sound of the piano into songs. He would send Clara his lieder, and she reciprocated by singing and playing them. Psychologically, the songs were like transitional objects, helping to maintain continuity through shared communication (Ostwald, 1989). While composing songs, Schumann was able to gain physical freedom, and he enjoyed being unrestrained. Accustomed to working always at the piano, he now found himself pacing and moving around the room, while singing and humming. "This is an entirely different sort of music," he wrote Clara; "it doesn't first have to be borne through the fingers—[it's] much more immediate and melodic" (Ostwald, 1989, p. 158).

Many of his songs also allowed Schumann to ventilate rage and grief over the possibility that, should Wieck be the victor in court, he might have to give Clara up. The first song cycle he completed, called *Liederkreis* (op. 24), dealt with the problem of sexual frustration and separation from the beloved. The words were taken from Heinrich Heine, that most complex, ironic, and enigmatic of German poets. He also wrote songs about madness and suicide, for example "Poor Peter" (op. 53, no. 3). A collection of twenty-six lieder, titled *Myrtles* (op. 25), was intended, ironically, as a wedding present for Clara. A second *Liederkreis* (op. 39) captured the essence of Schumann's anguish as he dealt symbolically with the loss of his parents, the terror of abandonment, and the danger of false friendships.

Then came the famous *Dichterliebe* (op. 48), an autobiography of the poet's love, sixteen songs filled with reminiscence of the past and apprehension of the future. The text, again, is by Heine, freely adapted by Schumann to serve his own needs (for example, he tried to tone down Heine's mysogyny, by eliminating verses which were too disparaging and transforming the rest into more positive statements about women). Two of the *Dichterliebe* songs are about dreaming, and one of these, the thirteenth in the cycle, is "Ich hab' im Traum Geweinet" ("I was Crying in my Dream"). This is the song of central interest to us here, since it suggests unmistakably Schumann's fantasies or memories of painful separation from his mother, reported when he was a small child, and demonstrates his remarkable capacity, during adulthood, for artistic sublimation.

The Song

The original key is E flat minor, marked "Leise" (softly). The singer starts alone, "I cried and cried while dreaming," in a sustained melody, monotonously, using only two tones, B flat and C flat, which give the impression of a wailing voice, a child's crying, followed by five staccato chords on the piano, alternating the tonic and dominant, in a slow, dotted rhythm. Dotted rhythms recur regularly, almost obsessively, throughout much of Schumann's music, like signature themes, or "Leitmotifs." In this instance, the muted drumming on the piano suggests a funeral march. Then the singer continues, again alone—"I dreamt that you lay in your grave"—now moving into another key, C flat, and followed once more by the pianist's gloomy death march. The singer continues with an upward and then downward wail, interrupted by accented chords, "I woke up, and the tears were still flowing down from my cheek." There is a return to the home key of E flat minor, with two chords. Then an ominous pause—fermata!—of unspecified duration.

The second stanza repeats the first, softly. "I cried and cried while dreaming." Again five lugubrious chords interrupt the lonely singer. "I dreamt you had abandoned me." Funeral march again. "I woke up" (slight crescendo, followed by a single chord) "and was still crying (chord) such long and bitter tears." At this point the pianist, still in the minor key, begins playing sustained, more drawn-out chords, echoing the wailing effect of the voice, acknowledging the singer's tears, and leading directly into the third stanza.

Even more softly, the singer now joins the pianist; they are together at last, the human voice supported by two voices from the keyboard. "I cried and cried while dreaming, I dreamt you were true to me still." For a few measures the mood is more hopeful, and there is a crescendo, while the tonality moves into A flat minor. "I woke up, and yet a flood of tears was still flowing forth." Two sustained chords, followed by ghastly silence. Emptiness! Then, pianissimo, the piano plays five-chords, the funeral march again. Another dreadful silence, punctuated by two staccato chords. The song is over.

INTERPRETATION

The song we have heard is part of a cycle devoted to "a poet's love," and his mood at this moment is clearly related to grief and mourning, recurring themes in Schumann's life and work. What has been happening? In the song, the dreamer first envisioned his beloved (mother? Clara?) dead and buried. While dreaming, he sensed her presence and felt close to her. But upon awakening, with tears in his eyes, he came to the painful realization that he is now truly alone, completely separated from her, a state reinforced by the audible disjunction between voice and piano. The prolonged fermata indicated the poignant uncertainty of this situation. He then fell asleep again, and started dreaming once more, this time not about her death, but about having been abandoned. When he woke, he again found himself alone, and crying bitterly. But at least there was the sound of the piano to keep him company for a while. In his third dream, she has returned and is true to him still (fantasy of reunion? hopes of marriage?). Tragically, when he woke up for the third time, it became only too clear that it had only been a dream, an illusory togetherness. He was still alone, and mournfully shedding tears. The sense of isolation was echoed by the mournful few chords of the piano, playing alone, interrupted by prolonged silences, until it all came to an end.

Schumann's song has replicated his deepest existential anxiety—reunion with the mother is possible only in death—and touched on his most immediate dread, that losing Clara could silence him forever. Considering the childhood traumas which predated Schumann's venture into songwriting and other forms of creativity, one can speculate that "Ich hab' im Traum Geweinet" symbolizes, as Donald J. Marcuse puts it, "a dialogue of mother and infant of the most distressing and dysfunctional kind." Let me cite Dr. Marcuse's penetrating interpretation, written after he heard the song:

> More specifically, the voice and the piano seemed to represent the mother and baby, and their prevailing discontinuity, proceeding painfully exclusive of one another [. . .] the reification of a rather hopelessly unempathic failure in rapport, or real physical absence. I can "hear" the singer easily as the cry of the baby, with all the implications of awakening and falling asleep [. . . .] Each time the infant pauses, the mother is heard briefly in the rhythmic chords on the keyboard, separated, removed. But equally, I can "hear" the sustained, affectively intense and self-contained voice of the mother in the vocal line, nearly impossible to join, to connect with the beat of the infant unattached, apart. That is, I can "read" the dialogue either way, the point of merger comes where they briefly "drown" in one another, illustrating the opposite danger (as Schumann tried to drown himself in the Rhine), before it is necessary for one to continue without the other into oblivion, following the passage where the held chords engulf the voice [. . . .] The affective peak of the song for me is "in" the fermata—leaving to the discretion of the pianist how long to dare to prolong that rest, that interruption (extended disruption) in the mother/child bond, "rapprochement," whatever [Donald Marcuse, personal communication].

CONCLUSION

Singing is a universal experience, intimately connected in every culture to the need for communication of emotion and meaning between songwriters, performers, and listeners. From the viewpoint of the composer, memories of different life events, as well as the talent and desire for creative work, contribute equally to the final product. As Stuart Feder has pointed out in his analysis of a song by Charles Ives, "distortion of memory and artistic inspiration go hand in hand in creating [artistic] forms, each pressing the other into the service of accomplishing its goals" (1989, p. 320).

In this paper I have tried to show that painful memories of Schumann's childhood, creatively transformed into song with the help of Mendelssohn's encouragement and Heine's poetry, allowed the composer to achieve two interrelated goals. One was the immediate personal goal of mastering an agonizing separation from his fiancée whose father, in a triangular, oedipal kind of rivalry, was threatening Schumann's reputation and blocking his contact with the woman who symbolized the continuity of his life and the vitality of his creative work. The other goal, a long-range and deeply aesthetic one, was to find solutions to the problem of how affects and ideas can be synthesized artistically. The affects he was dealing with in the song under discussion could be heard in the sound of voice and piano, playing separately and together, while the idea of a grieving dreamer yearning for contact with the beloved was symbolized through verbal imagery, borrowed from a great poet. Thus Schumann, in attempting to solve a personal problem, successfully contributed to a unique art form, the German Lied, rooted in the Middle Ages and carried (through Weber and Schubert) into the aesthetic dynamic of nineteenth century music. As a creative genius, he was able to communicate affects and ideas that reach us even today, across the barriers of his own culture and time, thus assuring Schumann's immortality.

REFERENCES

Bowlby, J. (1969), *Attachment and Loss,* Vol. 1. New York: Basic Books.
Feder, S. (1989), Calcium light nights and other early memories of Charles Ives. In: *Fathers and Their Families,* ed. S. Cath, A. Gorwitt, & L. Gunsberg, Hillsdale, NJ: Analytic Press.
Ostwald, P. (1985), *Schumann: The Inner Voices of a Musical Genius.* Boston: Northeastern.
—— (1987), Leiden und Trauern im Leben und Werk Robert Schumanns. In: *Schumanns Werke—Text und Interpretation,* ed. A. Mayeda & K. W. Niemoller. New York: Schott.
—— (1989), The healing power of music: Some observations on the semiotic function of transitional objects in musical communication. In: *The Semiotic Bridge—Trends from California,* ed. I. Rauch & G. F. Carr.
Ruesch, J., & Bateson, G. (1951), *Communication: The Social Matrix of Psychiatry.* New York: W. W. Norton.
Schumann, R. (1825), Autobiography. Robert Schumann, Haus, Zwickau, Germany. Manuscript.

Chapter 11

Notes on Incest Themes in Wagner's *Ring* Cycle

George H. Pollock, M.D., Ph.D.

Goldman and Sprinchorn (1964) note that "perhaps no artist in the history of Western art, has ever had so much to say about his own life, works, and ideas as did Richard Wagner" (p. 11). Prolific composer of massive operatic works, librettist, essayist, a political activist who spent many years in exile as a result of his activities, Wagner wrote extensively on drama, philosophy, opera, music, art, and politics. On the other side of the coin, Goldman and Sprinchorn point out that over ten thousand articles about Wagner's life and work have appeared over the past hundred years. If Wagner was a controversial figure in his own lifetime, he remains so today because of the major role his music played during the Third Reich. This came about not only because of Wagner's own virulent anti-Semitism and his son Siegfried's support of the Nazis (he was director of the opera house at Bayreuth and a prolific though minor composer), but because Hitler saw Wagner's operas in general, and the great *Ring* cycle in particular, with its use of Norse legends, its tales of gods and heroes, as fitting "theme music" for the fantasied Thousand Year Reich. (One wonders what the Nazis were doing during performances of *Götterdämmerung*. Had they truly understood Wagner's ideas, they would have predicted the firey end of the Third Reich. There was not to be an eternal fatherland populated by gods who control all, but instead, there would be a final curtain call with applause for the death of

Portions of this essay were presented at the symposium on "The Threat to the Cosmic Order: Psychological, Social, and Health Implications of Richard Wagner's *Ring of the Nibelung*," June 8–9, 1990, under the auspices of the Department of Psychiatry and the Health Program for Performing Artists of the University of California, San Francisco.

tyranny.) At any rate, Wagner's musical genius is such that today his work has come to be considered on its own merits as an essential part of the repertoire. Magee (1968), for example, believes that the deciding factor in the survival and popularity of a particular opera is the music alone. Certainly, one cannot dismiss a pivotal figure such as Wagner because of his biases and prejudices, without first considering what he had to say and create. Much has been written about Wagner's views on politics, revolution, philosophy, myths and their derivation, his anti-Semitism, his relationship to Nietzsche, vegetarianism, and his innumerable affairs with his closest friends' wives. But, as Magee also notes, were it not for Wagner's music, none of this would be of much interest.

Wagner himself knew that his music played a key role in "Bringing what had been unconscious to consciousness" (Magee, 1968, p. 80). This is the essential element that makes Wagner's ideas of interest in the context of this volume.

The focus of this essay will be on Wagner's life course as expressed in *The Ring* operas, with the attendant themes of incest, aging, immortality, and death. The discussion will be a discursive one in which the basic biographical facts of Wagner's life may, as it were, be read against the recurring themes that run throughout his body of work, most especially, of course, *The Ring*.

Wagner's parents were Carl Friedrich and Johanna Rosina Wagner; Richard was their ninth child (Millington, 1987). Carl was an amateur actor and costume designer. Both he and his wife Johanna had numerous extramarital affairs—Johanna, for example, was not, as she claimed, the illegitimate daughter of Prince Constantine of Saxe-Weimar-Eisenach, but his mistress. Thus, there is a question of whether Ludwig Geyer, an actor-painter-playwright friend of Carl's, slept with Johanna while her husband was alive. Certainly, Geyer was a close friend of both Wagners, and Johanna took the infant Richard to see Geyer, having to cross one hundred miles of enemy occupied territory to do so (this was in 1813 at the time of the Napoleonic Wars). Millington suggests "that Johanna urgently wished to show the baby to its father" (1987, p. 2). Carl Friedrich Wagner died on November 23, 1813, when Richard was 6 months old, and Geyer immediately took over the family. Johanna and Geyer were married on August 28, 1814, six months before the birth of their daughter, Cacilie, of whom Richard was later to become particularly fond. Geyer was a good father to his large family, and he insisted that Richard be sent to an excellent boarding school. But when Geyer's health became precarious because of tuberculosis, and he could no longer work, Richard returned home. Johanna would ask the boy to play the piano for his sick stepfather, and Geyer is known to have remarked on the boy's talent. Richard was 8 years old when Geyer died. No firm conclusions can be reached about Richard's paternity, but in practical terms, Geyer was the only father Richard knew. We must also assume, however, that there remained the distant but powerful image in the unconscious of Richard Wagner, of Carl Friedrich Wagner who had vanished so early, but whose existence inevitably would have continued to resonate throughout his son's life.

Richard was described as an abnormally sensitive and imaginative boy who suffered from nightmares. "Each night he would startle the household by wakening out of ghostly dreams and screaming" (Watson, 1979, p. 25). Loneliness had a special terror for him, and he continued to have grotesque nightmares all his life. The death of Carl Friedrich when Richard was 6 months old, and the death of his 5-year-old sister six months later, at a time when Johanna their mother was involved with Geyer and pregnant with his child, must have brought an atmosphere of anguish and turmoil to the household, and doubtless contributed to Richard's night terrors.

Wagner's abilities, which played so important a role in his later creative life, surfaced early. At the age of 4, he made his only appearance as an actor, in Schiller's *Wilhelm Tell*. (Both Wagner's father, an amateur actor, and particularly Geyer, who in addition to his other abilities, had occasional roles in the Dresden Opera company formed by the composer Carl-Maria von Weber, may be assumed to have been influential in Wagner's early development of artistic abilities—it was, as it were, in the air he breathed in childhood.) Not only was there the piano playing that Geyer had remarked upon, but compositions; in 1820, Richard wrote two overtures; he was 7 years of age.

Richard was strongly influenced by the world, musical criticism,
and tales of E. T. A. Hoffmann. Wagner's first opera, *The Wedding*, had occult themes related to Hoffmann's writings. Wagner
destroyed the libretto of this work, leaving only the music for
the opening scene and a synopsis of the plot. It is worth re-
counting the bare bones of the plot because the themes of love
and death that were to run through all of Wagner's operas are
present here in this very early work. Codolt, a family enemy,
sets his sights on Ada, who is marrying another. On the wedding night, he forces his way into her chamber where she awaits
her new husband. She struggles with him, and with superhu-
man strength throws him out of the tower window through
which he entered. He falls to his death. Revenge is demanded,
but the bride's father averts this by saying that God's judgment
will fall on the murderer at the time of Codolt's funeral. Ada
comes to the funeral, and when she sees Codolt's corpse, she
sinks lifeless upon the body. This first opera ends like so many
of Wagner's later operas, with the death of both the leading
male and female characters. The oedipal themes of the "outsider" trying to force his way into a marital relationship were
to be repeated in many of Wagner's later works (Codolt's death
plunge from the phallic tower after being expelled through a
window by Ada might be seen as a highly compressed birth
scene combined with punishment for oedipal wishes). It is my
belief that this thematic repetition and perseveration tells us
not only of Wagner's lifelong preoccupation with death as the
reward for incest, but foretells the fate that is presented in the
final opera of *The Ring*, *Götterdämmerung*. Here, it is not only
the individual, but the whole social order that is plunged into
the abyss. Reflected here also is the typical ending that Wagner
derived from his study of Sophocles' Oedipus trilogy, where
both female and male characters perish in the finale, leaving
no survivors. In other words, for the participants, it is truly the
end of the world, for when they die nothing of them remains.
The murder of Laius leads inexorably to the marriage of Oedipus and Jocasta, and after this is revealed, to the destruction of
Thebes itself. The actions of individuals bring down society.
    Even though Wagner never mastered classical Greek, his love
for Greek culture and legends began at age 8 in 1821 when he

heard about the Greek war of independence. The Greeks were fighting for their freedom after 400 years of Turkish rule. The Greek language was kept alive throughout that period by the Greek Orthodox priests who taught it secretly in mountain hideaways. This preservation of the language enabled the society to remain cohesive long enough to rise up and fight the oppressor. It was a war with enormous romantic appeal, which indeed attracted such people as the romantic poet Byron. Richard's fascination with Greek mythology and history, we may surmise, was reinforced by the stories of this real life struggle for freedom. This may not only have led him into Greek culture, to the Oedipus of Sophocles, and to Aeschylus and his Oresteia plays (see Ewans [1982] for a comparison of Wagner and Aeschylus and *The Ring* and the Oresteia), but also influenced in some measure his later political involvements. I have studied thematic perseveration in other musicians and artists (Pollock, 1982, 1989) and believe that the creator's basic themes get reworked and elaborated and the thread can be identified and then correlated with biographical details.

As we have seen, Wagner's early life included the deaths of his father, sister, and the man who was truly his father, Geyer, when Richard was 8 years old. At 14, when he was writing his first major dramatic work, Richard, having used Geyer's name throughout his childhood, again took his father's name, Wagner. Thus, we see a clear connection between loss, death, and creativity in Wagner's life. The first major work, taking place in adolescence, causes Wagner to effectively resurrect the dead father by taking his last name. In doing so he simultaneously acknowledges his loss whilst affirming the powerful and essential connection with Carl Friedrich Wagner. It may also have been a way of distancing himself from the oedipal issues that he would have been reworking at that age. By attaching himself to the mythological father, whom he knew only by repute, he could contain and minimize the dangerous feelings of oedipal triumph resulting from Geyer's death when the boy was 8 years old. At the same time, it is noteworthy that throughout his life, Wagner was accustomed to wear the painter's smock that was Geyer's preferred garb.

Had he not been a composer, Wagner would have been significant as an essayist and thinker. He wrote his principal prose
essays between the years 1848 and 1851, a period of profound
turmoil for him, with both internal and external crises. From
1847 to 1853, when he began *The Ring*, he wrote no music.
Goldman and Sprinchorn mention that during this time,
Wagner wrote "a series of theoretical treatises designed to explain the nature of his projected artwork and the circumstances,
political, cultural, and artistic, which made its realization necessary" (p. 13). This may perhaps be viewed less as a period when
he "couldn't write any music" and more as one of intellectual
reorganization. This was also the period when he was active
politically. He was involved in the May 1849 Dresden Revolution, as a result of which, he had to flee Germany. He settled
in Zurich where he lived until 1859, and it was there that he
composed two-thirds of *The Ring*, and began *Tristan*. In later
years, when Wagner no longer wrote formal essays, he still
addressed intellectual and philosophical topics in his many letters and had many conversations about these topics with his
friends. In his thinking, Wagner was both original and derivative. He was stimulated by the ideas of others, he could integrate
them into his own thoughts, he could formulate what he experienced at a very deep level, and he was very resourceful and
versatile.

His use of myths and legends as the basis of his work was
part of a major cultural trend in his day. The Brothers Grimm,
collectors of folktales, had been members of the Göttingen
seven, a group of university professors who had protested
against despotism in 1837, and their work must surely have
been familiar to Wagner. As Michaelis-Jena (1970) notes:
"[T]he Romantics. . . . saw folk literature as a product of natural
evolution, distinct from the deliberate culture of their age, an
expression of wisdom and fundamental truth . . ." (p. 5). The
Grimms, however, saw folktales "as the debris of myths, primeval beliefs, religion, early customs and law. . . . ancestral reminiscences to be collected for the investigation of ancient German literature, and to be treated with respect" (p. 5). It was
perhaps this latter view of folktales and myth that was closest
to Wagner's own. It may have been this grasping for historical

facts amongst myths and legends that has caused some commentators to accuse him of a kind of fake historicity. In his "making the unconscious conscious," the attention he paid to dreams and the "dreamlike" condensations of myth, and their role in his creative life as a composer, he broke new ground.

As we have seen, Wagner had been accomplished from an early age, playing the piano and writing music. Throughout his life he was notable for his all-round ability in every aspect of the staging of operatic works. He wrote the librettos as well as the music, had a hand in the design of costumes and scenery, and all the other innumerable technicalities involved in presenting an opera. In this we may see, perhaps, in addition to Wagner's innate abilities, the influence of the multitalented father, Geyer.

There are many frames of reference one can use in approaching Wagner: there were his operas, there was his place in the music of his time, there were myth and legend, philosophy, and the historical currents of the period and the effects they had upon his ideas and creativity. For example, George Bernard Shaw (1911) saw *The Ring* as a sociopolitical drama. Alberich, the dwarf, renounces love and beauty for gold and power. Others have seen *The Ring* as a reenactment of the ancient Greek drama of Oedipus; still others understand the cycle as a religious statement. Alternatively, it might be seen as symbolically portraying the life course: birth, growth and development, decline, death. There are those who would see *The Ring* as Wagner's autobiography. And indeed, we can perhaps only fully understand *The Ring* by considering each and every one of these aspects.

First, however, let us take a look at Wagner the man. Wagner's affairs with his friends' wives were legendary, yet paradoxically, Hans von Bülow, with whose wife Wagner had three illegitimate children and later married, spoke of " 'this glorious, unique man whom one must venerate like a god' " (Wagner, quoted in Magee, 1968, p. 32). Wagner's affairs, which were well known even during his marriages, did not appear to interfere at all with his creativity. Similarly, his revolutionary-political activities, and the fact that he lived in exile for a period of time, his fiscal problems, did not diminish his creativity, even though they did cause him some passing anguish. External traumas, which would otherwise demolish less "strong" individuals, seemingly did not impair Wagner's creativity—instead, they may even have contributed to it.

There were objections to Wagner's use of the incest theme in his own day. He dealt openly with incest on stage, and many people continue to be especially disturbed by the passionate love scenes between brother and sister which culminate in sexual intercourse and pregnancy. For example, in the second act of *Die Walkure*, where Wotan says:

> What wrong
> Did these two do
> When spring united them in love?

And when Fricka (goddess of marriage) cries out:

> My heart shudders,
> my brain reels;
> Marital intercourse
> Between brother and sister!
> When did anyone live to see it:
> Brother and sister *physically* lovers?

Wotan replies:

> You have lived to see it today.
> Learn from this
> That things can ordain themselves
> Though they never happened before.
> That these two love each other
> Is obvious to you.
>
> Listen to some honest advice:
> Smile on their love, and bless
> Siegmund and Sieglinde's union
> Their sweet joy
> Will reward you for your blessing [Magee, 1968, p. 35].

And then Wotan, speaking for Wagner, says:

> You want to understand always,
> Only what you are used to:
> My mind is reaching out towards
> Things that have never happened [Magee, 1968, p. 35].

Oedipal sexuality is an important theme in both *Siegfried* and *Parsifal*, as Magee notes (p. 36). Wagner anticipated Freud's observations in many ways, for example, libido theory, repression, the Oedipus complex, guilt and punishment. Magee refers to the fact that the operas of Wagner's artistic maturity are "like animated textbooks of psychoanalysis" (p. 36). Wagner had referred to music bringing the unconscious to consciousness and in this he captures, too, the essence of psychoanalytic thought. Ideas that are otherwise unexpressed and unknown in consciousness can be expressed in music, in which the essence of the emotions are represented in sound. Fifty years later Freud was to develop a scientific method of describing the functioning of the psyche through his clinical and theoretical formulations, not only regarding the Oedipus complex but in his writings about the unconscious and repressed—the essential source of all art. As Wagner had done, Freud turned to the plays of Sophocles for inspiration and instruction. In Wagner's works one finds the forbidden (such as incest) expressed openly, and the consciousness of performers and audience alike reverberates to its direct, clear presentation. I believe, as do others, that what Wagner produced stems thematically from what he perceived within himself and perhaps what he acted upon. Had he been involved in an incestuous relationship with one or more of his sisters? He is said to have been particularly close to Cacilie, his younger sister/stepsister, and to Rosalie. (As has been noted elsewhere, incestuous feelings for the parent are frequently expressed with a sibling, where the relationship is more manageable than it would be with a parent.) Whether or not there was a physical relationship between Wagner and one or more of his sisters is beside the point. What is significant is Wagner's ability to go straight to the sources within him and tap them in the service of his art. That he could take the reality of those overwhelming feelings and use their reality as the organizing theme in a series of works of art is undoubtedly true.

Wagner's impact on the society and culture of his time was extraordinary. His audiences were faced with the darkest, the most powerful, the most essential themes of human existence, and such was the power of Wagner's music, that it was impossible for listeners to see his operatic works as mere entertainments outside their own existence. Willy nilly, they, like audiences today, were drawn into the dramas of incest, love, murder, rape. They could see themselves as the flawed heroes and heroines, struggling with their impulses in a world they could not control, be forced to confront themselves as the Alberichts of this world, hungry for the power that comes with gold. They could see themselves as Siegfrieds and Sieglindes acting upon their feelings despite taboos against their expression. Wagner made his audiences confront their own mortality, their own frailty, the melding of power and helplessness in the face of the cosmos that lies at the center of human experience. As Magee (1968) notes: "Some were overwhelmed, and worshipped. Others regarded his almost incredible lack of restraint as shocking or frightening, or mad, or immoral, or in some other way deeply disturbing" (p. 40).

Wagner's idealization of the Greek theater was based on his ideas of what constitutes great art: "a religious occasion, the participation of the entire community, and the cooperation of all the arts in the dramatic representation of a mythic action" (Goldman and Sprinchorn, 1964, p. 19). Commenting on creativity, Wagner likened the birth of music to the birth of a child in all its cosmic power: "By virtue of its nature and origin, then, music carries an almost unbearable weight of meaning" (Wagner, cited in Rather, 1979, p. 138).

In his operatic works, Wagner focused on legends that were tragic in outcome and where suffering and death, and the total destruction of the protagonists' world, as in the story of Oedipus, are the major themes. Oedipus, the tragic hero, struggles, survives, kills, mutilates, and ultimately the line he created is destroyed (Pollock, 1986).

Despite, or perhaps because of, his intense relationship with dreams and the dreamlike condensations of myths and legends, Wagner could write, when he was in the midst of his most passionate romance, "I have at last found a quietus that in wakeful nights helps me to sleep. This is the genuine, ardent longing for death, for absolute unconsciousness, total non-existence. Freedom from all dreams is our only final salvation" (Wagner [1856], as cited in Goldman and Sprinchorn [1964, p. 27]).

There is a duality in all of human experience, between life and death, love and hate. But it seems particularly marked in Wagner, this larger than life figure, passionate in love and revolution, a man who truly lived in the world, and yet, as the quotation suggests, simultaneously longed for intrauterine oblivion.

We see and hear this in *Tristan and Isolde*, which is filled with the dualism of love (life) and death, love and hate, and I believe we can see these elements most clearly in *The Ring* and its underlying oedipal theme.

Wagner believed that Greek culture, with its roots in religion, and its direct expression of religious feeling through the drama, in which poetry, music, dance, song, were brought together to celebrate the glory and truth of existence, and with its roots firmly set in the Greek religion, reached its high point in Greek tragedy. This was a drama in which the whole community participated. Wagner like Freud believed that with the fragmentation of the arts and religion human beings came to look on their bodies and feelings with shame, suspicion, fear and guilt—especially in terms of instinctual love. Life became a burden, filled with sin and rewarded at death by an existence of eternal bliss. Wagner felt these religious beliefs, which had developed after the heyday of Greek classical culture, were anti-art. Man was alienated from his own nature, especially his emotions, and had the feeling that he was a "guilty worm."

Rightly or wrongly, Wagner felt that religion had come to be based on the celebration of death rather than life, and that inevitably this was hostile to the expression of spirituality.

The decline of the theater from the Greek pinnacle of religious experience to one where people came to be entertained with frivolity and emptiness, appeared to Wagner to be vulgar, socially exclusive, grotesque, and fragmented. He forbade the customary ballet to be performed before his operas began. Aside from being light entertainment to, as it were, warm up the audience, the ballet presumably allowed latecomers to be seated. Wagner wanted to return to the older, more meaningful Greek ideal where all the elements of the arts were unified in an enactment that was in essence religious. In addition to social and political dimensions, he was concerned with music-drama that expressed inner emotions and not just the outer motives that carry the plot. Myth was the ideal—ageless in that it could reach beyond time and place and deal with the core of universal truths. His sense of myth as speaking direct from the psyche of humanity, his intuitive grasp of symbolism (as Magee [1968], points out, he was the "progenitor of the Symbolist Movement in French poetry"), gave him the ability to unify all the elements into an artistic whole, as the Greeks had done. Drama was the means, music the end, and the participants, both performers and audience, could experience what was being communicated in a more total sense.

Wagner of all composers can only be understood by considering all aspects of his life: some regard him as politically naive, a utopian. The essence of a utopia, with its belief in the perfectibility of human institutions, laws, and social conditions, is that the human inhabitants become passive observers of laws which are agreed to be for the benefit of all. A utopia is not a place for individualists. This leads directly to Wagner's romantic idealization of ancient Greece. Central to Greek understanding of the human condition was its innate passivity. The gods were seen as controlling the lives of human beings entirely, as they fought and loved and connived on Mount Olympus. The Trojan War, for example, was understood by the Greeks as being entirely an artefact of politicking by the gods. Human beings could struggle to have control over their destiny, but they could never win against the power of the gods. This aspect of Greek thought is certainly apparent in Wagner's operas, particularly in *The Ring* cycle. Magee (1968) points out that even Wotan, the ruler of the gods, is "from the very beginning of *The Ring* at the mercy of forces he is powerless to control . . ." (pp. 14–15). He also says:

> [R]eality for Wagner is always found in the psyche, not in the external world. . . . It has been said of *The Ring* that in the deepest sense there is only one character, the different "characters" being aspects of a single personality, so that the work is a portrait of the psyche as well as a depiction of the world [Magee, 1968].

If we look at the passivity in the face of fate, along with the portrait of the inner world of the characters as aspects of the inner world of one character, we may with little difficulty conclude that we are looking into Wagner's spirit itself.

THE THEMES OF WAGNER'S OPERAS

We will now briefly outline the plots of Wagner's main operas:

1. *Rienzi* (1837–1840). The opera is filled with violence and rebellion, murder and plotting, assassination and treachery, fighting and killing. In the last act, Rienzi and his sister die together in the collapse of a burning building.

2. *The Flying Dutchman* (1840–1841). This is a music-drama rather than an opera, and it is based on Heine's version of the legend of the Flying Dutchman. The captain is condemned to sail the seas until Judgment Day unless he finds a woman who will love him faithfully until death. He finds Senta, who is loved by Eric. While she pledges her love for the Captain, Eric pleads with her to stay with him. Overhearing this and fearing he has been forsaken, the Captain flees to his ship. Senta throws herself off a cliff into the sea, the phantom ship sinks, and Senta and the Dutchman are seen rising in each other's embrace and floating upwards. Senta has sacrificed herself in order to be with the man she loves.

3. *Tannhauser* (1842–1845). Elisabeth and Tannhauser love one another. Elisabeth is loved by Wolfram. At the end of the opera, Tannhauser sees her body on a bier, and sinks down on her coffin and dies.

4. *Lohengrin* (1845–1848). Again a legend of battles and killing, ending with Elsa and her brother Godfrey joined. Elsa dies in her brother's arms while her husband, Lohengrin, departs

because she has betrayed him by asking him the forbidden questions about his name and birthplace. (The latter is a standard folklore motif.)

5. *Tristan and Isolde* (1854–1859). Tristan has been raised by his uncle, his parents having died while he was a baby. He slays a knight who is betrothed to Isolde, daughter of the Irish king. The wounded Tristan, keeping his identity secret, is cared for by Isolde, who is skilled in the healing arts. Isolde and Tristan fall in love, each believing their love is unrequited. Isolde decides to take a death potion; Tristan, thinking she will marry another, decides to share it with her. A love potion is substituted, and they declare their love for one another. Soon after arriving in Cornwall, Tristan is badly wounded by one of the followers of the slain knight. Tristan and Isolde die together.

6. *The Mastersingers of Nuremberg* (1845–1867). Beckmesser and von Stolzing both love Eva. Hanns Sachs is the kind father who helps von Stolzing in his quest for love and fulfillment with Eva—something perhaps that Wagner would have liked if he had had a father beyond his early years. Wagner may have seen himself as Walther, helped by an older man to achieve fulfilling adulthood and resolve his own oedipal competitions and conflicts. It is worth noting, that in this, the only one of Wagner's operas that is said to be based on a real life story, there is no death action.

7. *The Ring of the Nibelungs* (see below).

8. *Parsifal* (1845–1882). Here Wagner combined three legends together. This is an opera full of magic, deceptions, death, grief, the death of a former king. Kundry, the main female character, "sinks gently into the sleep of death" (Kobbé, 1919, p. 277).

9. *Leubald and Adelaide* (1827–1828). As noted earlier, this was Richard Wagner's first monumental romantic drama, begun when he was 14 years old. (He planned to set *Leubald* to music once he had learned about music theory.) Sabor (1989) notes that Wagner wrote to a friend that he remembered a dream from his youth in which he saw Shakespeare and spoke with him (p. 40). It was this fascination with Shakespeare that played an important role in Wagner's writing of *Leubald*. Wagner himself noted that the plot of the play was based loosely

on Hamlet. He said: " 'The difference was that my hero, con-fronted with the ghost of a father murdered in similar circum-stances and crying for vengeance, is roused to such violent action that he commits a series of murders and finally becomes insane' " (Wagner [1879] quoted in Sabor [1989]). It is of inter-est to see how the recurring themes of violence, death, and oedipal conflicts appeared in this the very first theatrical work that Wagner wrote. Wagner himself noted that in *Leubald* he killed off so many characters that he had to bring them back as ghosts in the last acts "for want of living characters" (Mander and Mitchenson, 1977, p. 24).

Finally, to conclude this brief discussion of the operas, let us note the themes of two operas that Wagner composed very early in his career. In *The Wedding* (1832–1833), treachery and mistrust are in evidence at the wedding to which former ene-mies are invited. In *The Fairies* (1832–1834), the themes include the death of a father king, loss of a wife and children, magical changes, deception, choices between a mortal's death on earth or immortality in fairyland, wars and death, the underworld and the eventual reunion with the hero and his wife who be-come the Fairy King and Queen. This was Wagner's first com-pleted opera, finished when he was aged 20. The reference to death is clear in the turning to stone of the key characters.

WAGNER, OEDIPUS, AND THE RING OF THE NIBELUNGS

The Ring of the Nibelungs

1. The Rheingold (1851–1854)
2. The Valkyries (1851–1856)
3. Siegfried (1851–1871)
4. The Twilight of the Gods (1848–1874)

Rank, in his magnificent 1912 monograph on *The Incest Theme in Literature and Legend* (1992), says that Wagner, by seducing other men's wives, avenged himself later in life for his mother's apparent infidelities. The winning of the sexual relationship with the wife of another and his fathering children with her

(Cosimá von Bülow, daughter of Franz Liszt) was an acting out of his oedipal triumph (the death of Geyer when Wagner was 8) and the consummation of the incestuous feeling toward the mother. Rank emphasized "that the incest complex plays the greatest role in the dramatic production of Richard Wagner" (1912, p. 534), and in his actual love life. His affair with Mathilda, the wife of his friend and supporter, Wesendonck, antedated his subsequent impregnations of Cosimá while she was still married to von Bülow, and again represented the oedipal triumph over the father. His subsequent marriage to Cosimá could be interpreted as the total possession of the mother—sexually and in all caretaking aspects. In his operas, we also frequently find the theme of the death of the father, completing what Wagner may have at first fantasied, and then in the case of father Geyer, came to pass in reality. This must indeed have been an overwhelming experience for an 8-year-old. (As noted earlier, perhaps his taking of his father's name when he was 14 was in part a way of offsetting this disturbing oedipal triumph, by connecting himself to a man he never knew.)

In *The Ring*, he also introduces sibling incest and pregnancy. Wagner was on extremely affectionate terms with his sisters, and especially with Rosalie, who died young. He apparently was not close to his brothers. In *The Valkyries*, Siegmund kidnaps his beloved sister from her husband and then kills him in battle. Rank sees this as the reworking of the older and more powerful drama of killing the father and possessing the mother. Sibling incest may reflect a displacement of the oedipal drama from the parents to the sibling. *The Ring* cycle concludes with the death of Siegfried and the suicide of Brunnhilde.

Rather discusses Wagner's understanding of the Oedipus story and how it was shaped by him into the operatic tetralogy that in allegorical and symbolic fashion depicts political, social, and psychological oedipal conflict. Rather quotes Wagner referring to Sophocles' Oedipus plays as a " 'depiction of the whole history of humanity, from the origins of society to the necessary downfall of the state' " (Wagner, cited by Rather, 1979, p. xviii). Was he in this expressing a view similar to that of Marx, who saw the eventual dissolution of the state as the ideal political development?

Rather (1979) asserts that Wagner's studies of the Oedipus trilogy are essential to an understanding of *The Ring*. As a former revolutionary, friend and admirer of the anarchist Bakunin, Wagner felt that the world in which he lived was too aggressive, egoistic (narcissistic), and superficial. He anticipated Freud by fifty years when he stated that the attainment of a more ideal world required the raising to consciousness of the unconscious. Wagner also felt music was related to dreams—his operas clearly make this point. He also felt that human beings were innately self-destructive, in effect that the world would inevitably end in ruins. The breakdown of culture, values, ideals can lead to the death of society—in short, Götterdämmerung.

The song of the Nibelungs has its origins in old Nordic tales and poems dating back to the pre-Christian era of northern Europe. The medieval version of the epic dealt only with mortal men and women (Rather, 1979, p. 3). Although it uses pagan myths and traditions, it is clearly a work that comes out of a courtly Christian tradition. Wagner rewrote the story for his own dramatic purposes, also incorporating material from the pre-Christian Volsungsaga and the Icelandic Poetic Edda. This search for Nordic cultural "roots" resulted in the use of myths and legends to give a unity and a supremacy to the Nordic people—the racial myth that fueled the Nazi movement. The downfall of the gods, clearly stated in the final opera of *The Ring*, indicates Wagner's belief that lack of love, along with envy, greed, lust for gold and power are the basic causes of the ultimate disaster—death to the human race and to the land which becomes ashes; if you wish, the cremation of man.

The story of the Nibelungs was in the cultural air in Wagner's time. Several other poets and writers worked on the story (including the composer Felix Mendelssohn), but clearly Wagner made it his own. Wagner introduced several new elements to it, of which the incest motif is the most important (Rather, 1979, p. 43). In the completed *Ring*, the incest theme was given further elaboration, although several elements were either changed or eliminated from Wagner's original outline. Wotan, the chief God, condemns Siegmund to die at the hands of Hunding, Sieglinde's husband, in order to expiate his crime of incest. Sieglinde also dies and their child, Siegfried, is raised by

Mime, who teaches him the smith's art. At Mime's behest, he kills the dragon guarding the hoard of gold, and hence, the source of power. Siegfried learns that Mime plans to kill him and thus possess the hoard. Siegfried kills Mime and finds the Valkyrie Brunnhilde (was this regression to the earlier mother?), who is in the forest in a deep sleep and surrounded by a ring of fire. He awakens her, and she gives him secret knowledge, warning him to be faithful and to avoid deception. Siegfried gives her the all-powerful Nibelung ring; they pledge their faith to each other and the hero departs in search of new adventures. Without going into further details of the story, we find magic, betrayal of Brunnhilde by Siegfried, the murder of Siegfried by a stab in the back, the only vulnerable point where he can be killed, the quarreling of the two half-brothers who plotted Siegfried's death, and the eventual murder of one, Gunther, by his half-brother, Hagen, who also killed Siegfried.

Brunnhilde finally returns the ring to the "sisters in the water," the Rhine maidens. She then steps into Siegfried's funeral pyre. Hagen makes one more attempt to seize the ring (genital? power?) but is drowned. After Siegfried's death, Wotan, Valhalla, and the Gods are destroyed. Wotan is both father of Siegfried and Sieglinde and of Brunnhilde. "And when Siegfried first awakens Brunnhilde, he takes her to be his mother" (Rather, 1979, p. 47). In *The Ring* Wagner interpreted the elements of Sophocles' Oedipus as archaic reality. This is the thread that connects the elements of this enormous work.

Wagner, the former revolutionary, called the revolution the sublime goddess. He used the word *revolution* more than ten times in a signed article:

> I will destroy [the whole present order] for it has sprung from sin, its flower is misery and its fruit is crime. [The present order] makes millions the slaves of the few, and makes these few the slaves of their own power, their own riches. [It] makes labour a burden and an enjoyment to vice; [it compels half of mankind to perform the useless and harmful work of] soldiers, officials, speculators and money-makers . . . while the other half must support the whole edifice of shame at the cost of the exhaustion of their powers and sacrifice of all joys of life. [Down to its last trace] this insane order of things, compact of force, lies, care, hypocrisy, want, sorrow, suffering, tears, trickery and crime [must be destroyed] [Wagner, cited by Rather, 1979, pp. 47–48].

It was the downfall of society which Wagner saw as the real meaning of the Oedipus story. Incest was merely one of several instruments that led to this inevitable end. Oedipus is abandoned as a small baby because his murder of his father has been foretold. Laius exposes him on a hillside where he is found by a shepherd who takes him to the king and queen of Corinth who adopt and raise him. In Laius' desperate act, we see the beginning of the end. Jocasta was either powerless to prevent this or entirely abrogated her responsibilities toward her child. Learning from the oracle at Delphi that he will kill his father and marry his mother, Oedipus fled Corinth hoping, like his father, to avoid his fate, but at a crossroads he met and killed Laius. At Thebes he correctly answered the Sphinx's questions and won the hand of Jocasta, Laius' widow, in marriage. They had two daughters and two sons. When a plague descended on Thebes an oracle declared that the only way to rid the city of the plague was to punish the murderer of Laius. Oedipus learned the truth, blinded himself, and was exiled by Creon, Jocasta's brother. Does Oedipus blind himself so that he cannot see what he has done, a symbolic castration displaced from below, so that he will be unable to see Laius and Jocasta when he meets them in the underworld? Or is it a regression to his own intrauterine blind state? Whatever the meanings, this is Oedipus' response to his being the patricide and then oedipal victor and sexual possessor of his mother. Jocasta, the mother-wife, commits suicide when she learns of what has occurred. Their two sons, Eteocles and Polynices at first agree to rule alternate years over Thebes, but they come to blows and are slain. Creon becomes king—he is both Oedipus' uncle and his brother-in-law. He permits Eteocles to be buried, but decrees that Polynices' body shall be left for the vultures. Antigone buries Polynices and is condemned to be buried alive, despite the pleading of Creon's son, who loves her. After Antigone's death, Creon's son attempts to kill his father, and then commits suicide. Creon's wife commits suicide, and the story ends when Creon acknowledges that the rule of his house has been destroyed—the twilight of the gods.

It is important to note that Wagner does not believe that the relationship between Oedipus and Jocasta is a crime. The crime is homicide—it is the murder of Laius that leads to the marriage

of Oedipus and Jocasta. Ultimately, the murder of Laius leads
to the destruction of the state. In a sense, by their suicide and
blinding, Jocasta and Oedipus abrogate all responsibility toward the state, preoccupied only with their own situation. The
ship of state with no one at the helm runs aground. In the end,
everyone is dead (Rather, 1979). They leave no descendants.

Without going into Wagner's extension of the Oedipus story
to political structures, the emphasis on death, murder, deception, and envy-greed in the operas can enable us to gain new
insights into the Oedipus plays themselves. Thus, the incestuous union between Siegmund and Sieglinde, like that between
Oedipus and Jocasta, "is unnatural only by convention and not
by nature" (Rather, 1979, p. 55). The overthrow of the state or
existing rule by Antigone, and of the corrupt order of the Gods
by Siegfried, are both acts of saviors (revolutionaries), and each
is the child of an incestuous union. Siegfried and Antigone
were Wagner's parallels.

Sabina Spielrein published a paper on "Destruction as the
Basis of Becoming" in 1912. Only when the world had returned
to its origins could it be saved. "In symbolic form this is represented by the return of the ring (life) to its original home, out
of which it was taken" (1912, cited by Rather, 1979, p. 149).
Perhaps this is the meaning of *The Ring*—beginning in water
and then returning to water—a life course trajectory. This includes the oedipal phase, where Siegfried renders Wotan impo-
tent by shattering his upraised lance with his sword, then passing through the magic fire and consummating his union with
Brunnhilde. In doing so, the boy recognizes that he must not
sacrifice his manhood in deference to his father.

Wagner wrote to Liszt in 1853 that *The Ring* encompassed
the beginning and the end of the world, and I would add, of
the life course. What is true of the individual, Wagner seems
to say, is true of society. The death of the gods, thus, is the end
of the life course of the individual and of society, and reflects
pessimism about human invulnerability and immortality. We
live today in a society with the highest prison population in the
world, greater than that of South Africa or the former Soviet
Union. Per capita, we use more of the world's resources than
any other nation, yet we harbor large populations of very poor
people; tuberculosis, the disease of poverty, is on the rise again.

The land, air, and sea have become seriously polluted in the name of "progress." Too many of our resources go to building armaments rather than providing such things as prenatal care. There is a loss of belief in the possibility of changing any of our problems. The government is no longer regarded as being an effective instrument of change. It is hardly surprising that the images we create in art, in painting, theater, poetry, fiction, and the movies, are images of darkness and destruction, of the end of the world. In other words, we live in a world very close in reality to Wagner's intellectual and artistic world as set out in *The Ring*.

Yet Wagner's final statement in *The Ring* is not one of despair. "Instead we hear in its closing bars a harmonious blending of motifs associated with Brunnhilde and Siegfried, with the feminine and masculine principles, a triumphant synthesis of opposites" (Rather, 1979, p. 182).

In retrospect then, it looks as if Wagner's life consisted of repeated oedipal victories and the emotions attendant upon them. His multiple affairs with the wives of men who supported his work were repeated enactments of the oedipal victory. His parents' infidelities were a part of Wagner's childhood, and became in a sense an organizing theme of their son's life. It is not surprising then that the punishment for oedipal victory would be death. This thematic perseveration runs throughout his music and may be the basis of his innate pessimism.

Again, I wish to emphasize that these possible linkages, correlations, and formulations do not explain his musical, literary, and philosophical genius; they may give direction to it and we have seen how Wagner attempted to explore these in his internal and his external creations.

One brief note about the use of myth. In prior work on Thomas Chatterton, a young man who committed suicide in his late teens and whose father died before Chatterton's birth, I found that Chatterton's need to invent a history that antedated his existence seemed to be related to his desire to re-create a life with a father that he did not know. In some ways, I believe Wagner may well have been drawn to myth for a similar reason. Behind Geyer, the more prosaic "psychological father" of Wagner's childhood, lay the mythic image of Carl Friedrich

Wagner, known and unknown, remembered and forgotten. It is possible to see in Wotan a synthesis of these two fathers, the mystical godhead, and the ruler with very ordinary human foibles, whose power is shattered by his grandson, who in the process drags down the whole social order into the abyss.

REFERENCES

Ewans, M. (1982), *Wagner and Aeschylus: The Ring and the Oresteia*. New York & Cambridge, U.K.: Cambridge University Press.
Goldman, A., & Sprinchorn, E. (1964), *Wagner on Music and Drama: A Compendium of Richard Wagner's Prose Works*, tr. H. Ashton Ellis. New York: Da Capo Press.
Kobbé, G. (1919), *The Definitive Kobbé's Opera Book*, ed. Earl of Harewood. New York: G. P. Putnam's Sons, 1987.
Magee, B. (1968), *Aspects of Wagner*. Oxford & New York: Oxford University Press, 1988.
Mander, R., & Mitchenson, J. (1977), *The Wagner Companion*. New York: Hawthorn Books.
Michaelis-Jena, R. (1970), *The Brothers Grimm*. New York: Praeger.
Millington, B. (1987), *Wagner*. New York: Vintage Books.
Newman, E. (1933–1947), *The Life of Richard Wagner*, Vol. 2. New York: Cambridge University Press, 1976.
Pollock, G. H. (1982), The mourning-liberation process and creativity: The case of Kaethe Kollwitz. *The Annual of Psychoanalysis*, 10:333–353. New York: International Universities Press.
——— (1986), Oedipus examined and reconsidered: The myth, the developmental stage, the universal theme, the conflict and the complex. *The Annual of Psychoanalysis*, 14:77–106. Madison, CT: International Universities Press.
——— (1989), *The Mourning–Liberation Process*, Vols. 1 & 2. Madison, CT: International Universities Press.
Rank, O. (1912), *The Incest Theme in Literature and Legend*. Baltimore: Johns Hopkins University Press, 1992.
Rather, L. J. (1979), *The Dream of Self-Destruction: Wagner's Ring and the Modern World*. Baton Rouge: Louisiana State University Press.
——— (1990), *Reading Wagner—A Study in the History of Ideas*. Baton Rouge: Louisiana State University Press.
Sabor, R. (1989), *The Real Wagner*. London: Sphere Books.
Shaw, G. B. (1911), *The Perfect Wagnerite: A Commentary on the Nibelung's Ring*, 2nd ed. New York: Brentano.
Wagner, R. (1856), Letter to August Rockel, August 23, 1856. In: *Richard Wagner an August Rockel*, ed. La Mara [Ida Maria Lipsius]. Leipzig: Breitkopf & Härtel Verlag, 1903.
——— (1895–1899), *Richard Wagner's Prose Works*, Vols. 1–8, tr. W. A. Ellis. London: Kegan Paul, Trench, Trubner.
——— (1870), *My Life*, tr. A. Gran, ed. M. Whittall. New York: Cambridge University Press, 1983.
Watson, D. (1979), *Richard Wagner*. New York: Schirmer Books.

Chapter 12

Wagner's Use of the Leitmotif to Communicate Understanding

Morton F. Reiser, M.D.

I

Richard Wagner, in his prose essays ([1848–1851], including "Opera and Drama" [1850–1851] and "The Artwork of the Future" [1849]) (Goldman and Sprinchorn, 1964), asserted that it is "the poet's" compelling need to express and communicate deeply felt—otherwise inexpressible—inner feelings and thoughts that impels the composition of music-drama. Only a combination of poetry, music, and ballet in the theatrical setting, he said, would make the work convincing, and the otherwise inexpressible thoughts and feelings communicable. Eventually he came to feel that all the elements were not equal—but rather that the music dominated. When asked why *Götterdämmerung* had to end as it did, his reply was that he could not explain in words, but added that the music would make it entirely clear. After experiencing a good performance, he said, one would "understand," would "*know*" why.

He was right—it does work. Experiencing the performance does generate for the audience an "understanding" of the meaning(s) embedded in it—the inner thoughts and feelings expressed in and by the combination of music, poetry, and drama that makes up the whole work. But the "understanding" created in the audience members is, for them, no more communicable in words than it was for Wagner, who composed *The Ring* cycle out of a compelling need to give expression to the inner problems within himself that impelled its creation.[1] This

[1]Of course there is no way to be certain that the audience member's understanding is *exactly* the same as Wagner's. I think that it probably is, but that it may well encompass additional more uniquely personal issues as well.

is a particularly striking instance of a not uncommon, but incompletely understood, class or genre of phenomena that is encountered in many other settings. For example, it is quite familiar to psychoanalysts. The practicing analyst repeatedly experiences instances when—through the medium, and with the aid, of words—he induces understanding in the analysand; but without the message coming more than fleetingly, if at all, into the full conscious view of either party. Psychoanalysis, in referring to its version of this class of phenomena, uses terms such as *insight* and *mutative interpretation*, but naming something doesn't explain it. Whether occurring in music drama or in psychoanalysis, the observable manifestations seem highly similar. I don't know if musicology has given its version of this phenomenon a name, but as I have just implied, finding an explanation for this genre may constitute a challenge for students of music as well as for students of psychoanalysis. Is it possible that common psychobiological mechanisms could account for the similarities?

It was inevitable that this issue would come to the front of my mind in 1989 and 1990 when I had my first opportunity to experience *The Ring* in live performance (in its revivals at the Metropolitan Opera in New York). During both of these years I was deeply involved in studying the relationship of psychological to neurobiological mechanisms of memory, asking how the brain functions to enable the memory functions of the mind as they can be observed in the course of the psychoanalytic process. Consequently, I was in the process of working toward formulation of a unified mind–brain principle of memory organization during the very same time period that I was experiencing intense emotional responses during *Ring* performances. It was this combination of experiences that generated the ideas I wish to discuss here. They concern the way in which Wagner's use of the leitmotif may exploit basic memory mechanisms of mind–brain to facilitate the development of implicit "understanding" of implicit meanings in *The Ring*. These ideas, which include a neurobiologic as well as a psychoanalytic dimension, should complement and perhaps enrich concepts already available in the vast literature on the leitmotif. Interestingly, they suggest: (1) that Wagner implicitly "understood" the psychobiology of memory as we know it now, and (2) that study of his elaborate musical manipulations of the motifs might very well generate new ideas about the psychobiology of emotion and cognitive–emotional interactions, perhaps even develop empirically testable hypotheses.

II

The Ring of the Nibelungs, twenty-six years in creation, offers its audience seventeen hours of exposure to a concatenation of musical, poetic, and visual stimuli intricately interwoven into a cycle of four operas—comprising thirty-seven scenes that depict the complex relationships and experiences of thirty-four characters (sixteen of them main ones) over a time span of about forty years. The librettos were written first—in reverse order, starting with the last one. The composition of the music followed completion of the librettos and was written forwards, but with a hiatus of twelve years between the second and third acts of the third opera of the cycle! It must have been a gigantic challenge to hold these monumentally complicated stories together and to present them in a way that would render them accessible and sufficiently understandable to hold the attention and engage the emotional participation of audiences. The problem of assisting the memory of the audience loomed large. Wagner utilized a number of devices to this end.

First, he insisted that the four operas be performed on consecutive nights. Second, as part of the plot and ongoing action, he introduced narrations in which the characters summarized what had gone before. Third, the characters, stories, and events were extensively drawn from mythology. This, he felt, would render the thematic content and action of the plot familiar to the audience. Fourth, he supplied highly specific stage directions. For example, in the first act of *The Valkyrie*, the characters, setting, and action are all new—in no way connected to the characters, setting, and action of *The Rheingold*, the opera that preceded it. In this act, Sieglinde drugs Hunding's bedtime drink. Wagner's stage directions instruct her at this moment to glance at Siegmund, and with her eyes direct his gaze (and presumably that of the audience) toward the shining knob of the sword embedded in the ash tree. The lighting instructions

specify illumination of this spot of light in an otherwise dark-
ened stage. This is reminiscent of the shining of the gold in the
dark waters of the Rhine when the first rays of the sun lit upon
it—a reference backwards to the opening scene of *Rheingold*.
And that sword will be of central significance in key events to
follow—a reference forward as well. In this same sequence of
the opera he uses the fifth, and I think most important, device:
the leitmotif.

Wagner's leitmotifs—melodic phrases expressive of certain
ideas, persons, or situations—in addition to their intrinsic musical qualities and functions, serve as musical remembrances and
foreshadowings to connect what is occurring on stage at the
moment with what has gone before and what will follow. For
example, at the same time that Sieglinde's eyes direct the audience's attention to the knob of the sword in the ash tree, the
orchestra briefly sounds the sword motif and shortly thereafter,
that of Wotan–Valhalla. Both motifs had been played in *Rheingold* as Wotan hesitated and inwardly formulated his secret
scheme just prior to the entrance of the gods into Valhalla.
Each motif will be heard again many times later, separately
and/or together, as various aspects of that scheme (to regain
possession of the ring and its power) develop or are anticipated
in subsequent stage events as the plot unfolds.

But even in this simplified example, these mnemic connections and promptings work *without the audience having to be consciously aware of them*, and as we shall see in a moment, there are
more complicated examples that would be impossible to think
through while paying attention to the performance. How could
this mysterious process work outside of consciousness? Musicologists answer that it works because of, or through the music.
Deryck Cooke (1979) puts it this way: "Only if the transformations of each motive are pursued carefully 'through all the
changing passions of the four-part drama' can the drama's true
significance be made clear" (p. 46). In his discussion of the
passage where Wotan is finally defeated in his argument with
Fricka in act 2 of *The Valkyrie*, Cooke traces the interrelation-
ships between the main motifs and the references each of them
carries for what has gone before and what will follow later in
the drama (1979):

The whole passage begins with a ferocious new thematic idea rising from the depths of the orchestra. . . ; this is an inverted transformation of the gloomy phrase recently introduced to express Wotan's sense of frustration at the thwarting of his will by Fricka, which is itself a broken, twisted form of the imperious descending scale associated with the spear, which symbolizes his will. The new idea finds a natural continuation in the thematic phrase attached to the curse which Alberich has put on the ring. . . . The sense of his whole being revolting against the frustration of his will, and against his entanglement in the curse on the ring, which he himself has coveted, is expressed with a power which no words could achieve. The musical allusion to the ring through the phrase attached to the curse on it, now becomes explicit—not through a statement of the idea attached to the ring itself, but in a more all-encompassing way . . . Wotan sings the words "Unending wrath, eternal grief" *to a long-drawn, grief-striken minor version of the second part of Freia's theme; and then, as the orchestral agitation ceases, he follows them with the words "I am the unhappiest of beings" to the melancholy falling cadence associated with the renunciation of love* [pp. 67–70].

Cooke then traces the connection of this motif to its prior appearances when it expressed:

1. the original despair of Alberich after his final rejection by the third Rhinemaiden
2. the lament as the newly love-bereft Alberich raced back to Nieblheim to forge the ring after renouncing love
3. the plight of Freia herself, whom Wotan had promised to barter away
4. Siegmund's sense of the hopelessness of his love for Sieglinde, even as he first grasped the handle of the sword [pp. 70–71].

Then, in Cooke's own words:

Finally, in Wotan's outburst, the sorrowful cadence associated with the renunciation of love speaks for itself, and sets its seal on the whole. . . . As can be seen, the whole meaning of Wotan's tremendous outburst is in the music, not in the words, which merely sketch a general mood of shame, distress, rage, and despair [p. 72]. . . . [I]t is an all-important moment in Wotan's development . . . it recurs twice with shattering effect—first when Brunnhilde temporarily rejects Siegfried in the final scene of *Siegfried*, and again when she refuses to give up the ring to Waltraute in Act 1 of *The Twilight of the Gods* [pp. 72–73].

Finally in this connection let me quote Bryan Magee's (1968) comments about the motifs:

> Scarcely anywhere else in music are there to be found themes that are both so short and so forceful. And yet—paradoxically for themes with this strength of character—they seem capable of infinite plasticity in Wagner's hands. He metamorphoses and transmogrifies them through countless incarnations and reincarnations, always different yet always related, *weaving them with seemingly infinite resourcefulness into the largest tapestries in the whole of music.* Into this process goes, it is true, a boundless fertility in harmony and orchestration, but his fullest genius is to be found in the free creation of the original material and the free creation of the structures then made out of it—and, when all is said and done, the sheer beauty of the resultant music [pp. 82–83; emphasis added].

III

Clearly musicologists agree that it is the music that carries the main burden of making the music-drama work in the way Wagner intended. This is done mainly, I think, through the complex development and treatment of the leitmotifs. That answer is cued by two words, one from each of the above quotations: *passions* (Cooke) and *tapestries* (Magee). Wagner himself in "On the Application of Music to Drama" (1879) used the expression "web of motifs." These words taken from the musicological analyses can serve as semantic bridges to appropriate conceptual and even empirical ground for engaging this question of how it works. Both psychoanalytic and cognitive–neuroscientific studies indicate that emotion plays a central role in laying down, organizing, and reactivating memories. The bridge becomes negotiable when we recognize that music is a powerful stimulant (or inducer) of emotion (as discussed by Rose [1991]). My hypothesis is that the leitmotif serves as a reminiscence because it induces emotions that in turn are connected to, and thus evoke, memories of earlier episodes that are meaningfully connected to the action developing on the stage at the moment. These connections do not have to be and usually are not conscious, but the feeling, tone, or mood induced by the musical reminiscence renders the situation familiar and (implicitly) understandable. For example, in the first act of *The Valkyrie*, when Siegmund bewails his desertion by his lost wild "wolf father," the Wotan motif sounds to tell us who that father really is. *Without having had to recognize the motif consciously*, we begin to "understand" how this up to now strange character fits into the story and is related to what has gone before. He is no longer a total stranger.

Let's look more closely into the way it could work. The account that follows draws upon information from three sources:

1. From clinical psychoanalytic data, especially from work with dreams;
2. From cognitive neuroscientific data which relates cognitive functions such as perception and memory to the underlying brain structures and functions that enable them;
3. From studies that combine the two, that is, psychophysiologic data pertaining to the psychology of dreams and the biology of the dreaming (REM) state of the brain.

Because of space limitations I will not be able to identify the data base for the individual features of this highly condensed overview account. I have discussed the supporting data in detail elsewhere (Reiser, 1990).

The Affective Organization of Memory: A Mind Principle

Memorable experiences are encoded in memory as perceptual residues of the sensations that accompanied them; that is, sensory stimuli that were registered during the experience. Experiences are memorable because they involve emotion—the stronger it is, the more memorable the experience. And these sensory registrations are "classified" or "filed," as it were, according to the nature or quality of the emotional meaning of the experience. Accordingly, sensory residues registered during experiences with the same or highly similar emotional meaning will be associatively linked or filed in the same section or file drawer (using the same metaphor). Later experience of the same emotion can reactivate or bring out the stored perceptual residues or images for perceptual reprocessing. This may occur *entirely outside of conscious experience* (perhaps accompanied by an unexplained mood), or the perceptually reprocessed image may appear unrecognized in waking consciousness as in a fantasy, or be experienced in dream consciousness as a dream image. Current life situations or experiences that evoke emotions common to several earlier meaningful life events or situations can reactivate stored images belonging to the earlier experiences that those images encode. Images common to several (similarly toned) experiences serve as nodes in a nodal memory network:

> Each of us carries somewhere within an enduring core network of stored memories—stored and linked in relation to a shared potential to evoke identical complexes of emotional experience. Such a network would be historically rooted in early and—for the child—cataclysmic events, either real or elaborated in fantasy. As development proceeds, the network would branch out with the occurrence of later events that set the earlier ones into resonance because they posed the same or similar problems. In this sense the later events could be thought of functionally as presenting emotional analogues or homologues of the earlier ones. Traces of such events and issues left encoded in memory could then be thought of as constituting *nodal* points as Freud conceived of them for the individual dream [Reiser, 1984, p. 67].

In other words, sensory residues in the mind are organized by affect and arranged as nodal memory networks.

The Affective Organization of Memory: A Brain Principle

As noted above, experiences are encoded in memory as perceptual residues of the sensations that accompanied them, that is, sensory stimuli that were registered during the experience. The sensory aspects may be in any of the sense modalities. It appears that visual registrations predominate, and they are the ones that have been studied in most detail, but it is considered that the same principles of processing the information they carry pertain to the other special senses as well. During processing of incoming sensory information in the brain, various modalities (and even different aspects of images in a single modality) are separated for processing by different circuits and ultimately routed for storage in widely distributed areas of the sensory cortex. This widely distributed information is functionally brought together or synchronized by corticolimbic system circuits in order for conscious perception of the whole image to occur, and the same "functional reassembly" is required for storage, and for reactivation or recall of the imagery at a later time.

The critically important point is this: The reassembly processing necessary (1) for perception, (2) for transfer into memory for storage, and (3) for recall, all intimately involve—in fact require—the participation of the very same subcortical limbic system structures that generate and regulate emotion. The result is that each percept encoding a memorable experience is inextricably linked by corticolimbic circuitry to the emotion that was generated as part of that experience. And that percept could then be expected to be sensitized or prepared for reactivation on later occasions when the same emotion is reexperienced.

In other words, perceptual and memory functions are carried out by the very same corticolimbic circuits and structures that process emotion. In this way, associative links are established between new percepts and older perceptual information that has been stored in the association cortex. Access to previous experiences via affect serves the adaptive purpose of matching new situations to previous experiences in order to respond appropriately in light of those previous experiences. It is apparent that brain circuits provide the mechanisms for emotional organization of memories in a way that is consistent with the nodal memory network pattern disclosed by psychoanalytic studies. This is not surprising, since emotions occupy both domains, those of mind *and* brain. Of course, Richard Wagner did not have access to this modern information, but could he have "known" it without "knowing" it, in the way we have been discussing? Was this another manifestation of his genius?

IV

How the Lietmotif Works, a Postulate

Music, as we know, can be a powerful inducer of emotion. Each leitmotif is heard from the first time on in association with an emotionally evocative scene. I postulate that this co-occurrence establishes associative links between the motif, the emotion, and the perceptual content of the scene with which it is associated. When the motif is heard again, the same emotions are induced, and these in turn reactivate the images which encode previous associated scenes in memory. As an example, when the Valhalla motif is first sounded in scene 2 of *Rhiengold*, we see the castle structure in all its splendor and witness–share Wotan's complex emotional response. When the motif is sounded again in subsequent scenes, the same emotions will be induced in the listener. Here is the key point of my hypothesis: the physiological changes that are part of the induced emotions will subliminally reactivate the stored perceptual image(s) which encode(s) relevant earlier scenes in memory. Such an affective reminiscence can and usually does occur without the cognitive memory itself having to become conscious. As we have seen, the stored image of the castle belongs to an extended complex of emotionally related images such as Wotan's spear, the sword, the ring, and Freia's flight, and so on. It is a nodal point in the memory network. Hearing it will induce affective reminiscences which will automatically orient the audience to the place of the current scene in the overall drama.

How the Leitmotif Works, a Metaphor

But there must be much more to it than orienting the audience within the story. The leitmotifs are sounded in an almost infinite series of variations and combinations. Remember Magee's phrasing (1968): ". . . they seem capable of infinite plasticity. . . . He metamorphoses and transmogrifies them through countless incarnations and reincarnations, always different yet always related . . . a boundless fertility in harmony and orchestration" (pp. 82–83). It is almost as if the emotions themselves are far more varied than we ordinarily think of them in psychology and physiology. Robert Guttman (1990) speaks of Wagner's work in refining

> [T]he *orchestral palette*, the poetic implications expressed by his harmonies being yet more subtly shaded by effects of timbre. . . . Wagner's orchestral color also functioned as yet another

unifying device. At a desired moment he was able to evoke the particular shades of a past scene. And *tone color is often a characteristic element of his motifs*. His hues, like Rubens', embrace the entire spectrum, the values scaling the ladder from pitch dark to blinding light, the chroma ranging from subtle neutrals to utmost brilliance [p. 383; emphasis added].

The music we have been discussing suggests that there may in fact be an extensive vocabulary of emotion—perhaps even a grammar. Is there a counterpart physiological vocabulary and grammar? How else could such communication be effected? Consideration of these issues gives rise to a hypothesis about the neurobiology of emotion; could there be an extended biological spectrum of affects and affective shadings corresponding to the musical one? The complexities of neurotransmission and neuromodulation are sufficient, I think, to lend a sense of face validity to such a notion.

Picture in your mind, if you will, an extended nodal memory network—perhaps like a complex three-dimensional spider web—continually being perturbed and set into vibration by being touched at various selected nodes. Each of them in turn transmits the vibration to nodes it is connected to by the delicate strands of the web.[2] If the perturbations occur with sufficient frequency and at a strategic variety of nodal points, the web will vibrate constantly or intermittently with the pattern varying according to the timing and distribution of stimuli. So it is, I think, with the mind–brain corticolimbic memory networks of each person in Wagner's audience. The leitmotifs—inducing emotion—continually play on the intricately arranged array of interrelated percepts contained in this mysterious inner instrument and, in this way, produce the intended effect and communicate the message.

To put it in an even more fanciful way, it is as if Wagner plays upon the inner memory instrument of each member of the audience by striking it with appropriate leitmotifs, and variants thereof, at strategic loci and times; thereby inducing in

[2]A parallel and distributed computer model would probably be a more apt metaphor—it more nearly approximates the anatomical and physiological arrangements in the brain. I find the spider web easier to visualize and so chose it. The purpose of any metaphorical model would be to aid in visualizing how a nodal network system could accommodate to the fourth dimension by adding a time function in the form of memory.

each member of the audience *the inner state* that he (Wagner) feels, and is compelled to communicate—in this, the only way he can.

REFERENCES

Cooke, D. (1979), *I Saw the World End: A Study of Wagner's Ring*. New York: Oxford University Press.
Goldman, A., & Sprinchorn, E. (1964), *Wagner on Music and Drama*. New York: Plenum/ Da Capo Press.
Guttman, R. W. (1990), *Richard Wagner: The Man, His Mind, and His Music*. New York: Harcourt Brace Jovanovich.
Magee, B. (1968), *Aspects of Wagner*, 2nd ed. New York: Oxford University Press, 1988.
Reiser, M. F. (1984), *Mind, Brain, Body: Toward a Convergence of Psychoanalysis and Neuroscience*. New York: Basic Books.
——— (1990), *Memory in Mind and Brain: What Dream Imagery Reveals*. New York: Basic Books.
Rose, G. (1991), Abstract art and emotion: Expressive form and the sense of wholeness. *J. Amer. Psychoanal Assn.*, 39/1:131–156.
Wagner, R. (1849), The artwork of the future. In: *Richard Wagner's Prose Works*, Vol. 1, tr. W. A. Ellis. London: Kegan, Paul, Trench, Trubner.
——— (1850–1851), Opera and drama. In: *Richard Wagner's Prose Works*, Vol. 2, tr. W. A. Ellis. London: Kegan, Paul, Trench, Trubner.
——— (1879), On the application of music to drama. In: *Richard Wagner's Prose Works*, Vol. 6, tr. W. A. Ellis. London: Kegan, Paul, Trench, Trubner.

Chapter 13

Erik Satie: Musicality and Ego Identity

Richard L. Karmel, Ph.D.

INTRODUCTION

Both compelling and troublesome, exalted and defiled by critics, the early, emerging musicality of Erik Satie deserves examination and consideration given its "out of the past," modern, yet, anachronistic style. From the perspective of developmental considerations which I will further elaborate upon, I believe it is "the music of disidentification," composed by a highly sensitive and introspective late adolescent–young adult under the influence of past reveries, drawn to state of meditative contemplation and ascetic withdrawal, working toward the creation and emergence of an ego identity which will carry him into the future.

MATERNAL LOSS IN CHILDHOOD

In characteristic fashion, Satie emphasized an unremarkable and unessential childhood in "Mémoires d'un amnésique" (Volta, 1981). However, the implications of maternal loss in childhood cannot be ignored.[1]

Born in 1866, in the Normandy coastal town of Honfleur, his father was employed as a shipbroker, though depicted as highly educated, fluent in nine languages, a one-time translator,

---

[1]Wolfenstein (1966, 1969, 1973) drew attention to the child's dilemma around parental loss: mourning appears to be "delayed by (developmental) necessity," held in abeyance until adolescence is underway.

and an amateur poet-musician. His Scottish mother[2] was portrayed as having "a very cultivated mind" and being artistically inclined (Volta, 1989, pp. 15–16). The parents married in England, honeymooned in Scotland, and in short order four children were born. In 1871, with the conclusion of the Franco-Prussian War, the family moved to Paris where tragedy struck. When Erik was aged 6, his mother died, whereupon he was sent back to Honfleur, rebaptized into the Catholic faith, and enrolled as a boarding student at the College of Honfleur. In effect, all ties with the maternal side were completely cut off. (Further discussions on the "fixated" or frozen image of the lost parent as an internal structure can be found in Dietrich and Shabad [1989].)

In 1873, Honfleur became the home of a young religiously trained musician named Vinot, who provided Satie with his first musical instruction from age 8 to 12. While biographers make no mention of special musical talent during this period, there seems to be unanimous agreement that, at the very least, these four years of musical instruction exposed him to the medieval world—"The visual and aural combined: the Gothic look of Vinot's church and the sound of the Gregorian mode . . ." (Harding, 1975, p. 13).[3]

His eccentric Uncle "Sea-Bird" was a nonmusical childhood influence. He suffered from "a sense of irresponsible, purely arbitrary fantasy . . . that was to appear later in the nephew" (Myers, 1948, p. 15). (An example of his uncle's mental state or self-object representation concerned the building of a magnificent sailboat, *The Wave*, which became an object of contemplation rather than function; e.g., he would not sail the boat for fear of damage from use.)[4]

[2]Their respective religious backgrounds—Catholic and Anglican—was a source of major conflict between Mrs. Satie and her in-laws, to be readdressed in 1872. The issue of religiosity and religious affiliation remained a significant one during Satie's late adolescent–young adulthood years influencing his characterology and musicality.

[3]As to the extent did such influences affect young Satie, and his musical compositions, Gillmor (1988) points out, "the diatonic lines of medieval monody, the serenity and haunting simplicity of plainchant, are never far beneath the surface of Satie's music . . ." (p. 9).

[4]A similar representation may have found its way into the 1913 composition *Enfantillages Pittoresques* (Sketches of Childishness). In his "Marche du Grand Escalier," Satie offered the following commentary: "It's a big staircase, a very big one. It has more than a thousand steps, all made of ivory. It is very beautiful. *Nobody dare use it for fear of spoiling it. The King himself has never used it.* When he leaves the room, he jumps out of the window. Consequently, he often says: I am so fond of this staircase that I'm going to have it stuffed. Don't you think he is right?" (emphasis added).

In short, Satie's childhood record shows no "flashes of musical brilliance," nor notable musicality, nor high scholastic potential, nor unusual or peculiar behavior (associated with childhood loss). Rather, he seems to have been both musically and scholastically unimpressive, perhaps, overly saturated with the aesthetics of medieval religiosity, and possibly overstimulated by his uncle's schizoid relationship to reality. But, was he "the prisoner of his childhood"? (Harding, 1975, p. 14).[5]

EARLY ADOLESCENCE

At age 12, his grandmother died accidentally while bathing in the sea and, concurrently, his music teacher Vinot left Honfleur for Lyon. Shortly thereafter, Satie was back in Paris, freed from formal educational requirements, accompanying his father to lectures on literature and philosophy. Thus, his early adolescence involved an introduction into his father's intellectual-aesthetic world,[6] which may have resulted in a particular adolescent oedipal constellation (Karmel, 1990).

In 1879, his father married Eugénie Barnetche, an accomplished pianist and "composer of pallid salon pieces" (Gillmor, 1988, p. 15), and Satie was enrolled in piano classes at the Conservatoire. This marked the beginning of a rather unsuccessful seven-year period of musical training. At the end of his second year, Professor Descombes' evaluation read, "The laziest student in the Conservatory—but gets a lovely sound" (Shattuck, 1968, p. 116).

During his adolescence, music permeated the Satie household and both parents tried their hand at composing for popular appeal.[7] Thus, for the Saties, one can infer that music-making was not a casual or recreational enterprise, but an integral

[5]A tentative and cautious "yes" is offered. Shattuck (1968) provides a "compensatory" explanation: "as if it offered consolation for all he had missed in his cheerless childhood" (p. 117). I assume the author is referring to the latency period following his mother's death. Nonetheless, Satie showed a marked propensity for "musical play" and music oriented to dance movement. The construction of musical pieces which denoted the child's capacity for fantasizing was also a predominate aspect to Satie's musicality.

[6]This might be regarded as his father's "wished-for self image" (Milrod, 1982); however, his talents seemed destined to be expressed on a lesser plane—he ran a stationery store.

[7]A composition representative of his stepmother's musicality is *Ronde de sorcieres* (Witches' Round), published in 1882. His father is represented by *Bulles de savon* (Soap Bubbles) published in 1885.

part of the family dynamics. While Eric was attending the Conservatoire, and barely getting by in his piano studies, the 1880s was a period of active musical productivity and marginal commercial success for his parents.

At the same time, in the midst of occasionally harsh criticism of his piano skills, Satie at 16 gravitated toward mystical religiosity and became a voracious reader, particularly drawn to the writings of Flaubert and Hans Christian Andersen. Furthermore, he seemed to attach himself to literary characters as if they were living and breathing.[8] Whatever might be attributed to his literary preoccupations, musical accomplishments in a formal sense remained essentially a marginal enterprise as his was described as "idle and frivolous" (Shattuck, 1968, p. 117). However, he did appear to be quite intentional with regard to musical taste as his inclination was decidedly oriented toward Bach and Chopin.

LATE ADOLESCENCE–YOUNG ADULTHOOD

As he moved into late adolescence, Satie's character development manifested itself in his dress which made him appear "austere and a little priggish . . ." (Shattuck, 1968, p. 117). At 18, on holiday in Honfleur, against the background of his father's part-time music publishing business and his stepmother's salon pieces, Satie produced his first known musical composition *Allegro* (for piano), which "reveals the slender musical resources of the salon composer" (Gillmor, 1988, p. 17). Shortly thereafter, he composed *Valse-ballet* and *Fantansie-valse*, the latter reflecting a somber, subdued, "resigned melancholy," which was to become a trademark of his early compositions (Templier, 1932).[9]

---

[8]This raises many interesting questions about Satie "the double" or what Myers (1948, p. 17) calls "the attraction of 'like to like,' " the background to the more public aspects of his character transformation and the nature of his identifications and efforts at disidentification. These writers are also believed to have had a significant influence on Satie's "inner" personality development and musical aesthetics in the sense of "imagery" or image-formation, the use of fairy tales, and his deep attachment to "the inner world of the child."

[9]Though Satie was later to be associated with the development of modern French music, as an adolescent his first compositions have been described as "unquestionably cut from the same cloth as the humorous and sentimental songs of his father and the shallow salon pieces of his stepmother" (Gillmor, 1988, p. 17). Thus, his first compositions approximated his parents' musical tastes and were rather conventional, consistent

At the age of 20, Satie collaborated with a religious, mystically inclined poet who employed the pseudonym J. P. Contamine de Latour, the latter laboring under the "delusion" of being related to Napoleon. This duo produced *Trois melodies de 1886* (for voice and piano) which spoke to the "perennial themes of disillusioned young love and the transience of earthly beauty" (Gillmor, 1988, p. 29). Perhaps, of greater significance was their assigning of pseudonyms, de Latour assuming the mantle "le Vieux Modeste" (The Humble Old Fellow) and Satie the title "Monsieur le Pauvre" (Mr. Poverty). No doubt, these were to be men who, in spite of their prodigious talents, had taken a secret oath that demanded for as long as they lived they would remain true to themselves and retain an air of deep humility whatever the cost! This manner of assigning life-roles holds special significance as an emerging ego identity (Erikson, 1956), involving a particular form of characterology; that is, pure artistry and the denial of material need or desire (Sharpe, 1935).

Concurrently, Satie is portrayed as spending considerable time "in silent contemplation" in the cathedral of Notre-Dame, immersing himself in the study of Gregorian Plainsong, housing himself in the Bibliothèque Nationale where he read on Gothic art. In the course of this period of ascetic-intellectual activity, he composed *Ogives* (for piano), which is described as an "overtly 'Gothic' work" (Gillmor, 1988, p. 34).[10] Ironically, at age 20, with the conclusion of a lackluster career as a conservatory music student—and certainly on this basis a future in music would be in question—Satie was a published composer, perhaps, in spite of himself.

Leaving the Conservatoire, his next stop was the military where he deliberately exposed himself to winter chills, contracted bronchitis, was hospitalized, and later discharged. During a three-month period of convalescence, he immersed himself in Flaubert's *Salammbô*, which Satie claimed inspired the *Gymnopédies*, his most familiar composition.

---

with the popular music of the period. "Had he been content . . . to follow in the footsteps of his father and stepmother and countless other minor tunesmiths of the day, he would have failed to earn a place in the chronicle of contemporary music" (p. 18).

[10]Satie's music is seen as "mystical" in style, reflecting "rebelliousness": "We note the refusal (or inability) to develop and manipulate musical material along traditional lines" (Gillmor, 1988, p. 32). From the perspective of this paper, I conceive it to be a musical expression (representation) of character transformation and a creative effort at achieving an ego identity via disidentification (Erikson, 1956).

THE EMERGENCE OF A CREATIVE STYLE: A FORMULATION

The portrait of the late adolescent Satie is that of a voracious reader who "took refuge" in the great libraries and churches of Paris, apparently in quest of admittance into that medieval world to which he had first been introduced by Vinot while living with his grandparents in Honfleur. While tentatively flirting with his parents' aesthetic sensibilities, he also collaborated (with a poet friend) and produced an "age appropriate" composition (e.g., mournful and idyllic). The latter might be conceived as a type of "mentor relationship" (Halperin, 1988). And though this relationship supported a mystical attitude toward life, it was not the type of object relatedness required—of the idealized type. For this object requirement to be realized a literary figure or motif was needed which met Satie's "totalistic" characterologic requirements (i.e., intellectualized asceticism). The text would have to satisfy his more introspective, ascetic, mystical leanings. Thus, I would hypothesize that Satie's "search for an object" (and his regressive requirements) was associated with specific intellectual and literary pursuits (which he would subsequently incorporate into his musical vocabulary). As a consequence, Satie at 20 was drawn to the author Joséphin Péladan and his novels on La Décadence latine.[11]

Satie's "use of the other" seemed to involve a particular form of object-seeking whereby a previously, though weakly, established character style and self-system seeks an "external collaborator" in order to strengthen characterologic requirements (e.g., asceticism). Upon military discharge, at age 21 Satie moved out of his parents' home, took a room in the Montmartre cafe district, and soon occupied the position of second pianist

[11]This literary series, which emphasized "that the Latin races have gone into a decline as a result of neglecting religion" (Harding, 1975, p. 23), begins with the novel Le Vice suprême, the story of a talented princess corrupted by education who is forced to become an accomplished linguist! She is intellectually perverse—so complete in her knowledge and in the experiences of life that she is dying of boredom! Seduction is her only release. Interestingly, the leading male character is "a magus" (with Jewish features), the ancestor of today's Portnoy or Woody Allen character: forced "to read pornography and to stay pure"! He is both an epicurean and an ascetic. He is "a good for nothing," idle and frivolous, and a brilliant metaphysician! In the end, he achieves mastery, control, and abstinence over "Le vice suprême"—the habit of smoking! In these literary excursions, one's fellow travelers are the mystic, the perverse, the hermaphrodite, and the cultist. In Péladan, the 20-year-old Satie had found a mentor.

at the infamous Chat Noir. Now, he was situated squarely at the center of Parisian bohemian life and the affectations often found in this milieu made their appearance.

At age 24, Satie took a further turn toward religiosity as a framework for his compositional activities. As if under the influence or spell of Péladan's literary renderings, upon personal introduction to the author he entered the world of medieval mystical religiosity, joining the Rosicrucian movement directed by Sâr Péladan. Leaving behind the bewitching debauchery of Parisian café life(?), Satie changed allegiances, which may be viewed as an effort at character (ego) synthesis (Richmond and Sklansky, 1984), and put himself and his music into a spiritual context thereby achieving improved self-regulation (Coppolillo, 1984), at least temporarily.

EGO IDENTITY AND COMPOSING: ITS INTERRELATIONSHIP

I am proposing that Satie's first "original" compositions, which departed considerably from his parents' aesthetic tradition, were creations associated with a newly emerging ego identity.

Beginning with the four *Ogives* (1886), "the first musical manifestation of Satie's neomedieval obsession . . . his first overtly 'Gothic' work" (Gillmor, 1988, p. 34), the *Sarabandes* (1887), "Satie's three archaic dances," the three *Gymnopédies* (1888), and the *Gnossiennes* (begun in 1889), Satie presented himself to (bohemian) Parisian society in the personage of "*gymnopédiste*," a rather strange title for a composer. (Note that Erik is substituted for Eric.) His profession, thus, reflected an "invented," magically conjured calling card, an idiosyncratic ego identity. He began to invent other identities, again idiosyncratic, obscure, and mysterious.

Satie via his musical talents, autodidactic excursions, and metaphysical voyages had arrived at a destination in the new world, the kingdom of Bohemia. Concurrently, he was able to take a giant leap backwards in time and place, catapult himself out of his parents' bourgeois musical establishment, and begin to work at establishing his "place in (musical) history" (Volta, 1989, p. 34).

With the composing of the *Ogives*, he took to self-advertisement and the creation of a mysterious, strange, and enigmatic personna, "the sphinx man":

Le Chat Noir
VIII, No 369, 9 February 1889

At last! Lovers of cheerful music can give themselves endless pleasure. The indefatigable Erik Satie, the sphinx man, the wooden-
headed composer, announces the appearance of a new musical work
which, up till now, he says, is the greatest. It is a series of melodies
conceived, in the mystico-liturgical mode beloved of the author, under
the suggestive title *Ogives*. We wish Erik Satie a success comparable to
the one he had already attained with his *Gymnopédie No 3*, currently
under all pianos.
On sale at 66 boulevard Magenta (His parents' address)

The discovery of a new compositional style produced excitement and a state of ironic intoxication in its author, giving rise
to the "authorization of musical testimonials" (Volta, 1989, pp.
34–35):

La Lanterne Japonaise
II, No 15, 23 March 1889
Japanese Salad

M. Erik Satie, musical composer, received the following letter, which
he asked us to print:

                    Précigny-les-Balayettes, 20 February 1889

Sir,
For eight years I have suffered from a polyp in the nose, compli-
cated by a liver disorder and rheumatic pains.
On hearing your *Ogives* my condition showed a clear improvement.
Four of five applications of your *Gymnopédie No 3* cured me com-
pletely.
I hereby authorize you, Monsieur Erik Satie, to make any use of
this testimonial you may wish.
In the meantime please accept the thanks of your grateful

                    Femme Lengrenage

Day worker at Précigny-les-Balayettes

As for us, our opinion of M. Erik Satie, whom we do not have the honour of knowing personally, can be summed up in four words: he's a hot rabbit!

Thus, his first "original" compositional efforts coincided with his "reconstructed" late adolescent character, Mr. Poverty, and to his public he was the mysterious and enigmatic "Sphinx Man." Soon, he was to achieve reputation as an emerging avantgarde stylist and in a few years he would make the acquaintance of young Ravel, influencing his early compositional style (1893). Shortly thereafter, Debussy would orchestrate two of his *Gymnopédies* (1897). Thus, the 1890s were important years where Satie would find company among "a small band of connoisseurs" sowing "the seeds of the modern spirit, seeds that lay largely dormant until the sudden climatic changes of 1914–1918" (Gillmor, 1988, p. 7).

ADOLESCENT NARCISSISM

In retrospect, though he was characterized as "indolent" within the conservatory milieu, we cannot rule out that possibility of a young adolescent's "thwarted narcissistic aspirations, hurts to one's pride, injuries to one's prestige needs . . ." (Kohut, 1975, p. 163).[12]

Was he "an adolescent thrust into a high-pressured conservatory setting against his will," who as a result remained narcissistically injured? At age 26, recalling "a huge, very uncomfortable and rather ugly building, a sort of local penitentiary without any exterior charm—or interior either," he continued to express his displeasure and indignation regarding this youthful period of musical instruction (Volta, 1989, p. 23):

---

[12]His school record showed fluctuations and "flashes of praiseworth comment . . . render less harsh the recurring lament over his chronic indolence" (Gillmor, 1988). On this matter I would speculate that Satie manifested "adolescent mood fluctuations" associated with narcissistic vulnerability (Spruiell, 1975). Asceticism and intellectualization among adolescents can also represent efforts at achieving regulation over disturbing affects, moods, and other internal tensions (A. Freud, 1946).

Erik Satie to the Conservatoire National
de Musique et de Déclamation
Paris, 17 November of 92

> Individual Theme of Liturgical Chastity
> by the High Wisdom with which I am filled,
> I speak to you

Hear ye:

A child, I entered your classes; My spirit so gentle that you could not understand it: and My way of walking around astonished the flowers, for they thought they were seeing an artificial zebra (the apparition of a sympathetic being).

And despite My extreme youth and My delicious agility, through your unintelligence you made Me detest the coarse art which you teach, by your inexplicable harshness you made me for a long time despise you.

Now that all the External Vegetation (this indicates My great sensitivity to the things of Nature) is in Me, I absolve you of your faults in regard to Me; I pray the Lord to forgive you; I bless the unhappy souls which you will educate until the day when the Capital Power will take them from your hands and restore them to the Seraphim of the Virgin Mary.

> I have spoken.
> Erik Satie

Whatever Satie experienced in terms of useful musical instruction, his letter speaks the "language of the misunderstood," the unempathically treated, and the individual subjected to enduring indignation (Segel, 1981). Perhaps, this explains in part his midadolescent literary excursions, that is, a turning away from external reality and a retreat into a fictional world or what has been termed "fictional space" (Baudry, 1990). In this letter, we also note how Satie has entered into the "space of the cleric" and has assumed a "borrowed identity," the character of "an ascetic pure soul." Thus, it seems plausible to state that Satie's turning to literature stimulated subsequent internalizations and character alterations which, I would suggest, can be noted in his musical compositions. Literary characters served as sources for identification—as "borrowed identities"—and, later, sources for compositional inspiration and collaboration. He was particularly drawn to the Danish writer Hans Christian Andersen, later to Flaubert, and it is on this point that the issue of adolescent character-formation and correlative defensive structures is worth considering.

Satie did not read simply for pleasure, nor recreation, nor escape; rather, his relationship to literature seems to assume (and permit) a regressive function involving ascetic withdrawal, identificatory modeling, and restructuring of his character, body-image, and mode of participation in the adult world. As Gillmor (1988) points out, "In a very short time Satie would cease to live the bohemian life vicariously through the pages of strange plays and novels; he would himself soon become part of the legend that is fin de siècle Montmartre" (p. 15).

LOSS, MOURNING, AND CREATIVITY IN ADOLESCENCE

To gain further insight into Satie's adolescent period, and his mode of coping and adaptation, Anna Freud's (1946) formulations on "Instinctual Anxiety During Puberty" provide an excellent mode of orientation. For example, there is the role of religiosity and mysticism, which has been cited as a feature of his earliest "original" musical compositions.

Aberbach (1987) cites the interrelationship between grief, mysticism, and creativity, which provides a conceptual link with the question of maternal loss (experienced by Satie in early childhood and puberty) and the formulation by Wolfenstein (1966) that "not only does adolescence resemble mourning, it constitutes the necessary precondition for being later able to mourn" (pp. 112–113). Thus, one can make the tentative formulation that Satie's late adolescent musical compositions reflected "a way of mourning the past" and a way of avoiding the affects associated with the mourning process, which was accomplished during adolescence via the strengthening of pre-existent (latency) defensive structures (the defenses associated with childhood mourning) which in adolescence were expressed in the form of asceticism and intellectualization.

This defensive mode represented a preferred mode of mourning and decathexis pertaining to object loss and enabled Satie to resurrect a preferred preadolescent, latency-based, pre-instinctual and presexual "purified" musical aesthetic. In this way, he would now return to a (latency-based) "Gothic aesthetic," a strangely interesting source for musical creativity—a retreat into both a humanized, though historical, and nonhuman environment resulting in "the objectification of spatial forms." As a means of countering the possibility of turning into a "normal" adolescent, replete with stereotypic sentimentality, young Satie reversed himself, renounced the aesthetic traditions of traditional youth, and produced "objectified music." Thus, in contrast to the adolescent (later conductor) Bruno Walter, whom I cited in a previous paper on adolescent musicality and idealization (Karmel, 1990), where the music of Wagner inspired passionate yearnings typical of young adolescents, Satie "turned against passion" as a musical aesthetic. Ultimately, he would seek to create a music for "the dispassionate listener": the "music of irony" (Chennevière, 1919).

COMPOSING, INTENTIONALITY, AND ACTION

On the subject of becoming a composer, Satie claimed he was "a victim of circumstances," and one might draw the rather sterile, unromantic conclusion that his father's music publishing business provided young Satie with the initial impetus. However, a "family romance perspective" suggests a more romanticized view of "the first inspiration to compose"—the return visit to his childhood home town by the sea—the stimulus for a 20-second miniature titled *Allegro* (for piano). This perspective emphasizes "affects associated with reunion and nostalgia" and the need or desire to express or represent an inner state (of heightened fantasy and affectivity) by way of a musical language. Another perspective might raise the issue of "creative action" in reaction to an earlier state of passivity and the beginning efforts at "resynthesizing early modes of functioning" (Nass, 1971). In that sense, he was in effect saying: "I want to show you that I am no longer the 'victim of circumstances' nor

Shattuck, R. (1968), *The Banquet Years*, rev. ed. New York: Vintage.

Spruiell, V. (1975), Narcissistic transformations in adolescence. *Internat. J. Psychoanal. Psychotherapy*, 4:518–536.

Templier, P-D. (1932). *Erik Satie*, tr. E. L. French & D. S. French. New York: Dover Publications, 1980.

Volta, O. (1981), *Erik Satie: Écrits*. Paris: Éditions Champ Libre.

—— (1989), *Satie Seen Through His Letters*. London: Marion Boyars.

Wolfenstein, M. (1966), How is mourning possible? *The Psychoanalytic Study of the Child*, 1:93–123. New York: International Universities Press.

—— (1969), Loss, rage, and repetition. *The Psychoanalytic Study of the Child*, 24:432–460. New York: International Universities Press.

—— (1973), The image of the lost parent. *The Psychoanalytic Study of the Child*, 28:433–456. New Haven, CT: Yale University Press.

IV

HISTORICAL ESSAYS

Chapter 14

Richard Wagner's Life and Music: What Freud Knew

Cora L. Díaz de Chumaceiro, Ph.D.

Sigmund Freud was quite familiar with different aspects of Richard Wagner's (1813–1883) life and with some of his works. Wagner's popularity was so extensive that it was difficult for a highly cultured individual to ignore the controversy he had created in musical, literary, and political circles in Europe. Wagner societies were founded worldwide during his lifetime; before his death, he and his work had been discussed in over ten thousand publications (Magee, 1968). It is also true, however, that while some idolized him for his music, his anti-Semitism engendered the hatred of many (Wistrich, 1989). Freud apparently despised the man, but at least appreciated his *Meistersinger von Nürnberg* (Roazen, 1971).

On December 12, 1897, Freud wrote to Fliess about his recent positive reaction to a performance of *Die Meistersinger* (1862–1867): "I was sympathetically moved by the 'morning dream interpretation melody'; I would have liked to add the '*Parnosse*' to 'paradise' and 'Parnassus.' Moreover, as in no other opera, real ideas are set to music, with the tones of feeling attached to it lingering on as one reflects upon them" (Masson, 1985, p. 286).

Interpretation of the first clause to mean "as in no other [*Wagner*] opera" implies, then, that by 1897, Freud's knowledge of Wagner's music was greater than has been underscored in the psychoanalytic literature to date; during his lifespan he learned even more. In this presentation, then, some striking omissions in terms of data that have been overlooked are briefly highlighted, followed by a chronological amplification of the summarized comments made about Wagner in the *Minutes of*

249

the Vienna Psychoanalytic Society (Nunberg and Federn, 1962, 1967, 1974, 1975).

CASES OF OVERLOOKED DATA

I

In his letter of December 12, 1897, before writing about *Die Meistersinger*, Freud made the following request to Fliess: "May I ask you to bring for me to Breslau the dream examples I sent you (insofar as they are on separate sheets)" (Masson, 1985, p. 286). Freud was already working on his ideas for *The Interpretation of Dreams* (1900), actually published in November of 1899.

In view of Freud's positive reaction to this opera, one wonders why he did not mention it later in his works (Guttman, Parrish, and Jones, 1984) nor to others; he would repeatedly recall the Mozart operas he liked (Diaz de Chumaceiro, 1992a). He certainly had the opportunity in "Notes Upon a Case of Obsessional Neurosis" (1909a), because the Rat Man had recalled *Die Meistersinger*—as was later revealed in the "Original Record" (1909b), found in London after Freud's death, and not meant for publication (Strachey, 1955). On November 30, 1907, Freud wrote: "The first performance he [the Rat Man] went to was the *Meistersinger*, where he heard the name of 'David' repeatedly called out. He had used the David *motif* as an exclamation in his family" (1909b, p. 291; see Mahoney, 1986).

Is there a plausible reason for Freud's silence? The musicologist Theodor Adorno (1952) has underscored that Wagner's " 'psychoanalytic' motifs—incest, hatred of the father, castration—have been pointed out often enough; and Sach's [sic] apothegm about 'true dream interpretation' seems to bring the work of art close to the analytic ideal of making the unconscious conscious" (p. 121). In Act III, sc. ii, of *Die Meistersinger* after Walther has expressed his fear that if he thinks about the beautiful dream he dreamt he may forget it, Sachs sings in response that the poet's exact task is "to interpret and record his dreamings. Believe me, man's truest madness is disclosed to him in dreams: All poetry and versification is nothing but true dream interpretation" (Branscombe, 1974, p. 197).

It can be hypothesized, then, that if when Freud attended the performance in 1897 he found that Wagner's ideas about Walther von Stolzing's dream of the prizewinning song were too close to his material, consequently, he refrained from citing this opera elsewhere. Sulloway (1979) has pointed out that Freud wrote to Fliess in a previous letter of November 14, 1897, referring to a different issue: "(Privately I concede priority in the idea to no one)" (Masson, 1985, p. 279). Was this opera a similar case? More recently, Chessick (1986) stated about Wagner: "In attempting to use art to probe the unconscious, he stood between Schopenhauer and Freud" (p. 467). Clearly then, this issue of priority deserves further study.

II

According to Jones (1953), "Freud's aversion to music was one of his well-known characteristics" (pp. 17–18). In his report on Freud's personal life during the decade of 1890 to 1900, his opinion was that "Freud paid only very occasional visits to the theater or opera. The operas had to be by Mozart, though an exception was made with *Carmen*" (1953, p. 329). In view of this statement, then, it is hardly surprising that *Die Meistersinger* was also, perhaps unwittingly, omitted in the chapter on the Fliess period (1887–1902), even though Jones had access to the then unpublished Freud–Fliess correspondence (p. xiv). However, also as a result of omitted data, his narrative about the few operas Freud attended during the period 1880 to 1890 is erroneous (Jones, 1953; Díaz de Chumaceiro, 1990a).

History was rectified almost two decades later, when Roazen (1971) wrote: "Even though he [Freud] detested Richard Wagner, he loved *Die Meistersinger*, and in the late 1920's could point out many aspects of it which had escaped the notice of at least one highly musical patient" (p. 32). Roazen's source was an interview with Mark Brunswick, on January 25, 1966. Unless biographers base their reports exclusively on Jones (e.g., Vitz, 1988), this opera is now included in the lists of the music Freud liked (e.g., Anzieu, 1975; Gay, 1988). Uniquely, Anzieu (1975) added *Tannhaüser* (1843–1845) to his list, but omitted his source.

III

Also in 1953, Reik published *The Haunting Melody*, yet his discussion on Freud's (by now famous) disclaimer that he "was almost incapable of obtaining any pleasure" from music (1914, p. 211), seems to have remained unnoticed (Díaz de Chumaceiro, 1991). Reik, who met Freud in 1910 (Gay, 1988), also commented: "Twice I had the opportunity to observe that Freud sometimes enjoyed music (He told me once that Wagner's *Ring des Nibelungen* did not mean anything to him, but that he liked the *Meistersinger*)" (1953, p. 4). To date, however, it is unknown when and where Freud attended a performance of *The Ring*, or if he just read the libretti.

This remark may well be an instance of denial. It is difficult to believe, for example, that Freud remained indifferent to the following passage in *Siegfried* (Act III, sc. i) when Erda sings: "I have wakened from the sleep of wisdom: who has dispelled my slumber?" (Salter, 1969, p. 137). Wotan answers that it is he, searching for knowledge. Erda then replies: "My sleep is dreaming, my dreaming meditation, my meditation mastery of wisdom" (Salter, 1969, p. 137).

In synthesis, Wagner began to outline the *Nibelungen* saga combined with the *Eddas* (in prose and verse drafts) in 1848; the result was *Siegfrieds Tod* (*Siegfried's Death*) (later *Götterdämmerung*). In 1852, this was extended with *Der junge Siegfried* (*The Young Siegfried*) (later simply *Siegfried*); the following year, wanting to amplify the two parts into four, *Walküre* and *Rheingold* were created to present the prehistory of the rise and fall of Siegfried, an innocent, noble, and fearless hero. Wagner dedicated over a quarter of a century to the conception and development of his masterpiece (Deathridge and Dahlhaus, 1984).

Interestingly, in "Some Character-Types met with in Psycho-Analytic Work" (1916), Freud asked: "Why did not Nature give us the golden curls of Balder or *the strength of Siegfried*?" (p. 315; emphasis added). Was he referring to the opera, to the saga, or to both in this instance? *The Interpretation of Dreams* (1900) reveals that Freud certainly had been attracted to the saga of Siegfried at the turn of the century (see p. 515). Furthermore, with the recent publication of the correspondence with his friend Eduard Silberstein (1856–1925) during 1871 to 1881, it is now clear that Freud was familiar with the *Nibelungenlied* since 1875 (Boehlich, 1990).

IV

The publication of the Freud–Jung correspondence in 1974 revealed allusions to Wagner's *Parsifal* and *Siegfried* in the following contexts. In the first case, on November 29, 1908, Freud wrote to Jung, defending Brill's (1908) paper, "Psychological Factors in Dementia Praecox: An Analysis," against his criticism: "I thought it was very good; of course, I don't know how much of what you recommended to him he omitted. Penns-Parcival looks good to me. I have ventured to translate it from the paranoiac. Then it reads: Am I still in love with**, who is (in) Penns (with) Thaw? Have I still a right to identify myself with her?" (Freud's Letter 116, McGuire, 1979, p. 182). A footnote explains "Penns" as the abbreviation of Pennsylvania. A patient in Zurich, whom Brill had formerly treated at the Burghölzli, was sent a letter by his former girl friend—a servant to the Thaw family in Pittsburgh. "Pennsylvania, Thaw" had its role in his hallucinations. Brill interpreted that the patient transformed "Pa (abbr. of Pennsylvania) into 'Parsifal' and 'Thaw' into 'Thor.' " Praying on his knees, in a psychotic state, he frequently repeated: " 'Am I Parsifal the most guileless fool?' (In Wagner's music-drama, Parsifal is called *reiner Thor*, 'guileless fool.')" (McGuire, 1979, p. 182). On December 3, 1908, Jung answered Freud on this issue, affirming that his opposition to Brill's analysis did not imply that for him "Penns-Parsifal" was not possible. Although agreeing from a theoretical viewpoint, he thought it inadvisable to present to laymen "such inconclusive parallels in a beginner's works," and thus advised Brill to exclude it. "What he omitted was important" (Jung's Letter 117, McGuire, 1979, p. 184).

In the second case, on December 11, 1908, Freud wrote to Jung (a few days after the birth of Jung's son, Franz Carl) stating: "I must say, your regret at being unable to play the ideal hero-father ('My father begot me and died') struck me as

very premature. The child will find you indispensable as a father for many years, first in a positive, then in a negative sense!"
(Freud's Letter 118, p. 186). The footnote reads: "Allusion to
the hero of Wagner's music drama *Siegfried*; see Act II, scene
iii" (p. 186). In this instance, Siegfried sings: "*meine Mutter
schwand, mein Vater fiel: nie sah sie der Sohn!*" ("My mother is
dead, my father was slain: their son never saw them" [Salter,
1969, p. 131]). With respect to Freud's wording of the allusion,
according to Howard (1988), "Wagner is the most successful
German poet since Goethe just because no one can remember
his words (except, one trusts, the singers)!" (p. 25). In both
cases, Freud and Jung were familiar with Wagner's operas.

V

With the discovery over a decade ago of Sabina Spielrein's diary
and her letters to Jung and Freud (which had remained hidden
in Geneva for over sixty years), the significance of Wagner and
Siegfried's legend in her life were revealed. Apparently, during
her treatment with Jung they became lovers; she was obsessed
about having a child named Siegfried with him (Carotenuto,
1980). Although on October 23, 1906, Jung had first mentioned
to Freud his treatment of his 20-year-old Russian student, it
was not until his letter of June 4, 1909, that he revealed Spielrein's name (McGuire, 1979; see also Lehmann, 1986). By then,
however, in her letter of May 30, 1909, she had already con-
tacted Freud seeking his help. Spielrein and Jung loved
Wagner's music; *Das Rheingold* was a favorite. On June 20, 1909,
she wrote to Freud: "It was Wagner who planted the demon in
my soul with such terrifying clarity" (Carotenuto, 1980, p. 107).
    Jung betrayed her love and she married Pavel Scheftel. Freud
wrote to Spielrein on August 12, 1912: "I must confess, after
the event, that your fantasy about the birth of a Saviour to a
mixed union did not appeal to me at all. The Lord, in that anti-
Semitic period, had him born from the superior Jewish race.
But I know these are my prejudices" (Carotenuto, 1980, pp.
116–117). Furthermore, after the birth of Renate, on September 29, 1913, Freud congratulated her: "It is far better that the
child should be a 'she.' Now we can think again about the blond

Siegfried and perhaps smash that idol before his time comes"
(Carotenuto, 1980, p. 121). However, Spielrein continued to
correspond with Jung until 1918.

In discussing this case, Bettelheim (1989) remarked that in
view of the deep and frequent discussions that Spielrein and
Jung had about Wagner's works, "they could not possibly disregard that in the *Ring* cycle Siegfried is the son of Siegmund,
whose name is a variant of Freud's first name, Sigmund. Spielrein thus desired a son whose physical father would be Jung,
but whose name would symbolize that his spiritual father was
Freud" (pp. 67–68). Could Freud, knowing *The Ring*, disregard
this connection?

VI

Anzieu (1975) commented on Freud's motives for having short-
ened his name from "Sigismund to Sigmund at about the age of
19" (p. 7). He suggested that besides desiring social acceptance,
"there was another, and possibly more important unconscious
echo in Freud's mind. The legendary hero, Siegfried, who became well-known to the public through two operas by Richard
Wagner (1848 and 1876), was 'pure' because he was the son of
twins (Siegmund and Sieglinde)—in other words, the issue of a
'super-incest' between brother and sister" (p. 8). Was *The Ring*
really as meaningless to Freud as he wanted Reik to believe?

VII

When Freud changed his name, he was already a member of
the Leseverein der deutschen Studenten Wiens (Reading Society of the German Students of Vienna), a German radical na-
tionalistic group that proclaimed Schopenhauer (1788–1860),
Wagner (1813–1883), and Nietzsche (1844–1900) as their ideational leaders. His membership lasted from 1873 to 1877
(McGrath, 1967). However, after Freud's affiliation with this
group ended, Theodore Meynert (1833–1892), his later, deeply
venerated teacher, was an active member who often lectured on
psychiatry (Freud, 1900, p. 437; McGrath, 1967). Presumably,

then, members of this reading society would have been familiar with at least some of Wagner's personal and theoretical works, as well as with his music.

Wagner's early operas are based on literary texts: *Die Feen* (1833–1834); *Das Liebesverbot* (1835–1836); *Rienzi* (1838–1840); and *Der fliegende Holländer* (1841). His later works for which he wrote both text and music include: *Tannhäuser* (1843–1845); *Lohengrin* (1846–1848); the tetralogy *Der Ring des Nibelungen* (1853–1874); *Tristan und Isolde* (1857–1859); *Die Meistersinger von Nürnberg* (1862–1867); and *Parsifal* (1877–1882) (Deathridge and Dahlhaus, 1984). With the exceptions of *Parsifal* and *Die Feen*, the rest of Wagner's music had been premièred before Freud left the Leseverein in 1877. The first complete *Ring* cycle was held at Bayreuth, on August 13, 14, 16, and 17, 1876 (Deathridge and Dahlhaus, 1984). However, after poor attendance at the subsequent two cycles, the festival was discontinued until 1882 (Strobel, 1938). The complete cycle was presented for the second time at Bayreuth by Cosima Wagner in 1896 (Bowers, 1988).

Schopenhauer's influence on Wagner and Nietzsche has been well documented, as well as the impact of Schopenhauer and Nietzsche on Freud (McGrath, 1967; Ellenberger, 1970; Rudnytsky, 1987). However, in another inexplicable case of omission, the influence of Wagner on Freud has yet to be extensively explored in historical psychoanalysis. Wagner has been treated like a neglected middle child!

But in 1952, Adorno wrote: "It is as if Wagner had anticipated Freud's discovery that what archaic man expresses in terms of violent action has not survived in civilized man, except in attenuated form, as an internal impulse that comes to the surface with the old explicitness only in dreams and madness" (p. 117). Moreover, in 1968, Magee contended that, except for *Die Meistersinger*, Wagner's mature operas appeared to be "like animated textbooks of psychoanalysis." In his view, "while archetypal psycho-sexual situations are being acted out and discussed on stage at exhaustive length, the orchestra is pouring out a flood of the otherwise inexpressible feelings associated with them" (p. 36).

VIII

In "An Autobiographical Study" (1925), Freud wrote: I read Schopenhauer very late in my life. Nietzsche, another philosopher whose guesses and intuitions often agree in the most astonishing way with the laborious findings of psycho-analysis, was for a long time avoided by me on that very account; *I was less concerned with the question of priority than with keeping my mind unembarrassed* (p. 60; emphasis added).

What about Wagner? Clearly, Freud's omission may well be quite significant in view of the overlooked fact that, aside from the special case of *Die Meistersinger* omitted in 1909(a), and of another nameless Wagner opera presented in *The Interpretation of Dreams* (1900) and only recently identified as *Der fliegende Holländer* (Díaz de Chumaceiro, 1990b), Freud specifically mentioned in his works *Tannhäuser* in 1900, *Lohengrin* in 1905, and *Tristan und Isolde* in 1911 (Guttman, Parrish, and Jones, 1984).

Gedo and Wolf (1976) have underscored that an "interesting revelation of the correspondence in Stanescu's [1971] possession is the fact that in 1873 the 17-year-old Freud was quite familiar with what Nietzsche had written up to that point" (p. 13). Moreover, Sulloway (1979) has stressed that Freud's denial "contrasts vividly with his complaints to Fliess in the 1890's upon finding himself anticipated by someone else" (p. 468; *Origins*, 1887–1902, pp. 126, 135, 231, 262). In spite of Freud's repetitive denials in 1908 (Nunberg and Federn, 1962), the fact remains that during his early maturity these three genial individuals received so much exposure in the media and cultural circles in Vienna that it was not necessary to have studied their works in detail to be influenced by their ideas (Ellenberger, 1970). Thus, until evidence to the contrary appears, the data suggest that Freud initially may well have become acquainted with many of Wagner's works during his membership at the Leseverein, and later continued to absorb data from his cultural milieu.

IX

In 1942, the musicologist Max Graf (1875–1958) wrote a brief article in which he reminisced about meeting Freud and the circumstances of his invitation to join the Wednesday evening meetings at 19 Bergasse. However, in concentrating on honoring Freud, Graf merely mentioned in passing his own presentations of papers "on the psychological processes of Beethoven and Richard Wagner in writing music" (p. 471). He did state, however, that he gave Freud the manuscript of his work on "an attempted analysis of Richard Wagner's The Flying Dutchman; in this the poetic imagery of Wagner was connected with his childhood impressions" (p. 471). He was referring to *Richard Wagner im "Fliegenden Holländer"; Ein Beitrang zur Psychologie künstlerischen Schaffens* (Richard Wagner in the "Flying Dutchman." A Contribution to the Psychology of Artistic Creation), written in 1905(a). Recognizing its value, Freud kept his friend's "first of its kind" piece and later published it in 1911, under his editorship. According to Deathridge (1982), "Graf throws new light on the character of Eric (who does not appear in Heine's account of the story) and Wagner's reasons for inventing him" (p. 21). Five years later, in 1910, Graf (1910) also applied Freud's theories "for the interpretation of creative musical work" in *The Inner Workshop of the Musician* (p. 471). Unfortunately, to date, Graf's seminal works on the application of psychoanalysis to music have not been translated into English.

X

Twenty years after the publication of Graf's article, Nunberg and Federn (1962) ended the introduction to the first volume of the *Minutes of the Vienna Psychoanalytic Society* with a translation of Graf's (1905a) foreword to his work on Wagner. Therein he stated: "The ideas which I develop here are *the result of an uninterrupted exchange of thoughts with Professor Freud*, and of many suggestions which slowly ripened over the years" (p. xxxii; emphasis added). He also clarified: "it would be impossible to separate those which I owe to the guidance of Professor Freud, and those which should be attributed to the criticism of several of my colleagues" (p. xxxii).

Curiously, although Nunberg and Federn (1962) in their notes on the members of the Psychological Wednesday Evening

Society mentioned the previous works they had published, in the case of Graf, they only stated that he "was an eminent musicologist and author, a personal friend of Freud" (p. xxxiv), omitting the titles of his works. Interestingly, when Graf met Freud in 1900, he had already written *Die Musik der Frau in der Renaissancezeit* (The Music of Women in the Renaissance) in 1896 for his dissertation at the University of Vienna—later published in 1905(b) as *Die Musik in Zeitalter der Renaissance* (Music in the Renaissance Period). In 1898, he had published *Deutsche Musik in neunzehnten Jahrhundert* (German Music in the Nineteenth Century), followed by *Wagner Problems und andere Studien* (Wagner Problems and Other Studies) in 1900. "From 1902 he taught musicology and musical aesthetics at the Conservatory of the *Gesellshaft der Musikfreunde* and when this became a state academy he was appointed to a lectureship in music history (1909–1938)" (Sadie, 1980, pp. 611–612). Would it not have been quite natural for Freud to have read some of his personal friend's works? This aspect of their relationship merits further study.

It is well known that Freud's (1909c) famous case of "Little Hans" was Graf's son, Herbert (1904–1973), who after graduating with a Ph.D. from the University of Vienna in 1925, and having also attended the Opera School of the State Academy for Music, became a stage director and opera impresario. He was stage director of the Metropolitan Opera in New York in 1936 (Thompson, 1938).

Given Freud's supposed "aversion" to music (Jones, 1953; H. Freud, 1956) and Graf's musicological status, it could easily have been assumed that Freud really knew little about Wagner and this opera, except for what his friend may have told him. From this perspective, then, in his foreword Graf was merely reflecting his idealizing transference. Graf (1942) himself had remarked that "Freud was a man of great artistic sensibilities, but to his great regret he was quite unmusical" (p. 474).

XI

As previously mentioned, in *The Interpretation of Dreams* (1900), Freud included a unique example given to him by a lady of his acquaintance that contained an untitled Wagner opera in its manifest content, which he interpreted without the dreamer's associations. In 1925, however, he added a footnote indicating that the dreamer's paramour in the dream had been the composer Hugo Wolf (1860–1903). Evidently, the omission of the title of this opera failed to attract curiosity and it remained overlooked in *The Standard Edition* (Strachey, 1953–1974) for over ninety years.

The recent identification of *Der fliegende Holländer* in this dream, however, expands the still quite limited view of how much Freud knew about Wagner's oeuvre (Díaz de Chumaceiro, 1990b). Just in connection with Graf's (1905a) work on Wagner, for example, it is now clear that Freud, having previously interpreted a dream containing this opera, had much to contribute on his own—in spite of his inability to sing on pitch (Díaz de Chumaceiro, 1990c). It is absurd to assume that Freud, without his friend's associations, would have analyzed this dream without consulting the libretto if he was not very familiar with the opera.

XII

Only recently has Graf's musical contribution to the field of applied psychoanalysis been acknowledged:

> Graf's approach involved an investigation of Wagner's autobiographical writings, including letters and reported dreams, a detailed study of the opera and its "poetic imagery," the women in Wagner's life, and the nature of each relationship as it could be determined. It utilized certain psychoanalytic views prevalent at that time about "the typical family history of neurotics" emphasizing the concepts of repetition compulsion, identification, early object loss, maternal fixation, and the reality conflicts resolved through (adolescent) fantasy. Graf also considered concepts such as artistic creativity as a source for conflict expression and conflict resolution where solutions in reality cannot be found.
>
> Graf brought considerable knowledge and sophistication to the Wednesday discussion groups and he can be thought of as the first musicologist to apply Freud's clinical findings and theoretical formulations to the study of an operatic work, delineating the many motifs employed by the composer and relating

them to the vicissitudes of the composer's complex life [Feder, Karmel, and Pollock, 1990, p. x].

MINUTES OF THE VIENNA PSYCHOANALYTIC SOCIETY

The discussions of the early years of the Wednesday Psychological Society (1902–1906) were not recorded (Nunberg and Federn, 1962). In this attempt to add data to the existing brief extracts on Wagner, Nunberg's (1962) warning to readers must be kept in mind: "Some of the Minutes are not easy to understand; some papers are rendered in a form that is too abbreviated, while others are mentioned only by their titles. Some speakers discuss one part of an unrecorded paper, others comment on another part. Thus, the Minutes are, at times, difficult to read" (p. xviii).

In addition to Graf, there were other members who had varying degrees of musical interests and knowledge. In the initial group, Rudolf Reitler (1865–1917), who was a highly respected physician and therapist, also composed songs. Alfred Adler (1870–1937) had several patients who were musicians; he was quite familiar with the lives of Beethoven, Mozart, and Schumann which he underscored in support of his theory of organ inferiority. Wilhelm Stekel (1869–1940) played duets with his wife, "a form of spiritual communication which he found deeply satisfying" (Brome, 1967, p. 20); he left the group shortly after Adler's exit in 1911 (Nunberg and Federn, 1962).

David Josef Bach (1874–1947) had studied philosophy and philology at the Vienna University. On his return to Vienna in 1900—after studying in London with Helmholtz and in Leipzig with Wundt—he initiated the Workers' Symphony Concerts. He was music critic for the *Frankfurter Zeitung, Die Zeit*, and the *Arbeiter Zeitung* (Thompson, 1938). Adler introduced him to Freud in 1902 (Nunberg and Federn, 1962); he withdrew from the group on October 11, 1911 (Nunberg and Federn, 1974, p. 146). He published *Die Wiener Volksoper* in 1911 (cited in Thompson, 1938, p. 100). One wonders whether this work will ever be published in English.

In 1902, Hermann Nothnagel, professor of internal medicine, introduced Paul Federn (1871–1950), who in turn

brought Eduard Hitschmann (1871–1958) to the group in 1905
(Nunberg and Federn, 1962). Hitschmann's wife Hedwig sang
with the Vienna opera; she successfully tutored Freud's daughter Anna in singing for her teacher's examinations in 1915
(Young-Bruehl, 1988).

Among the members who joined in 1908 or after, noteworthy
for their interest in music were Ferenczi, Sachs, Reik, and
Spielrein. Sandor Ferenczi (1873–1933), who became a member in 1908, wrote a brief paper entitled "On the Interpretation
of Tunes that Come into One's Head" (c. 1909), which was
published only posthumously. Hanns Sachs (1881–1947), a very
cultured lawyer with deep interests in art and literature, met
Freud in 1904 and joined the group in 1909. He coedited *Imago*
with Otto Rank (1844–1939) and later founded *American Imago*
(Nunberg and Federn, 1975; Sachs, 1945). Theodore Reik
(1888–1969) began to attend the meetings on November 22,
1911 (Nunberg and Federn, 1975). His early musical interest
was later developed in works that included clinical uses of thera-
pists' musical associations (1948, 1952, 1953). Finally, Sabina
Spielrein (1885–1941), initially Jung's patient, later attended
medical school, and joined the group in October 1911 (Nunberg and Federn, 1974). She played the piano and shared with
Jung an intense attraction to and passion for Wagner's music
(Carotenuto, 1980).

1906

On October 17, 1906, during the discussion of Rank's paper
on "The Incest Drama and Its Complications, Part II: The
Incestuous Relationship Between Siblings" (*Das Inzest-Motiv in
Dichtung und Sage: Grundzüge einer Psychologie des dichterischen
Schaffens* [The Incest Motif in Poetry and Saga: Fundamentals
of a Psychology of Poetic Creation]), Graf called attention to
the love Wagner had for his younger sister and to his anxiety
dreams in childhood, when he would wake up screaming and
calling her name. In addition, he was not able to clarify in the
least "the mysterious obscurity" surrounding the figures of
Erda and Kundry, assuming, however, "that repressed unconscious impulses lay behind the creation of these characters"
(Nunberg and Federn, 1962, Min. 2, p. 16).

In the first observation, since Richard was the youngest of seven surviving children, Graf was probably referring to Ottilie (1811–1883), the youngest of four females, who later married Hermann Brockhaus. With respect to the anxiety dreams, Wagner revealed in *My Life* (1870) that from early childhood to late boyhood, he awakened every evening screaming as a result of having dreamt about ghosts and only became silent when a human voice told him to do so. He welcomed as kindness being severely scolded or corporally punished; consequently, his siblings refused to sleep near him. As Wagner wrote: "they tried to bed me down as far from the others as possible, not stopping to think that by so doing my nocturnal call to be saved from the ghosts would become even louder and more enduring, until they finally accustomed themselves to this nightly calamity" (p. 13). In this instance, however, Wagner did not mention the name of the person he called.

Clearly, data are missing between Graf's two comments; the two operatic protagonists do not have siblings. In *The Ring* (*Das Rheingold* and *Siegfried*), Erda is Mother Earth, a goddess knowing everything, who conceives and brings to life the Norns (three fates representing past, present, and future) and the nine Valkyries. The paternity of the Norns (*Götterdämmerung*) is mysterious; however, Wotan is the father of the Valkyries, of whom Brünnhilde is the most famous.

Graf's curiosity about Kundry (in *Parsifal*) was hardly unfounded. She has been described as "one of Wagner's most striking creations. She is a sort of female Ahasuerus—a wandering Jewess" (Kobbé, 1919, p. 265). *Parsifal* is based on three sources: Chrétien de Troyes' (1190) *Perceval le Galois, ou li Contes del Graal*; Wolfram von Eschenbach's (c. 1195–1225) *Parzival*; and the fourteenth century collection of stories, *The Mabinogion*. As a result of combining elements from these sources, Wagner condemns Kundry for having laughed in front of the Saviour when he carried the cross. Wanting to be forgiven, Kundry offers her services as horseback messenger to the Grail knights, but is driven by a curse; Klingsor (a magician) then transforms her into a beautiful temptress who is to seduce the Knights of the Grail in order to destroy them. Only the man immune to her temptations can free her—Parsifal (Kobbé, 1919). The theme of salvation through compassionate enlightenment is a radical change from the earlier themes of salvation through the faithful love of a woman in *Der fliegende Holländer, Tannhaüser*, and *Tristan und Isolde*.

Not surprisingly, the only other recorded comment about Wagner in 1906 was also made by Graf. On November 28, Isidor Sadger discussed a recent publication on Nikolas Lenau (1802–1850) and Sophie (née von Keyle) Löwenthal. Graf then highlighted the similarity between the relationship of this couple with that of Wagner and Mathilde Wesendonck (Nunberg and Federn, 1962, Min. 8). In his previous work of 1905, Graf had already discussed Wagner's love life (Feder, Karmel, and Pollock, 1990).

Graf was referring here to the well-known scandal in which Wagner, while married to the actress Christine Wilhelmine ("Minna") Planer (1809–1866), had a love affair with Mathilde—the wife of the rich silk merchant, Otto Wesendonck. At this time, the latter was helping Wagner extricate himself from financial problems (Deathridge and Dahlhaus, 1984). Wagner recognized his debt to her inspiration in *Tristan* and in *Walkure* (Seglinde). In 1857 and 1858, he composed five songs for her: *Der Engel, Träume, Schmerzen, Stehe still*, and *Im Treibhaus* (Strobel, 1938).

1907

On January 23, 1907, Graf's paper, "Wagner's letters to his family—Art and Life," was announced (Nunberg and Federn, 1962, Min. 10, p. 82). However, no further record remains of this presentation. On February 6, in response to Stekel's review of Willmans's (1906) *Zur Psychopathologie des Landstreichers* (On the Psychopathology of the Vagabond), Rank (in addition to mentioning Kleist, Schiller, Goethe, Hebbel and Shakespeare) included "Wagner's flight from Dresden" when he linked "the flightlike travels of many of our greatest poets and 'vagrancy' " (Nunberg and Federn, 1962, Min. 12, p. 106).

Rank was referring, of course, to Wagner's involvement in the Dresden Revolution of 1849, with the arrest warrant of May 16, and to his subsequent escape to Switzerland on May 24, with the help of Franz Liszt—an exile that lasted for eleven years (Deathridge and Dahlhaus, 1984). In Rank's view, "in most poets this flight is really . . . emancipation not from father, mother, and siblings but from his own family: from his wife and child (this, however, is merely a displacement). The same is true of Wagner" (p. 106). Freud then reminded the group "of his division of love into object love and autoerotism, and furthermore of the retrogression mentioned before (regression of the libido) which also has a bearing on paranoia. The vagabond who runs away has a similar motive: to *flee* from his instincts; from *object love*" (Nunberg and Federn, 1962, pp. 108–109).

In Wagner's case, Minna later joined him in Switzerland, in September 1849; however, on January 29, 1850, Wagner again left her behind when he went to Paris. He then had an affair with Jessie Laussot from March until May, when their plans to escape (elope) to Greece and Asia Minor were ruined by her husband. Wagner returned to Minna on July 3 (Deathridge and Dahlhaus, 1984). Afterwards, he had his famous affair with Wesendonck. Apparently he also had an affair with Friederike Meyer—mentioned to Hans von Bülow in a letter on February 16, 1863 (Wagner, 1870, p. 743).

On April 17, 1907, during his presentation on Jean Paul Richter (1763–1825), among other issues, Bach underscored the difficulty and high risks involved in using a composer's music to draw conclusions about the individual. He proposed that "one moves on somewhat firmer ground when there is a text [written by the composer for his music], as in Wagner's case. The literary tastes of the composer might also give us some clues to his personality" (Nunberg and Federn, 1962, Min. 20, p. 167). Nevertheless, in spite of Bach's recommendation, *Der fliegende Holländer* was the opera most frequently discussed by this group. Then, in the ensuing free discussion, Freud remarked:

> The mother-etiology can be inferred with certainty only in those individuals (1) who have already began in puberty to make a peculiar separation of sex objects. On the one hand, they put the woman in such an exalted position that they dare not think of her in connection with sexual enjoyment. On the other hand, they open what we might call a separate account for the common wench: they look to her for sexual gratification. If these two

attitudes finally meet, various conflicts can arise: either they sublimate the harlot or they suffer disappointment with the lofty
object and then become misogynists.

(2) who show a strange mixture of faithfulness and unfaith-
fulness. They are always in search of the deliveress, the re-
deemer (Wagner), and put all kinds of women to the test.

(3) who are interested only in women who belong to other
men. The unattached woman does not attract them.

Only those who have all three characteristics can with certainty
be considered as cases of mother-etiology. Wagner is an exquisite
case [in point]. Not one of these conditions is present in the case
of Jean Paul [Nunberg and Federn, 1962, p. 172].

Graf did not limit his attention to just one opera. On December 11, 1907, he presented his paper on "Methodology of the
Psychology of Poets" (manuscript annexed to the original pro-
tocol). In his view, Cesare Lombroso's works on "the pathological roots of creative writing" had been presented "in a distorted
and amateurish manner" (Nunberg and Federn, 1962, Min. 33,
p. 260). Graf also rejected the French psychologists, with their
term *dégenéré supérieur* who only see a neurotic in a poet. Freud,
by contrast, "is interested in the human soul, the psychic organism" (p. 260). Graf believed that, "All artistic creation is rooted
in the repressed. But the repressed will offer resistances when
the autobiographer is about to relate his most important experiences. Precisely the most significant questions therefore will
remain unanswered. The artist overcomes his psychic inhibi-
tions only by creating, and whoever wishes to know the poet
must seek him out in his works" (p. 262).

In addition to mentioning several artists and their works,
referring specifically to Wagner, Graf then wrote:

Richard Wagner's Dutchman, Wotan and Amfortas are one figure. In the *Dutchman*, Senta leaves her betrothed to follow the
Dutchman; in the *Walküre*, in *Tristan*, the wife leaves the *husband*
in order to follow the lover, a kindred being. It is only here that
this motif is completely elucidated.

The desperate man, torn by discord, redeemed by the love of
a woman, is a dominant motif in all of Wagner's works.

The central themes of the poet's creations betray the inner-
most mechanisms of the poet's mind. Here we are in the center
of the unconscious [Nunberg and Federn, 1962, p. 263].

Furthermore, in his view, "it is also important to compare kindred personalities among the poets and artists, to establish *types of artists*. Richard Wagner and Euripides, Beethoven and Michelangelo, Raphael and Mozart are kindred, identical personalities. What may not be transparent in one becomes clear in the other" (p. 264; emphasis in original). Graf concluded that "second-rate geniuses who show pathological traits produce little or after long intervals. Their creative process is changed, is destroyed, is inhibited by the illness" (p. 264). In the discussion section, Freud elaborated on his paper, "Creative Writers and Day-Dreaming," which he had presented on December 6, 1907. There are no recorded comments about Wagner's operas.

1908

On January 29, 1908, discussing Adler's paper, "A Contribution to the Problem of Paranoia," Freud argued: "Paranoia can be studied very well in nonmorbid cases. The reformer, as long as he is alone, is considered a paranoiac (lately Richard Wagner). The fact that he has followers protects an individual against being declared ill" (Nunberg and Federn, 1962, Min. 38, p. 295).

Then, on March 4, 1908, Adolf Deutsch shared "an anecdote about Wagner to demonstrate how close love comes to art in the state of ecstasy" (Nunberg and Federn, 1962, Min. 43, p. 341). However, unfortunately, this example was not recorded. Nevertheless, these discussions seem to have been echoed two years later in Freud's (1911) "Psycho-Analytic Notes on an Autobiographical Case of Paranoia," where in a footnote he wrote: "An 'end of the world' based upon other motives is to be found in the climax of the ecstasy of love (cf. Wagner's *Tristan und Isolde*)" (p. 69n; see Chessick, 1983, 1986).

The meeting on April 1, 1908, was most significant. In the reading and discussion of Nietzsche's (1887) *On the Ascetic Ideal* (Part 3 of *Genealogy of Morality*), parallels were drawn between Schopenhauer and Nietzsche. Graf remarked that Nietzsche's development lacked "a sudden shift in the midst of life (as, for instance, in Wagner). His is a thrice-broken line: first, he

abandons philology when he becomes a Wagnerian and a Scho-
penhauerian; at this point, something must have broken
through, which perhaps is a consequence of the repudiation
and repression of sex following in the wake of his infection"
(Nunberg and Federn, 1962, Min. 45, pp. 358–359). Freud,
however, denied knowing Nietzsche's work; "occasional attempts at reading it were smothered by an excess of interest"
(p. 359). He then assured the group that, in spite of the similarities that had been stressed, "Nietzsche's ideas have had no influence whatsoever on his own work" (pp. 359–360). Clearly,
Freud protests too much; however, if he said anything about
Wagner, it was omitted. Then, turning to another point, Rank
added that Nietzsche's "relationship to Wagner becomes clearer
when one knows of his love for Cosima" (p. 361).

The background to Rank's comment is as follows: Cosima
(1837–1930), Franz Liszt's daughter, met Wagner in Paris in
1853 when she was 16 years old. Hans von Bülow, her first
husband, originally met Wagner in 1846. In 1864, von Bülow
began to conduct Wagner's works and the latter fell in love with
Cosima. In 1866, the lovers lived together in Switzerland, but
the following year, to keep up appearances, she rejoined her
husband for a short period; afterwards, however, she returned
to Wagner. In 1870, after having had three children with
Wagner (Isolde, Eva, and Siegfried) Cosima obtained an
annullment and married Wagner on August 25 of that year
(Strobel, 1938).

Wagner, the disciple of Feuerbach and Schopenhauer, met
Nietzsche at the home of his brother-in-law, Hermann Brockhaus (married to his sister Ottilie), on November 8, 1868.
Wagner was then 58 years old and Nietzsche (already a pro-
fessed Wagnerian highly impressed by *Tristan* and *Die Meistersinger*) was aged 24. The latter soon gained the confidence of
Wagner and Cosima, who entrusted him with the details of
the publication by *My Life* (1870). When Nietzsche became a
frequent house guest at Wagner's home at Tribschen, Wagner
was living with 31-year-old Cosima von Bülow, who had already
had two illegitimate children and was pregnant with the third
without having yet obtained a divorce. The external signs of
the deterioration of their relationship only became apparent

after the first Bayreuth Festival in August, 1876 (Deathridge and Dahlhaus, 1984)—before Freud left the *Leseverein*!

According to Rudnytsky (1987), Cosima reinforced Nietzsche's oedipal dynamics—envy of Wagner's successes—in this triangle. Nietzsche apparently was successfully able to repress his attraction to Cosima until his breakdown. In 1889 he wrote to her: "Ariadne, I love you. Dionysius"; in March of the same year, in the asylum he said: "My wife, Cosima Wagner, has brought me here" (Kaufmann, 1950, p. 32; Rudnytsky, 1987).

Over six months later, on October 28, 1908, Adolf Häutler presented a paper on Nietzsche's "Ecce Homo." He referred to Nietzsche's regrets about his *Der Fall Wagner. Nietzsche Contra Wagner* (1895). Nietzsche accused Wagner of "dramatizing"—a trait he himself possessed—"forever discovering himself in a superior being: in Schopenhauer, Wagner, Zarathustra, and finally, in Dionysius" (Nunberg and Federn, 1967, Min. 56, p. 28). In a long intervention in the discussion period, however, Freud, again, "would like to mention that he has never been able to study Nietzsche, partly because of the resemblance of Nietzsche's intuitive insights to our laborious investigations, and partly because of the wealth of ideas, which has always prevented Freud from getting beyond the first half page whenever he has tried to read him" (p. 32).

Clearly, these comments on Nietzsche and Wagner could have reminded Freud of his days at the *Leseverein*! Ellenberger (1970), for example, has underscored "a noteworthy parallelism" of Nietzsche's (1887) *Genealogy of Morals* with Freud's (1930) *Civilization and Its Discontents* (p. 277). By contrast, referring to the latter, Magee (1968) has stated that Wagner "expressed its central thesis in his book *Art and Revolution* [1849]" eighty years before Freud (p. 38). Evidently, this issue requires more study.

Wagner was also mentioned in more general contexts. On November 18, 1908, Isidor Sadger's nephew Fritz Wittels (1880–1950), in his paper on "Sexual Perversity," contrasted a lover with a "rake" (incapable of love). Among other issues, he made a lengthy musical parallel and compared "lovers to those who, being connoisseurs, see in Wagner a great advance over

the older musicians and for that reason hold him in high esteem, whereas the rake, who knows nothing about the nature
of love, is comparable to the overenthusiastic Wagner fans who
do not have any notion of music." In the middle, lie those
lacking deep comprehension who "assert that Wagner means
the end of all music—they like Mozart" (Nunberg and Federn,
1967, Min. 59, p. 56).

Oscar Rie (1863–1931), a prominent pediatrician, close
friend and coauthor with Freud, considered that this comparison was "a good one, but unfortunate for Wittels, for it proves
him to be wrong: the rakes are just as far from being sick—unless they are anesthetic—as the unmusical person is from
healthy enjoyment" (Nunberg and Federn, 1967, p. 63; also see
Freud's Letter 116, McGuire, 1979, p. 182; Wittels, 1931).

Then, on December 9, 1908, Freud mentioned an interpretation by Brill—six days after receiving Jung's reply (see page
253). In his view, it is "very daring, but it does seem plausible":

> The patient constantly reiterates the question: 'Am I Parsifal,
> the pure *Tor*?'. . . We could go further and ask: What is the
> meaning of this question, which has become the substitute for
> another question? Obviously the question that torments him is:
> Is she faithful to me? This question has been transformed, as it
> were, into the homosexual [counterpart]. The word 'purest,'
> used with regard to faithfulness, contains a hint of what is ani-
> mating, so to speak, the entire obsession [Nunberg and Federn,
> 1967, Min. 61, p. 79].

1909

On January 13, 1909, when discussing Stekel's work on "Poetry
and Neurosis," Graf remarked: "The finest characterization of
poetic creation is found in [Richard] Wagner's dictum: 'The
poet is he who knows the unconscious' " (Nunberg and Federn,
1967, Min. 64, p. 103). Freud undoubtedly agreed.

Four months later, in his presentation on May 19, 1909, of
"On a Specific Type of Male Object-Choice," Freud declared:
"The individual deliverer (*not* the world-saviour, the deliverer
of mankind) who appears also in Wagner's '*Flying Dutchman*'
and elsewhere in literature, can be traced back to the mother,
[who comes] in the wish-fantasy to liberate [the son] from mas-
turbation. But the motif of rescue has another source" (Nun-

berg and Federn, 1967, Min. 80, p. 242). Interestingly, Freud changed his mind in his final version for publication. In "A Special Type of Choice of Object Made by Men" (1910), this reference to Wagner was eliminated.

1910

On March 16, 1910, Graf commented that in his first work on Wagner's *Flying Dutchman* (1905a), he had not been successful in his attempt to unravel the dominating motif in Wagner's life and works: "intruding into a marriage and snatching the woman away toward himself" (Nunberg and Federn, 1967, Min. 101, p. 461). His new explanation, instead, is based on the rumor that Ludwig (Heinrich Christian) Geyer (1779–1821) was Wagner's father—wedding Wagner's mother when the infant was 6 months old. These rumors, spread by Wagner, revealed his fantasy. "If this is true, then that Wagnerian main motif is to be traced back to an identification with Geyer (throughout his life Wagner wore the painter's garb that was characteristic of Geyer)—whom he assumed to have committed adultery with his mother" (p. 461). Freud observed: "The Wagner-motif goes back to the 'maternal aetiology': (1) the wife of another man; (2) ill-repute = fantasy of adultery" (p. 462).

According to Deathridge and Dahlhaus (1984), however, Richard Wagner was born on May 22, 1813; his father died when he was 6 months old (November 23, 1813), and his mother Johanna married Geyer on August 28, 1814—nine months after Richard's father's death. Thus, Richard was *15 months old* when his mother remarried, not 6 months as recorded here. Until January 21, 1828, when Richard (*almost 15 years old*) entered the *Leipzig Nicolaischule*, his name was Richard Geyer. His later repetition of the name "Wagner" on his manuscripts has suggested his doubt about his name.

1911

On November 15, 1911, during the discussion of Reik's paper, "On Death and Sexuality," Spielrein commented on "the fear of the dissolution of the ego or the fear of the transformation into a different personality; further, the problem of eternal life

(Glaukos; the flying Dutchman), which is thought of as being as terrible as birth, and in which death represents nothing but birth." The editors clarified: "Glaukos Pontios, Greek sea-divinity, a fisherman who had been transformed into a merman and endowed with the gift of unerring prophecy" (Nunberg and Federn, 1974, Min. 150, p. 316).

Two meetings later, on November 29, 1911, Spielrein presented a paper on "Transformation," as a part of her work, *Die Destruktion als Ursache des Werdens* (Destruction as a Cause of Coming into Being). Addressing life and destruction in myths, she traced them to earth and water symbolisms. For her, "the tree of knowledge" had this duality, represented in "the wood of Christ's cross"; "the tree of life" symbolized "the bridge over the water, which is a procreative primeval force like the earth." She then linked these parallels to "the Siegfried myth and the legend of the *Flying Dutchman*; in this connection it is pointed out that it is in the manner of Freud's savior type that Wagner's heroes love, in that they sacrifice themselves and die" (Nunberg and Federn, 1974, Min. 152, p. 330; see Kerr, 1988). In view of the significance of Siegfried in Spielrein's personal life at this time, as was previously underscored, it is not surprising that this issue would also surface in her work.

This was the last time that mention of *The Flying Dutchman* was recorded in the *Minutes*. The final meeting Graf attended in 1911 was on January 4; this explains the absence of his remarks to Spielrein's statements. (Apparently he withdrew from the group after having attended only one meeting in 1912, on March 27) (Nunberg and Federn, 1975).

In the discussion, Sachs remarked: "In one of the older songs of the Edda, Wotan hangs as a sacrifice from the world-ashtree" (p. 331). Sachs is alluding to the fact that in the *Elder Eddas*, Yggdrasil was a huge ash tree that supported the cosmos. Odin (Wotan or also Woden), the one-eyed chief of the gods, usually is depicted with two ravens perched on his shoulders (Memory and Thought); his thirst for knowledge and wisdom was described as intense and unending. To rejuvenate themselves, the gods ate magic apples given to them by Idun. Odin, instead, selected a more difficult way of preventing aging: "He freely wounded himself with his own spear and hung himself for nine days from the cosmic tree Yggdrasil, which was shaken by the winds. In this manner, he renewed his youth, but he also became the master of the magic runes, inscriptions that could accomplish any mortal purpose, whether beneficial or baneful" (Weigel, 1973, p. 156). Freud was familiar with Odin's legend, which he had previously linked to a childhood scene with his own father (1900, p. 216).

1913

In 1912, Wagner was not mentioned in the records. The final statement about Wagner was made on January 22, 1913, when Lorenz, in his presentation of "The Story of the Miner of Falun," mentioned among others, Wagner's outline of the text for an unfinished opera, *Die Bergwerke zu Falun* (*The Miner of Falun*) published in 1905 (Nunberg and Federn, 1975, Min. 186, p. 151).

SUMMARY

Freud's indifference toward the music world is legendary (Díaz de Chumaceiro, 1992b,c; 1993a,b,c); nevertheless, data reflecting his knowledge of Wagner's life and music merit attention. Thus, Freud's reaction to *Die Meistersinger* was highlighted, a preliminary consolidation of data that had previously been overlooked, and the historical records of the Wednesday evening meetings that mentioned Wagner were chronologically underscored and amplified. Presumably, Freud was acquainted with Wagner's works during his membership at the *Leseverein*, and later continued to acquire data from his milieu. Wagner's impact on Freud, the extent of which has yet to be determined, is reflected in the fact that brief references to *Der fliegende Holländer*, *Tannhäuser*, *Lohengrin*, and *Tristan und Isolde* were included in his writings; the case of *Die Meistersinger* requires further study. Clearly, Freud knew more about Wagner than previously assumed.

REFERENCES

Adler, A. (1908), A contribution to the problem of paranoia. In: *Minutes of the Vienna Psychoanalytic Society*, Vol. 1, ed. H. Nunberg & E. Federn, tr. M. Nunberg. New York: International Universities Press, 1962, pp. 288–297.

Adorno, T. (1952), *In Search of Wagner*, tr. R. Livingstone. U.K.: Thetford Press Ltd., 1981.

Anzieu, D. (1975), *Freud's Self-Analysis*, tr. P. Graham. Madison, CT: International Universities Press, 1986.

Bach, D. J. (1911), *Die Wiener Volksoper*. In: *The International Cyclopedia of Music and Musicians*, 10th ed., ed. B. Bohle. New York: Dodd, Mead, 1975.

Bettelheim, B. (1989), A secret asymmetry. In: *Freud's Vienna and Other Essays*. New York: Alfred A. Knopf, 1990, pp. 57–81.

Boehlich, W., ed. (1990), *The Letters of Sigmund Freud to Eduard Silberstein 1871–1881*. Cambridge, MA: The Belknap Press/Harvard University Press.

Bonaparte, M., Freud, A., & Kris, E., eds. (1954), *The Origins of Psychoanalysis: Letters to Wilhelm Fliess, Drafts and Notes, 1887–1902*, by Sigmund Freud. New York: Basic Books.

Bowers, F. (1988), Ring tales. In: *The Ring: Metropolitan Opera*. New York: Metropolitan Opera Guild, pp. 41–64.

Branscombe, P., tr. (1974), *Die Meistersinger von Nürnberg*. German libretto of R. Wagner's (1867) opera in 3 acts. Hamburg: Polydor International GmbH [CD 415 278-2].

Brill, A. A. (1908), Psychological factors in dementia praecox: An analysis. *J. Abnorm. Psychol.*, 3:219–239.

Brome, V. (1967), *Freud and His Early Circle: The Struggles of Psycho-Analysis*. London: William Heinemann Ltd.

Carotenuto, A. (1980), *A Secret Symmetry: Sabina Spielrein between Jung and Freud*, tr. A. Pomerans, J. Shepley, & K. Winston. New York: Pantheon Books, 1982.

Chessick, R. D. (1983), The Ring: Richard Wagner's dream of preoedipal destruction. *Amer. J. Psychoanal.*, 43:361–374.

———— (1986), On falling in love: The mystery of Tristan and Isolde. In: *Psychoanalytic Explorations in Music*, First Series, eds. S. Feder, R. L. Karmel, & G. H. Pollock. Madison, CT: International Universities Press, 1990, pp. 465–483.

Chrétien de Troyes (1190), *Perceval le Galois, ou li Contes del Graal*, 6 vols., ed. C. Potvin. New York: French & European Publications, 1970.

Deathridge, J. (1982), An introduction to 'The Flying Dutchman.' In: *Opera Guide Series: Der fliegende Holländer. Richard Wagner*, ed. N. John. New York: Riverrun Press, pp. 13–26.

———— Dahlhaus, C. (1984), *The New Grove Wagner*. New York: W. W. Norton.

Díaz de Chumaceiro, C. L. (1990a), A brief report on Freud's attendance at opera performances: 1880–1890. *Amer. J. Psychoanal.*, 50:285–288.

———— (1990b), The identification of Wagner's *Der fliegende Holländer* in a dream Freud reported. *Amer. J. Psychoanal.*, 50:337–350.

———— (1990c), Was Freud really tone-deaf? A brief commentary. *Amer. J. Psychoanal.*, 50:199–202.

———— (1991), Sigmund Freud: On pianists' performance problems. *Med. Prob. Perform. Art.*, 6:21–27.

———— (1992a), A brief note on Freud and Mozart's *Magic Flute*. *Amer. J. Psychoanal.*, 52:75–78.

———— (1992b), On Freud's admiration for Beethoven and his 'splendid creations.' *Amer. J. Psychoanal.*, 52:175–181.

—— (1992c), On the identity of Sigmund Freud's "prima donna." *Amer. J. Psychoanal.*, 52:363–369.

—— (1993a), Transference–countertransference implications in Freud's patient's recall of Weber's *Der Freischütz. Psychoanal. Rev.*, 80 (in press).

—— (1993b), Review of *Psychoanalytic Explorations in Music.* First Series by eds. S. Feder, R. L. Karmel, & G. H. Pollock. International Universities Press, 1990. *J. Mus. Ther.*, 30 (in press).

—— (1993c), Freud, three operas, and the affair with Minna Bernays. *Amer. J. Psychoanal.*, 53:85–91.

Elder Edda, The. In: *The Harvard Classics*, Vol. 49, *Epic and Saga*, ed. C. W. Eliot, tr. E. Magnússon & W. Morris. New York: P. F. Collier & Son Corporation, 1938, pp. 361–438.

Ellenberger, H. F. (1970), *The Discovery of the Unconscious.* New York: Basic Books.

Eschenbach, W. von (1195–1225), *Parzival*, tr. A. T. Hatto. New York: Penguin Books, 1980.

Feder, S., Karmel, L., & Pollock, G. H., eds. (1990), *Psychoanalytic Explorations in Music*, First Series. Madison, CT: International Universities Press.

Ferenczi, S. (1909), On the interpretation of tunes that come into one's head. In: *Final Contributions to the Problems and Methods of Psycho-Analysis*, ed. M. Balint. New York: Brunner/Mazel, 1980, pp. 175–176.

Freud, H. (1956), My uncle Sigmund. In: *Freud As We Knew Him*, ed. H. M. Ruitenbeek. Detroit: Wayne State University Press, 1973, pp. 312–313.

Freud, S. (1900), The Interpretation of Dreams. *Standard Edition*, 4/5. London: Hogarth Press, 1953.

—— (1905), Jokes and Their Relation to the Unconscious. *Standard Edition*, 8. London: Hogarth Press, 1960.

—— (1908 [1907]), Creative writers and day-dreaming. *Standard Edition*, 9:141–153. London: Hogarth Press, 1959.

—— (1909a), Notes upon a case of obsessional neurosis. *Standard Edition*, 10:155–318. London: Hogarth Press, 1955.

—— (1909b), Addendum: Original record of the case (of obsessional neurosis). *Standard Edition*, 10:254–318. London: Hogarth Press, 1955.

—— (1909c), Analysis of a phobia in a five-year-old boy. *Standard Edition*, 10:5–147. London: Hogarth Press, 1955.

—— (1910), A special type of choice of object made by men. Contributions to the psychology of love I. *Standard Edition*, 11:163–175. London: Hogarth Press, 1957.

—— (1911), Psycho-analytic notes on an autobiographical account of a case of paranoia (Dementia paranoides). *Standard Edition*, 12:163–175. London: Hogarth Press, 1958.

—— (1914), The Moses of Michelangelo. *Standard Edition*, 13:211–238. London: Hogarth Press, 1955.

—— (1916), Some character-types met with in psycho-analytic work. *Standard Edition*, 14:311–315. London: Hogarth Press, 1957.

—— (1925 [1924]), An autobiographical study. *Standard Edition*, 20:3–74. London: Hogarth Press, 1959.

—— (1930 [1929]), Civilization and its discontents. *Standard Edition*, 21:64–145. London: Hogarth Press, 1961.

Gay, P. (1988), *Freud: A Life for Our Time.* New York: W. W. Norton.

Gedo, J. E., & Wolf, E. S. (1976), From the history of introspective psychology: The humanist strain. In: *Freud: The Fusion of Science and Humanism*, ed. J. E. Gedo &

G. H. Pollock, *Psychological Issues*, Vol. 9, 2/3, Monograph 34/35. New York: International Universities Press, pp. 11–45.

Graf, M. (1896), *Die Musik der Frau in der Renaissancezeit (The Music of Women in the Renaissance)*. Doctoral Dissertation, University of Vienna.

—— (1898), *Deutsche Musik in neunzehnten Jahrhundert (German Music in the 19th Century)*. Berlin: S. Cronbach.

—— (1900), *Wagner Problems und andere Studien (Wagner Problems and Other Studies)*. Wiener: Verlag.

—— (1905a), Richard Wagner im *fliegende Holländer*: Ein Beitrag zur Psychologie künstlerischen Schaffens (Richard Wagner in *The Flying Dutchman*: A contribution to the psychology of artistic creation). *Schriften zur angewandten Seelenkunde*, 9. Vienna: Franz Deutike, 1911.

—— (1905b), *Die Musik im Zeitalter der Renaissance (Music in the Renaissance Period)*. Berlin: Bard, Marquardt.

—— (1907a), Wagner's letters to his family. Art and life. In: *Minutes of the Vienna Psychoanalytic Society*, Vol. 2, ed. H. Nunberg & E. Federn, tr. M. Nunberg. New York: International Universities Press, 1962, p. 82.

—— (1907b), Methodology of the psychology of poets. In: *Minutes of the Vienna Psychoanalytic Society*, Vol. 2, ed. H. Nunberg & E. Federn, tr. M. Nunberg. New York: International Universities Press, 1962, pp. 260–265.

—— (1910), *Die innere Werkstatt des Musikers (The Inner Workshop of the Musician)*. Stuttgart: Ferdinand Enke.

—— (1942), Reminiscences of Professor Sigmund Freud. *Psychoanal. Quart.*, 11:465–476.

Guttman, S. A., Parrish, S. M., & Jones, R. L. (1984), *The Concordance to the Standard Edition of the Complete Psychological Works of Sigmund Freud*. New York: International Universities Press.

Howard, R. (1988), Wagner as poet. In: *The Ring: Metropolitan Opera*. New York: Metropolitan Opera Guild, pp. 24–28.

Jones, E. (1953), *The Life and Works of Sigmund Freud*, Vol. 1. New York: Basic Books.

Kaufmann, W., ed., tr. (1950), *Nietzsche: Philosopher, Psychologist, Antichrist*. Princeton, NJ: Princeton University Press, 1974.

Kerr, J. (1988), Beyond the pleasure principle and back again: Freud, Jung, and Sabina Spielrein. In: *Freud: Appraisals and Reappraisals. Contributions to Freud Studies*, Vol. 3, ed. P. E. Stepansky. Hillsdale, NJ: Analytic Press, pp. 3–79.

Kobbé, G. (1919), *The Definite Kobbé's Opera Book*, ed. Earl of Harewood. New York: G. P. Putnam's Sons, 1987.

Lehmann, H. (1986), Jung contra Freud/Nietzsche contra Wagner. *Internat. Rev. Psycho-Anal.*, 13:201–209.

Lorenz, E. F. (1914), The story of the miner of Falun. *Imago*, 3:250–301.

Mabinogion, The. tr. G. Jones & T. Jones. New York: Everyman Library, 1950.

Magee, B. (1968), *Aspects of Wagner*, rev. ed. New York: Oxford University Press, 1988.

Mahoney, P. J. (1986), *Freud and the Rat Man*. New Haven, CT: Yale University Press.

Masson, J. M., ed. & tr. (1985), *The Complete Letters of Sigmund Freud to Wilhelm Fliess (1887–1904)*. Cambridge, MA: The Belknap Press/Harvard University.

McGrath, W. J. (1967), Student radicalism in Vienna. *J. Contemp. Hist.*, 2:183–201.

McGuire, W., ed. (1979), *The Freud/Jung Letters*, tr. R. Manheim & R. F. C. Hull. Cambridge, MA: Harvard University Press, 1988.

Nibelungenlied, The (1200), tr. A. T. Hatto. London: Penguin Books, 1965.

Nietzsche, F. (1887), Genealogy of Morals. In: *The Birth of Tragedy and The Genealogy of Morals*, tr. F. Golffing. New York: Doubleday/Anchor Books, 1956, pp. 147–299.

—— *Werke und Briefe*, 9 vols., ed. H. J. Mette. Munich: Beck, 1934.

Nunberg, H., & Federn, E., eds. (1962), *Minutes of the Vienna Psychoanalytic Society*, Vol. 1: 1906–1908. tr. M. Nunberg. New York: International Universities Press.

—— (1967), *Minutes of the Vienna Psychoanalytic Society*, Vol. 2: 1908–1910. tr. M. Nunberg. New York: International Universities Press.

—— (1974), *Minutes of the Vienna Psychoanalytic Society*, Vol. 3: 1910–1912. tr. M. Nunberg. New York: International Universities Press.

—— (1975), *Minutes of the Vienna Psychoanalytic Society*, Vol. 4: 1912–1918. tr. M. Nunberg. New York: International Universities Press.

Rank, O. (1906), *Das Inzest-Motiv in Dichtung und Sage: Grundzüge einer Psychologie des dichterischen Schaffens (The Incest Motif in Poetry and Saga: Fundamentals of a Psychology of Poetic Creation)*, 2nd ed., enlarged & rev. Vienna: Franz Deuticke, 1926.

Reik, T. (1911), On death and sexuality. In: *Minutes of the Vienna Psychoanalytic Society*, Vol. 3, ed. H. Nunberg & E. Federn, tr. M. Nunberg. New York: International Universities Press, 1974, pp. 310–319.

—— (1948), *Listening with the Third Ear*. New York: Farrar, Straus & Giroux.

—— (1952), Refrain of a song. *Psychoanal.*, 1:25–35.

—— (1953), *The Haunting Melody: Psychoanalytic Experiences in Life and Music*. New York: Farrar, Straus & Young.

Roazen, P. (1971), *Freud and His Followers*. New York: Meridian, 1974.

Rudnytsky, P. L. (1987), *Freud and Oedipus*. New York: Columbia University Press.

Sachs, H. (1945), *Freud, Master and Friend*. London: Imago Publishing.

Sadie, S., ed. (1980), *The New Grove Dictionary of Music and Musicians*, Vol. 7. London: Macmillan Publishers Limited.

Salter, L., tr. (1969), *Siegfried*. Part 2 of R. Wagner's Trilogy *Der Ring des Nibelungen*. German libretto (1853) of music drama in 3 acts. Polydor International [CD Stereo 415 150-2] GmbH, Hamburg.

Sams, E. (1980), Hugo Wolf. In: *The New Grove Late Romantic Masters*. New York: W. W. Norton, 1985, pp. 303–389.

Spielrein, S. (1912), Die Destruktion als Ursache des Werdens (Destruction as a cause of coming into being). *Jahrbuch für Psychoanalyse*, 4:465–503.

Stanescu, H. (1971), Young Freud's letters to his Rumanian friend, Silberstein. *Israel Ann. Psychiat.*, 9:195–207.

Stekel, W. (1909), Poetry and neurosis. Contributions to the psychology of the artist and of artistic creative ability. *Psychoanal. Rev.*, 1923, 10:73–96, 190–208, 316–328, 457–466; 1924, 11:48–60.

Strachey, J., ed. (1953–1974), *The Standard Edition of the Complete Psychological Works of Sigmund Freud*. London: Hogarth Press.

—— (1955), Editor's Note to Addendum: Original record of the case (of obsessional neurosis). *Standard Edition*, 10:253–257. London: Hogarth Press.

Strobel, O. (1938), Richard Wagner. In: *The International Cyclopedia of Music and Musicians*, 10th ed., ed. B. Bohle. New York: Dodd, Mead, 1975, pp. 2397–2408.

Sulloway, F. J. (1979), *Freud, Biologist of the Mind*. New York: Basic Books.

Thompson, O., ed. (1938), *The International Cyclopedia of Music and Musicians*, 10th ed., ed. B. Bohle. New York: Dodd, Mead, 1975.

Vitz, P. C. (1988), *Sigmund Freud's Christian Unconscious*. New York: Guilford Press.

Wagner, R. (1834), *Die Feen*. German libretto of opera in 3 acts, based on G. Gozzi's *La donna serpente*. Mannheim, 1888.

—— (1836), *Das Lievesverbot oder Die Novize von Palermo*. German libretto of opera in 2 acts, based on Shakespeare's *Measure for Measure*, Leipzig, 1911.

—— (1840), *Rienzi der Letzte der Tribunen*. German libretto of opera in 5 acts, based on E. Bulwer Lytton's *Rienzi: The Last of the Roman Tribunes*. Dresden, 1842.

—— (1841), *Der Fliegende Holländer*. German libretto of opera in 3 acts, based on *Heine's Memoiren des Herr von Schnabelewopski*, tr. S. Robb. New York: G. Schirmer, 1964.

—— (1842), *Die Bergwerke zu Falun (The Miner of Falun)*. Text for unfinished opera in three acts. Gleichzeitig in Ermisch, 1905.

—— (1845), *Tannhäuser und der Sängerkrieg auf Wartburg*. German libretto of opera in 3 acts, tr. F. Rullman. New York: Fred Rollman, 1953.

—— (1848), *Lohengrin*. German libretto of opera in 3 acts. Weimar, 1850.

—— (1849), *Die Kunst und die Revolution (Art and Revolution)*. Leipzig.

—— (1853a), *Das Rheingold*. German libretto of Prologue in one act to the Trilogy *Der Ring des Nibelungen*. tr. S. Robb. New York: G. Schirmer, 1960.

—— (1853b), *Die Walküre*. Part 1 of Trilogy *Der Ring des Nibelungen*. German libretto of music drama in 3 acts, tr. S. Robb. New York: G. Schirmer, 1960.

—— (1853c), *Götterdämmerung*. Part 3 of Trilogy *Der Ring des Nibelungen*. German libretto of music drama in 3 acts, tr. S. Robb. New York: G. Schirmer, 1960.

—— (1859), *Tristan und Isolde*. German libretto of opera in 3 acts, tr. S. Robb. New York: G. Schirmer, 1965.

—— (1870), *My Life*, tr. A. Gray, ed. M. Whittall. Cambridge, MA: Cambridge University Press, 1983.

—— (1877), *Parsifal*. German libretto of opera in 3 acts. Mainz, 1882.

Weigel, J., Jr. (1973), *Mythology*. Lincoln, NE: Cliff Notes.

Willmans, K. (1906), *Zur Psychopathologie des Landstreichers (On the Psychopathology of the Vagabond: A Clinical Study)*. Leipzig [publisher not given].

Wistrich, R. S. (1989), *The Jews of Vienna in the Age of Franz Joseph*. New York: Oxford University Press.

Wittels, F. (1908), Sexual perversity. In: *Minutes of the Vienna Psychoanalytic Society*, Vol. 2, ed. H. Nunberg & E. Federn, tr. M. Nunberg. New York: International Universities Press, 1967, pp. 53–64.

—— (1931), *Freud and His Time*, tr. L. Brink. New York: Liveright Publishing Corporation.

Young-Bruehl, E. (1988), *Anna Freud: A Biography*. New York: Summit Books.

Chapter 15

Freud and Max Graf: On the Psychoanalysis of Music

David M. Abrams, Ph.D.

INTRODUCTION

Vienna was long the world's capital of music. Composers who lived there included Mozart, Haydn, Beethoven, Gluck, Schubert, Brahms, Johann Strauss, father and son, Richard Strauss, Bruckner, Mahler, Goldmark, Hugo Wolf, Alban Berg, Anton von Webern, and Arnold Schoenberg. Historian William Johnston (1972, p. 132) writes that "Vienna's favorite entertainment was undoubtedly music. In homes, music making was so popular that a law forbade playing an instrument after 11:00 P.M. Many families staged musicales on Sunday afternoon inviting young musicians to perform." For many centuries, then, it was as much a part of the daily lives of Viennese children and adults to play music as it is today for most people to regularly engage in sports and physical exercise.

Freud's closest musical colleague was Max Graf, who has been described as "the foremost music historian of his time" (Gartenberg, 1978, p. 48). Born on October 1, 1873, he was a prominent music critic for several leading newspapers in Vienna, professor of music history and esthetics at the Academy of Music, organizer of music festivals, and author of many books and articles. A good introduction to Graf and to his style of writing is to be found in this description of Vienna's musical life and the thrill for its young people of attending the opera:

Acknowledgments. The author wishes to acknowledge the help of Helen Levine, Peter Deri, Phyllis Sloate, Judy Levy, Werner Graf, Lydia Sobolev, Gertrude Lessem, Ruth Rosenfield, and Stuart Feder.

We became musicians without knowing why or how. Everywhere we went we encountered music. We sang and fiddled. As a student in high school, I took my violin every evening and went to other homes and played classical string quartets with minor officials, teachers or business people, just as if that were self-understood. On Sundays, I played Haydn's or Mozart's Masses in church choirs. On excursions, we all sang choruses and canons. Or we stood, evenings, in front of restaurant gardens or in the parks and listened to band concerts. Thus, we prepared ourselves for the holiday when we went for the first time to the opera palace on the Ring. From noontime on we stood, boys and girls, in front of the small entrance to the Opera House, which still remained locked, with piano scores in our hands, heatedly debating about music. When the door at last was opened, we would storm excitedly to the box office, and then up four flights of stairs like competing foot racers—up the still dimly-lighted passageway to the fourth gallery from where we could look down on the stage.

Slowly, after some time, the musicians came into the comfortable orchestra pit. The violinists tuned their instruments and little runs rose high like butterflies. Woodwinds tried passages, and the low brasses tossed growling, antedeluvian tones into the bustle of the orchestral voices. The sounds kept swelling louder and louder, like the buzzing of a teakettle about to boil. Then the lights in the hall were extinguished, the great chandelier went slowly out and one could see only the ghostly glow of the lights over the musicians' desks. When all had become silent and one's heart pounded excitedly, the conductor came, sat at his desk, opened the sorcerer's book and raised his magic wand. This was a festive moment. For then, for the first time, were we taken in to the great Viennese music community which assembled every evening in the new opera house. A new generation of musicians and of music had joined itself to the old. We had become full-fledged citizens of the old music city [1945, pp. 67–68].

Given this environment, it is striking that as cultured and educated a man as Freud neither played a musical instrument nor regularly attended musical concerts and that so few of his early followers were musical. Joining Freud's circle in 1923, Richard Sterba (1982, pp. 96–97) was surprised to find that "for a Viennese group, there were conspicuously few amateur musicians among the members," and he suggests that "one reason for this may have been that many of them had not grown up in Vienna." Freud (1914) emphasized that literature and sculpture had a powerful effect on him, but of music said, "I am almost incapable of obtaining any pleasure" (p. 211). The few references to music in his writings are mostly to Mozart's *Don Giovanni* and *The Magic Flute*, and Jones (1953, Vol. 1) reports that the rare occasions Freud attended the opera, it "had to be by Mozart, though an exception was made with *Carmen*" (p. 329).

While such inability to appreciate Vienna's greatest art form might be traceable to some auditory-related trauma in his early life, another possibility is that Freud might have been "tone deaf." For he wrote Fliess on August 31, 1898, that he had to stop reading a philosophical book when the author began discussing the topic of "sound relationships that has always vexed me, because I lack the most elementary knowledge, thanks to the atrophy of my acoustic sensibilities" (1887–1904, p. 325). His sister, Anna, who was two-and-a-half years younger than Freud, also points out that, "When I was eight years old, my mother, who was very musical, wanted me to study the piano, and I began practising by the hour. Though Sigmund's room was not near the piano, the sound disturbed him. He appealed to my mother to remove the piano if she did not wish him to leave the house altogether. The piano disappeared and with it all opportunities for his sisters to become musicians. Nor did any of [Sigmund's] children ever receive musical instruction where he would have to hear it" (Bernays, 1940, p. 142).

In view of this history, it is a testament to Freud's pioneering spirit that for well over a decade he engaged in a very productive collaboration with Max Graf on the psychoanalysis of music, which resulted in several works (Graf, 1906, 1907a,b, 1910, 1911). At that time, Graf was an active member of Freud's early circle and from 1906 to 1908, regularly sent him reports on the psychosexual development and later treatment of his son, Herbert Graf. Freud (1907, p. 135) first referred to Graf's son as "Little Herbert" and later (1909) as "Little Hans." With so much focus on the child, it is easy to overlook the fact that over half of the case report was actually written by Graf in the form of weekly letters to Freud, providing the verbatim process of his treatment sessions much as an analytic candidate would report to a supervisor today. However, comparing these letters with the sessions of most analytic candidates, it is impossible to overlook the inspiring level of creative exploration, depth of analytic insight, humane humor, and emotional sensitivity in the therapeutic work of Freud's (1909, p. 5) anonymous collaborator, who is identified simply as "a father and a physician united in a single person." The case is all the more remarkable, since it appears to be the only one Graf seems to have undertaken.

OVERVIEW OF THE WORK ON MUSIC

The beginning of Graf's involvement in psychoanalysis was at the turn of the century, when a young woman told him about her treatment sessions with Freud. Graf went to meet Freud and had many individual consultations. Graf (1957) reports:

> Freud did not appear to have any doubt about devoting a great deal of his precious time to an unknown young man, who came for explanations of many questions about which he was in the dark. Better yet, he encouraged me to keep coming, and in these private conversations taught me a lot and encouraged me continuously. The stimulation I derived from his writings illuminated many areas of music for me and also helped clarify what takes place in the psyche of creative people. Freud himself was not musical, which he regretted. He derived his artistic experiences from literature, in which he was well versed, and from paintings, which he loved. He travelled to see paintings in Holland and Italy. Freud welcomed conversations with a musician, which gave him access to a field unfamiliar to him, and our initial acquaintance developed into friendship. I had married the young woman he had treated, and Freud often climbed the four flights to our small apartment and had simple evening meals with us to which I often invited the composer, Eduard Schütt, whom Freud loved as I did [p. 163].[1]

When Freud started the Wednesday night meetings at his home in 1902, he wanted to broaden the work he had begun individually in psychoanalysis as a method of treatment and to explore its application to other fields, such as art, literature, or sociology. In addition to psychiatrists, therefore, he invited

[1]It is possible that Graf's (1955, pp. 201–203) life-long enthusiasm for the fourth gallery of the Vienna Opera, to which he devoted a separate chapter of one of his last books, may have influenced his choice of floor in this apartment building.

Graf and two of Graf's music colleagues—Leher, who also taught esthetics at the Academy of Music, and David Bach. Bach regularly wrote on music for the *Oesterreichische Rundschau* (Austrian Review), as did Graf, and for the socialist newspaper, *Arbeiter Zeitung* (Worker's Newspaper), which had been founded by the socialist leader Victor Adler, who had lived at Berggasse 19 prior to Freud moving there. When Victor Adler died in 1918, the next leader of the Socialist Party in Vienna was Otto Bauer, whose younger sister Irma had been the subject of Freud's (1905) Dora case. It is important to note that of the three music scholars in the original members of the Wednesday Night meetings, Graf (1942a) was the primary person to apply Freud's ideas to music: "I took over the task of investigating the psychology of great musicians and the process of composing music, utilizing psychoanalysis for this task" (p. 470).

The transcript of the Vienna Psychoanalytic meetings from the years 1906–1918 recorded by its secretary Otto Rank (Nunberg and Federn, 1962–1975) provides another view of Graf's relationship with Freud. When Graf speaks, Freud usually agrees with him or suggests how he might develop his ideas further. On December 4, 1907, when Isodor Sadger presents an analysis of the Swiss poet Konrad Meyer, Freud criticizes him and states that, "Graf has come closer to suggesting the correct way" (Nunberg and Federn, 1962, Min. 32, p. 257). On February 10, 1909, when Graf reports "his self-analysis of so-called 'spontaneous emerging melodies,' which he regularly found to be associatively linked with the text," Freud suggests that "one should perhaps make a distinction between associations that are connected with the wording of the text, with the content, or with the situation" (Nunberg and Federn, 1967, Min. 68, p. 151).

The next week on February 17, 1909, when Graf makes a comment on Mozart's Don Juan, Rank records that, "Freud suggests to Graf that he work up the theme of 'Mozart and his relationship to *Don Juan*' for the *Sammlungen Kleiner Schriften zur Neurosenlehre* (Shorter Writings on the Theory of the Neurosis)" (Nunberg and Federn, 1967, Min. 68, p. 159).[2] A further example of Freud's friendly way of encouraging Graf comes at the end of the meeting of March 16, 1910:

[2]The *Sammlungen* was a collection of Freud's papers originally published in Germany in 1906, then later in English as Freud's *Collected Papers*. There does not appear to have been such an article by Graf or by Freud and Graf together.

In an earlier paper on *The Flying Dutchman*, Graf tried in vain to find an elucidation of the motif that plays such a crucial role in Wagner's poetic work and in his life—intruding into a marriage and snatching the woman away toward himself. Graf is now in a position to offer an explanation for this. It was repeatedly rumored that Geyer, who married Wagner's mother when the child was six months old, was Richard's father. Wagner himself spread these rumors abroad, and one gets the impression that a fantasy of Wagner's is involved in this. If this is true, then that Wagnerian main motif is to be traced back to an identification with Geyer (throughout his life Wagner wore the painter's garb that was characteristic of Geyer), whom he assumed to have committed adultery with his mother [Nunberg and Federn, 1967, Min. 101, p. 461].

At the end of the meeting, Freud (p. 462) voiced his agreement that, "The Wagner-motif goes back to the 'maternal etiology': (1) the wife of another; (2) ill-repute = fantasy of adultery." Perhaps the best example of Freud's generosity in assisting Graf is when Freud (1905 or 1906) wrote an essay entitled, "Psychopathic Characters on the Stage," and gave it to Graf apparently as a guide, since Freud never published the essay and Graf's first two psychoanalytic publications were on the same general subject ([1906] on Wagner's dramatizations and [1907a], a more general paper on theater). Herbert Graf also made good use of it in a section entitled, "Die psychologischen Wurzeln der Kunst des Theaters" (The Psychological Roots of the Art of the Theater), of his doctoral dissertation (Graf, H., 1925, pp. 11–13). Fortunately, Graf (1942a) preserved Freud's article and later arranged for it to be published in the *Psychoanalytic Quarterly* and in the *Standard Edition* of Freud's works.

Graf noted that his (1900) first publication under Freud's influence was *Wagner Probleme und andere Studien* (Wagner Problems and Other Studies). It discusses some of the personality characteristics of Wagner, Mahler, and others in the style and manner of a scholarly essay, but does not yet show much use of Freud's ideas.[3] The next five works, however, do show an increasing use of psychoanalytic thinking.

---

[3]Its only connection to psychoanalysis may be the fact that after Graf dedicated the book to Gustav Mahler, the composer reciprocated by becoming the godfather to his son, when Herbert Graf was born in 1903.

In the paper Freud (1905 or 1906) gave to Graf, he hypothesizes that drama is a sublimation of an artist's own conflicts and
a corresponding identificatory working-through experience for
the audience. A work of theater is successful, Freud suggests,
to the extent that this sympathetic concordance between the
conflicts of dramatist and audience is successful. This becomes
the main theme of Graf's (1906) article, "Richard Wagner und
das dramatische Schaffen" (Richard Wagner and Dramatic Creation), which may well be the first published article on the psychoanalysis of music. Graf argues that dramatists such as Euripides, Schiller, and Wagner form a "group by themselves," since
their lives are full of dramatic conflict that tends to match the
grand conflicts of their time. The display of their psychic conflicts on the stage enables the audience to follow the unfolding
of a psychic conflict that coincides with aspects of their own
conflicts and thereby to have an experience of "recovery from
a serious illness" (p. 112), as these conflicts are resolved in the
drama. Taking a position worthy of the object relations theory
of today, Graf (p. 115), then, writes: "Ist schon jeder grosse
Mann eine Versammlung von Individuen, so ist der grosse Tra-
giker eine Versammlung von Individuen, die sich gegenseitig
bekämpfen, und seine Seele der Kampfplatz" ("If every great
man is a gathering of individuals, so the great tragedist is a
gathering of individuals who struggle against each other in the
battleground of his psyche").

Graf's next paper (1907a), "Probleme des dramatischen
Schaffens" (The Problems of Dramatic Creations) adds to the
idea of dramatic sublimation of current life conflicts by also
considering the sublimation of early childhood experiences in
authors from antiquity through Shakespeare, Goethe, and the
later Austrian playwright, Franz Grillparzer.

On December 11 of the same year, Graf (1907b) presented a
paper to the Wednesday Night Psychoanalytic Society entitled,
"Methodology of the Psychology of Poets," suggesting that his
colleagues not only consider that artistic works are due to the
psychopathology of their creators, but also to healthy aspects
of their personalities. He also suggests that in attempting to
understand a particular character in a literary work, it is helpful
to look for examples of a similar character in other works of
the same author (Freud's [1920] later concept of the repetition

compulsion) as well as examples of such a character in the works of other authors, who may resemble the personality of the original author, as Michelangelo's fits of fear and trembling, melancholy moods, and the way he attacked the marble with gigantic force in an "aggressive state akin to destruction" resemble similar traits in Beethoven. As he had earlier suggested in his paper of 1906, Graf recommends the group "compare kindred personalities among poets and artists to establish *types of artists*. Wagner and Euripides, Beethoven and Michelangelo, Raphael and Mozart are kindred personalities. What may not be transparent in one becomes clear in the other. The mystery of Beethoven's copybooks became intelligible to me only when I learned about Michelangelo's method of working" (p. 264).

In 1910, Graf published the first book on the psychoanalysis of music entitled, *Die innere Werkstatt des Musikers* (The Workshop of a Musician's Mind), in which he presents in-depth analyses of the psychodynamics of Mozart, Beethoven, and Wagner and important ideas on the relationship of stages of music composition to Freud's (1900) topographic levels of consciousness. Finally in 1911, Graf published the monograph, "Richard Wagner im fliegenden Hollander. Ein Beitrag zur Psychologie künstlerischen Schaffens" (Richard Wagner in the *Flying Dutchman*: A Contribution to the Psychology of Artistic Creation), which Freud accepted in his own journal, *Schriften zur angewandten Seelenkunde* (Writings on Applied Psychology). In this first full-length analytic study of a work of music (Feder, Karmel, and Pollack, 1990, p. xi), Graf applied an idea Adler had suggested to him in a Wednesday night meeting (followed by Freud's agreement) that an artist's earliest work should be studied "with special care," since it is often most revealing of the artist's overall character (Nunberg and Federn, 1962, Min. 33, 68, 101). Graf's monograph illustrates how Wagner's childhood and other life experiences are condensed in *The Flying Dutchman* and how the themes and issues of this early work are repeated throughout the rest of his operas. His fellow Wednesday night colleague, Wilhelm Stekel (1911), commended Graf in a laudatory review. Graf was so aware of his debt to Freud and the Wednesday night group that he wrote in the foreword that it "would be impossible to separate the ideas which I owe to the guidance of Professor Freud and those which should be attributed to the criticism of several of my colleagues. Thus, I dedicate this study to the memory of those stimulating and exciting hours spent in mutual intellectual strivings with this circle of friends" (1911, p. ii). Not long after publishing this monograph, Graf withdrew from Freud's circle, having attended his last Wednesday night meeting on March 27, 1912.

However, 30 years later, he spent much of World War II near New York City, where a neighbor was Dr. Marion Kenworthy, who has the distinction of having been the first woman president of the American Academy of Child Psychiatry and of the American Psychoanalytic Association (1958–1960). She asked him to write an article on his earlier work with Freud, and this moving tribute has become an oft quoted article on the atmosphere of the earliest hours of the Wednesday night meetings (Graf, 1942a). Another memorable work from this period in the United States was *Legend of a Musical City* (1945), a modern tragedy of Vienna's rise to prominence in the history of music, which Graf was afraid the Nazis had destroyed on the single fateful day of the Anschluss, when they marched into the city on March 13, 1938. This was followed by *Modern Music* (1946a) on the history of contemporary music and *Composer and Critic* (1946b) on the role of music critics over the last 200 years. After the war, just before Graf left New York to return to live the rest of his days in Vienna, he (1947) briefly returned to the period of his early psychoanalytic writings on music and reworked his 1910 book into *From Beethoven to Shostakovitch: The Psychology of the Composing Process*. Two collections of his essays followed, *Die Wiener Oper* (The Vienna Opera) in 1955 and *Jede Stunde War Erfüllt* (Every Hour was Fulfilled) in 1957. This last book contains a slightly amended version of his 1942 reminiscences of Freud (1942a). Graf died on June 24, 1958, at the age of 84 years.

GENERAL THEMES AND IDEAS

I will now present Graf's psychoanalytic music concepts in more detail. A first impression in reading his work is of his flowery, romantic style replete with metaphors and images evoking different moods, which occasionally detracts from the ideas he is presenting. Graf (1947, p. 37) makes a distinction between the "epic poetry" style of writing, which uses a lot of visual description, and "lyric poetry," in which the poet "luxuriates in moods, the word itself is taken from music, and for whom words and rhythm have above all musical meaning." An example of the epic style is when Graf (1947) writes that "Debussy's piano has its picturesque color specks that hover in the air, in the fog, in the rain" (p. 57), while an example of a more lyrical style is "the tone of Palestrina's masses shine like silver, just as the sound of Mozart's tones has a golden glimmer" (p. 54). As a musician turned writer, it appears that Graf primarily modeled his own writing style on that of lyric poetry as well as on that of the French novelist Romain Rolland, whose early, poetically moving works on music Graf translated into German (1905).

Another influence on his writing style is a mystical thread that runs throughout his work. For example, he (1910) compares the action of a conductor lifting his baton to signal the orchestra to begin to a witchdoctor shaking a rattle to dispel evil spirits or to a priest quietly ringing his bell during the moment of transubstantiation in the Catholic Mass, when silence envelops the church, the devout kneel down, and the priest raises the chalice, the moment when God descends and the souls of the pious unite with the Divine. Graf (1942b) suggests that Bruckner placed this moment of the descent of the Holy Ghost during Catholic Mass in the finales of all his symphonies, which also reminded Graf of the way Bruckner would suddenly kneel down and pray during university lectures, whenever he heard a church bell ring outside the classroom. Beneath Graf's musically rhapsodic writing style, then, there is this mystical element that he believes must ultimately remain beyond the grasp of scientific reason. Following Kant's *Critique of Pure Reason* (which Herbert Graf [Rizzo, 1972] said was his father's favorite book), Graf (1947) writes that the spiritual light that gives a piece of music its greatest beauty and vitality, "belongs to the mysteries of creation, and can no more be explained than the growing of a plant" (p. 458).

Therefore, a main function of music in Graf's view is to enhance the listener by bringing about a feeling of connectedness with other people and with God. For the moment music begins in a concert hall, everyone becomes silent, everyday life seems to vanish, the audience's emotions become intensified, and everyone feels united on this deep, emotional level. In advance of his time, Graf (1910) precedes what is currently called the "narcissistic dimension" of music in writing of this ability to transport the listener from the ordinary world of worries and fallibilities to a more idealized one. He maintains that listening to a work such as Beethoven's *Ninth Symphony* one feels identified with a powerful composer, conductor, outstanding group of musicians, and the rest of the audience, who all seem to be having the same experience. Moreover, the structure of great artistic works, like the structure of the Catholic Mass, encapsulates a spiritual pathway from the more mundane realm of life to a divine world of beauty and truth, as in Dante's *Divine Comedy*, Goethe's *Faust*, Bach's *St. Mathew's Passion*, Haydn's *Adagios*, Mozart's *Magic Flute*, Beethoven's *Ninth Symphony*, and Wagner's *Parsifal*. In this way, music inspires the listener to a higher order of living. While composers of the classical period, such as Bach and Handel, reported feeling divinely inspired in the process of creating, Graf (1910) suggests that the Renaissance brought a shift toward viewing artistic inspiration as coming less from an external source like God speaking to Moses through a burning bush and more from one's own strong inner feelings, as Wagner likened intense creative activity to being "in heat" or Goethe to being in love.

Another function of music according to Graf (1910) is as a way of gaining access to unconscious processes, since it often relaxes the listener and resonates within the unconscious. Hence many painters and writers listen to music while creating in order to liberate the creative unconscious. In Freud's work, the child is described as developing from infantile states of awe, playful fantasy, and nightmarish fears more under the predominance of the unconscious to the increasingly controlled rationality of adult life under the predominance of the conscious. Freud similarly described the path of Western civilization from its more primitive beliefs in magic, witchcraft, and mythology to the advent of the scientific method. Since music can be listened to on unconscious, preconscious, and conscious levels simultaneously, Graf proposes that this experience recapitulates and narcissistically enhances the listener's history from birth to maturity and culture from primitive savagery to the

technocratic age. Therefore, he (1910) identifies four psychological functions of music to (1) lift the listener to a more moral
and spiritual level of experience; (2) narcissistically enhance the
listener's sense of self and connection to others; (3) help the
listener gain access to his or her own unconscious; and (4) give
the listener an experience of healthy psychic balance between
the past and present and among the three levels of the psyche.

CLASSICAL AND ROMANTIC STYLE

Comparing musical styles, Graf (1910, p. 34; 1947, p. 41) draws
upon August Wilhelm Schlegel's view that, "The art and poetry
of antiquity insists upon strict separation of the dissimilar, while
romantic art delights in combinations," and Freud's (1900) description of the way consciousness makes clear separations
among elements and logically organizes them together, while
the unconscious is characterized by an easy displaceability and
tendency to seemingly illogical condensations of different elements. Graf (1910) suggests that the classicist Bach lived a very
bourgeois, ordered life, with his wife and many children, and
composed on a more conscious level, using the strict Baroque
fugue, cantata, chorales, and other prescribed forms of his time
and further purifying his composing "into a simple great style"
with technical devices of Italian composers such as Vivaldi. On
the other hand, Graf suggests that romantic composers, such
as Beethoven and Wagner, compose more on an unconscious
level and tend to change the basic forms of music, which is a
reflection of their restless, revolutionary life-styles.

He further suggests that the classicist's tendency to maintain
strict separation of the dissimilar can be seen in a tendency to
stick to only one art form, while the romanticist mixes not only
dissimilar elements within one art form, but mixes many art
forms together, often creating music, poetry, and painting, as
in Wagner's desire to create a "Gesamtkunstwerk" (universal
work of art). Following Nietzsche's *Birth of Tragedy from the Spirit
of Music*, Graf notes that the classicist is also more "Apollonian,"
being more graphic and relying more on the eye, as in the
epic poetry of Goethe, while the romanticist is a more musical

"Dionysian," relying more on the ear, as in the more lyrical poetry of Novalis.

This difference may also be seen over the stages of normal development. Graf observes that an adolescent may create art, poetry, and music due to the heightening of unconscious drives during puberty. But as the intensity of the drives gradually diminishes, the adolescent may eventually give up creative productions. This leads to Graf's suggestive hypothesis that it is not the unconscious of an artist that develops over the life span, but rather the artist's increasingly conscious level of technical mastery. He gives the example of Goethe, whose work shows an increasing level of technical maturity, but who may have sought out frequent affairs in order to infuse his later work with the emotional intensity of an adolescent in the passions of first love.

Another one of his favorite examples is Brahms, whom he sees as a romantic composer prior to 1854, who stopped composing for six years to contemplate the artistic problems of the age, only to reemerge to compose for the rest of his life in a style of "classical severity." In his old age the confidant of Eduard Hanslick, the powerful, conservative music critic for the *Neue Freie Presse*, Vienna's most widely read newspaper, Graf (1945) writes that Brahms became "the bête noir' of every composer, for he was a sharp and scurrilous censurer." As an adolescent, Graf once took his own compositions to the elderly Brahms, who harshly advised him to take out his more romantic middle voices, which had been influenced by Richard Strauss, and concentrate only on the melody and bass notes. However, Graf concludes that Brahms' rudeness and ascetic simplicity in living were defensive covers for a tenderness and inward shyness still discernible in his later music that "conceals his romantic sentiment behind a classic façade" (p. 109).

STAGE I OF THE COMPOSING PROCESS: THE UNCONSCIOUS

Graf (1910) then proposes three stages of composing that roughly follow Freud's topographic levels of the unconscious, preconscious, and the conscious: (1) the preliminary work done by the unconscious; (2) the combined work of unconscious and

conscious mental powers; and (3) the conscious final polishing
of the form. He finds evidence for the first phase of composing
work done by the unconscious by examining the composer's
use of (a) unconscious drives, (b) psychic complexes, (c) early
childhood memories, and (d) external and internal experiences.

On the influence of unconscious drives in artistic works, Graf
(1910) primarily relies upon Freud's (1900) libidinal drive,
which he sees especially in Goethe and Wagner, who felt they
could not compose unless they were in love. But Graf was also
exposed in the Wednesday night meetings to Adler's (1908)
suggestion of an aggressive drive, which he feels Beethoven
proclaims with a musical gesture of an upheld, clenched fist, as
in the four beginning notes of Beethoven's *Fifth Symphony*, and
to Rank's (1907) notion of a "creative, playful impulse," which
he feels inspires much of the light-hearted, humorous music of
Mozart and Haydn. As he earlier suggested that God enhances
music with special vitality, he suggests that these different unconscious drives also give a composer's music its identifiable
intensity and liveliness.

Due to an artist's particular life experiences, temperament,
level of drive intensity, and struggle to repress a particular
drive, unconscious fantasies tend to coalesce into a "psychic
complex," which Graf feels organizes the majority of the artist's
works around a single, unifying theme. Graf sees the chief
motif of "salvation through love" throughout Wagner's operas
as the result of a "love complex," which represents Wagner's
attempt to sublimate his strong libidinal drive. Graf suggests
that an attempt to sublimate the aggressive drive can be seen
in Beethoven's "death complex," in which moods of sorrow,
destitution, and melancholia inspired the Adagio of the string
quartet in F major, opus 18, as he pondered the "derniers
soupirs" (last sighs) of the grave scene in Shakespeare's *Romeo
and Juliet*, and in Gustav Mahler, whose father was physically
abusive and who experienced the early death of six of his siblings.

Graf (1910, p. 9) notes that the childhood of composers often
reveals a precocious sexual interest, as in Mozart and Wagner,
and a high sensitivity to sound, as in Chopin and Tchaikovsky,
who reacted so strongly to tones as children they began to weep.
Graf hypothesizes that such early sensitivity may lead to the

child becoming a prodigy and perhaps later a great composer. A year before this publication of Graf, Freud with unusual prescience had compared Little Hans's intellectual and psychosexual precocity with the similar "records of the childhood of men who have later come to be recognized as 'great' " (1909, p. 142). Freud (1909) had also noted that "from the time of the beginning of his anxiety [in January 1908 he was 4 years, 9 months of age], Hans began to show an increased interest in music and to develop his inherited musical gift" (p. 138). Herbert Graf later became a highly innovative pioneer in operatic stage direction, stage design, and the televising of performances, and education of opera singers (Abrams, 1992b). In retrospect, when reading Graf's similar writing about the childhood of Mozart, one cannot avoid wondering if Graf might have sensed a similarity between his faithful recording of his son's psychosexual discoveries in his copious letters to Freud and the faithful work of Mozart's father's in transcribing his son's early childhood compositions and guiding his career.

Graf further points out that as children, Schubert was a competent player of the piano, violin, and organ; Mendelssohn played the piano at age 7; Schumann portrayed his elementary school classmates' personalities in compositions at the piano; Mozart played piano and composed at the age of 7; Handel composed at age 10; and Beethoven, Schubert, and Carl Maria von Weber composed musical works at 12 and 13 years of age.

This intensity of unconscious biological drives, Graf suggests, also makes these individuals extremely sensitive to traumatic experiences and provides a ready access to these traumatic memories for their later artistic life. He (1907a) gives the example of Raphael's series of paintings of the Madonna holding her child in her arms, playing with him, or looking down at him playing. Since Raphael's mother had died when he was 8 years old and was also named Maria, his memory of her associated itself with the pictures of the Divine Mother and, as Raphael himself relates, the picture appeared to him in dreams repeatedly. Graf writes:

> Raphael as a child became melancholy when the name of the Mother of God was mentioned, and when one thinks of the tenderness with which he always painted the child nestled in the

arm of the mother, one recognizes this longing of the boy for
the mother. The longing for his mother hides behind the picture
of the Virgin Mary, his highest wish by his own confession being
to paint the Heavenly Virgin. Day and night, he thought of her
picture, and out of this desire in his unconscious was formed
the dream and the work of art [p. 332].

Since artists have a higher sensitivity to the contents of their
unconscious, Graf finds they also have ample access to memories that are not traumatic and can later incorporate them into
their compositions, such as a favorite folk song enjoyed during
a traditional family gathering (Bach), a lullaby or favorite song
sung by one's parent (Haydn), the rhythm of a passing
marching band (Mahler), a hymn heard in church (Wagner),
or the mistakes of local musicians in a tavern (Richard Strauss).

Current experiences may further influence the content of
the unconscious. Graf (1910, pp. 105–106) compares Mozart's
Don Giovanni to Shakespeare's *Hamlet*, pointing out that both
were written after the recent death of their fathers. In *Hamlet*,
Graf points out that Shakespeare has the father stride across
the stage as a ghost, letting his spectral voice be heard, as later
Mozart was to have the Commander do. Happy events in a
composer's current life also stir the creative unconscious, as in
1783 when Mozart was inspired to write the Minuet and Trio
of the String Quartet in D minor in the same room in which
his wife was giving birth to their first child.

He contrasts such "external experiences" that occur in the
outside environment with "internal experiences," which he de-
fines as psychic or physical changes in the body, such as Beethoven conceiving the idea for the *Eroica Symphony* soon after he
had become aware of his deafness. The symphony's Napoleonic
theme of military conquest became a way to fight against increasing fears of physical defectiveness, an interpretation supported by an entry in Beethoven's notebook of the time, "Cour-
age! No matter what the weaknesses of my body, my spirit shall
dominate." He composed the "Hymn of thanks to God" in the
A minor String Quartet, opus 132, feeling grateful for having
just recovered from an abdominal ailment, again writing in his
diary, "Thank you hymn to God by a sick man on his recovery.
Feeling of new strength and reawakened sensation." Graf finds

this very different from Smetana, who expressed his own discovery of impending deafness in the plaintive string quartet, "From My Life."

STAGE II: FROM THE UNCONSCIOUS TO THE PRECONSCIOUS

In the second stage of composing, Graf addresses (1) repression's opposition to unconscious expression in a "composer's block"; (2) productive moods; (3) sublimation; (4) the first appearance of the unconscious in the preconscious level; and (5) the combining of the unconscious with conscious, critical work.

As in Freud's description of dream formation, Graf explains that elements in the composer's unconscious, such as sexual and aggressive thoughts, impulses, and fantasies and repressed memories of childhood and other traumatic events, must first find their way into a composer's preconscious. They may come bursting forth very freely, as in Mozart's ability to compose very quickly like an uninhibited child at play, and in Handel, whom Graf suggests was perhaps the fastest of all composers. Or they may emerge in bits and pieces written in notebooks, shaped and reshaped, remembered and forgotten, as in the extensive notations of Beethoven, whose method of composing he sees as a constant struggle between the unconscious that pushes for expression and repression that blocks against unconscious discharge. Graf notes that Beethoven once remarked that he had to write his musical ideas down as quickly as possible in order to, as he put it, "save them from submerging in the 'active gap.'" Graf gives extensive examples of this musical repression in Beethoven, in which a musical idea at one point in his work may recede into memory, often for several years at a time, only to reappear in a later work, as the *Choral Fantasy* later became the final movement of the *Ninth Symphony* (1910, pp. 83–85).

Graf (1947, pp. 278–279) reports Brahms as saying that an idea first germinated unaware within him and, when he got an idea, he went for a walk or did something different, and then he might return unexpectedly to it taking shape. Richard Strauss said he would tuck an idea away for a year, and then later "find that quite unconsciously something within me—the

imagination—has been at work on it." Graf points out that composers often experience the force of repression's ability to block
the emergence of creative ideas, much as Freud describes the
way neurotic patients push uncomfortable impulses, feelings,
and thoughts into the unconscious realm of forgotten memories. Goethe wrote down poems immediately upon awakening
from the dream state, "else he would not find them anymore";
hence the diaries, journals, and notebooks of writers, artists,
and composers. Graf hypothesizes that the more composers
tend to repress the unconscious, the more they may utilize notebook sketching and other means of gaining access to the content
in their unconscious, as in the obsessive musical sketches Beethoven was constantly elaborating and editing. If repression is
too successful, a composer may experience a partial or total
inhibition of creative work similar to "writer's block" in literature. Graf finds that this is often due to depression, as in periods
of work stoppage in Michelangelo, Hebbel, Wagner, and Debussy or the manic depressive cycles of Hugo Wolf, whose medical chart at a sanitorium Graf later consulted after Wolf's death
in 1903.

As Freud recommended that patients in psychoanalysis re-
cline on a comfortable couch surrounded by a dim light and
free associate in order to get into the preconscious level where
access to the unconscious can more readily occur, Graf finds
that composers often employ another art form to enhance the
creative flow of ideas and feelings. Schubert thought of a melody for a song while reading Shakespeare's *Anthony and Cleopa-
tra* and Goethe and Leonardo da Vinci often listened to music as
they worked. In the chapter "Productive Moods," Graf (1910)
discusses these free association methods of different composers, later expanding on this in one of his strongest chapters
(1947). For example, he points out that Debussy grew up as a
child on the coast of Cannes, often dreaming of becoming a
sailor. Later on in Paris, he would enable this unconscious childhood longing to emerge into the conscious level of his musical
compositions by contemplating the waters of the Seine by sun-
set, after which he would go inside to compose in a room with
a green carpet and green walls full of fragile and precious
objects, such as butterflies, Japanese woodcuts, and valuable
canes. Thus, Debussy brought to the surface elements from his

unconscious in his orchestral work *La Mer* with, as Graf writes rhapsodically, "its wonderful sea moods, the pictures of the waves in the morning light and midday reflection, the play of the waves, and the dialogue between wind and water" (1947, p. 174).

Wagner worked in a room full of fine furniture, silk, and perfumed fragrances, dressing as his stepfather, a painter, and stroking the silk as he composed in order, as he put it, "to feel complimented" (1910, p. 57). For others, the experience of physical motion helps get their unconscious imagination moving, as in vigorous walking (Goethe, Nietzsche, Carl Maria von Weber, Brahms, Wagner, and Berlioz) or driving an automobile (Richard Strauss). Beethoven went on long walks, humming and singing, and stopping now and then to quickly jot down different fragments of musical ideas as they came to him. Some utilized the freeing experience of piano improvisations (Bach and Mozart), while others (Wagner and Richard Strauss) never used a piano for composing. Some feel freer during the night to do their work (Debussy, Johann Strauss), while others prefer the day or early morning (Haydn, Mozart, Beethoven, Richard Strauss). Some compose only during spring or summer, while others, such as Hebbel, who actually felt oppressed by the infinite sprouting of nature, work best in fall or winter. Still others employ stimulants, such as alcohol (Moussorsky, Beethoven, Schubert, Max Reger), tea (Debussy), or snuff (Wagner) to free the unconscious.

The healthy alternative to either expressing unconscious processes maladaptively or rigidly repressing them in an immobilized depression, Graf reminds us, is through adaptive sublimation of the unconscious, which is different from composer to composer. Mozart was so uninhibited he made ribald jokes while composing. Schumann wrote music at night, as if making love to his wife sleeping nearby, telling her that his Sonata in F sharp minor was "a single cry of the heart for my beloved" and, "Romantic girl that you are, your eyes follow me everywhere, and I have often thought to myself that without such a fiancée one cannot write such music" (1910, pp. 55–56).

While always in love with one woman or another, Graf suggests that Beethoven seemed instead to sublimate more the aggressive drive in his music, which he identified with Napoleon and other conquerors battling against men and the storms of nature. Throughout his music, there is often a rise toward a tumultuous battle, followed by a period of relative calm. Defiant of authority and given to unceasing restlessness, frequent changes of residence, emotional outbursts, and occasional violence, Graf believes that Beethoven managed to express these urges in music of the most sublime and moving vitality. Moreover, he considers that Beethoven's life-long hatred of tyrants stemmed from early childhood mistreatment by his father, who beat him and locked him in a cellar, and concludes that Beethoven "had been made a revolutionary by the brutality suffered as a child" and that "the quiet boy, who was made an introvert by brutal treatment and who as such dreamed of love and liberty, became one of mankind's mightiest fighters for freedom" (1947, p. 187).

While Wagner was also constantly having romantic affairs, often with the wives of his friends, Graf suggests that his work nevertheless shows a struggle to suppress these erotic urges in the extreme themes of total renunciation, celibacy, self-castration, and self-sacrificing death.

When a musical idea first takes its step from the unconscious to the preconscious level in this sublimatory process, Graf suggests that it may first appear in a shadowy, indefinite form, as just a piece of melody without much form, the thought of a musical key to employ, or a fragment of rhythm or chord progression. He gives as examples Schubert's indefinite first sketch for the third movement of his Piano Sonata in A minor that later develops into a more definite filled-in form, Beethoven's sketches that often start at the very beginning of a piece or in the middle, and Wagner's vision of the character of Parsifal as he was composing *Siegfried*. Applying Freud's identification of an obsessive idea that keeps reappearing as an "idée fixe," Graf refers to the way Beethoven earlier composed a melody out of the letters of Bach's name, and shows how this little four-note melody also keeps reappearing in Beethoven's music notebooks and in the String Quartets in A minor, B flat, and C sharp minor. Graf suggests that this musical association to Bach from his unconscious seems to reappear in the level of Beethoven's preconscious at times when he is looking for religious serenity, much as he planned to write a tenth symphony at the end of his life around ancient church modes, and that glimpses of these religious moods can be heard in the many prayer adagios he wrote during the period of the *Ninth Symphony* and these last string quartets (1910, p. 77).

In the chapter "Critical Work," Graf (1910) further discusses how traumatic experiences, feelings, and wishes in a composer's unconscious are combined with the more conscious work of technical musical expression. In order to develop, order, and polish the final composition, a composer needs to have a good working combination of feeling and thought. Many have the impression that artists and composers primarily work from a spontaneity of powerful emotions and that intellectual thinking is not part of this process. Graf refers to incisive musical critiques and reflections written by Mozart, Weber, Schumann, Berlioz, and Wagner and the ever-developing musical sketches in Beethoven's notebooks to demonstrate that this is a mistaken notion.

STAGE III: THE LAST STAGE OF COMPOSING

In the last stage of composing, the work becomes increasingly more logical, reflective, analytical, and conscious. Considering that he did not have the benefit of Freud's (1923) ego psychology, Graf makes a worthy attempt to specify for this stage what in that later theory might be called the "ego functions" of composing. He suggests that a composer starts and ends with a "principle of unity," beginning with a rough overall picture of the piece in the unconscious, as in Albrecht Dürer's statement, "A painter is inwardly full of diagram." In the last stage of composing, this inward unity becomes a conscious level mechanism to "unify the grand design," as Gustav Mahler compares putting together musical elements in composing to assembling pieces of a picture puzzle. Graf bases this creative idea on Freud's (1900) dream mechanism of condensation; but in speaking of the conscious level of this organizing activity, he anticipates Nunberg's (1930) later concept of the "synthetic function of the ego." Building on Freud's other dream mechanism of displacement, he identifies a mechanism of moving a musical idea from one location to another, which he calls the "elaboration and expansion" of elements often seen in fugues and the form of a theme and variations. Another is "intensification and accentuation" of elements to give the music rhythmic and dynamic power, and the last is "simplification and final editing" to communicate musical ideas as simply and directly as possible. Brahms said that, "The pen is not just for writing, but for crossing out as well," which Graf suggests is illustrated in Bach's improvements of the *St. John's Passion* after its first performance.

CONCLUSION

These suggestive writings of Graf lay out a good beginning for a psychoanalysis of music. While his expansive, lyrical writing style may detract from some of the points he is making, this impression should be tempered by the fact that he was writing in his early thirties about a field he had just begun studying, which itself was only in its earliest beginnings.

His mystical comparison of Freud's unconscious with Bergson's *élan vital* or with the power of God that Kant felt can never be fully described by human reason is very far from Freud's position. Since the unconscious tends to be covered over by repression. Freud's point was that it is usually not directly observable, but can be scientifically studied through its appearance in the preconscious level of dreams, slips of the tongue, parapraxes, and the sequence of free associations to these and other phenomena in psychoanalysis. It may have been Graf's strong dislike for repressive external authority and his own religious conflicts that influenced his desire to replace an external deity for an inspirational power that resides within the human unconscious. However, it was Rolland, whom Graf translated, who later criticized Freud for leaving out of his view of religion the "oceanic feeling" that is the same mystical feeling Graf describes in inspiring part of the creation and enjoyment of music.

While Freud openly disclaimed such beliefs, recent research of Frieden (1990), Rice (1990), and Yerushalmi (1991) suggests that Freud was influenced by mystical elements in his own Jewish background. Both life-long members of the Jewish B'nai

B'rith society, Graf is clearly more religious and mystical than Freud. But as a young man writing at the beginning of the twentieth century in Vienna, he had to come to terms with his own Jewish background, the religious belief system of the Catholic-centered Hapsburg Monarchy, a conservative anti-Semitic political climate, divergent socialist ideas, and the more humanistic exploration of man's inner life in Freud's description of the unconscious. This may explain the contradiction between Graf at times stressing music's spiritual function to lift the listener toward God and at other times stressing its narcissistic function to enhance the self through intensifying human emotions and providing an experience of omnipotent power, beauty, and truth. Since he believes that music can be listened to on all topographic levels simultaneously, Graf suggests that it also functions for the listener as a way to gain access to the unconscious and as a way to develop increasing psychic balance between the unconscious, preconscious, and conscious levels of the psyche.

There are similar contradictions in Graf's attempt to make a psychoanalytic contrast between classical style, in which the composer works more on the conscious level, maintains a strict separation between art forms and of elements within an art form, is better adjusted to the outside world, but more conservative and less creative in the invention of new forms; and the romantic style, in which the composer works more on the unconscious level, mixes art forms together and mixes elements within an art form, is less adjusted psychologically, but more radical politically and basically more creative. At times, Graf seems to prefer the romanticists, as "creators of their own lives," his special favorites being Beethoven and Wagner, who "break the bonds of conventional rules, because their imagination drives them beyond life" (1947, p. 51). At other times, he seems to prefer classicists, describing Bruckner as "the last great musician of the Baroque" and classes with him as "the greatest experience of my life" (1945, p. 152). His overall conclusion is that all artists possess more emotional passion and vitality and access to childhood memories and to other elements of their unconscious.

While Freud's topographic theory helps distinguish artists who mix dissimilar elements and seem less adjusted psychologically, it may be a less adequate explanation of their politics. Graf compares Bach's political conservatism in living a bourgeois ordered life and writing music that remained within the pre-scribed forms of his time to Beethoven's revolutionary political stance reflected in his challenging of traditional musical forms. But this conflicts with Graf's own fascinating analysis of Beetho-ven's later study of the works of Bach and the ancient church modes in the search for inner peace. His idea of measuring creativity by the degree to which an artist has access to the unconscious, can remember early memories, can freely com-bine the dissimilar, mix art forms, and draw upon an intensity of unconscious drives is also debatable. Romantic composers may not be as well adjusted as classicists. But is Beethoven genuinely more creative than Bach, simply because Bach did not also create new forms?

More convincing is Graf's similar contrast of Adler and Freud: "[Freud] was a born discoverer and investigator, and his imagination was that of an artist. Freud's best pupil cannot be compared to this creative imagination and real genius. Adler possessed clarity, poise, and a fine psychological feeling; he went along his path in slow steps, ever testing. He remained on the surface of the earth. Unlike Freud, he never rose into the air in a flight of imagination, nor did he ever dig deep shafts into the bowels of the earth" (1942a, p. 475). However, if a romanticist is able to mix the dissimilar, then he may also com-bine aspects of the past with that of the present. Thus, the romanticist may be just as capable of adaptively working through past and present identifications as the classicist. As Bach incorporated aspects of Vivaldi, Beethoven later incorpo-rated aspects of Bach. Living a fairly apolitical, bourgeois life, Freud possessed exemplary access to the unconscious, was poet-ically imaginative, and was truly revolutionary in his work. The more left-wing politically, Adler was a highly competent psychi-atrist; yet as Graf correctly points out, Adler was not as deeply probing, radical, or creative in his work.

Graf's psychoanalytic studies of individual composers are very thought-provoking. After reading the extensive analyses of Mozart, Beethoven, and Wagner, one might consider that they all had elements of attention deficit hyperactivity disorder (ADHD), since they tended to be in constant motion and activ-ity, rarely stood still, had an overabundance of energy and impulsivity, had many romantic affairs, often worked on more than one composition at the same time, had a high level of emotional sensitivity to their environment, and were rather immature socially and emotionally. Many of Graf's observations could be further developed, such as considering whether Beethoven's associations to the four-note melody on Bach's name, Napoleon's conquests, and to ancient church modes might have functioned as a narcissistic grandiose defense against feelings of defectiveness, loss, and fear of death. For as the child of an abusive father, Beethoven might have reached for the fantasy of an idealized father as a source of strength at times in his life of greatest vulnerability. Other intriguing analytic observations of Haydn, Debussy and Hugo Wolf, the writers Goethe, Shakespeare, Schiller, and Hebbel, and the artists Michelangelo and Raphael stand out in the landscape of Graf's early writings and warrant further investigation in terms of more current concepts of psychiatric diagnosis and later concepts of Freud and later psychoanalytic theorists.

As Kris (1952) was many decades later to provide the first comprehensive psychoanalytic consideration of the visual arts, Graf's greatest contribution to the psychoanalysis of music is his in-depth application of Freud's topographic theory to the composing process. He considers the first stage to be the "work of the unconscious," illustrated in the appearance in the lives and work of composers of the different unconscious drives, early childhood memories, and of external and internal experiences. The second stage is the unconscious just coming into the level of the preconscious, seen in the indefinite formlessness of musical elements, as they are first written down in a composer's notebook, and in reappearing "idée fixes." The task of getting the unconscious into the preconscious realm and of "combining unconscious and conscious" together is then seen in the way a composer struggles against unconscious inhibition, repression, and what could be called "composer's block" by doing sketches, walking, driving, donning different clothes, decorating their work place in different ways, and by other such ways of getting into what Graf calls "productive moods." The comparison of these methods to Freud's method of free association is an important reminder that treatment for both analyst and patient is also fundamentally a process of free expression and creative discovery, perhaps the best lesson of Freud's earliest case histories.

The last stage of composing in Graf's scheme is the increasingly conscious stage of critical work involving mechanisms, which he identifies as "elaboration," "accentuation," "augmentation," "unification," "simplification," and "editing" of elements into the final form of the musical composition. These resemble the "ego functions" of Freud's structural theory, which Graf did not have available to him in the first decade of the twentieth century. His hypothesis that art and music represent an artist's attempt to develop and express a psychic balance of the unconscious, preconscious, and conscious is also a refreshing viewpoint in a psychoanalysis of the creative arts that has all too often viewed a final work of art as a sublimation of psychopathology, rather than as also an expression of creative health.

Many of the ideas Graf expressed in his early psychoanalytic writings were later expressed by others: (1) That artists are born with relatively higher levels of sensitivity is found in Greenacre (1957) and Nass (1975). (2) That many artists tend to mix art forms together in their process of creating is found in Nass (1984). (3) Graf's suggestion of studying Gustav Mahler as a classic example of the influence of death and depression in musical creations is found in Feder (1981) and Pollock (1989). (4) That listening to music provides an experience of narcissistic enhancement is suggested in Kohut (1957). (5) That Freud's dream mechanism of condensation can be seen in the conscious level of organizing elements into a composition is similar to Nunberg's (1930) synthetic function of the ego. (6) That psychoanalysis should consider creative works as expressions of health, rather than only as sublimations of psychopathology, was a point of departure for the interesting work of Susan Deri (1982).

Many of Graf's other ideas are also worthy of further investigation. Since he worked so closely with Freud for such an extended period, Graf (1911, p. ii) points out that it is difficult to determine which were his own ideas and which were those of Freud and his colleagues in the Wednesday night group. If a correspondence of letters between Freud and Graf exists and could be published, it might clarify the origin of these valuable ideas. Graf himself made a valiant early effort at sketching out what a psychoanalysis of music might entail, and it is not surprising that the high level of creative exploration, analytic insight, and sense of humanity in these early writings are the very same qualities to be valued in his work in the case of Little Hans.

REFERENCES

Abrams, D. M. (1991), Looking at and looking away: Etiology of preoedipal splitting in a deaf girl. *The Psychoanalytic Study of the Child*, 46:277–304. New Haven, CT: Yale University Press.

——— (1992a), The dream's mirror of reality. *Contemp. Psychoanal.*, 28/1:50–71.

——— (1992b), Origins of innovation: Freud, Little Hans, and the Grafs. Paper presented, Div. 39 of Psychoanalysis, American Psychological Association Spring Meeting, Philadelphia, PA.

Adler, A. (1908), Der Aggressionstrieb im Leben und in der Neurose (The aggressive drive in life and in neurosis). *Fortschritte der Medizin*, No. 19.

Bernays, A. F. (1940), My brother, Sigmund Freud. In: *Freud As We Knew Him*, ed. H. M. Ruitenbeck. Detroit: Wayne State University Press, pp. 140–147.

Deri, S. (1982), *Symbolization and Creativity*. New York: International Universities Press.

Feder, S. (1981), Gustav Mahler: The music of fratricide. *Internat. Rev. Psychoanal.*, 8:257–284.

——— Karmel, R. L., & Pollock, G. H., eds. (1990), *Psychoanalytic Explorations in Music*, First Series. Madison, CT: International Universities Press.

Freud, S. (1887–1904), *The Complete Letters of Sigmund Freud to Wilhelm Fliess*, ed. J. Masson. Cambridge, MA: Harvard University Press.

——— (1900), The Interpretation of Dreams. *Standard Edition*, 4 & 5. London: Hogarth Press, 1953.

——— (1905), Fragment of an analysis of a case of hysteria. *Standard Edition*, 3:3–112. London: Hogarth Press, 1962.

——— (1905 or 1906), Psychopathic characters on the stage. *Standard Edition*, 3:305–310. London: Hogarth Press, 1962.

——— (1907), The sexual enlightenment of children. *Standard Edition*, 9:131–139. London: Hogarth Press, 1959.

——— (1909), Analysis of a phobia in a five-year-old boy. *Standard Edition*, 10:1–149. London: Hogarth Press, 1955.

——— (1914), The Moses of Michelangelo. *Standard Edition*, 13:209–236. London: Hogarth Press, 1955.

——— (1920), Beyond the pleasure principle. *Standard Edition*, 18:1–64. London: Hogarth Press, 1955.

——— (1923), The ego and the id. *Standard Edition*, 19:1–60. London: Hogarth Press, 1961.

Frieden, K. (1990), *Freud's Dream of Interpretation*. Albany, NY: State University of New York Press.

Gartenberg, E. (1978), *Mahler*. New York: Schirmer Books.

Graf, H. (1925), *Richard Wagner als Regisseur: Studien zu einer Entwicklungsgeschichte der Opernregie* (Richard Wagner as a Stage Director: Studies for a Development of the History of Opera Staging). Doctoral dissertation, University of Vienna.

Graf, M. (1900), *Wagner Probleme und andere Studien* (Wagner Problems and Other Studies). Wien: Zweites Tausend, Wiener Verlag.

—— tr. (1905), Rolland, Romain. *Paris als Musikstadt* (Paris Musical), *Die Musik*, Vol. 11. Berlin: Bard, Marquardt.

—— (1906), Richard Wagner und das dramatische Schaffen (Richard Wagner and Dramatic Creation). *Oesterreichische Rundschau.* 9:111–121.

—— (1907a), Probleme des dramatischen Shaffens (Problems of Dramatic Creations). *Oesterreichische Rundschau,* 10:326–337.

—— (1907b), Methodology of the psychology of poets. In: *Minutes of the Vienna Psychoanalytic Society,* Vol. 1, ed. H. Nunberg & E. Federn. New York: International Universities Press, 1962, pp. 259–269.

—— (1910), *Die innere Werkstatt des Musikers* (The Workshop of a Musician's Mind). Stuttgart: Verlag von Ferdinand Enke.

—— (1911), Richard Wagner im Fliegenden Hollander. Ein Beitrag zur Psychologie künstlerischen Schaffens (Richard Wagner in the Flying Dutchman: A Contribution to the Psychology of Artistic Creation). *Schriften zur angewandten Seelenkunde,* Vol. 9. Nandeln/Liechtenstein: Kraus, 1970.

—— (1942a), Reminiscences of Professor Sigmund Freud. *Psychoanal. Quart.,* 11:465–476.

—— (1942b), Anton Bruckner's Catholicism. *Commonweal,* 36:486–488.

—— (1945), *Legend of a Musical City.* New York: Philosophical Library.

—— (1946a), *Composer and Critic: Two Hundred Years of Musical Criticism.* New York: W. W. Norton.

—— (1946b), *Modern Music: Composers and Music of Our Time.* New York: Philosophical Library.

—— (1947), *From Beethoven to Shostakovitch: The Psychology of the Composing Process.* New York: Philosophical Library.

—— (1955), *Die Wiener Oper* (The Vienna Opera). Vienna & Frankfurt: Forum-Verlag.

—— (1957), *Jede Stunde War Erfüllt: Ein halbes Jahrhundert Musik- und Theaterleben* (Every Hour Was Fulfilled: A Half-Century of Life in Music and the Theater). Wien-Frankfurt: Forum-Verlag.

Greenacre, P. (1957). Childhood of the artist: Libidinal phase development and giftedness. *The Psychoanalytic Study of the Child,* 12:47–72. New York: International Universities Press.

Johnston, W. M. (1972), *The Austrian Mind: Intellectual and Social History 1848–1938.* Berkeley, CA: University of California Press.

Jones, E. (1953), *Life and Work of Freud,* Vol. 1. New York: Basic Books.

Kant, E. (1848), *Critique of Pure Reason.* London: Pickering.

Kohut, H. (1957), Observations on the psychological functions of music. *J. Amer. Psychoanal. Assn.,* 1–4/5:398–407.

Kris, E. (1952), *Psychoanalytic Explorations in Art.* New York: International Universities Press.

Nass, M. L. (1975), On hearing and inspiration in the composition of music. *Psychoanal. Quart.,* 44:431–449.

—— (1984), The development of creative imagination in composers. *Internat. Rev. Psychoanal.,* 11:481–492.

Nietzsche, F. W. (1872), *Birth of Tragedy from the Spirit of Music.* New York: Vintage Books.

Nunberg, H. (1930), The synthetic function of the ego. In: *Practice and Theory of Psychoanalysis.* New York: International Universities Press, 1960, pp. 120–136.

——— Federn, E., eds. (1962), *Minutes of the Vienna Psychoanalytic Society*, Vol. 1. New York: International Universities Press.

——— (1967), *Minutes of the Vienna Psychoanalytic Society*, Vol. 2. New York: International Universities Press.

——— (1974), *Minutes of the Vienna Psychoanalytic Society*, Vol. 3. New York: International Universities Press.

——— (1975), *Minutes of the Vienna Psychoanalytic Society*, Vol. 4. New York: International Universities Press.

Pollock, G. (1989), Mourning through music: Gustav Mahler. In: *Psychoanalytic Explorations in Music*, ed. S. Feder, R. L. Karmel, & G. H. Pollock. Madison, CT: International Universities Press, 1990, pp. 321–339.

Rank, O. (1907), *Art and Artist: Creative Urge and Personality Development*. New York: Agathon Press, 1968.

Rice, E. (1990), *Freud and Moses: The Long Journey Home*. Albany, NY: State University of New York Press.

Rizzo, F. (1972), Memoirs of an invisible man. *Opera News*, February 5:25–28.

Stekel, W. (1911), Review. *Zentralblatt für Psychoanalyse und Psychotherapie*, 1:252–254.

Sterba, E., & Sterba, R. F. (1954), *Beethoven and his Nephew: A Psychoanalytic Study of Their Relationship*. New York: Pantheon Books.

Sterba, R. F. (1965), Psychoanalysis and music. *Amer. Imago*, 22:96–111.

——— (1982), *Reminiscences of a Viennese Psychoanalyst*. Detroit: Wayne State University Press.

Yerushalmi, Y. H. (1991), *Freud's Moses: Judaism Terminable and Interminable*. New Haven, CT: Yale University Press.

Name Index

Aberbach, D., 239
Abrams, D. M., xii, 293
Ackerman, D., 88
Adler, A., 261, 267, 286, 292, 302
Adler, G., 7
Adler, V., 283
Adorno, T., 250
Aeschylus, 199
Allen, W., 234n
Alvarez, X., 98n
Anderson, E., 155, 156, 161, 174
Anderson, H. C., 239
Anzieu, D., 251, 255
Arco, Count, 174
Arenberg, I. K., 24
Arnheim, R., 68, 84
Augustine, St., 61

Bach, C. P. E., 164
Bach, D., 283
Bach, D. J., 261
Bach, J. A., 164
Bach, J. C., 164, 165
Bach, J. S., xi, 153–169, 171–176, 265, 289, 294, 298–300, 302, 303
Bach, P. E., 83
Bach, Q., 83
Barnetche, E., 231
Barth, K., 158
Bartók, B., 43–46, 48–49, 51–52
Bartók, P., 48
Basch, M. F., 74, 140
Bateson, G., 179
Baudry, F., 11, 238
Bauer, O., 283
Beethoven, L. van, 27, 58, 67, 70–72, 97, 128–129, 267, 286, 289–290, 292–295, 297–299, 301–303
Benet, M., 22
Berger, K., 53
Bergson, H., 300
Berlioz, L. H., 135–136

Bernays, A. F., 281
Bernstein, L. M., 24, 70
Berte, H., 17
Bettelheim, B., 255
Blake, W., 52
Boehlich, W., 253
Bollas, C., 78
Boretz, B., 94
Bowers, F., 256
Bowlby, J., 183
Brahms, J., 55, 71, 111, 131, 291, 295, 300
Branscombe, P., 250
Brenner, C., 74, 98n
Brill, A. A., 253, 270
Brockhaus, H., 268
Brockhaus, O., 263
Brome, V., 261
Bruckner, A., 288, 301
Bruhn, H., 95
Brunswick, M., 251

Cage, J., 72
Carotenuto, A., 254–255, 262
Carus, A., 185
Carus, E. A., 185
Castelnuovo-Tedesco, P., 74, 77
Chasseguet-Smirgel, J., 21
Chatterton, T., 215
Chennevière, R. D., 240
Chessick, R. D., 251, 267
Chipp, H. B., 66
Chopin, F., 292–293
Clynes, M., 95
Codolt, 198
Coker, W., 7–8
Colloredo, H. von, 161, 174
Coltrera, J. T., 25
Cone, E. T., x, 4, 6, 8–17, 94–95, 110n
Cooke, D., 220–222
Coppolillo, H. P., 235
Countryman, L. F., 24

Crafat, R., 69

da Vinci, L., 296
Dahlhaus, C., 67, 83, 153n, 252, 256, 264, 265, 269, 271
Dante, 289
David, H., 164–166
Davies, P. J., 160, 171
de Latour, J. P. C., 233
Deathridge, J., 252, 256, 258, 264, 265, 269, 271
Debussy, C., 237, 288, 296–297, 303
Deri, S., 304
Deutsch, A., 267
Deutsch, D., 95
Deutsch, F., 11
Diaz de Chumaceiro, C. L., xii, 250–252, 257, 260, 273
Dickens, C., 43
Dietrich, D. R., 230
Dürer, A., 299

Ehrenzweig, A., 130
Eidelberg, L., 12
Einstein, A., 26, 93, 166–167
Eliot, T. S., 53, 85
Ellenberger, H. F., 256, 257, 269
Emde, R. N., 77–78
Epstein, D., xi, xii, 71, 84, 86, 116, 119, 122n
Erdmann, G., 165
Erikson, E., 233
Ewans, M., 199

Fauré, G. U., 27
Feder, S., ix, x, xi, 3, 9, 29, 63, 71–72, 75, 76, 99, 114n, 139, 172, 176, 192, 260–261, 264, 286, 304
Federn, E., 250, 257, 258–259, 261, 262, 264–273, 283–284, 286
Federn, P., 261–262
Ferenczi, S., 262
Feuerbach, A., 55
Fisher, C., 64
Flaubert, G., 233, 239
Fliess, J., 257, 281
Forkel, J. N., 164

Freud, A., 237n, 239, 262, 281
Freud, H., 259
Freud, S., xii, 6–7, 12, 63, 64–65, 73–74, 176, 203, 211, 249–273, 279–305
Fricken, E. von, 187
Frieden, K., 300
Friedman, S. M., xii, 130

Galile, V., 126
Gartenberg, E., 279–280
Gay, P., 251, 252
Gedo, J. E., 257
Geyer, H. C., 271
Geyer, L., 196–197, 199, 201, 210, 215–216, 284
Gillmor, A., 230n, 231–233, 235, 237, 239, 241, 242
Goethe, J. W. von, 16, 168, 254, 289, 290–291, 292, 296, 303
Goffman, E., 67
Goldberg, E. L., xi
Goldman, A., 195, 200, 204, 205, 217
Goodman, N., 73
Gradenwitz, P. E., 128–129
Graf, H., 259, 281, 284, 288, 293
Graf, M., xii, 257–264, 266, 267, 270–272, 279–305
Green, D. B., 99n
Greenacre, P., 25, 173, 176, 304
Guck, M. A., 94–95
Guttman, R. W., 226–227
Guttman, S. A., 250, 257

Hadamard, J., 26
Halperin, D. A., 234
Handel, G. F., 153n, 295
Hanslick, E., 54, 291
Harding, J., 230, 231
Harries, K., 66
Hartmann, H., 144
Häutler, A., 269
Haydn, F. J., 70–71, 131, 157, 280, 289, 292, 294, 303
Hebbel, F., 296, 297, 303
Heine, H., 189–190, 192
Hevner, K., 137

Hildesheimer, W., 173
Hilmar, E., 17
Hindemith, P., 72, 73, 84, 106
Hippocrates, 160
Hitler, A., 195
Hitschmann, E., 262
Hoffmann, E. T. A., 185, 198
Howard, R., 254
Hulsker, J., 24

Ingarden, R., 52–53
Ives, C., 29, 75, 192

Jahn, O., 173
Johnston, W., 279
Jones, E., 251, 259, 281
Jones, R. L., 250, 257
Joseph, Emperor, 157
Jung, C. G., 253–254, 255

Kant, I., 288, 300
Karmel, R. L., ix, xii, 3, 63, 231, 240,
    260–261, 264, 286
Katan, A., 242
Kaufmann, W., 269
Kenworthy, M., 287
Kerman, J., 7, 56, 61
Kerner, J., 186
Kerr, J., 272
Kierkegaard, S., 60
Kimmelman, M., 24
Kinney, D. K., 22
Kivy, P., 9, 72, 105–106n, 126, 134, 139,
    141
Klein, G., 78
Kneif, T., 6
Kobbé, G., 263
Kohut, H., 24–25, 127, 143–144, 147,
    237, 304
Kretchmar, H., 6
Kris, E., 303

Langer, S., 9, 96, 101n, 106n, 110n, 116,
    119, 126–127, 133, 138–141
Laussot, J., 265
Lehmann, H., 254
Lenau, N., 264

Levarie, S., 127, 143–144, 147
Lifton, R. J., 59–60
Ligeti, G., 30
Lipps, Th., 140
Liszt, F., 214, 264–265, 268
Lockwood, L., 59
Lombroso, C., 266
Lorenz, E. F., 273
Louschin, B., 179
Löwenthal, S., 264
Lunde, I., 22

Magee, B., 196, 201, 202–204, 206–207,
    222, 226, 249, 256
Mahler, G., 71–72, 97, 111, 284, 292,
    294, 299, 304
Mahoney, P. J., 64, 250
Malatesta, C., 77
Malevich, K., 66
Mander, R., 209
Marcuse, D. J., 191–192
Marshall, R. L., xi, 153n, 167, 168,
    171–176
Masson, J. M., 249–251
Matisse, H., 22
Maus, F. E., 46, 95
McClary, S., 15–16
McDonald, M., 85
McGann, J., 59
McGrath, W. J., 255, 256
McGuire, W., 253, 254, 270
Mendel, A., 164–166
Mendelssohn, F., 102–105, 117, 119,
    188, 192, 211, 293
Merzel, A. P. C., 22
Meyer, F., 265
Meyer, K., 283
Meyer, L. B., 70, 72, 84, 95, 131,
    144–145
Meynert, T., 255
Michaelis-Jena, R., 200–201
Michelangelo, 267, 286, 296, 303
Micznik, V., 95
Millington, B., 196
Mitchenson, J., 209
Modell, A. H., 78
Mozart, A. M. P., 172–173

Mozart, C., 156, 161, 163, 173
Mozart, L., 157, 158–159, 162, 173–175, 293
Mozart, M. A. T., 162
Mozart, W. A., xi, 49–51, 71, 78–79, 112–118, 135, 146, 153–169, 171–176, 251, 267, 280, 281, 283, 288, 292–295, 297, 302
Myers, R. H., 230, 232n

Narmour, E., 95
Nass, M. L., x, xii, 21, 25, 27, 30–32, 33, 85, 240, 243, 304
Newcomb, A., 46, 53
Newton, I., 167–168
Nietzsche, F., 196, 255, 256, 257, 267–268, 269, 290
Nothnagel, H., 261–262
Noy, P., 130, 135, 136–137, 138, 140, 145–146
Nunberg, H., 250, 257–259, 261–262, 264–273, 283–284, 286, 299, 304

Oerter, R., 95
Olds, C., 87
Ostwald, P. F., xi, 87–88, 183, 188, 189

Paganini, N., 22–23
Parrish, S. M., 250, 257
Pater, W., 3–4
Péladan, J., 234–235
Péladan, S., 235
Planner, C. W., 264
Plato, 58, 66–67, 91
Polk, J., 179
Pollock, G. H., ix, xi–xii, 3, 29, 63, 141, 199, 204, 260–261, 264, 286, 304
Pöppel, E., 111
Posèq, A. W. G., 72
Pratt, C. C., 126–127, 133, 138, 139–140
Prentky, R., 21–22
Proust, M., 76
Puchberg, M., 161

Rahm, J., 93
Ramana, C. V., 130
Rank, O., 209–210, 262, 264–265, 268, 283, 292
Raphael, 267, 293–294, 303
Rather, L. J., 204, 210–211, 212, 214–215
Ravel, M., 97, 237
Rechardt, E., xii
Reik, T., 252, 255, 262, 271
Reiser, M. F., xii, 223, 224
Reitler, R., 261
Rice, E., 300
Richards, R., 22
Richmond, M. B., 235
Richter, J. P., 185, 265–266
Rie, O., 270
Riepel, J., 55
Rizzo, F., 288
Roazen, P., 249, 251
Rochberg, G., 86
Rochlitz, F., 154
Roehmann, F. L., 86
Rogers, C., 88
Rolland, R., 288
Rose, G. J., xi–xii, 11, 63–64, 76, 78, 83–89, 97–98, 99, 222
Rosen, C., 69–71, 72, 84
Rosing, H., 95
Ross, N., 74
Rossini, G. A., 29
Roth, H., 23–24
Rothstein, E., 15
Rudnytsky, P. L., 256, 269
Ruesch, J., 179
Ruppius, Frau, 179–183

Sabor, R., 208–209
Sachs, H., 250, 262, 272–273
Sacks, O., 86, 89
Sadger, I., 264, 269, 283
Sadie, S., 7, 174, 259
Salter, L., 252, 254
Salzer, F., 84
Sandblom, P., 21, 22–23, 24
Satie, E., xii, 229–244
Schachter, C., 60

Schafer, R., 12–13
Scheftel, P., 254
Schilder, P., 243
Schiller, J. C. F. von, 303
Schlegel, A. W., 290
Schoen, M., 137
Schöenberg, A., 55, 57–58, 84
Scholes, R., 67
Schopenhauer, A., 92n, 255, 256, 257, 267–268
Schubert, F., 4–11, 13–17, 94–95, 185, 293, 296, 298
Schumann, C., 186–189, 191
Schumann, E., 184
Schumann, R., xi, 27, 46, 55, 176, 179–193, 293, 297
Schunke, L., 187
Schwartz, D. W., 29
Segel, N., 238
Seiber, M., 48
Sessions, R., 26, 28–29, 69, 87, 110n, 120
Shabad, P. C., 230
Shakespeare, W., 10, 208–209, 292, 294, 296, 303
Shambaugh, G. E., 24
Sharpe, E. F., 233
Shattuck, R., 231, 232, 241–242
Shaw, G. B., 201
Shelter, D. J., 87
Silberstein, E., 252–253
Sklansky, M. A., 235
Sloboda, J., 95
Smetana, B., 27, 295
Solomon, M., 13, 16, 154
Sophocles, 198, 199
Spielrein, S., 214, 254–255, 262, 271–272
Spitz, E. H., xii
Sprinchorn, E., 195, 200, 204, 205, 217
Spruiell, V., 237n
Stafford, W., 173
Stanescu, H., 257
Stekel, W., 261, 286
Sterba, R., 280
Stern, D., 84–85
Storr, A., 160, 166–167, 171

Strachey, J., 250, 260
Strauss, R., 139, 291, 294, 295–296
Stravinsky, I., 69, 93–94n, 97
Strobel, O., 256, 264, 268
Suchoff, B., 48
Sulloway, F. J., 251, 257
Sweetman, D., 24

Tchaikovsky, P. I., 143, 292–293
Templier, P.-D., 232
Thompson, O., 259, 261
Toch, E., 68
Tovey, D. F., 7
Treitler, L., xi, 46, 58, 60, 61

Van DeCarr, R., 87
van Gogh, V., 24
van Swieten, Baron, 155
Várnai, P., 30
Verdi, G., 140
Vinot, 231, 234
Vitz, P. C., 251
Vivaldi, A., 290, 302
Volta, O., 229–230, 235–236, 237–238
von Bülow, C.. See Wagner, C.
von Bülow, H., 201, 265, 268
von Stolzing, W., 251
von Weber, C. M., 184–185, 197, 293

Waelder, R., 12, 13–14
Wagner, C., 209–210, 256, 268, 269
Wagner, C. F., 196–197, 199, 215–216
Wagner, J., 271
Wagner, J. R., 196–197
Wagner, R., xii, 106–112, 118, 119, 195–216, 217–228, 240, 249–273, 284–285, 286, 289, 290, 292, 294, 296–298, 301–302
Walter, B., 240
Wasielewski, W., 184
Watson, D., 197
Weigel, J., Jr., 273
Wesendonck, M., 210, 264, 265
Wesendonck, O., 264
Wieck, C.. See Schumann, C.
Wieck, F., 186, 188
Wiedebein, G., 186

Willmans, K., 264
Wilson, A., 77
Wilson, F. R., 86
Winnicott, D. W., 75, 85–86
Wistrich, R. S., 249
Wittels, F., 269, 270

Wolf, E. S., 257
Wolf, H., 260, 296, 303
Wolfenstein, M., 229n, 239

Yerushalmi, Y. H., 300
Young-Bruehl, E., 262

Subject Index

Acceleration/ritard rhythm, 120–121
Active gap, 295
Aesthetic approach, 66
Aesthetic form. *See* Form
Affect. *See also* Emotions
  as communication, 43–61, 140
  in music, xi, 4–8, 43–61
  musical motion and, 91–122
  psychoanalytic theories of, 137
  symbolic, 96–97
  through Schumann's songs, 9–10,
    179–193
  tonal center and, 114–115
Affections, doctrine of, 53n, 92
Affective core, 77
Affective signaling, biological basis of,
  77–78
Age, creativity and, 29–30
Allegro (Satie), 240
Ambiguity
  capacity to tolerate, 33–37
  in *Tristan and Isolde*, 109–110
Amusia, 88
Anxiety dreams, 263
Appeal, 156–157
Art. *See also* Music
  communication of emotion in,
    125–148
  content versus form of, 63–66
  as expression of religion, 65–67
  from mental life, 10–11
  pleasure provided by, 145–147
  psychoanalytic interpretation of, 125–
    126
  as transmuter, 63–79
Art and Revolution (Wagner), 269
The Art of Fugue (Bach), 155–156, 176
Artist. *See also* Composers
  childhood of, 158–159
  disease in, 21–24
  empathic abilities, 25
  establishing types of, 285–286

  experience of and creativity in, 21–39
  family romance of, 176
  mother of, 172–173
  personalities of, 266–267
  self-knowledge of, 33–38
  sensitivity of, 304
Artistic choice, 13
Artistic missions, 153–169
On the Ascetic Ideal (Nietzsche), 267–268
Attunement, 85
Auditory sensitivity
  hyperacuity in, 27–29
  in infants, 87–88
Auditory sensory style, 26–29
Auditory stimuli, prenatal responses to,
  86–87
"An Autobiographical Study" (Freud),
  257
Autobiography (Stravinsky), 93

Bachian personality, 166–167
Baroque period, 92
Bäsle letters (Mozart), 162
From Beethoven to Shostakovitch (Graf),
  287
Beethoven's Piano Concerto No. 4, op.
  58, 128–129
Beginning, styles of, 34–35
Birth of Tragedy from the Spirit of Music
  (Nietzsche), 290–291
Borrowed identity, 238–239, 241
Brain, in affective organization of mem-
  ory, 224–225
Brandenburg Concertos (Bach),
  157–158

Character, expressive pathway of, 171–
  172
Childhood
  of artist, 158–159
  of Bach, 164–165
  maternal loss in, 229–231

transformation of memories of in
      song, 192–193
Choral Fantasy (Beethoven), 295
Civilization and Its Discontents (Freud),
      269
Classical period
   emotion in, 92
   style of, 290–291, 301
Cognition, in psychology of music, 95
Cognitive organization, 144–147
Collaborator, 234–235
Communication
   art as, 125
   through leitmotif, 217–228
   through song, 179–193
   two-level system of, 135
Communicational matrix, infant-care-
      giver, 77–78, 84–85
Composer and Critic (Graf), 287
Composers
   auditory sensory style of, 26–29
   biography and musical themes of,
      195–216
   experience of, 21–39
   inspirational sources for, 30–31
   musical styles of, 153–169
   musicality and ego identity of,
      229–244
   psychoanalytic studies of, xi–xii,
      302–303
   self-knowledge of, 33–38
   working styles of, 33–36, 38–39
Composer's block, 303
Composing process
   conscious stage of, 299–300, 304
   ego identity and, 235–237
   intentionality and action in, 240–242
   preconscious in, 295–299
   unconscious in, 291–295
Composition
   beginning of, 34–35
   dealing with problems of, 33–35
Congeneric musical meaning, 8
Connectedness, 288–289
Connotation, 95
   affective, 96–97
Conscious, in composing, 299–300, 304

Content
   arts of, 128–133
   versus form, 63–66
   interpretation of, 126
   untranslatability of, 96
Contour theory, 134
Convention theory, 134
*The Corded Shell: Reflections on Musical
      Expression* (Kivy), 9, 141
Core self, 85
Corpse Fantasy (Schumann), 188
Craft of Musical Composition (Hinde-
      mith), 84
Creative imagination, elements in, 27–
      28
"Creative Writers and Day-Dreaming"
      (Freud), 267
Creativity
   composer's experience and, 21–39
   disease and, 21–24
   of everyday life, 63–64
   external traumas and, 201–203
   internal-external sources of, 30–33
   loss and, 29–30
   measurement of, 302
   preconscious mind in, 295–299
   risk taking and, 39
Creativity and Disease (Sandblom), 21–23,
      24
Creativity and Perversion (Chasseguet-
      Smirgel), 21
Creativity and Psychopathology (Prentky),
      21–22
Crescendo/decrescendo, 105
Criticism
   affect in, 57–60
   Mozart's response to, 160–161
Cubist revolution, 66
Cyclothymic personality, 160

D minor, Mozart's works in, 112–117
Death
   causes of, 211
   creativity and, 304
"On Death and Sexuality" (Reik), 271–
      272
Death complex, 292

Death theme, 115
Defensive organization, 144
Depressive personality, 160
Dichterliebe (Schumann), 189–190
Direct interpretation, 128, 133–142
Disease, creativity and, 21–24
Disidentification, music of, 229–231
Don Giovanni (Mozart)
    death theme in, 115
    unconscious in, 294
Drama, Wagner and, 285
Dream
    formation of, 295
    symbolism in, 15
Dream work, 130
Das Dreimaderlhaus (Berte), 17
Dresden Revolution, 264–265
"The Dry Salvages" (Eliot), 85
The Dynamics of Creation (Storr), 166–167

Effect, 157
Ego
    art and development of, 63–64
    functions of, 299, 304
    musicality and identity of, 229–244
Ego mastery activity, 144
Ego mastery theory, 127, 128
    problem with, 147
Emotion and Meaning in Music (Meyer),
        84, 144–145
Emotional communication, Langer-
        Pratt theory of, 138–140
Emotional response, 140–141
Emotions. *See also* Affect
    anlage of, 83–89
    anxiety over, 59, 61
    communication of in music, 125–148
    conscious and unconscious ideas asso-
        ciated with, 73–75
    direct route to, 133–142
    etymology of, 100
    familiarity and, 72–73
    form and, 63–79
    indirect route to, 142–147
    infective, 140
    memories of, 73, 75–76, 77–79
    memory and, 223–225

in music, 4–8
    musical motion and, xi
    patterns signaling, 138–139
    through narrative content, 128–133
Empathy
    in artist, 25
    primary, 140
Endorphins, musical response and, 88
Epic poetry, 288
Eroica Symphony (Beethoven), 294
Erwartung (Schoenberg), 57
Essays in Musical Analysis (Tovey), 7
Experience, creativity and, 21–39
Expression, musical, 46–48
Extrageneric musical meaning, 8

The Fairies (Wagner), 209
Family, music in dynamics of, 231–232
Family heritage, Bach's, 175–176
Family romance, 176
    falsified, 242
"The Farewell Song of a Fool" (Schu-
        mann), 188
Father
    of Mozart, 158–160, 162, 173–176
    need for, 174–175
    Oedipus myth and, 212–215
    of Wagner, 197, 199, 215–216, 271
Feeling. *See* Affect; Emotions
Feeling-memories, 73, 75–76, 77–79
Fifth Symphony (Beethoven), 292
Fingal's Cave Overture (Mendelssohn),
        102–105
"The Fly" (Blake), 52–53
Flying Dutchman (Wagner)
    Freud on, 258
    psychoanalysis of, 270–271, 272,
        286–287
    theme of, 207
Form, 67–68
    arts of, 125
    versus content, 63–66
    direct effects of, 126
    feeling and, 63–79, 83–89
    in Freud's prose style, 64–65
Freud-Fliess letters, 251
Freud-Jung correspondence, 253–254

Fugues
    of Bach, 155–156
    of Mozart, 156

Genealogy of Morals (Neitzsche), 269
Genius
    as source of meaning, 166–167
    styles of, 153–169
Gothic art, 233
Götterdämmerung (Wagner), 195–196,
    198
    ending of, 217
Göttingen seven, 200–201
Gradus ad Parnassum (Bartók), 43–49
Greek theater, Wagner's idealization of,
    204–207
Gregorian chants, 57–58
Grimm's folktales, 200–201
Gymnopédies (Satie), 233, 235–237
György Ligeti in Conversation, 30

Hamlet (Shakespeare), 294
Harmonia, 66–67, 83
Harmonic structure, imbalance in, 69–
    70
Harmonic struggle, 117
The Haunting Melody (Reik), 252
Haydn Variations, op. 56 (Brahms), 131
Hearing disturbances, 26–27
Hermeneutics, x
    in music and affect, 4–8
Historical factors, in music analysis,
    54–57
Holding environment, 85–86
Human condition, Greek understand-
    ing of, 206–207

"I Was Crying in My Dream" (Schu-
    mann), 179, 190–191
    composition of, 188–190
    interpretation of, 191–192
Iconoclastic composition, 243–244
Ideas
    communication of through music,
        43–61
    versus form, 65–66
    through Schumann's songs, 179–193

Idée fixes, 298–299, 303–304
Identity, borrowed, 238–239, 241
Imbalance, 69–70
"The Incest Drama and Its Complica-
    tions" (Rank), 262–263
Incest theme, in Wagner's Ring cycle,
    195–216, 262–263
The Incest Theme in Literature and Legend
    (Rank), 209–210
Indirect interpretation, 128, 142–147
Infinite displaceability, 15–16
Infinite representation, 16–18
Information theory, 95
The Inner Workshop of the Musician
    (Freud), 258
Insight, 218
Inspiration
    process of, 27–31
    sources of, 26, 30–31
"Instinctual Anxiety During Puberty"
    (A. Freud), 239
Instrumentation, 32–33
Intentional fallacy, 57–58
Intentionality, 240–242
Interdisciplinary meetings, x
The Interpretation of Dreams (Freud),
    252–253, 259–260
Intertextuality, 95
Introverted personality, of Bach,
    165–166
Isomorphism, 75, 128
    theory of, 126, 127

Janissary chorus, 156–157
Jupiter Symphony, fourth movement
    (Mozart), 146

"Lacrymosa," Berlioz Requiem, 135–
    136
Language, 135
    musical, 136
Legend of a Musical City (Graf), 287
Leitmotif
    processing of, 225–228
    in Wagner, xii, 217–228
Leubald and Adelaide (Wagner), 208–209
Liederkreis (Schumann), 189

"Light as Fluttering Sylphs" (Schumann), 185
Lines, 68
Listener
  active participation of, 142–147
  capacity of to respond emotionally, 133–137
Little Hans case, 259
Logical positivism, 93–94
Logos, 67, 83
Lohengrin (Wagner), 207–208
Loss, creativity and in adolescence, 239–240
Love, ecstasy and, 267
Lyric poetry, 288

Madeleine phenomenon, 76
Madonna, 293–294
Mahler's Second Symphony, latent intent in, 71–72
Manic-depressive temperament, 160–162
Maternal etiology, 284
Meaning, in music, 4–8
Die Meistersinger (Wagner)
  Freud on, 249, 250–252, 257, 273
  theme of, 208
Memory
  affective organization of, 223–225, 226
  nodal network of, 226–227
Mental function, fluidity and flexibility in, 15–16
"Methodology of the Psychology of Poets" (Graf), 266, 285–286
Mikrokosmos (Boosey and Hawkes), 48
Mind
  in affective organization of memory, 223–224
  leap to art from, 10–11
Mind-set, 94–95
The Miner of Falun (Wagner), 273
Modern Music (Graf), 287
Moment Musical in A flat, Op. 94 (Schubert)
  content and affect in, 9–10
  poignancy of, 4–6

structural analysis of, 8–18
Mother
  early loss of, 229–231
  good enough, 172–173
  in Raphael's paintings, 293–294
  reunion with in death, 191–192
  of Schumann, 182–183
  in Wagner's work, 265–266
Motion
  affect and, 97–122
  structural role of, 100–101
  tension-release rhythm in, 98–99
Mourning
  creativity and, 29, 239–240
  in response to music, 77
Mozart Piano Concerto No. 23, affect in, 49–51
Mozart Piano Concerto No. 20, Movement I, 112–118
Multiple function principle, 13–14
Music
  absolute, 67
  affect in, xi
  as communication and expression, 156–157
  communication of affect and idea through, 43–61
  communication of emotion in, 125–148
  eclectic, 163
  ego identity and, 229–244
  form and feeling in, 63–79
  functions of, 288–290
  hermeneutics of, 4–8
  history of, 54–57
  imbalance in, 69–70
  intuitive grasp of, 119
  in life of Freud, xii, 279–305
  meaning in, 4–8
  motion in structure of, 100–101
  narrative content of, 128–133
  narratological interpretations of, 46n
  as object of study, 154
  Platonic structure of, 83
  prenatal exposure to, 87
  processing of in brain, 88
  psychoanalysis of, 3–18, 137, 279–305

psychoanalytic themes and ideas in, 287–290
quasi-religious function of, 83
revelation through, 157–158, 166–168
as secondary language system, 86
sensuous in, 91–92
structure of, 66–67
Music aesthetics, 54
Music and Meaning (Coker), 7–8
Music and the Historical Imagination (Treitler), 58
Music-psychoanalysis interface, xi
Music structuralism
    emergence of, 92–94
    inadequacies of, 94
    selectivity of, 95
Musical analysis, subjectivity and, 58–59
Musical Experience of Composer, Performer and Listener (Sessions), 87
Musical genre, destruction of, 97
Musical hallucinations, 89
Musical language, 136
Musical motion, phenomenon of, 96–122
Musicologists, wild, 7
Musicology, 7
Mutative interpretation, 218
My Life (Wagner), 263
Myrtles (Schumann), 189
Mysticism
    in Freudian theory, 300–301
    grief and, 239–240

Narcissism, adolescent, 237–239
Narcissistic dimension, 289
Narration-imagination-identification theory, 128–133
Narrative
    of life, 131–132
    in music, 46
    rhythm of, 132
Narrative interpretation, 128–133
Narrative strategies, 53
Neural proclivities, 120–122
Neurology, music processing and, 88–89

Neurotransmission, complexities of, 227
New Criticism, 94
New Journal for Music, 186
Niberlungs, song of, 211
Niberlungs story, 211–212
Nightpieces (Schumann), 188
Ninth Symphony (Beethoven), 289, 295
Nonfigurative art, 66
Nonrepresentational music, 138–142
Nonverbal signs, 135–136
Nordic tales, 211
Nostalgia, mood structure of, 75

Object loss, Schumann's, 184–185
Object replacement, forced, 242–243
Obliqueness, 68
Observer effect, 94–95
Obsessive idea, 298–299
Odin legend, 272–273
Oedipal sexuality
    in Wagner's life, 268–269
    in Wagner's work, 202–204
Oedipus myth
    downfall of society and, 213–214
    in Ring cycle, 209–216
    in Wagner's music, 204–205, 271
Oedipus trilogy, 198–199
Ogives (Satie), 235–236
Open system model, 74
Opera
    Freud and, 250–252, 281
    incest theme in, 195–216
    Wagner's, 256
Oresteia myth, 199
Organization-provoking theory, 147
Organizational activity, emotional communication through, 142–147
Organizing processes, 143–144
Oriental music, emotions in, 72
Overdeterminism, 12–14

Parody, 97
Parsifal (Wagner), 203
    themes in, 208, 263–264
Passion-desire, struggle between, 58–59
Perception
    brain in processing of, 224–225

expressive forces in, 68–69
Performance
  motion and problems of, 101
  nature and problems of, xii
Periodicity, innate, 120–122
Personality, style of, 171–172
Phaedrus (Plato), 58–59
Philosophy in a New Key (Langer), 96
Pleasure, from art, 145–147
Pleasure/unpleasure experience, 120
Plot archetypes, 53
Poetics of Music (Stravinsky), 69, 93
"Poetry and Neurosis" (Stekel), 270
Poignant, definition of, 4–6
Positivism, 56
Preconscious, 295–299
Preverbal affective interactions, 77–79
Preverbal communication, 136, 137
Primary affectivity, 77
Primary process transformation, 130–
  131, 146
Problems of Dramatic Creations (Graf), 285
Productive mood, 296–297
Promissory E-natural, 14
"Protean Man" (Lifton), 59
Protean style, 59–60
Proteus myth, 59–60
Psychic compromise, 17–18
Psychic conflict, in Schubert, 15–16
Psychoanalysis
  applied to arts, 3–18
  in interpretation of arts, 125–126
  of music, 279–305
  principles for application of, 11–18
Psychoanalysis and Music, Colloquium
  in, x
Psychoanalytic Explorations in Music
  (Feder, Karmel, Pollock), 63
Psychoanalytic motifs, 250
Psychoanalytic themes, 287–290
Psychobiology, in *Ring* cycle, 218–228
Psychopathology, creativity and, 21–22

Rage, patterns of, 139
Reason, versus impulse, 58–59
Regression in service of ego, 64
Religion

art as expression of, 65–67
  Greek theater and, 205–206
  music and, 83
Renaissance, aesthetics of, 126
Repetition
  to build tension, 70
  compulsion, 285–286
Representational music, 134–137
Repression, 64
Requiem (Mozart), 115
Responsive resonance, 74–75
Revelation, art as, 155–158, 166–168
Revolution, Wagner and, 212, 264–265
Rheingold (Wagner), 219–220, 226
Rhythm, 67
  musical motion as, 97n
Rhythmos, 67, 83
Rienzi (Wagner), 207
Ring cycle (Wagner)
  as expression of inner problems,
    217–218
  Freud on, 252–255
  incest themes in, 195–216
  leitmotif in, 218–228
  Oedipus myth in, 209–216
  themes in, 263–264
Risk taking, 39
Rite of Spring (Stravinsky), 57
Romantic music
  emotion in, 92
  style of, 290–291, 301
Rubato, 121

Sadness, patterns of, 139
Sarabandes (Satie), 235
Satire, 97
Schenkerian analysis, 84
Schubert and the Peacocks (Solomon), 13
Schwammerl, 17
Science, evolution of, 93–94
Scientific verification, 93
Scientists, Bachian personality of, 166–
  167
Sebastian complex, 165
Secondary process, 145–146
Self, development of, 85–86
Self-observing function, 33–38

Self-trust, 37–38
Sensory stimuli
    hyperacuity to, 24–25, 27–29
    processing of, 224–225
Sensuality, 91–92
Separation
    creative act and trauma of, 32
    for Mozart, 174–175
    new ideas and, 34
"Sexual Perversity" (Wittels), 269–270
Sexuality. *See also* Incest theme; Oedipal
        sexuality
    in Schubert's music, 15
    in Wagner's work, 202–204
Shapes, 68
Siegfried (Wagner), 203, 221
    Freud on, 254
Society, downfall of, 211–214
Song
    affect and idea communicated
        through, 179–193
    childhood memories in, 192–193
    universality of, 192
Songwriting, Schumann's, 184–186
"A Special Type of Choice of Object
        Made by Men" (Freud), 271
"On a Specific Type of Male Object-
        Choice" (Freud), 270–271
Speech
    affinity of for music, 136
    musical aspects of, 77–78
Spiritual connectedness, 288–289
Story and discourse theory, 95
Structure, transduction of, 97–98
Styles
    of Bach and Mozart, 153–169
    classical and romantic, 290–291
    emergence of, 234–235
    as expressive pathway of character,
        171–172
Subjective self, 85
Subjectivity, exclusion of from judg-
        ment, 58–59
Sublimation, 64, 297–298, 304
Suprematist art, 66
Symbolic feelings, 96–97
Symbolic representation, 141

Symbolic self, 86
Symbolism, affect and, 104–105, 116
Symmetrical unbalanced structure,
        69–70
Synthesizing impulse, 166–168, 304

Tale of Two Cities (Dickens), 43
Tannhauser (Wagner), 207
Temperaments, 160
Tempo, cognitive aspects of, 120–121
Tension, 69–70
    building, 70
    dynamic of, 72
    resolution of, 70–71, 73–75
    in *Tristan and Isolde*, 108–112
Tension-release
    balance of, 69–79
    rhythms of, 98, 99
    symmetrical, 83–84
Third Reich, Wagner and, 195–196
Till Eulenspiegel (Strauss), 139
Tonality
    affect and, 116–118
    death of, 106–112
Topographic theory, 301–302, 303–304
Transduction, 97–98
"Transformation" (Schumann), 185
Transformations
    primary process, 130–131
    in unconscious processes, 129–130
Tristan and Isolde (Wagner), 200, 205
    prelude of, 106–112
    theme of, 208
Tritone, 91–92
Twilight of the Gods (Wagner), 221

Unclosure, ability to tolerate, 33–37
Unconscious
    access to processes of, 289–290
    in composing, 291–295
    language of, 130
    sublimation of, 297–298
Unfinished Symphony (Schubert), 15, 16
Unifying principle, 168, 304
Unity principle, 299–300

Valhalla motif, 226

Valkyrie (Wagner), 219, 220–221, 223
Vienna, musical life of, 279–281
Vienna Psychoanalytic Society, minutes
    of, 249–250, 261–273, 283–284
Vision, content of, 68
Visual perceptual categories, 68

Wagner Problems and Other Studies (Graf),
    284
"Wagner's Letters to His Family--Art
    and Life" (Graf), 264
Die Walkure (Wagner), 202–203

The Wedding (Wagner), 198
  theme of, 209
Wednesday   Psychological   Society,
    258–259, 261
The Well-Tempered Clavier (Bach), 154–
    155, 168
"Why Do We Enjoy Art?" (Noy),
    145–146
Die Wiener Volksoper (Adler), 261
Wild psycho-analysis, 7
Workers' Symphony Concerts, 261
Workshop of a Musician's Mind (Graf), 286
Writer's block, 296